Falling Backwards:

Stories of

Fathers and Daughters

Falling Backwards:

Stories of

Fathers and Daughters

Gina Frangello
Guest Editor

Stacy Bierlein
Kathryn Kosmeja
Allison Parker
Assistant Editors

With a Foreword by
Elissa Schappell

CHICAGO

www.hourglassbooks.com

Cover Artwork by Randi Layne Scheurer
www.randiworks.com

ISBN 0-9725254-2-4
LCCN 2004101294

Printed in the United States of America
on acid-free paper

Hourglass Books ... time to read
Publishers of short story anthologies

www.hourglassbooks.com

Contents

Contents

Contents

Foreword

Elissa Schappell

I realize now that I have always written about my father. Save for a few early childhood stories, such as the adventure story of a jellybean stowed away in a man's pocket, and some dirty limericks involving goats and boys named Buck. But maybe I was writing about my father then too; my desire to see the entire world but under his protection, or complicated ways in which my father's sexuality influenced my own sense of self and sexual curiosity.

Fathers are often far more of an enigma than mothers. They have more time for double lives, girlfriends, thievery, gambling. Mothers have always toiled in the grimy and intimate trenches of domesticity, the constant nurse *and* constant witness to the battles and victories of their children's childhood. The father's beat is more removed, securing the stockade, putting money in the bank, patrolling the perimeter for snipers.

A mother's love for her daughter, long celebrated in song and countless weepy blockbusters, seems easier to manage on the page. After all, mothers are supposed to love their children, if only because they have given them life. The father's role in it all is far murkier—save a DNA test. It is not an evolutionary accident that babies so resemble their fathers at birth. Surely that is all that saves some of them from being eaten by a father who presumes they might be a bastard.

Mothers aren't supposed to leave. The mother who abandons her child, or hates her child, is the lowest of all creatures, the subject of Shakespearian tragedies. Fathers it is understood *can* leave. They shouldn't, but they can. A father, like a lover, can turn on a dime, disown or destroy you.

As a kid, writing was the one skill that was mine, and mine alone. It wasn't like making art exactly, which both my parents did. It wasn't like athletics; my father was a good squash player and scuba diver, my mother a human rubber band at yoga. Writing was the first thing I alone did well.

I was in graduate school working on the stories that would become my novel-in-stories, *Use Me*, when someone pointed out the proliferation of fathers in my stories. A plague of fathers held court, center stage and off-stage, on the telephone and only by mail. They were different sorts of fathers, or father figures, carousing, misunderstood, silent, or charming with all sorts of daughters, or sons who were really stand-ins for daughters. I couldn't escape my father, and I didn't want to.

"How do you think this stuff up?" my father once asked me after reading a story in which a woman is cruel to a man, because although he's a nice man, he isn't really nice to her. He refuses to see her for who she really is. She isn't enough for him so she punishes him.

"This is sad, heavy stuff," my father said, "It's not funny at all." He looked at me sadly, curiously, and shook his head. It was clear that he was proud that I was publishing, but still.

"Those are my stories," I said, my heart beating in my throat. "That's what I know."

"Well," he sighed. "You're very creative." Then he got up and got some more ice for his drink.

He was upset. I was furious.

In the last real conversation I had with my father, he told me, "I know you are going to be successful. You just have to get out of your own way."

"You can't imagine how hard that is," I joked, but he didn't laugh.

A few days later, he died. It seemed that my father, once assured of my fate, had decided he could now go. I was angry and confused. I wasn't ready for him to leave. I couldn't imagine ever being ready. It's a bitter irony that my father had to die for me to write my book—that I literally had to *use him* to make art.

So the sword he gave me—his faith—was the one I used to run him through, then resurrect him. After the tortured man conversation, I hadn't shown my father any more stories, although he spied another in a magazine.

I'd like to show this to our friends ... he said with a small laugh—but, Jesus do you have to use the word fuck ten times on a page?

On the page, my father belonged to me, not to my mother or my sister or his friends or the people who worked for him. He was my hostage. On the page, we had time alone. I could do the talking and he could do the listening, or lack of listening. I could control his misunderstanding. I could make it clear that I was right.

Often our fathers are the first great loves of our lives. Some of us never get over them. Their love, or lack of love—whether they tell us we are beautiful, make us feel safe in our bodies, whether they stay—determine how a woman sees herself. For many women sexuality becomes directly related to how her father treated her. He was the first person to be in love with her, to kiss her toes, perhaps, to slap her. So, it is the daughter's destiny that all future connection or lack of connection with men is shaped by the relationship with her father.

I didn't want to write about my father. I *had* to write about him. All my life—or at least since I was a teenager and he was diagnosed with the cancer the first time—I have been memorizing him, taking notes, preparing for the day when he'd leave me, and all I'd have was what I'd stolen or saved of him. I wanted his company, and after he died, I wanted his voice in my head. I wrote him because I didn't want the conversation to be over. I needed to continue, to have the last word.

I wanted him alive, to raise him from the dead. I wanted to introduce my father, or this fictional jazzed-up version of him, to people that mattered to me, and strangers. On the page I could move my father around, figure him out. Take us on trips, see things we'd never seen. The daughter character could do and say things I would never do or say, make the father respond in a way my father wouldn't. I'd create two of us, the not-really-us, then two more not-really-us, and two more, and so on and on.

Certainly there were people who wondered at my desire to write about my father, the intensity of my attachment. There is something dangerous and unseemly about a daughter's love for her father. There is something improper and unsettling in what people imagine to be her desire to unseat her mother—to become the queen to her father's king. No one mistakes mothers and daughters for lovers, the way people do fathers and daughters. A stranger who notices a young woman and older man together sees a connection that could be sexual.

Fiction feels like the appropriate place to explore father daughter relationships. I don't think I could write truthfully about my father in nonfiction. I wouldn't dare. By hiding behind the blazing shield of fiction—all fiction is a lie—I was protected from my father's wrath and the scorn of those who think such stories should go untold. If the writer's job is to tell the stories that should be told, to report back on experiences many have but can't or won't talk about, then the writers represented in this anthology are doing their job.

Two stories that deftly explore sexual themes are Heather Sellers' "My Life as a Delicious Peach," which sees the narrator being shanghaied to a convention by her abusive alcoholic father who passes her off as his wife, and Tony Houghton's "Night Train," in which a father is drawn to a hooker his daughter's age and torn by the desire to possess and protect her. The desires of fathers are explored in Bliss Broyard's "Mr. Sweetly Indecent" and Amy Wilkinson's "Green Cubes," where ideas of connection and commitment are thrown into relief against the backdrop of a father's faithlessness.

In many of these stories the mother is dead or conspicuously absent. These capture the Be-Careful-What-You-Wish-For-Elektra fantasy/horror of being marooned with your father. In this universe, widowed fathers are poor substitutes for mothers. Their hearts already broken, they seem unable to love their children or anything else—save the cat in Pam Houston's "Waltzing the Cat"—to fail to make a difference.

Fathers drink and sink into murky bottomless depressions. They blink blind as moles at daughters who are nearly bursting their buttons with ripeness, like the heroine of Steve Almond's "The Problem of Human Consumption," who imagines she and her father somehow conspired to kill her mother. Motherless daughters such as the heroine of Aimee Bender's "The Girl in the Flammable Skirt" and Joan Corwin's

"Sinners" imagine passions so strong they are possible of self-immolation, able to create disaster when desire ignites. Such is the power of the daughter. Such is the power of the father.

At the end of Dan Chaon's title story "Falling Backwards," structured in retrograde, he takes the now seven-year-old narrator onto the skeleton of a bridge he is helping to construct. He shows his frightened daughter how it is possible to jump off the bridge and fall safely into the net stretched out below. Though she doesn't understand what their purpose is in being there, and can't understand what this moment means to her father, what she feels, and what is clear, is that these two beings, father and daughter, are inexorably linked, forever, and throughout time.

"She does not understand the look in his eyes, when he clasps her hand. She doesn't think she will ever understand it, though for years and years she will dream of it, though it might be the last thing she sees before she dies.

"'This is something you're never going to forget, baby-girl,' he says. And then they plunge backward into the air."

These nineteen stories, like the stories of our own fathers, are ones you'll never forget.

Introduction: The End of an Archetypical Father

Gina Frangello

My father was an anomaly. In the mostly Italian and Latino neighborhood where I grew up—inner-city Chicago in the 1970's—fathers came in several common varieties: absent, drunk or addicted; abusive, or at the very least domineering, macho Kings of their households. It was not unusual for fathers to be involved in some kind of criminal undertaking as a profession, whether dealer, thief, bookie, or some vague companion or runner for somebody said to be in the Mob.

Amidst this environment, my father, one of seven Italian brothers (and by the time I was growing up, one of the neighborhood patriarchs), wanted to be Cary Grant. He wore wool caps and tweed blazers that he fancied British (despite our lack of money he scouted Brooks Brothers for bottom-out sales) and was fanatically devoted to jazz. A book of photographs of England sat on our coffee table. He had an ulcer prone to violent hemorrhaging, and so avoided coffee, drinking only endless cups of tea. Though he owned a bar, he didn't touch alcohol; he never raised his voice unless yelling at other drivers on the road with his windows up so the recipients of his rage couldn't hear. While most of the men in our neighborhood never went further than a couple miles radius, my father had a penchant for taking me and the other neighborhood kids on road trips outside the city to obscure small towns like Cherry Valley so we could sample the resident diner's homemade apple pie.

My favorite story about my father (told to me by my mother, from whom I received most of my information about him since he rarely talked much about himself) involved one of the "neighborhood sluts" coming into the club where all the men shot craps and played cards. She was looking for money—just a few dollars—for some unclear end: maybe food, maybe drugs, maybe a pack of cigarettes. The other men began to mock and proposition her, offering money in exchange for some sexual service although she was young enough to be their daughters. My father, never one to make a scene, quietly stood up among them, went to the girl and handed her a twenty, patted her on the arm and walked her out of the club and back onto the street. At eighty-two now, that anecdote may still embody him best. He is a gentle soul, mild and introspective, artistic in disposition though he never even finished the eighth grade. Never one to challenge systems overtly, he still managed always to conduct himself with a certain kind of dignity in an environment that made such actions difficult at best. He was admired by everyone for his generosity. When I look back at my childhood, my father was the quietest of mythic heroes: the kind who followed his own drummer and encouraged me—never by preaching but by his own inner sense of what was right—to do the same.

It would seem, then, that with this sort of man for a father, I would have grown into a fiction writer for whom positive portrayals of fathers—as caretakers and role models— came easily and naturally. Yet looking back over my body of writing for the past twenty years, since my first short stories as a teenager, the exact opposite is true. Despite being the only daughter of a gentle man, my Father Archetype, so to speak, became the dozens of other men in my neighborhood for whom violence often substituted reason, who were jealous and misogynistic, intoxicated by various substances, loose with the family money, and casually unfaithful. My earliest stories involved a gang rape covered up by a neighborhood crime boss, and fathers who were mostly sadistic in their dealings with their wives and children. In college I majored in psychology and then pursued my M.A. in order to work with battered women and sexually abused foster girls—I was compelled to this career direction by the things I'd seen growing up. Even though my own father passed his days clipping out Mike Royko columns or laughing at Woody Allen films, leaving the world in its peace, the fathers in my fiction work were brutes who dominated those around them, especially their daughters. It seemed that, at least in my experience, my *actual* father could not quite rise above the Archetypal Father of my childhood—that for me, something about what it was to be a grown man in relationship to a young girl had been tainted by the environment in which my own peaceable father had, perhaps unwisely and definitely over my (non-Italian) mother's protests, chosen to raise me.

Being offered the editorship of this anthology, then, could not have come at a more coincidental moment in my personal and writing life. With twin daughters of my own now, watching the fiercely intelligent and independent—but also nurturing and open-hearted—man I married beginning to fit into his role as Father, I have finally begun to confront my twenty-year war with the fathers on the pages of my fiction. Last year I began writing a novel as close to autobiographical as I dare get, with a man much like my own father at its center, juxtaposing him (just as in "real life") against the senseless brutality around him. My struggle to overcome my fears, prejudices and anger against Fathers as a group, and to begin to embrace all that is beautiful and tentative and touching in this crucial relationship, has been playing out on the pages of that text. And so it was particularly fascinating, and helpful, for me to sit back here and watch the way other writers, male and female, have grappled with this dyad of father and daughter too. As this anthology goes to press, so I am completing a first draft of that novel, and it has begun to seem to me as though the two projects are inextricably linked: that I could not have made the leaps of faith I did, and paid my own father the homage he has long deserved, without the writers of this book as my models and muses.

What I feared most in coming to this project with the responsibility of choosing the "best" stories was that I would be bombarded with homogeneous submissions that were either sentimental eulogies of perfect Hallmark dads, or bitter rants about disapproving jerks who had ruined their daughters' lives—that it would be difficult for me as an editor to find the kind of subtle variety of experiences that makes both life and fiction great. But to my relief—and excitement—what I found instead (albeit amidst much of the former and latter, of course) were stories that grappled mightily with the "fathers in the middle"—those well-meaning but flawed human beings who love their daughters and yet, like my own father, have a hard time putting their feelings into words, have a hard time inserting themselves into the private bond between mothers and their girls, have a hard time knowing how to deal with their daughters' fledgling sexuality just as their own aging process picks away at their youthful prowess and identities. What I found—from correspondence with the writers who ended up in this book and the many who did not—was that fathers are perhaps the most provocative and personal topic of all, and that writers cannot escape them and yet often feel they cannot quite pin them down.

Likewise, what struck me immediately as I began to compile the strongest stories I received was that writers are fascinated with the way fathers are perceived *by* their daughters and daughters impacted by their fathers, so that even male writers often chose to write from a female voice in tackling this relationship. Maybe this is why some of the most fascinating stories in this book will be those that *do* approach the father-daughter bond from the perspective of often befuddled—but equally intense—dads. Stories like "The Minor Wars" by Kaui Hart Hemmings, "Dry Falls" by Heather Brittain Bergstrom, and "Pepper Hunt" by Kate Blackwell, which tackle head on the dangerous ground fathers can find themselves on when venturing—usually by sad necessity—where mothers and daughters usually tread, trying to forge their way to love and understanding on a terrain where there has never been any reliable map.

What struck me too—I am thrilled to say—is that in editing this book I found barely a glimmer of traditional literary notions of fatherly influence—no doting Cordelias or virginal Rosa Coldfields here. In fact, as Elissa Schappell points out in her foreword, even the Electra fantasy of being marooned with one's father has become, for the contemporary writer, partially a "horror" and ultimately unsatisfying; fathers are "poor substitutes" for mothers who are no longer competitors in the father-daughter arena but more like necessary buffers. It is impossible not to note the proliferation of dead mothers in these stories, of the need to remove that powerful maternal figure in order for writers and characters to see the elusive father clearly—yet somehow the outcome as it plays here is often the exact converse of former Oedipal thinking: not a man and girl who unite in any quasi-sexual marriage after ousting the mother, but instead a father and a daughter who timidly approach each other in grief, who cannot quite move through the shadow cast by Mother and so continue to move tentatively around her, even in her absence. In story after story, old truths are given new spins: grown daughters are protective of mothers when fathers stray; a father and daughter who, to the eyes of their town seem to be husband and wife, secretly despise one another. In "The Other Daughter" by Antonya Nelson, a father and his younger daughter unite in annoyed, almost *male* camaraderie to worship of the family's eldest, charismatic girl. At one point the editors and publisher of this book even bandied around the title *Electra Doesn't Live Here Anymore,* so fascinated were we by how Greek, psychoanalytic and Shakespearean visions of daughters' attraction to their fathers were being readdressed on our pages. Clearly, contemporary American writers are meeting the age-old enigma of the father-daughter bond—not with a dismissal of tradition, but fiercely on their own terms—and with this book a collection of the best of them have made this subject wholly their own.

There is no shortage of unappealing dads in this book—men who would do the lesser fatherly models of my old neighborhood proud. Yet even these dads were chosen for inclusion for their humanity, for their refusal to be two-dimensionally pinned down on the page—who, even when the voice we hear is their daughter's, like in Heather Sellers' "Myself as a Delicious Peach," insist on inserting their own messy humanity and pain so that we *care* why they act as they do, so we feel for them even as they hurt their children. And likewise even the most noble of dads—the doting dentist of Peter Ho Davies' "Brave Girl," the political teacher of Lan Tran's "Lone Stars," or the ex-Air Force outdoorsman of Ashley Shelby's "In a Cold Climate," have foibles and weaknesses that make them complicit in their daughters' wounds, failures and losses.

Some stories here may be familiar to readers, as they are near canonical already. Pam Houston's protagonist Lucy of "Waltzing the Cat" has perhaps one of the most memorable fathers in the contemporary short story, a man we alternately pity, hate, and like Lucy, seek desperately to love. Sandra Cisneros' Papa, excerpted from her brilliant *The House on Mango Street*, is perhaps the embodiment of all immigrant fathers, a man who works himself to the bone in the face of grief after failure after grief, constantly on the move and unable to be held the way his daughter—the one for whom he toils—wishes to hold him in place and keep him to her. Other stories here may not be ones that would traditionally be conceived of as "father-daughter" stories—perhaps most notably Michael Knight's "Smash and Grab," where dad never even makes an appearance but is, off-stage, the powerful motivator for his savvy but ignored daughter's extreme actions, or Lisa Stolley's "Everything is Going to Be So Good," where pregnant, drug-addled Olivia spins further and further out of control as she seeks in every misguided way her powerful and distant father's approval. In such cases where daughters behave badly—as they often do—it is impossible not to wonder, even though we never receive the fathers' point of view, what these men—these pillars of their communities—would think if they realized the extent of their daughters' thrashing around in search of their love, thrashing that can in truth only confuse their fathers and hurt them in turn.

This anthology is not complete, as no anthology on this powerful and universal relationship could be. Many wonderful stories could not be included, and if we had an honorable mentions section it would go on for pages. *Falling Backwards* is, more than anything, a beginning, an approaching, a circling of one of life's three fundamental bonds: father-child, mother-child, lover-lover—and maybe the most challenging of the three. Like all that is best in literature, perhaps these stories, individually and collectively, ask more questions than they answer—questions that each of us has faced or still faces in our lives with our own fathers or daughters. For that reason, my biggest hope as the editor of this book is that it will be something that fathers and daughters not only enjoy and grapple with alone, but will meet each other to share.

Waltzing the Cat

Pam Houston

For as long as I can remember, my parents have eaten vicariously through the cat. Roast chicken, amaretto cheese spread, rum raisin ice cream: there is no end to the delicacies my parents bestow on Suzette. And Suzette, as a result, had developed in her declining years a shape that is at first glance a little horrifying. It isn't simply that she is big—and she *is* big, weighing in at twenty-nine pounds on the veterinarian's scale—but she is alarmingly out of proportion. Her tiny head, skinny tail, and dainty feet jut out from her grossly inflated torso like a circus clown's balloon creation, a nightmarish cartoon cat.

I remember choosing Suzette from a litter of mewing Pennsylvania barn cats, each one no bigger than the palm of my hand. I was sixteen then, and I zipped Suzette inside my ski jacket and drove back to the city with my brand new license in the only car I ever really loved, my mother's blue Mustang convertible—the old kind—passed on to me and then sold, without my permission, when I went away to college.

At first Suzette was tiny and adorable, mostly white with black and brown spots more suited to a dog than to a cat, and a muddy-colored smudge on her cheek that my mother always called her coffee stain. But too many years of bacon grease and heavy cream have spread her spots across her immense and awkward body; her stomach hangs so low to the ground now that she can only waddle, throwing one hip at a time out and around her stomach, and dragging most of her weight forward by planting one of two rickety front paws.

Suzette has happily accepted her role as family repository for all fattening foods. She is, after all, a city cat who never did much exploring anyway, even when she was thin. She didn't really chase her tail even when she could have caught it. My parents are happy now to lift her to the places she used to like to get to under her own power: the side board in the dining room table or the middle of their king-sized bed. Suzette has already disproved all the veterinarian's warnings about eating herself to death, about my parents killing her with kindness. This year Suzette turns seventeen.

The cat and I were always friends until I left home and fell in love with men who raised dogs and smelled like foreign places. Now when I come home for a visit the cat eyes me a little suspiciously, territorial, like an only child.

I don't have any true memories of my parents touching each other. I have seen pictures of them the year before I was born when they look happy enough, look maybe like two people who could actually have sex, but in my lifetime I've never even seen them hug.

"Everything was perfect with your father and me before you were born," my mother has told me over and over, confusion in her voice but not blame. "I guess he was jealous or something," she says, "and then all the best parts of him went away. But it has all been worth it," she adds, her voice turning gay as she fixes the cat a plate of sour cream herring chopped up fine, "because of you."

When I was growing up there was never anything like rum raisin ice cream or amaretto cheese spread in the refrigerator. My mother has always eaten next to nothing: a small salad sprinkled with lemon juice, or a few wheat thins with her martini at the end of the day. (One of my childhood nightmares was of my mother starving herself to death, one bony hand extended like those Ethiopian children on late-night TV.) My father ate big lunches at work and made do at night with whatever there was. When I came home from school I was offered carrots and celery, cauliflower and radishes, and sometimes an orange as a special treat.

I have forgotten many things about my childhood, but I do remember how terrified my parents were that I would become overweight. I remember long tearful conversations with my mother about what my friends and teachers would say, what everyone in the world would say, behind my back if I got fat. I remember my father slapping my hand at a dinner table full of company (one of the few times we pretended to eat like normal people) when I got caught up in the conversation, forgot the rules, and reached for a warm roll. I remember my mother buying the family clothes slightly on the small side so we were always squeezing and tucking and holding our breaths. My mother said that feeling the constant pressure of our clothes would remind us to eat less.

What I know now is that I was never fat, that none of us was ever fat, and I have assembled years of photographs to prove it. The first thing I did when I went away to college was gain fifteen pounds that I have never been able to lose.

After college, when I left home for good, my father, in a gesture so unlike him that my mother attributed it to the onset of senility, began to listen with great regularity to the waltzes of Johann Strauss, and my mother, for reasons which are for me both unclear and all too obvious, started overfeeding the cat.

In my real life I live in California and volunteer twice a week at a homeless shelter, where I stir huge pots of muddy-colored stew and heap the plates with it, warm and steaming. My friend Leo stays over at my house every Saturday night and we watch movies until daylight and then we get up and work all day in my garden. I love watching the tiny sprouts emerge, love watching them develop. I even love weeding, pulling the encroaching vines and stubborn roots up and away from the strengthening plants, giving them extra water and air. I love cooking for Leo entire dinners of fresh vegetables, love the frenzy of the harvest in August and September when everything, it seems, must be eaten at once. I love taking the extra food to the shelter, and at least for a few months, putting the gloomy canned vegetables away.

What I love most of all is lying in bed on Sunday mornings thinking about the day in the garden and hearing Leo puttering around making coffee. It's never been romantic with Leo and I know it never will be, but still, on those mornings I feel a part of something. With the moon sliding behind the sunburnt hills, the sun up and already turning the tomatoes from green to red, the two of us get our hands dirty together, pulling out the dandelions, turning the rich dark soil.

Aside from the weight issue, which always gets us in trouble, my mother and I are very close. I told her the first time I smoked a cigarette, the first time I got drunk, the first time I got stoned, and at age sixteen when I lost my virginity to Ronny Kupeleski in the Howard Johnson's across the border in Phillipsburg, New Jersey, I told my mother in advance.

It's just as well," my mother said, in what I regard now as one of her finest moments in parenting. "You don't really love him, but you think you do, and you may as well get it over with with someone who falls into that category."

It wasn't the last time I followed my mother's advice, and like most times, she turned out to be right on all counts about Ronny Kupeleski. And whatever I don't understand about my mother always gets filed away behind the one thing I do understand: my mother believes she has given up everything for me; she will always be my harshest critic, she will always be my biggest fan.

My father has had at least three major disappointments in his life that I know of. The first is that he didn't become a basketball star at Princeton; his mother was dying and he had to quit the team. The second is that he never made a million dollars. Or, since he *has* made a million dollars if you add several years together, I guess he means he never made a million dollars all at one time. And the third one is me, who he wanted to be blonde, lithe, graceful, and a world-class tennis champion. Because I am none of these things and will never be a world-class sportsman, I have become instead a world-class sports fan, memorizing batting averages and box scores, penalties and procedures, and waiting for opportunities to make my father proud. Fourteen years after I left home sports is still the only thing my father and I have to talk about. We say, "Did you see that overtime between the Flyers and the Blackhawks?" or "How bout them Broncos to take the AFC this year," while my mother, anticipating the oncoming silence, hurries to pick up the phone.

My mother believes that her primary role in life has been to protect my father and me from each other: my rock music, failed romances and teenage abortion; his cigarette smoke, addictive tendencies toward gambling, and occasional meaningless affairs. My mother has made herself a human air bag, a buffer zone so pliant and potent and comprehensive that neither my father nor I ever dare, or care, to cross it.

The older I get, the more I realize that my father is basically a good person who perceives himself as someone who, somewhere along the line, got taken in by a real bad deal. I am not completely unlike him—his selfishness, and his inability to say anything nice—and I know that if it were ever just the two of us we might be surprised at how much we had to say to each other—that is, if we didn't do irreparable damage first. Still, it is too hard for me to imagine, after so many years of sports and silence, and he is ten years older than my mother. He will, in all likelihood, die first.

My parents, I have noticed in my last several visits, have run out of things to say to each other. They have apparently irritated and disappointed each other beyond the point where it is worth fighting about. If it weren't for the cat, they might not talk at all.

Sometimes they talk about the cat, more often they talk to the cat, and most often they talk *for* the cat, responding to their own gestures of culinary generosity with words of praise that they think Suzette, if she could speak, would say.

On a typical afternoon, my mother might, for example, drop everything to fry the cat an egg. She'll cook up some bacon, crumble the bacon into the egg, stir it up Southwestern style, and then start cooing to Suzette to come and eat it.

The cat, of course, is smarter than this and knows that if she ignores my mother's call my mother will bring the egg to her on the couch, perhaps having added a spot of heavy cream to make the dish more appetizing.

At this point my father will say, in a voice completely unlike his own, "She's already had the milky-wilky from my

cereal and a little of the chicky-chick we brought from the restaurant."

"That was hours ago," my mother will say, although it
hasn't been quite an hour, and she will rush to the cat and
wedge the china plate between the cat's cheek and the sofa.
My parents will hold their breath while Suzette raises her
head just high enough to tongue the bacon chips out of the
egg.

"We like the bak-ey wak-ey, don't we, honey," my father will say.

"Yes, yes, the bak-ey wak-ey is our fav-ey fav-ey," my
mother will say.

I will watch them, and try to search my conscious and
unconscious memory for any time in their lives when they
spoke to me this way.

The more years I spend living on the other side of the
country, the better my mother and I seem to get along. It is
partly an act of compromise on both our parts: I don't get angry every time my mother buys me a pleated Ann Taylor
skirt, and my mother doesn't get angry if I don't wear it. We
had one bad fight several years ago Christmas Eve, when my
mother got up in the middle of the night, snuck into my room
and took a few tucks around the waist of a full hand-painted
cotton skirt I loved, and then washed it in warm water so it
shrank further.

"Why can't you just accept me the way I am?" I wailed,
before I remembered that I was in the house where people
didn't have negative emotions.

"It's only because I adore you, baby," my mother said,
and I knew not only that this was true, but also that I adored
my mother back, that we were two people who needed to be
adored, and the fact that we adored each other was one of

life's tiny miracles. We were saving two other people an awful lot of work.

When I am at home in California I don't communicate with my parents very much. I live a life they can't conceive of, a life that breaks every rule they believe about the world getting even. I have escaped from what my parents call reality by the narrowest of margins, and if I ever try to pull the two worlds together the impact will break me like a colored piñata, all my hope and humor spilling out.

One Saturday night, when Leo and I have stayed in the garden long after dark, planting tomatoes by the light of a three-quarter moon, I feel a tiny explosion in the core of my body, not pain exactly, or exactly joy, but a sudden melancholy relief.

"Something's happened," I say to Leo, though that's all I can tell him. He wipes the dirt off his hands and sits down next to me and we sit for a long time in the turned-up dirt before we go inside and get something to eat.

When the phone rings the next morning, so early that the machine picks it up before Leo—sleeping right beside it on the couch—can get to it and I hear my father say my name once with something I've never heard before in his voice, something not quite grief but closer to terror, I know my mother is dead.

I hear Leo say, "She'll call you right back," hear him pause just a minute before coming into my bedroom, watch him take both of my hands and then a deep breath.

"Something bad?" I say, shaking my head like a TV victim, my voice already the unfamiliar pleading of a motherless child.

Later that day, I will learn that sometime in the night my mother woke up my father to ask him what it felt like when he was having his heart attack, and he described it to

8

her in great detail, and she said, "That isn't like this," and he offered to take her to Emergency, and she refused.

But now, sitting in my bed with the sun pouring in the skylight and Leo holding my hands, I can only see my mother like a newscast from Somalia, cheeks sunken, eyes hollow, three fingers extended from one bony hand.

My mother was scheduled to go to the dentist that morning, and my father tried to wake her up several times, with several minutes in between—minutes in which the panic must have slowly mounted, realization finally seeping over him like a dark wave.

On the phone he says, "I keep asking the paramedics why they can't bring one on those machines in here." His voice loses itself in sobs. "I keep saying, why can't they do like they do on TV?"

"She didn't have any pain," I tell him, "and she didn't have any fear."

"And now they want to take her away," he says. "Should I let them take her away?"

"I'll be there as soon as I can get on a plane," I tell him. "Hang in there."

"There's a lady here who wants to talk to you, from the funeral home. I can't seem to answer her questions."

There is a loud shuffling and someone whose voice I have never heard before tells me, without emotion, how sorry she is for my loss.

"It was your mother's wish to be cremated," the voice goes on, "but we are having a little trouble engaging reality here, you know what I mean?"

"We?" I say.

"Your father can't decide whether to hold up on the cremation till you've had a chance to see the body. To tell you the truth, I don't think he's prepared for the fact of cremation at all."

"Prepared," I say.

"What it boils down to, you see, is a question of finances."

I fix my eyes on Leo, who is outside now. Bare-chested, he has started the lawn mower and is pushing it in ever-diminishing squares around the garden and in the center of the yard.

"If we don't cremate today, we'll have to embalm, which of course will wind up being a wasted embalming."

I count the baby cornstalks that have come up already: twenty-seven from forty seeds, a good ratio.

"On the other hand, you have only one chance to make the right decision. So if you are willing to handle the expense of embalming, well, it's your funeral."

"I don't think she would have wanted anyone to see her, even me," I say, maybe to myself, maybe out loud. I want only to get back in bed, wait for Leo to bring me my coffee and re-plan my day in the garden. I think about the radishes ready for dinner and the spinach that will bolt if I don't pick it in a few days.

"In this heat, though," the voice continues, "time is of the essence. The body had already begun to change color, and if we don't embalm today ..."

"Does she look especially thin to you?" I ask, before I can stop myself.

I cannot leave, I think suddenly, without planting the rest of the tomatoes.

"Go ahead and cremate her," I say. "I can't be there until tomorrow."

"They're going to take her away," I tell my father. "It's going to be okay though. We have to do what she wanted."

"Are you coming?"

"Yes," I say, "soon. I love you," I say, trying the words out on my father for the first time since I was five.

There is a muffled choking, and then the line goes dead.

I hang up the phone and walk out to the middle of the yard. I say to Leo, "I think I am about to become valuable to my father."

After a lifetime of nervous visits to my parents' house, I walk into what is, I remind myself, now only my father's house, as nervous as I've ever been. I can hear Strauss, *The Emperor's Waltz*, or is it *Delirium*, streaming from my father's study.

The cat waddles up to me, yelling for food. No one ever comes to the house without bringing a treat for Suzette.

"I thought cats were supposed to run away when somebody dies," I say, to no one.

"Run?" Leo would say if he were here, "That?"

My father emerges from his study, looking more bewildered than anything else. We embrace the way people do who wear reading glasses around their necks, stiff and without really pressing.

"Look at all these things, Lucille," my father says when we separate, sweeping his hand around the living room, "all these things she did." And he is right, my mother is in the room without being there, her perfectly handmade flowered slipcovers, her airy taste in art, her giant, temperamental ferns.

"I told the minister you would speak at the service," my father says. "She would have wanted that. She would have wanted you to say something nice about her. She said you never did that in real life."

"That will be easy," I say.

"Of course it will," he says quietly. "She was the most wonderful woman in the world." He starts to sob again, life-time-sized tears falling onto the cat who sits, patient as Buddha, at his feet.

The night before the funeral, I dream that I am sitting with my mother and father in the living room. My mother is wearing my favorite dress, one that she has given away years before. The furniture is the more comfortable, older style of my childhood, my favorite toys are strewn around the room. It is as though everything in the dream has been arranged to make me feel secure. A basket full of garden vegetables adorns the table, untouched.

"I thought you were dead," I say to my mother.

"I am," my mother says, crossing her ankles and folding her hands in her lap, "but I'll stay around until you can stand to be without me, until I know the two of you are going to be all right." She smoothes her hair around her face and smiles. "Then I'll just fade away."

It is the first in a series of dreams that will be with me for years, my mother dissolving until she becomes as thin as a sheet of paper, until I cry out, "No, I'm not ready yet," and my mother solidifies, right before my eyes.

On the morning of the funeral, all I can think of is to cook, so I go to the market across the street for bacon and eggs and buttermilk biscuits, and come back and do the dishes that have already begun to accumulate.

"If you put the glasses in the dishwasher right side up, I discovered, they get all full of water," my father says.

I excuse myself, shut the bathroom door behind me, and burst into tears.

I fry bacon and eggs and bake biscuits and stir gravy as if my life depends on it. My father gives at least half of his breakfast to the cat, who is now apparently allowed to lie right on top of the dining room table with her head on the edge of his plate.

We talk about the changes that will come to his life, about him getting a microwave, about a maid coming in once a week. I tell him I will come east for his birthday next month, invite him west for a visit next winter. We talk about the last trip the three of us took together to Florida. Did I remember, he wants to know, that it had rained, like magic, only in the evenings, did I remember how we had done the crossword puzzle, the three of us all together? And even though I don't remember, I tell him that I do. We talk about my mother, words coming out of my father's mouth that make me believe in heaven, I'm so desperate for my mother to hear. Finally, and only after we have talked about everything else, my father and I talk about sports.

Before the funeral is something the minister calls the "interment of the ashes." My father and I have our separate visions of what this word means. Mine involves a hand-thrown pot sitting next to a fountain; my father, still stuck on the burial idea, imagines a big marble tomb, opened for the service and cemented back up.

What actually happens is that the minister digs up a three-inch square of ivy in an inconspicuous corner of the church garden, digs a couple of inches of dirt beneath it, and sprinkles what amounts to little more than a heaping table-spoon of ashes into the hole. I can feel my father leaning over my shoulder as I too lean over to see into the hole. Whatever laws of physics I once knew cannot prepare me for the minis-cule amount of ashes, a whole human being so light that she could be lifted and caught by the wind.

The sun breaks through the clouds then, and the minister smiles, in cahoots with his God's timing, and takes that opportunity to refill the hole with dirt, neatly replacing the ivy.

Later, inside the parish house, my father says to the minister, "So there's really no limit to the number of people who could be cremated and inter ... ed," his voice falling around the word, "in that garden."

"Oh, I guess upwards of sixty, eighty thousand," the minister answers with a smile I cannot read.

My father has that bewildered look on his face again, the look of a man who never expected to have to feel sorry for all the things he didn't say. I pull gently on his hand and he lets me, and we walk hand in hand to the car.

After the reception, after all the wellwishers have gone home, my father turns on the Strauss again, this time *Tales from the Vienna Woods*.

People have brought food, so much of it I think they are trying to make some kind of point. I sort through the dishes mechanically, deciding what to refrigerate, what to freeze.

It has begun raining, huge hard summer raindrops, soaking the ground and turning my mother, I realize almost happily, back to the earth, to ivy food, to dust. I watch my father amble around the living room, directionless for a while, watch a smile cross his lips, perhaps for the rain, and then fade.

"Listen to this sequence, Lucille," he tells me, "Is it possible that the music gets better than this in heaven?"

Something buzzes in my chest every time my father speaks to me in this new way, a little blast of energy that lightens me somehow, that buoys me up. It is a sensation, I realize, with only a touch of alarm, not unlike falling in love.

"She would have loved to have heard the things you said about her," my father says.

"Yeah," I say. "She would have loved to hear what you said too."

"Maybe she did," he says, "from … somewhere."

"Maybe," I say.

"If there is a God …" he says, and I wait for him to finish, but he gets lost all of a sudden as the record changes to the *Acceleration Waltz*.

"I love you so much," my father says suddenly, and I turn, surprised to face him.

But it is the cat he has lifted high and heavy above his head, and he and the cat begin turning together to the tryptic throb of the music. He holds the cat's left paw in one hand, supporting her weight, all the fluffy rolls of her, with the other, nuzzling her coffee-stained nose to the beat of the music until she makes a gurgling noise in her throat and threatens to spit. He pulls his head away from her and continues to spin, faster and faster, the music gaining force, their circles bigger around my mother's flowered furniture, underneath my mother's brittle ferns.

"One two three, one two three, one two three," my father says as the waltz reaches its full crescendo. The cat seems to relax a little at the sound of his voice, and now she throws her head back into the spinning, as if agreeing to accept the weight of this new love that will from this day forward be thrust upon her.

The Minor Wars

Kaui Hart Hemmings

The sun is shining, mynah birds are hopping, palm trees are swaying, so what. I sit down in my easy chair. I've brought it here from home. I pick up the spoon from my lunch tray. I'd like to fling this spoon into the air, catch it in my mouth and say, "Look at that, Boots." Boots is my wife, although I haven't called her that since the early seventies when she used to wear these orange knee-high boots in eighty-six degree weather. She'd top my utensil act by using a fork or a steak knife. Her real name is Joanie, and she's barefoot. She's in a coma. Dying the slowest of deaths. Or perhaps I'm wrong. Perhaps she has never felt more alive.

"Shut this crap off," I tell Scottie, my ten-year old daughter. Her real name is Scottie. She turns off the television with the remote.

"No, I mean this." I point to the stuff in the window — the sun and the trees.

Scottie slides the curtain across the window, shutting all of it out. "This curtain is sure heavy," she says.

She needs a haircut or a brushing. There are small tumbleweeds of hair rolling over the back of her head. She is one of those kids who always seem to need a haircut. I'm grateful that she isn't pretty, but I realize this could change.

"It's like the bib I have to wear at the dentist when he needs x-rays of my gums," Scottie says. She knocks on the hard curtain. "I wish we were at the dentist."

"Me too," I say, and it's true. A root canal would be a blast compared to this. Life has been strange without Joanie's voice commanding it. I have to cook now and clean and give Scottie orders. That's been weird. I've never been that full-time parent, supervising the children on weekdays, setting schedules and boundaries. Now I see Scottie before school and right after school, and I'm basically with her until she goes to bed. She's a funny kid.

The visitor on my wife's bed looks at Scottie standing by the shaded window and frowns, then turns on a light with a remote control and goes back to work on Joanie's face. My wife is in a coma and this woman is applying make-up to her lips. I have to admit that Joanie would appreciate this. She enjoys being beautiful, and she likes to look good whether she's canoeing across the Molokai channel or getting tossed from an offshore powerboat. She likes to look *luminous* and *ravishing*—her own words. Good luck, I always tell her. Good luck with your goals. I don't love my wife as I'm supposed to, but I love her in my own way. To my knowledge, she doesn't adore me either, but we are content with our individual schedules and our lives together, and are quite proud of our odd system.

We tried for a while to love each other normally, urged by her brother to subject ourselves to counseling as a decent couple would. Barry, her brother, is a man of the couch, a believer in therapy, affirmations and pulse points. Once, he tried to show us exercises he'd been doing in session with his new woman friend. We were instructed to trade reasons, abstract or specific, why we stayed with one another. I started off by saying that she would get really drunk and pretend I was someone else and do this really neat thing with her tongue. Joanie said tax breaks. Barry cried. Openly. Joanie and Barry's parents are divorced and his second wife had recently left him for a man who understood that a man didn't do volunteer work. Barry wanted us to reflect on bonds and promises and love and such. He was tired of things breaking apart. Tired of people resigning so easily. We tried for Barry, but our marriage only seemed to work when we didn't try at all.

The lady with the make-up (Tia? Tara? Someone who models with Joanie) has stopped her dabbing and is looking at Scottie. The light is hitting this woman's face giving me opportunity to see that she should perhaps be working on her own make-up. The color of her face, a manila envelope. Specks of white in her eyebrows. Concealer not concealing. I can tell my daughter doesn't know what to do with this stare.

"What?" Scottie asks.

"I think your mother was enjoying the view," Tia, or Tara, says.

I jump in to protect my daughter who is silent and confused.

"Listen here, T. Her mother was not enjoying the view. Her mother is in a coma."

"My name is not T," T says. "My name is Allison."

"Okay then, listen here, Ali. Don't confuse my daughter."

"I'm turning into a remarkable young lady," Scottie says.

"Damn straight," I say.

This Ali person gets back to business. Scottie turns the television back on. Another dating show. I'm running out of toys. I can usually find a toy in anything. A spoon, a sugar packet, a quarter. Our first week here, I made up this game:

who could get the most slices of banana stuck to the ceiling. You had to put a piece on a napkin and then try to trampoline it up there. Scottie loved it. Nurses got involved. Even the neurologist gave it a go. But now we're nearing the end of our fourth week here and I'm running out of tricks. The neurologist says her scores are lower on the various coma scales. She says things, uses language I don't understand, and yet I understand her—I know what she's telling me.

"Last time you were the one on the bed," Scottie says.

"Yup."

"Last time you lied to me."

"I know, Scottie. Forgive me." My motorcycling accident. I insisted I was okay, that I wasn't going to go to the hospital. Scottie had issued me these little tests to demonstrate my unreliability. Joanie participated. They played bad cop, worse cop.

"How many fingers?" Scottie had asked, holding up what I thought was a pinky and a thumb: a shaka.

"Balls," I had said. I hadn't wanted to be tested this way.

"Answer her," Joanie said.

"Two?"

"Okay," Scottie said warily. "Close your eyes and touch your nose and stand on one foot."

"Balls, Scottie. I can't do that regardless, and you're treating me like a drunk driver."

"Do what she says," Joanie yelled.

I had stood still in protest. I knew something was wrong with me, but I didn't want to go to the hospital. I wanted to let what was wrong with my body run its course. I was curious. I was having trouble holding up my head.

"Look at yourself," Joanie said. "You can't even see straight."

"How am I supposed to look at myself, then?"

"Shut up, Matthew. Get in the car."

I had damaged my fourth nerve, a nerve that connects your eyes to your brain, which explained why things had been out of focus.

"You could have died," Scottie says. She's watching Allison brush color onto Joanie's cheeks.

"No way," I say. "A fourth nerve? Who needs it?"

"You lied. You said you were okay. You said you could see my fingers."

"I didn't lie. I guessed correctly. Plus, for a while there I got to have twins. Two Scotties."

Scottie nods. "Well. Okay."

I remember when I was in the hospital Joanie put vodka into my Jell-O. She wore my eye patch and teased me and stayed with me. It was very nice. I'm wondering what my accident has to do with anything. Lately, Scottie's been pointing out my flaws, my tricks and lies. She's interviewing me. I'm the back-up candidate. I'm the dad.

Scottie touches her mother's hair. It's slippery looking. It looks the way it did when she gave birth to Scottie and our other daughter, Alexandra. Allison is now looking at me as if I'm disturbed. "You have an odd way of speaking to children," she says.

"Parents shouldn't have to compromise their personalities," Scottie says.

It's something I've heard Joanie tell our other daughter. I catch a glimpse of my wife's face. She looks so lovely. Not ravishing, but simply lovely. Her freckles rise through the blush, her closed eyes fastened by dark, dramatic lashes. These lashes are the only strong feature left on her face. Everything has been softened. She looks pretty, but perhaps too divine; too bone china white, as if she's underwater or cased in glass. Oddly, the effect makes me like all the things I usually don't like about her. I like that she forgets to wash the lettuce and our salads are always pebbly. Or sometimes we go to this restaurant that's touristy, but the fish is great, and without fail she ends up at the bar with these Floridian spring-break sorts for a drink or ten and I'm left at the table all alone. I usually don't enjoy this, but now I don't mind so much. I like her magnetism. I like her courage and ego. But maybe I only like these things because she may not wake up again. It's confusing.

The manager of that restaurant once thanked me. He said that she always livened up the place and made people want to drink. I'm sure if she died, he'd put her picture up because it's that kind of restaurant—pictures of local legends and dead patrons haunting the walls. I feel sad that she has to die for her picture to go up on the wall, or for me to really love everything about her.

"Allison," I say. "Thank you. I'm sure Joanie is so pleased."

"She's not pleased. She's in a coma," Allison says.

I'm speechless.

"Oh my God," Allison says and she starts to cry. "I can't believe I said that. I was just trying to sound like you. To get you back."

She leaves the room with her beauty tools.

"Oh mercy. I need to change some habits. I'm an ass," I say.

"You're my dad," Scottie says.

"Yes," I say. "Yes."

"You're a dad-ass. Like a bad-ass but older."

"Mercy," I say.

Scottie wants me to step into the waiting room with her. She has something to tell me. This is routine. She's afraid of speaking to her mother. She's embarrassed of her life. A ten year old, worried that her life isn't interesting enough. She thinks that if she speaks to her mother, she should have something incredible to say. I always urge her to talk about school or the dogs, but Scottie says that this would be boring, and she wouldn't want her mother to think she was a walking yawn. For the past few weeks or so, Scottie has been trying to have these worthy experiences after school at the beach club.

"Okay, Scottie," I say. "Today's the day. You're going to talk to mom. You can read an article, you can sing a song, or tell her what you learned in school. Right-o?"

"Okay, but I have a story."

"Talk to me."

She smiles. "Okay, pretend you're mom," she says. "Close your eyes."

I close my eyes.

"Hi mom. Yesterday I explored the reef in front of the public beach by myself. I have tons of friends, but I felt like being alone. There's this really cute guy who works the beach stand there. His eyes look like giraffe eyes."

I'm trying not to smile.

"The tide was low. I could see all sorts of things. In one place the coral was a really cool dark color, but then I looked closer and it wasn't the coral. It was an eel. A moray. I almost died. There were millions of sea urchins and a few sea cucumbers. I even picked one up and squeezed him."

"This is good, Scottie. Let's go back in. Mom will love this."

"I'm not done."

"Oh." I close my eyes again.

"I was squatting on the reef and lost my balance and fell back on my hands. One of my hands landed on an urchin and it put its spines in me. My hand looked like a pincushion."

I'm grabbing her hands, holding them up to my face. The roots of urchin spines are locked in and expanded under the skin of her left palm. They look like tiny black starfish that plan on making this hand their home forever. I notice more stars on her fingertips. "Why didn't you tell me you were hurt? Why didn't you say something?"

"I'm okay. I handled it. I didn't really fall."

"What do you mean? Are these pen marks?"

"Yes."

I look closer. I feel her palm and press on the marks.

"Ow," she says and pulls her hand back. "Just kidding," she says. "They're real. But I didn't really fall. I did it on purpose. I slammed my hand into an urchin. But I'm not telling mom that part."

"What?" I can't imagine Scottie feeling such terrible pain. "Why would you do this? Scottie?"

"For a story, I guess."

"But Christ, didn't it hurt?"

"Yes."

"Balls, Scottie. I'm floored right now. Completely floored."

"Do you want to hear the rest?" she asks.

I push my short fingernails into my palm just to try to get a taste of the sting she felt. I shake my head. "I guess. Go on."

"Okay. Pretend you're mom. You can't interrupt."

"I can't believe you'd do that."

"You can't speak! Be quiet or you won't hear the rest."

Scottie talks about the blood, the needles jutting from her hand, how she climbed back on to the rock pier like a crab with a missing claw. Before she returned to shore, Scottie describes how she looked out across the ocean and watched the swimmers do laps around the catamarans. She says that the ones with white swimming caps looked like runaway buoys.

Of course, she didn't see any of this. Pain makes you focused. She probably ran right to the club's medic. She's making up the details, making a better story for her mother.

My eldest daughter had to do the same thing—knock herself out to get some attention from Joanie. Or perhaps to take the attention away from Joanie. Now Scottie is realizing what needs to be done. I'm afraid it's all going to start again.

"Because of dad's boring ocean lectures I knew these weren't needles in my hand but more like sharp bones— calcitic plates, which vinegar would help dissolve."

I smile. Good girl, I think to myself.

"Dad, this isn't boring, is it?"

"Boring is not the word I'd use."

"Okay. You're mom again. So I thought of going to the club's first-aid."

"Good girl."

"Shh," she says. "But instead, I went to the cute boy and asked him to pee on my hand."

"Excuse me?"

"Yes, mom. That's exactly what I said to him. *Excuse me*, I said. I told him I hurt myself. He said, *Uh-oh. You okay?* Like I was an eight year old. He didn't understand so I placed my hand on the counter. He said a bunch of swear words then told me to go to the hospital or something. *Or are you a member of that club?* he asked. He told me he'd take me there, which was really nice of him. He went out through the back of his stand and I went around to meet him. I told him what he needed to do and he blinked a thousand times and used curse words in all sorts of combinations. He wondered if you were supposed to suck out the poison after you pulled out the needles, and if I was going to go into seizures. He told me he wasn't trained for this, and that there was no way he'd do that to my hand, but I told him what you always tell dad when you want him to do something he doesn't want to do. I said, 'stop being a pussy,' and it did the trick. He told me not to look and he asked me to say something or whistle."

"Scottie," I say. "Tell me you've made this up."

"I'm almost done," she whines. "So I talked about the records you had beaten in your boat. And that you were a model, but you weren't all prissy, and that every guy at the club was in love with you but you only love dad because he's easy like the easy chair he sits on all the time."

"Scottie. I have to use the bathroom." I feel sick.

"Okay," she says. "Wasn't that a hilarious story? Was it too long?"

"Yes and no. I have to go to the bathroom. Tell your mom what you told me. Go talk to her." She can't hear you anyway, I think. I hope.

Joanie *would* think that story was hilarious. This bothers me. The story bothers me. Scottie shouldn't have to create these dramas. Scottie shouldn't have to be pissed on. She's reminding me of her sister, someone I don't ever want her to become. Alex. Seventeen. She's like a special effect. It wows you. It alarms you, but then it gets tiresome and you forget about it. I need to call Alex and update her. She's at boarding school on another island, not too far but far enough. The last time I called, I asked her what was wrong and she said, 'The price of cocaine.' I laughed, asked 'Seriously, what else?' 'Is there anything else?' she said.

She's very well known over at Hawaii's Board of Tourism. At fifteen, she did calendars and work for Isle Cards whose captions said things like Life's a Damn Hot Beach. One-pieces became string bikinis. String bikinis became thongs and then just shells and granules of sand strategically placed on her body. The rest of her antics are so outrageous and absurd, it's too boring to think about. In her struggle to be unique, she has become common: the rebellious, privileged teen. Car chase, explosion, gone and forgotten.

Despite everything, her childishness, her utter wrongness, she makes me feel so guilty. Guilty because I catch myself believing that if Joanie were to die, we'd make it. We'd flourish. We'd trust and love each other. She could come home. We used to love each other so much. I don't call her even though I need to tell her to fly down tomorrow. I can't bear to hear any accidental pitch of joy or release that may slink into her voice or my own.

Scottie is sitting on the bed. Joanie looks like Sleeping Beauty.

"Did you tell her?" I ask.

"I'm going to work on it some more," Scottie says. "Because if mom thinks it's funny, what will she do? What if the laugh circulates around in her lungs or in her brain somewhere since it can't come out? What if it kills her?"

"It doesn't work that way," although I have no idea how it works.

"Yes, but I just thought I'd make it more tragic, that way she'll feel the need to come back."

"It shouldn't be this complicated, Scottie." I say this sternly. I sit on the bed and put my ear to where Joanie's heart is. I bury my face in her gown. This is the most intimate I've been with her in a long time. My wife, the speedboat record holder. My wife, the motorcyclist, the model, the long-distance paddler, the tri-athlete. What drives you Joanie? I say into her chest. I realize I've copied one of her hobbies and wonder what drives me as well. I don't even like motorcycles. I hate the sound they make.

"I miss mom's sneezes," Scottie says.

I laugh. I shake with laughter. I laugh so hard it's soundless and this makes Scottie laugh. Whenever Joanie sneezes, she farts. She can't help it. This is why we are hysterical. A nurse comes in and opens the curtain. She smiles at us. "You two," she says. She urges us to go outside and enjoy the rest of the day.

Scottie agrees. She looks at her wristwatch and immediately settles down. "Crap, dad. We need to go. I need a new story."

Because the nurse is still in the room I say, "Watch your language."

At the beach club, the shrubs are covered with surfboards. There has been a south swell, but the waves are blown out from the strong wind. I follow Scottie into the dining room. She tells me that she can't leave until something either amusing or tragic happens to her. I tell her that I'm skipping practice and am not letting her out of my sight. This infuriates her. I tell her I'll stay out of her way, but I'm not going to paddling practice. I tell her to pretend I'm not there.

"Fine, then sit over there." She points to the tables on the perimeter of the dining room. There are a few ladies playing cards at one of these tables. I like these ladies. They're around eighty years old and they wear tennis skirts even though I can't imagine they still play tennis. I wish Joanie liked to play cards and sit around.

Scottie heads to the bar. The bartender, Jerry, nods at me. I watch Scottie climb onto a barstool and Jerry makes her a virgin daiquiri, then lets her try out a few of his own concoctions. "The guava one is divine," I hear her say, "but the lime makes me feverish."

I'm pretending to read the paper that I borrowed from one of the ladies. I've moved to a table that's a little closer to the bar so I can listen and watch.

"How's your mom?" Jerry asks.

"Still sleeping." Scottie twists atop her barstool. Her legs don't reach the metal footrest so she crosses them on the seat and balances.

"Well, you tell her I say hi. You tell her we're all waiting for her."

I watch Scottie as she considers this. She stares at her lap. "I don't talk to her," she says to Jerry, though she doesn't look at him.

Jerry sprays a swirl of whipped cream into her drink. She takes a gulp of her daiquiri then rubs her head. She does it again. She spins around on the barstool. And then she begins to speak in a manner that troubles me. She is yelling as if there's some sort of din in the room that she needs to overcome.

"Everybody loves me, but my husband hates me, guess I'll have to eat the worm. Give me a shot of Cuervo Gold, Jerry baby."

Jerry cleans the bottles of liquor, trying to make noise.

I wonder how often Joanie said this. If it's her standard way of asking for tequila. It makes me wonder how we managed to spend so much time at this place and never see each other at all.

"Give me two of everything," Scottie yells, caught in her fantasy. I want to relieve Jerry of his obvious discomfort, but then I see Troy walking towards the bar. Big, magnanimous, golden Troy. I quickly hide behind my newspaper. My daughter is suddenly silent. Troy has killed her buzz. I'm sure he hesitated when he saw her, but it's too late to turn around.

"Hey Scottie," I hear him say. "Look at you."

"Look at you," she says, and her voice sounds strange. Almost unrecognizable. "You look awake," she says.

"Uh thanks, Scottie."

Uh thanks, Scottie. Troy is so slow. His great grandfather invented the shopping cart and this has left little for Troy to do except sleep with lots of women and put my wife in a coma. Of course, it's not his fault, but he wasn't hurt. He was the driver and Joanie was the throttle-man because Troy insisted he wanted to drive this time. Rounding a mile marker, their boat launched off a wave, spun out and Joanie was ejected. When Troy came in from the race alone he kept saying, "Lots of chop and holes. Lots of chop and holes."

"Have you visited her?" Scottie asks.

"Yes I have, Scottie. Your dad was there."

"What did you say to her?"

"I told her the boat was in good shape. I said it was ready for her."

What a Neanderthal.

"Her hand moved, Scottie. I really think she heard me. I really think she's going to be okay."

Troy isn't wearing a shirt. The man has muscles I didn't even know existed. I wonder if Joanie has slept with him. Of course she has. His eyes are the color of swimming pools. I'm about to lower the paper so he'll stop talking to Scottie, until I hear her say, "The body has natural reactions. When you cut off a chicken's head, its body runs around, but it's still a dead chicken."

I hear either Troy or Jerry coughing.

"Don't give up, Scottie," Jerry says.

Golden Troy is saying something about life and lemons and bootstraps. He is probably placing one of his massive tan paws on Scottie's shoulder.

I see Scottie leaving the dining room. I follow her. She runs to the beach wall and I catch her before she jumps off of it. Tears are brewing in her eyes. She looks up to keep them from falling, but they fall anyway.

"I didn't mean to say dead chicken," she cries.

"Let's go home," I say.

"Why is everyone so into sports here? You and mom and Troy think you're so cool. Everyone here does. Why don't you join a book club? Why can't mom just relax at home?"

I hold her and she lets me. I try to think if I have any friends in a book club. I realize I don't know anyone, man or woman, who isn't a member of this club. I don't know a man who doesn't surf, kayak or paddleboard. I don't know a woman who doesn't jog, sail or canoe paddle, although Joanie is the only woman I know racing bikes and boats.

"I don't want mom to die," Scottie says.

"Of course you don't." I push her away from me and bend down to look in her freckled brown eyes. "Of course."

"I don't want her to die like this," Scottie says. "Racing or competing or doing something marvelous. I've heard her say, 'I'm going out with a bang.' Well, I hope she goes out choking on a kernel of corn or slipping on a piece of toilet paper."

"Christ, Scottie. How old are you? Where do you get this shit? Let's go home," I say. "You don't mean any of this. You need to rest." I imagine my wife peaceful on her bed. I wonder what she was thinking as she flew off the boat. If she knew it was over. I wonder how long it took Troy to notice she wasn't there beside him. Scottie's face is puffy. Her hair is greasy. It needs to be washed. She has this look of disgust on her face. It's a very adult look.

"Your mother thinks you're so great," I say. "She thinks you're the prettiest, smartest, silliest girl in town."

"She thinks I'm a coward."

"No she doesn't. Why would she think that?"

"I didn't want to go on the boat with her and she said I was a scaredy-cat like you."

"She was just joking. She thinks you're the bravest girl in town. She told me it scared her how brave you were."

"Really?"

"Damn straight." It's a lie. Joanie often said that we're raising two little scaredy-cats, but of all the lies I tell, this one is necessary. I don't want Scottie to hate her mother as Alexandra once did or maybe still does. It will consume her and age her. It will make her fear the world. It will make her too shy and too nervous to ever say exactly what she means.

"I'm going swimming," Scottie says.

"No," I say. "We've had enough."

"Dad, please." She pulls me down by my neck and whispers, "I don't want people to see that I've been crying. Just let me get in the water."

"Fine. I'll be here." She strips off her clothes and throws them at me, then jumps off the wall to the beach below and charges towards the water. She dives in and breaks surface after what seems like a minute. She dives. She splashes. She plays. I sit on the coral wall and watch her and the other kids and their mothers and nannies. To my left is a small reef. I can see black urchins settled in the fractures. I still can't believe Scottie did such a thing.

The outside dining terrace is filling up with people and their pink and red and white icy drinks. An old man is walking out of the ocean with a one-man canoe held over his head; a tired yet elated smile quivering on his face as if he's just returned from some kind of battle in the deep sea.

The torches are being lit on the terrace and on the rock pier. The soaring sun has turned into a wavy blob above the horizon. It's almost green flash time. Not quite yet, but soon. When the sun disappears behind the horizon, sometimes there's a green flash of light that sparkles seemingly out of the sea. It's a communal activity around here, waiting for this green flash, hoping to catch it.

Children are coming out of the water.

I hear a mother's voice drifting off the ocean. It's far away yet loud. "Get in here, little girl. They're everywhere."

Scottie is the only child still swimming. I jump off the wall. "Scottie!" I yell. "Scottie get in here right now!"

"There are Portuguese manowars out there," a woman says to me. "The swell must have pushed them in. Is she yours?" The woman points to Scottie who is swimming in from the catamarans.

"Yes," I say.

My daughter comes in. She's holding a tiny man-of-war—the clot of its body and the clear blue bubble on her hand, its dark blue string tail wrapped around her wrist.

"What have you done? Why are you doing this?" I take the man-of-war off of her with a stick; pop its bubble so that it won't hurt anybody. My daughter's arm is marked with a red line. I tell her to rinse her arm off with seawater. She says it's not just her arm that's hurt—she was swimming amongst a mass of them.

"Why would you stay out there, Scottie? How could you tolerate that?"

I've been stung by them hundreds of times; it's not so bad, but kids are supposed to cry when they get stung. It's something you can always count on.

"I thought it would be funny to say I was attacked by a herd of minor wars."

"It's not minor war. You know that, don't you?" When she was little I would point out sea creatures to her but I'd give them the wrong names. I called them minor wars because they were like tiny soldiers with impressive weapons—the gaseous bubble, the whip-like tail, the toxic tentacles, advancing in swarms. I called a blowfish a blow-pop; an urchin, an ocean porcupine, and sea turtles were salt-water hard-hats. I thought it was funny, but now I'm worried that she doesn't know the truth about things.

"Of course, I know," Scottie says. "They're manowars, but it's our joke. Mom will like it."

"It's not manowar either. It's man-of-war. Portuguese man-of-war. That's the proper name."

"Oh," she says. She's beginning to itch herself. More lines are forming on her chest and legs. I tell her I'm not happy and that we need to get home and put some ointments and ice on the stings. "Vinegar will make it worse, so if you thought giraffe boy could pee on you, you're out of luck."

She agrees as if she was prepared for this—the punishment, the medication, the swelling, the pain that hurts her now and the pain that will hurt her later. But she's happy to deal with my disapproval. She's gotten her story, and she's beginning to see how much easier physical pain is to tolerate. I'm unhappy that she's learning this. She's ten years old.

We walk up the sandy slope towards the dining terrace. I see Troy sitting at a table with some people I know. I look at Scottie to see if she sees him and she is giving him the middle finger. The dining terrace gasps, but I realize it's because of the sunset and the green flash. We missed it. The flash flashed. The sun is gone. The sky is pink and violent like arguing little girls. I reach to grab the offending hand, but instead I correct her gesture.

"Here, Scottie. Don't let that finger stand by itself like that. Bring up the other fingers just a little bit. There you go."

Troy stares at us and smiles a bit. He's completely confused.

"All right, that's enough," I say, suddenly feeling sorry for Troy. He may really love Joanie. There is that chance. I place my hand on Scottie's back to guide her away. She flinches and I remove my hand, remembering that she's hurt all over.

We are at the hospital again even though it's late at night. Scottie insisted on it. She practically had a tantrum.

"I'll forget the exact sensations that I need to communicate to mom!" she had screamed.

She still hasn't showered. I wanted the salt water to stay on her. It's good for the wounds. She cried on the way over here, cried and scratched at herself. Her stings are now raised red lesions. A nurse gave them attention. She gave her some antibiotics as well. Scottie has a runny nose; she's dizzy and nauseous though she won't admit it's from swimming with poisonous invertebrates. She's miserable, but I have a feeling she won't do anything like this again. The nurse shaved her legs to get rid of any remaining nematocyst. Now Scottie is admiring her smooth, woman legs.

"I'm going to start doing this all the time," she says. "It will be such a hassle."

"No, you're not," I say. I say it loudly and it surprises both of us. "You're not ready." She smiles, uncomfortable with my authority. So this is what it's like.

We're going to stay the night. I'm sitting on the end of the bed putting eye drops in my eyes. We don't even look like visitors. We look like patients; defeated, exhausted from the world outside. We have come in for shelter and care and a little rest. The staff here has been so kind and lenient towards us. It's nine-o-clock in the ICU. We have walked in unannounced; Scottie has received free medical attention. This can't be standard practice. It's over. I know their indulgence of us is because they have no hope, or they've been advised by Dr. Johnston to scratch hope off of their charts. People become so kind right before someone dies.

Scottie opens the curtain and lets the night in—the dark palm trees and the lights of other buildings. She asks me if she hurt the urchin as much as it hurt her. She asks me why everyone else calls them manowars. I tell her I don't know, in reply to the first question. I don't know how that works. For the second question I answer, "Words get abbreviated and we forget the origins of things."

"Or fathers lie," she says, "about the real names."

"That too."

She climbs up on the bed and we look at Joanie in the half-moon light. She leans back against my chest. Her forehead is beneath my chin. I move my head around. I nuzzle her. I don't talk about what we need to talk about.

"Why is it called a jellyfish?" Scottie asks. "It's not a fish and it's not jelly."

I say that a man-of-war isn't a jellyfish. I don't answer the question, but I tell her that she asks good questions. "You're getting too smart for me, Scottie."

I can feel her smiling. Even Joanie seems to be smiling, slightly. I feel happy, though I'm not supposed to be, I guess. But the room feels good. It feels peaceful.

"Water," I say. "And blankets." I leave the room to get water and blankets.

When I come back towards the room, I hear Scottie say, "I have a remarkable eye." I stop in the doorway. Scottie is talking to her mother. I watch.

She is curled into her mother's side and has maneuvered Joanie's arm so that it's around her. "It's on the ceiling," I hear her say. "The most beautiful nest. It's very golden and soft-looking and warm, of course."

I see it too, except it isn't a nest. It's a browning banana, the remnant of our old game still stuck to the ceiling.

Scottie props herself onto an elbow, then leans in and kisses her mother on the lips, checks her face, then kisses her again. She does this over and over; this exquisite version of mouth to mouth, each kiss expectant, almost medicinal.

I let her go on with this fantasy, this belief in magical endings, this belief that love can bring someone to life. I let her try. For a long time, I watch her effort. I root for her even, but after awhile I know that it's time. I need to step in. I tap lightly on the door. I don't want to startle her too badly.

Papa Who Wakes Up Tired in the Dark

Sandra Cisneros

Your *abuelito* is dead, Papa says early one morning in my room. *Esta muerto,* and then as if he just heard the news himself, crumples like a coat and cries, my brave Papa cries. I have never seen my Papa cry and don't know what to do.

I know he will have to go away, that he will take a plane to Mexico, all the uncles and aunts will be there, and they will have a black-and-white photo taken in front of the tomb with flowers shaped like spears in a white vase because this is how they send the dead away in that country.

Because I am the oldest, my father has told me first, and now it is my turn to tell the others. I will have to explain why we can't play. I will have to tell them to be quiet today.

My Papa, his thick hands and thick shoes, who wakes up tired in the dark, who combs his hair with water, drinks his coffee, and is gone before we wake, today is sitting on my bed.

And I think if my own Papa died what would I do. I hold my Papa in my arms. I hold and hold and hold him.

The Other Daughter

Antonya Nelson

"Who," my father asked me, "would pay fifteen bucks for that crap?" We were waiting for my beautiful sister in the masseur's lobby. Before us towered shelves of oils and creams, anemic blue bottles with labels in French script. It was a crowded little anteroom. Price tags hung on gold thread. Lutes played, seagull sounds. "Better be the frigging elixir of the universe, worth that much," he grumbled. "Right, Patty?" he prodded, looking for me to agree.

I shrugged, though I did not doubt the value, only my father's false, old-fashioned innocence about it. On the glass table against which our knees were jammed there lay fanned-out business cards. Made of heavy paper, they were designed to look torn, and although the address they specified was on a rue in Paris, France, this was First Street, Wichita, Kansas. An air conditioner went on and on; everything smelled of essence of almonds and had a slippery quality to it. My sister had introduced us to places neither my father nor I would ever have reason to seek out on our own, offices without signs, without receptionists, whose business hours seemed arbitrary and crooked. Now she was in the room beyond the closed door, beyond the window and its slender, sealed blinds, lying naked on a table.

A man named Ascenzo, emaciated with a rotten tooth, would be running his thumbs up and down her spine locating pressure points and meridians. If I was thinking this, knowing it, what was my father thinking? I moved my knees away from his. Of course he would be thinking of Janice, too, his beauty. This summer he was unemployed—like us, Janice and me, free from high school—bored and self-hating, waiting for prime time TV. Every afternoon he would step onto the back porch of our house to tell her, as she tried to tan in the muggy sunlight, that her skin was so perfect, why was she ruining it with ultraviolet rays? She wouldn't even look at him, just yanked her tube top higher, adjusted the inside elastic of her thong, and listened to him plead.

"Thank you, Father," she would call indulgently. "I wear screen, you know." But what she wore was a chemical designed to turn her more quickly orange, a stain that smelled like soy sauce. Over her eyes sat a green plastic device like two spoons. She accepted neither parent's advice, though she was far kinder to my father than to my mother. The hostility between Janice and Mom was our family's crux, the thing we all orbited and negotiated: who was tormenting the other more? And whose displeasure could we better endure?

Our mother most often lost. She was no fun, especially in recent times. "Menopause," Janice diagnosed. My father greeted Mom in the mornings with the same stale line: "Look who took her ugly pills," seeming to believe it so outrageous as to be endearing. It was true she woke up with rumpled face skin and liquid eyes that leaked unchecked. True she muttered and bristled and wished most sincerely to be left alone. None of us was who she wanted. We had turned out wrong.

Dad and I could have read magazines while we waited for Janice, but I was afraid of what I might find in their pages while sitting next to my father, all those bodies in clothes, and out, girls not like me but like Janice. His reason for not reading them might have been the same. Our mutual shame left us staring at the svelte bottles for sale on the shelf, signed by Ascenzo, the masseur, containing pricey oils used to anoint bodies like my sister's. In the company of my father, even these benign vessels made me look aside blushing.

When her hour was up, the inner door opened just wide enough to let Ascenzo escape. He squeezed out and closed it softly behind him, showing his gray tooth as he greeted us. I watched his hands, which shone with oil. He continued to wipe them on a towel as we made small talk and waited for Janice to dress. It was a stubborn oil, like cooking oil, and Ascenzo had to run the towel between his fingers, rub down his wrists. This scrubbing was the only movement in the room, a vaguely masturbatory massage of his own. I knew my father was watching it as closely as I, thinking of those smug hands, that oil, on Janice.

My sister clattered out of the inner room, trailing her purse on her injured hand, as if to draw attention to it. She was a teenage model. Her hair was a glossy white curtain she swung with exaggeration, as if it were heavy, though in reality it was thin hair inclined to stringiness. She had to have just this moment brushed it for it to swing as it did.

"Ready?" she asked us, leaning into Ascenzo's open arms. Their embrace was for us to witness; they were dear friends, this gesture implied, dear and sympathetic like kin of another plain. Janice gave me and Dad a little glance, just to make sure we beheld her worldly, uninhibited, unKansan affection.

I was like my father, shy, embarrassed by my own presence, as if I were large or ugly or uninvited, though I was none of those things. But my sister was superior on all three counts: lithe, pretty, welcome. And damaged, her right hand shredded and ruined.

She held it up to slide her leather bag onto her shoulder. Where her three fingers had been were cherry-like buds, suture scars along the rims. Only her forefinger and thumb remained, so that she appeared constantly to be making a point.

"That's eighty-seven eighty-seven, even," Ascenzo told Janice, "including the drops," handing her a bottle of his oil. My father made out the check, crossing his sevens with a terse jerk of his wrist, and then leaving the paper on the table instead of in Ascenzo's open palm.

If I'd been brave, I would have answered my father's earlier question: "*You* pay fifteen bucks for that crap, that's who."

"Drink water," Ascenzo advised Janice. "I thought those kidneys would never clear. I had to do some *talking* to those fellows," he told me.

It was July, and though Janice glistened with massage oil and smelled of almonds, I sweated. In the car, she rode up front while our father drove us to her next appointment. She cracked her neck, side to side with her eyes closed. I wondered where *my* kidneys were, my liver and all the rest. How had she become so exotic? My life had sprung from the same source, fed on the same kibble, been exposed to the same Midwestern rays, and yet—the chasm between us.

"What did you think of Ascenzo?" Janice had asked my father and me after the first session, in June, her hand then a white plaster-cast club, a big wrapped drumstick stuck on the end of her slender arm.

"His name sounds like somebody sneezed," I had answered, without thinking. She'd given up expecting much from me. When she was whole, we'd spatted; it had been fair to do so. But now I felt a chilling, dumb guilt for the injustice done her.

My father said, "Uh-huh," trying not to sound judgmental. Later, when Janice wasn't around, he said to me, "That Ascenzo was a fairy." He made declarations of these sort only occasionally, as if to release dangerous pressure, and only to me, as far as I could tell. Why? Because he knew I was thinking the identical thing? But shouldn't he have had the befuddled respect for me that he did for Janice and my mother, the same masculine mock impatience, the same restraint? Instead, something about me generated confidence in him, as if I were his son instead of younger daughter. The other daughter.

Today my father leaned his elbow on the ledge of the open Falcon window, holding a cigar in his fingers. He'd done this so regularly, for so long, that the paint on the door had worn away, revealing a smooth silver beneath. I always thought the whole car might have looked pretty, rubbed down to this hue, a blinding chrome. At the tip of the cigar, his wing window glass had a halo of unctuous brown smudge. In the back, I smelled myself. I shook my head to see if it hurt. I tried to focus on the painted lines of First Street to quell carsickness. Had I ridden in the front seat since Janice's accident? I had *driven*—learning, in the graveyard; later today, I would finally take the test for my license—but had not been a passenger up there.

"You girls want some lunch?" he asked us as we passed Pitt's Barbecue.

"Frozen yogurt," Janice answered, gazing out her window as the crowded, shimmering parking lot of Pitt's disappeared behind us. "Salad and a Diet Coke, don't you think, Patty?"

I shrugged; nothing sounded appetizing, though I would eat more than she would, once we arrived at the table.

They consulted me as if they might actually take my advice, my father looking in the rear view, my sister turning her ear my direction. I might have mediated between them, if it had been called for, having a foot squarely in each of their worlds. But it was never called for.

"I could circle round to Pitt's," he said, edging the Falcon toward the right lane.

"Grease," Janice said, motioning with her good hand for him to swim back into thru traffic. "I'm nothing but a greased pig myself. Let's don't eat one, too."

"What do you want, Pats?"

"Nothing, a Coke, some Tylenol. My *hair* hurts."

"If we eat at the yogurt shop, I'll have fries," Janice said. "If the air's not greasy, I could eat some fries and yogurt."

"Air conditioning," I agreed. The yogurt shop appeared in my mind like a mirage, bright green and white.

My father did not belong in a yogurt shop. He belonged at Pitt's, where he could bring in his cigar, not here where little stickers with puffin penguins on them declared the place anti-smoker. Janice ate a yogurt cone with her left hand, her tongue moving concentrically, sexily, around the white cream. I couldn't seem to maintain my posture in my seat, slumped and suddenly chilled by the rush of Coke up my straw. That icy ache flew to my forehead. My father pulled a hairy mound of bean sprouts from his avocado sandwich and left it on his plate. ("Bean sprouts smell like sperm," he'd declared to me once. Was I supposed to know enough to praise such an insight?) We all checked our watches; Janice's next appointment was at the Danish furniture store where she would be photographed displaying teak end tables and high-tech chairs that looked like praying mantises. This shoot had been delayed for two weeks to allow her stitches to heal and her gauze to be removed; I was just happy not to have to anticipate seeing her in bras and underwear in the Sunday newspaper pullouts.

Why had they waited for her? I studied her to try to learn why, what people saw in her that commanded their submission. She was not merely beautiful. That wouldn't have been enough. And now she would have to tuck away her right hand, behind cushions, in her pocket, leaving perhaps her thumb poised outside like a cowgirl. She was blessed with something far better than simple beauty, a kind of fickle, charmed affection that made you feel lucky when she turned it on you, and flawed when she withdrew it. She would choose to leave you, and you would deserve it.

Men stared at her here, as they did everywhere, and Janice did not seem to differentiate between those who ogled her intact, and those who fixated on her sudden deformity. She ignored them all unless it became necessary to do otherwise. "Take a picture," she would say. "It'll last longer." If only I could have adopted her assurance, I often thought, but of course it was inseparable from the rest of her. She had earned her indifference.

After lunch we returned to our wretched hot car. Later I was going to drive it around with a stranger and obtain my license. Dusty bits of the old cushion stuffing would stay like fine sand on the examiner's pants. Janice sat in the front again and brushed her hair with her clumsy left hand. "My shoulders are killing me," she told us. "My relationships are a wreck, Ascenzo said, that's why they hurt right here." She stretched to tap her right shoulder blade with her hair brush.

"Which relationships?" I asked, as I was supposed to. The air was so hot that my words seemed to come out composed of a gaseous substance.

"All of them," she said. "Family, friends, lovers, all of them."

Dad snorted and re-lit his cigar. He only made it through one or two of them a day, constantly extinguishing and tamping, the butt end in his mouth growing soggy, its leafy origins becoming grotesquely clear, little remnants like lawn debris on his tongue.

"Who'd believe insurance would cover this stuff?" he announced. Janice and I had heard this before; I listened as if in a trance. He digested topics of conversation like a cow, constantly bringing them back up for a chew. "*I* wouldn't believe it if I hadn't seen it with my own eyes. This *Ascenzo*, the guy with no last name, or maybe no first name, who has the Blue Cross, Blue Shield okay, this guy knows from your *back* you have trouble? He consults with your kidneys, they say 'send water'?" But Dad wasn't really annoyed. He found Janice gratifyingly mysterious, and her fierce defense of the bizarre amusing. He tolerated all manner of what he called *flake lore* as long as it came from her. He'd allowed her to glue a large, many-spired crystal right in the center of the dashboard, stuck there with a green substance like Silly Putty, because she said it would protect his ride. The crystal was almost exactly the size of the fat compass that had used to be attached to the windshield, its slow watery slosh something to focus on from the backseat when I grew bored, the green letters slipping serenely from N to NE to E. This had been my mother's compass, something she'd ordered by mail for no apparent reason; she never traveled anywhere she might have needed one, and besides that, she'd stuck it in our father's car instead of hers. Also for no apparent reason, the compass simply dropped off one hot day, rolling to the floorboard and disappearing out the passenger door when Janice opened it, the plastic ball cracking open as it hit the parking lot pavement and spilling out its viscous fluid. Oddly, it fell off only hours after Janice's crystal had been affixed beneath it, as if they'd waged a turf battle in the stuffy, summer interior of our closed car. On the windshield where the compass had been remained a cloudy circle of left-over glue, something Janice picked at in traffic with her bad hand.

What had Ascenzo made of that hand, anyway, free from its bandages at last? Her mangled hand—I stared at it endlessly—those sutured buds like boys' testicles with their funny seams, three in a row.

We arrived at Danish By Design and pulled in behind the white panel van that belonged to Marty, Janice's photographer. "He's probably sleeping with that masseur fag," my father had said to me privately. Privately, while Janice had been posing for a girdle ad, a still for Macy's, the bottom half of a girl who didn't need a girdle. Red and black girdles, spread on our Sunday breakfast table, the newspaper sticking in the syrup. I'd never known girdles came in colors. But mostly, why did my father feel he could say things like that to me?

"You guys waiting, or coming with?" Janice asked. She had to reach over herself to open her car door, her right forefinger not yet strong enough to pull the stiff handle by itself. A yawn suddenly overtook her: her mouth flexed open wide like a cat's to reveal her impeccable teeth—as she shook her head, rolled her shoulders, cracked her neck—then closed with a little peep.

"I'll bring your stuff," I told her, unhooking the drycleaner bag holding her pressed skirt and blouse. The blouse was silk, and she would wear it without a bra, her large breasts quivering like gelatin beneath. My father had already stepped from the car. He wouldn't sit outside waiting, "like a dog," as he put it, "a damned drooling dog."

Yet he reminded me of something ferocious and canine, a boxer or bulldog. And then there was me, the mutt. Janice led us inside where it was air conditioned. Customers watched her as they moved on the periphery, fingering floor lamps that looked like microphones. I sagged in my poor-postured way onto an ottoman with Janice's clothes on my lap. Marty's assistant, Roid, was playing with his shields and reflectors, snapping them open like big round silver fans, then checking his light meter, retracting the reflector, checking the meter. Roid, like Janice, was another South High student, a doper looking for a way out of class. Marty taught photography there, a buzz-cut redhead, tense and tangerine-freckled from top to bottom, also a doper. He'd brought Janice drugs when she was in the hospital, a French candy tin full of pretty pills that she'd given to me. She'd given me her legitimate meds, too, the codeine and seconal. Marty had no patience for Janice's family, us, my father the watchdog and me, the gape-mouthed dimwit.

"Yo, Patty," said Roid, who only had clout here. His biggest function was to shoot Polaroids—hence, his name—in advance of Marty's real shots. At school, he was nobody.

"Scum," I said to him, not unkindly. "Freak."

Janice motioned for me to follow her to the back, to the closet-like bathroom where she changed. I had to button her blouse, zip her skirt, smell again the warm perfume of almonds. It was her dominant hand that was ruined; her physical therapist would train the other fingers to take up the slack. Soon, she wouldn't need my help. When I'd heard about her accident at school, during algebra, my first thought had been that she would die, that I would be a celebrity. My imagination was grotesque that way, greedy and ruthless.

"I look okay?" Janice asked me. In our previous life, I would have lied and said no.

"Great," I said, which was true, but which didn't feel true.

"Thanks," she said, dismissing me. I left her to apply her own lipstick and found a leather armchair to sink into, momentarily comfortable in its pristine coolness. Marty's lights had cast an over-bright, beach-like atmosphere in the place, and I closed my eyes as if sunbathing. Through a drooping pair of eyelids I watched Janice's shoot. She floated through the showroom, caressing a teak highboy, sprawling over a cream-colored chaise, crossing her beautiful legs as she perched on a mahogany computer center shaped like a dressmaker's dummy, her bad hand behind her, supporting her. My father sat at a dining table across the showroom, reading Danish By Design literature, biting his damp extinguished cigar. Marty marched from his camera to Janice's knees and lifted her skirt. "Scooch," he told her, wiggling his own ass. She pulled the skirt higher. Roid giggled. "Thankee," Marty said, restored behind the lens of his camera. "Isn't that the way we say it out here, in Kansas? Thankee?"

"That's right," Roid told him.

Janice said, "You bet" without moving her smiling lips.

It was clear to me that Marty wanted to provoke my father. What would happen if Dad reacted? Janice would patiently hop down from the table and calm him. Marty would step outside to his van and take a toot, pop a diet soda, return when the air was clear again, red-eyed fox. Janice had taken several Independent Studies with Marty at South, leaving the grounds to visit developing labs and museum exhibits, to sit in his panel van and tell him about herself, to earn A's by virtue of her sophisticated flat affect and her natural beauty.

Outside of Danish By Design's tinted showroom glass, a traffic jam evolved around the overheated engine of a red Celica. I watched languidly as the driver put his face in the white vapor, everything wavering around him like a dream. My driving exam was our next stop today, and I wondered if I were prepared to navigate a snarl like this. I ran groggily through rules of the road while Janice finished up with her shoot. Signal at 100 feet. Two seconds space between your vehicle and the one in front of you. At breakfast—pancakes for the rest of us, milky coffee in a bowl for Janice—Dad had asked in his bright expectant morning voice, as he did every morning this summer, "What's on the agenda for today?" Janice couldn't drive because of her hand; I was useless unless accompanied by one of my parents. My mother worked. Dad had to take us. In better times, he was a general contractor. But his temper defeated him, over and over. He'd been supposed to supervise the construction of a car lot this summer— a sultry, asphalt-heavy prospect. A fight over his office space—the air-conditioned trailer parked at the site—had lost the job. This was what my mother called shooting his mouth and foot off at the same time. *Her* position at Southwestern Bell was secure—she *liked* to work; she liked it better than she liked us—and we got telephone perks. For example, Janice had her own line, her own unlisted number, and her own calls that came late at night to keep her murmuring in the room beside mine, her indistinct voice telling other people her secrets.

"Wrap, wrap, we gotta wrap," Marty sang out after an hour of flashes, to the tune of "Ding Dong the Witch is Dead." Janice pulled down her skirt and shook her breasts. Roid lowered his head like an industrious mole and began collapsing equipment.

Janice and Marty were intimate in a different way than she and Ascenzo were. With Marty she exchanged little pecks to the cheeks, both of them, their arms not involved, like birds nipping seeds. How did one know these things, I wondered? What in his appearance led Janice to behave this way and not another? And to be always correct?

"See ya, Dick," Marty called to my father, who preferred to be called Richard, or, if one absolutely had to shorten it, Rich. "Pat and Dick," Marty continued, meaning me and my father, "the dead Nixons."

"Yeah," my father said. "Ha ha."

Marty raised both his hands as we left, two-fingered victory signs, "I am not a crook," he called, "I am not a crook."

"Later, Babe," Roid yelled out to me.

Restored by my doze in the chair and by test anxiety, I climbed into the stifling back seat. Now we were headed for my appointment. Now it was my turn.

"You want to try to drive?" my father asked.

"Sure," I said.

"I meant your sister," he said. "I thought maybe she'd like to practice."

"No thanks," Janice said from the front passenger seat. "I'm happy just to ride. Let the munchkin drive."

"Nah, we're already going," Dad said, swinging the Falcon into traffic.

They did not wait for me. They relinquished the car because I had to drive it to pass the test, but there was a coffee shop down the block, so they walked there, my sister still in her modeling clothes, my father with his new cigar. Of course, the Department of Motor Vehicles was not air conditioned. Old-fashioned floor fans whirred, orange streamers flying straight out as if to prove they were doing their best.

My examiner was a woman named Officer Davies. She sat in front of me as I took, and passed, the written and eye exams, and then, afterwards, motioned with her fingernail at her own front teeth. "You have something right there," she said, looking cross-eyed at my mouth. A chocolate sprinkle, there since lunch, had lodged itself beside an upper canine. Then she asked me to lead her to my vehicle.

The Falcon was blistering. I felt obliged to explain the crystal, though she hadn't asked. "My sister's superstitious," I told her. "She thinks this crystal will bring good luck to the driver."

"We'll see," said Officer Davies. She buckled, I buckled. Before we even left the parking lot I had failed to stop at the sidewalk, and she had made a demoting little black mark on her clipboard.

I piloted my father's car slowly down the street, past the coffee shop where I dared not glance; would they see me, sailing sluggishly by? Obtaining my license was our last errand today, and if all went well, tomorrow it would be I who ferried Janice from doctor to physical therapist to voice lesson, and we would go in my mother's car, the one with a stereo and air conditioning, first dropping her off downtown at Bell headquarters. Everything would be different, once I could drive. My father, with nothing else to do, would be obliged to call on his contacts in the world of construction. He would go to Pitt's Barbecue and do some lunchtime hustling. He would lose track of Janice's commitments and adventures. Between tomorrow's errands and today's lay a brief but important fissure of time: my passing the test, and our waiting tonight for Janice while someone else took her away from the house.

My sister had two boyfriends, and this evening's date was with the college guy, Trevor. "How can she go out with him?" my father would ask my mother and me while we moved around the house in her absence. "Who can take seriously this *Trevor*, the boy named from a soap opera?" We would occupy ourselves in front of electrical appliances—TV, stereo, refrigerator, microwave—while we waited for her, rotating every thirty minutes or so. Before the accident, my mother would have predicted the hickeys Janice might arrive home bearing on her neck, the liquor on her breath, the tardy hour. Never mind that it was I who sneaked cigarettes (Janice wouldn't risk the stains or stench), or that Janice never went without her full eight-hours' rest. These facts merely compounded my mother's annoyance. She seemed not to want a beautiful daughter, after all, nor an unbeautiful one, either. Maybe she wished she'd had sons.

Janice's other boyfriend, Teddy, was Janice's age, and my father preferred him. Teddy's parents had the same names as our pets, Max and Emma (dog and cat, respectively) and Dad liked this about Teddy; it kept him in a proper place.

But tonight was Trevor, and then when we all woke tomorrow things would be different. That's what I thought as I performed my head-check before changing lanes, as I scrupulously entered intersections and on-ramps and parking spaces when Officer Davies instructed. Everything waffled in the miserable Midwest heat; the sky above us was featureless, not blue but simple empty white. Pets and children and red rubber balls all stayed put in their yards; wheelchairs weren't rolling into crosswalks, taillights weren't flashing on ahead of me unexpectedly. I drenched myself, jumping these mild hoops only adequately, but Officer Davies was going to confer my reward.

At our house it had always been I who'd come home marked and scarred and broken, from sunburn or wind chill, the V on my chin from the rock I hadn't seen, an apostrophe at my scalp-line from which a fish-hook had been pulled, the chicken pox and acne dimples, the fractured femur after skiing, the grisly flesh on my hand where the iron had once fallen, the bruised lips and genitals from boys I let manhandle me.

On the hot steering wheel, I tucked my three lesser fingers till they were hidden away. In my nightmares, it had happened to me, and I had deserved it.

Who had done this to Janice, our beauty? A stranger had, an ugly girl with no stature at our school, no notoriety until now. Now, she had plenty. She was the one who'd stood beside Janice in Mr. Tilbino's Shop class, who'd been designated Janice's building buddy, who'd held the end of Janice's two-by-four as they used the radial arm saw, who'd shoved her sideways into the blade. There was jealousy involved, as you might expect, a boy this ugly girl loved in a sickening unrequited way, this boy who loved Janice in the same pathetic way, lonely desperation begetting lonely desperation.

Couldn't you sympathize with that luckless girl's desire to do damage? Couldn't you imagine the self-preserving instinct that would guide her lurching into my sister?

When we got our bodies, Janice and I, when we bloomed, my mother took me aside to offer consolation. Janice had gotten Grandma's big breasts and slender legs. She had gotten a confident swing in her hips and large clean teeth, a flare for higher math, a spontaneous wit, a knack for combining unlikely clothes. She'd gotten things I ought obviously to desire, and now she'd gotten something I could not have known to wish for.

Officer Davies said, "*Both* hands on the wheel, please."

It would become an enduring habit of mine: using my thumb and forefinger, I made my own gun.

The Problem of Human Consumption

Steve Almond

Paul, in this case, is a widower. His wife died thirteen years ago. He kept their daughter away as much as he could. There were relatives around to play with her, to shower her with gifts and praise. His wife grew pale in the study. Her hair fell out. The disease ate her body in delicate bites. How do you explain such things to a four year old?

Paul has not moved or remarried. He has not taken a new job or dated a pretty secretary. To become unstuck has proved more than he can manage. He took his one grand risk of love. He met his desire and clung to her and she dissolved in his arms.

He lives with his daughter in this same house, which is a little too big for the two of them. (There were plans for a second child.) Jess has grown into an awkward beauty. She has a great head of hair, which she wears long down her back. Paul watches her on occasion, speaking to one of her suitors on the phone. She has aspects of her mother, an easy, unexpected laugh; that hair, which floats behind her like the train of a gown. But she is burdened with his bones—stolid, heavy. She dresses to conceal her figure, the broad pallid curves. Her young body swims inside baggy jeans and sweaters.

The moment in question is a Saturday night. Paul is alone in his home. Jess is out on a date, with a boy, or perhaps a group of them all together, at a bowling alley or movie house, chattering about the people they fear they are, or wish to become.

Jess has given herself over to this second life, among her peers, and Paul makes every effort not to hold her back. It is vital that she find happiness where she can.

Paul occupies himself by acquiring expertise: airplanes, butterflies, the history of the labor movement. He reads articles in his study, by the dozens, and sends electronic messages with his new computer. He imagines them flying from his fingertips, lighting the dark circuits of the world with knowledge.

But on this particular evening an ancient restlessness has stirred within Paul and he wanders from the soft lamps of his study into the kitchen and makes a sandwich. The fridge is divided by shelves, because Jess has decided, of late, to become a vegetarian. He admires this decision. It strikes him as the only sustainable solution to the problem of human consumption. (Six billion mouths to feed. The energy required to raise a calf versus a field of beans. He has studied the problem.) Paul has even considered telling her how much he admires her decision. But this would deprive Jess of the pleasure of her righteousness. And it would expose him as a hypocrite, because meat is one of his few pleasures. He gazes at the items on her shelf—the bumpy soups and mysterious chutneys, a jar of green liquid that appears to be growing spores— and reaches for the smoked ham.

The first sandwich only serves to make him hungrier, so he eats a second. The phone rings and he goes to pick it up, but there's only a dial-tone. These hang ups are a new development. They make Paul feel embarrassed, as if Jess is ashamed of him.

He wanders the house, unable to attach himself to a task. He turns on the TV and allows the colors to wash over him for a few minutes. They make his eyes tear up. He doesn't worry about his daughter. There is something ruthless in her sensibility. He pities the boy who mistakes her for an easy mark.

Paul arrives at Jess's room. He's not sure how he got here. A minute ago, he was watching the History Channel—that terrible siege at Stalingrad, grown men feeding on the soles of their children's shoes—and now he's standing in his socks before her room. The door is open a crack, because Jess knows her father isn't a spy. He has always kept himself from such obvious curiosities.

Her room is much larger than most of her friends', because, in fact, he's given her the room that once served as the master bedroom. He sleeps downstairs, in the room that used to be his study. And his study is the room that she slept in as a child. All these changes were made hastily, after the funeral, and they never seemed odd or unnatural to him. Jess has always required more room than him.

As it is, she's expanded her possessions to fill the room. She has a set of drums in one corner, which she rarely plays anymore, thank God. There are two desks, one devoted to her schoolwork, the second to her recent fanatical interest in astrology. There are a few sweaters on the bed, which is half-made, and a stack of books on her nightstand, all devoted to astrology.

The room is warm, unexpectedly so, and filled with the sweet, slightly burnt residue of sandalwood incense. Paul turns this way and that. He lopes into Jess's bathroom and pees and wipes the rim and stares at the bulky makeup bag beside the sink, afraid to touch it. He walks back into her room and glances at the possessions on her dresser—an ivory chopstick, a tube of something called *Spirit Gel,* a tiny tin of breath mints—strange relics of her personhood scattered in the low light.

There is another object there, glimmering beneath a pile of scrunchies. Paul doesn't want to disturb the pile. He doesn't want to snoop. But he does want to know what that might be glimmering, so he turns on the light and peers into the pile. The object is his wife's wedding band.

Paul's reaction is one of terror. He hurries over to turn off the light and sits on the edge of the bed and his heart is galloping. He has always assumed his wife was buried with her ring. He has an image of her laid out, the slender gold band on her finger. This is ridiculous, though, because she insisted that her body be used for medical research, and they didn't bury her at all. There had been a memorial service.

He tries to remember the last time he saw his wife, but cannot. He remembers only the rails of the bed, the steel of them, and the humiliating smell of decay. At some point, she must have given Jess the ring. But why had she done this? And how had Jess managed to keep this from him? And why? Was this a secret between the two of them? And if so, what was the ring doing on her dresser, left out like a bit of costume jewelry?

These are the mysteries that consume him as he sits on his daughter's bed with his hands in his lap. They matter as much as any of the others, the fact that people die for no good reason, that they choose to hate when love becomes unbearable, that a certain part of them, starved of happiness, gives up, shuts down, goes into hibernation.

Paul can feel the squeeze of panic in his chest. He has worked so hard to avoid the traps of mourning, the self-pity and rage. He has made sure his daughter feels loved. He has given her all the gifts of compassion she will bear. But this ring, it feels like a betrayal, a cruel stirring.

He wants to leave her room, shut the door, drift back to his study. Instead, he gets up and walks to the dresser and stares at the ring. He removes the scrunchies one by one, with the chopstick. He picks the ring up and puts it down and picks it up again and it's heavier than he expected or denser or something and he notices a hair, a single strand of his daughter's hair, clinging to metal. The hair is looped through the band, actually, in such a way that when he holds both ends the ring is suspended. He lifts one end and then the other and the ring slides back and forth and this simple motion, in the somber light of the room, strikes him as miraculous: the ring defying the law of gravity.

It is at this precise moment that his daughter appears in the doorway. She often finds her father asleep at this hour, in the chair in his study. The habit has become a joke between them. He denies in mock indignation, she gently accedes. *Whatever you say, dad.*

Jess is in the doorway for a second before her father realizes she's there, and for a portion of that second she's not even entirely sure what she's seeing—a stranger in her room, a thief, should she be frightened?—but then she recognizes his socks and the bedraggled clumps of the hair above his ears, which she has always wanted to trim.

She sees that he is hunched over something shiny and that this shiny thing is sliding back and forth, between her father's fingers. There is an instant, the tiniest of instants, in which she too believes the object is floating in the air and this possibility of magic is a thread that joins them.

Then she sees that the object is the ring, her mother's ring, and she is furious at herself for being so careless and a little frightened of what her father might do, and a little frightened, also, of what her father might not do, that he may be too cautious at this point to express what she would consider an appropriate rage. Because she did not, after all, receive this ring from her mother. She stole the ring from her father, from a shoebox tucked away on a high shelf in the closet in his study, where it was stashed, along with the results of a blood test and a yellowed marriage license and a ribbon which she imagines her mother wore on her wedding day, though she has never been able to find it in the photos.

Jess is considering all this when her father looks up.

Remember: the light is low. It is difficult to read precise expressions. These two are, more than anything, familiar shapes in the dark.

Paul feels dizzy with shame. He has been caught in his daughter's room, playing with his wife's ring, a ring which now belongs to Jess. The transfer of this object between the two women is, in his mind, an ancient secret he had no business discovering. He wishes he had slipped away a few minutes earlier, as he intended.

Jess doesn't say anything. She is capable of excruciating silences. It hasn't yet occurred to her to feel betrayed. She doesn't quite know how she should react, though she does have a vague sense that her father should take the lead here, he is the adult and the rightful owner of the ring and the person whose actions have initiated the moment.

But her father is standing there, frozen. The ring is quivering. Jess waits for him to speak. She still hasn't figured out exactly how the ring is able to float there between his fingers. She wants to switch on the light, solve the mystery, confess to her secret theft, get everything out into the open. And then again, she wants to back away quietly and run to where her friends are waiting in a car by the curb. Her father might never say anything. He might suppose he had dreamed the entire thing. She would not put that past him.

Paul looks at his daughter, looks her flush in the face, that soft pink swirl of youth, and suddenly he is hungry again, famished. He wants to prepare himself another sandwich, heavy on the ham, and settle into his sleeping chair. But his legs won't move and he remembers, rather too suddenly, that he used to feel this same way after making love to his wife, a queer, short-lived paralysis which overtook him as he lay in a pool of his own heat.

Jess sees her father begin to smile and she takes this as a bad sign. He looks a bit touched actually, and this worries her and this worry causes her to take a step into the room. Not a whole step, just an experimental little half-step, as if testing the temperature of a bath.

"Dad?" she says. "Are you all right?"

He nods, or tries to nod. She can't tell.

"Is something the matter?" Jess steps closer. "What's going on?"

Paul is shaking a little. He is looking at his daughter and smelling the sandalwood and remembering a trip they took years ago to the beach, to San Gregorio, south of Half Moon Bay, remembering the sandy hollow where they built a fire to roast hotdogs and marshmallows. He is thinking of his wife, who was not ill yet, not diagnosed, though she was tired more than usual, and despite this, the cooling breeze off the water and the rhythm of surf made them both amorous. Jess was there, too, in a little white bikini which she quickly shed. She ran about naked, chasing the gulls all the way down to the shore, until Paul was forced to go after her. He picked her up and swung her so that her toes swept across the water and she shrieked. The sun beat down on both of them. Later, her mother combed out her hair until she grew drowsy enough for a nap. Paul ate the last of the hot dogs and his wife lay beside him and set her hand on his chest and they whispered to one another, *Should we? Do you think?* though they already were (beneath their blanket) engaged in the soft panic of love. It was a weekday afternoon. There was no one else around. Their daughter slept beside them. Her hair, still blond, fell across her small brown shoulders.

Jess is still calling his name and she has, by now, stepped close, close enough to smell the meat on his breath, the tang of mustard, and she, too, is thinking about that trip to the beach, though she isn't quite certain where she was, only that it was some place outdoors that smelled of fire and burned meat and that she woke to find her father on top of her mother, moving against her with a wet desperation, as if to devour her, while her mother smiled delicately in profile. Then her father looked over and saw her watching and seemed to want to say something to her, to yell or apologize, she couldn't tell which, and she shut her eyes and turned the other way and soon after her mother got skinnier and skinnier and they locked her in the study. This is when all the aunts began to arrive and to give Jess gifts, one every morning. They told her she was beautiful again and again.

Jess would have no idea, at this point in her life, that she has associated this memory with her mother's death, that, in some hidden cavern of her heart, she regards her father as having killed her mother, or, more precisely, that she regards she and her father as having collaborated in the murder of her mother.

She knows only that she has arrived home to find her father in her room, that he is shaking, his eyes clouded over with sorrow, and because she loves her father she moves to embrace him, not a full hug, just a brushing of their two bodies in the dark. Her hair is shining like some wild flag and he is staring down at the ring, breathing heavily. What is this embrace—a gesture of condolence, of forgiveness?

Paul is so hungry now he could eat a pig, a cow, an entire farm of useless beasts. All the fields of crops in all the countries of the world would not fill his belly. He can smell the smoke of the fire and the meat and he is lying with his wife on the warm sand and he is holding on to his only given daughter and he is starving to death.

It is important to remember that this is only a single moment, this tentative caress, nothing they will speak of again, an *interlude*.

It is important to remember that their crimes are not really crimes. They are simple human failings, distortions of memory, the cruel math of fractured hopes. The only true crime here is one of omission. The woman they both loved has been omitted from their lives. She is a beautiful ghost, a floating ring.

In less than a second, a horn will sound from below. Jess will fall back, swing herself away from her father and toward the rest of her life, her friends waiting in a car by the curb, the night to come, the boy who has told her she is beautiful, who will, in a few hours, in the basement of another home, slip his hand inside her pants and whisper again that she is beautiful.

As for the ring, it will be replaced, first by Paul, on the dresser, under the scrunchies, then by Jess, in the box on the shelf in her father's closet.

Paul will return to the kitchen and make himself a sandwich, but the meat will taste rotten and this taste will haunt his tongue, even after he rinses with mouthwash, and he will drink warm milk instead and take a sleeping pill, and then a second, until he can feel the convincing blur of his dreams. In the days to follow, he will swear off meat, a gradual transition, so as not to attract the notice of his daughter.

But this, of course, is what lies ahead for them, as they race away from the hot center of themselves. Decent lives. Reasonable consumption.

For now, they are still together. Her arms are around him, one hand on his shoulder, the other touching the padding of his waist. He is staring at the ring. Hunger is surging inside him as he sways with her, once, through the dimness of the room. What are they doing here, exactly? Who can say about such things? They are weeping. They are dancing. They are prisoners of this moment and wonderfully, terribly alive.

Mr. Sweetly Indecent

Bliss Broyard

I meet my father in a restaurant. He knows why I have asked to meet him, but he swaggers in anyway. It's a place near his office, and he hands out hellos all around as he makes his way over to my table. "My daughter," he explains to the men who have begun to grin, and he can't resist a wink just to keep them guessing. "Daddy," I say; his arms are around me. He squeezes a beat too long, and I'm afraid I might cry. He kisses me on both cheeks, my forehead, and chin. "Saying my prayers," he has called these kisses ever since he used to tuck me into bed each night. They started as a joke on my mother, who is French and a practicing Catholic. Because my mother always kept her relationship with God to herself, the only prayer I knew is one my father taught me.

> *Now I lay me down to sleep.*
> *I pray the Lord my soul to keep.*
> *If I should cry before I wake,*
> *I pray the Lord a cake to bake.*

I only realized years later that he had changed the words of the real prayer so I wouldn't be scared by it.

My father orders a bottle of expensive red wine. He's had this wine here before. When it arrives, he insists that I taste it. He tells the waiter that I'm a connoisseur of wines. The truth is that I worked one summer as a hostess in a French restaurant where I attended some wine-tasting classes. We learned that a wine must be tasted even if it's from a well-known vineyard and made in a good year because there could be some bad bottles. I could never tell the good wines from the bad ones, but I picked up some of the vocabulary.

I make a big fuss, sniffing the cork, sloshing the wine around in my mouth. "Fruity. Ripe," I say.

The waiter and my father smile at my approval. I smack my lips after the waiter leaves. "But no staying power. Immature, overall."

My father gets a sour look on his face. He's taken a big sip so that his cheeks are puffed out with the liquid. After he gulps it down, he says, "It's fine." And then he adds, "You know, it's all right for you to like it. It costs forty dollars."

"I'll drink it, but I don't really like it."

He looks ready to argue with me and then thinks better of it, glancing instead around the restaurant to see if anyone else he knows has come in.

We don't say anything for a bit. I'm hesitating. I sip the wine, survey the room myself. I've recently begun to realize that my father's life exists outside the one in which I have a place. Rather than viewing this outside life as an extension of the part that I know, I choose to see it instead as a distant land. Some of its inhabitants are here. Mostly men, they chuckle over martini glasses; one raises his eyebrow. They all look as if they have learned something that I have yet to discover.

Finally, I put my glass down and smooth some wrinkles in the tablecloth. "Dad, what are we going to do?" I ask without looking up.

He takes my hand. "We don't need to do anything. We should just put it behind us. We can pretend that it didn't even happen, if that's what you want."

"That's what you want," I say. I'd caught him, after all, kissing a woman on the street outside his apartment.

As long as I can remember, my father has kept an apartment in this city where he works and I now live. In his profession, he needs to stay in touch, he has always said. That has meant spending every Monday night in the city having dinner with his associates. Occasionally, it had occurred to me that his apartment might be used for reasons other than a place to sleep after late business dinners. Then one night, while I still lived at home, my mother confided that a friend of my father's contributed $100 a month toward the rent to use it once in a while. I remember that my mother and I were eating cheese fondue for dinner. On those nights my father was away, my mother made special meals that he didn't like. She ripped off a piece of French bread from the loaf we were sharing and dipped it in the gooey mixture. "This friend brings his mistress there," she explained. "I hate that your father must be the one to supply him with a place to carry out his affair." I didn't say anything, my suspicion relieved by this sudden confidence. My mother tilted back her head and dropped the coated bread into her open mouth. When she finished chewing, she closed the subject. "His wife should know what her husband is up to. I'm going to tell her one day."

When I was walking down my father's street early last Tuesday morning, it didn't even occur to me that my father would be at his apartment. I was on my way to the subway after leaving the apartment of a man with whom I had just spent the night. This man is a friend of a man at work with whom I have also spent the night. The man at work, call him Jack, is my friend now—he said that working together made things too complicated—and we sometimes go out for a drink at the end of the day. We bumped into his friend at the bar near our office. The friend asked me to dinner and then asked me to come up to his apartment for a drink and then asked if he could make love to me. After each question, I paused before answering, suspicious because of the directness of his invitations, and then when he would look away as if it didn't really matter, I would realize that, in fact, I had been waiting for these questions all night, and I would say yes.

When we walked into this man's living room, he flicked a row of switches at the entrance, turning on all the lights. He brought me a glass of wine and then excused himself to use the bathroom. I strolled over to the large picture window to admire the view. Looking out from the bright room, it was hard to make out anything on the street. The only movement was darting points of light. "It's like another world up here," I murmured under my breath. I heard the toilet flush and waited at the window. I was thinking how he could walk up behind me and drape his arm over my shoulder and say something about what he has seen out this window, and then he could take my chin and turn it toward him and we could kiss. When I didn't hear any movement behind me, I turned around. He was standing at the entrance of the room. "I'd like to make love to you," he said. "Would that be all right?" There was no music or TV, and it was so silent that I was afraid to speak. I smiled, took a sip of wine. He shifted his gaze from my face to the window behind me. I glanced out the window, too, then put my glass down on the sill and nodded yes. "Why don't you take off your coat," he said. I slipped my trench coat off my shoulders and held it in front of me. He pointed to a chair in front of the window, and I draped the coat over its back. Then he asked me to take off the rest of my clothes.

Once I was naked, he just stood there staring at me. I wondered if he could see from where he was standing that I needed a bikini wax. I wanted to kiss him, we hadn't even kissed yet, and I took a small step forward and then stopped, one foot slightly in front of the other, unsteady, uncertain what to do next. "Beautiful," he finally whispered. And then he kept whispering *beautiful, beautiful, beautiful* ...

I had just reached my father's block, though lost in my thoughts I didn't realize it, when from across the street, I heard a woman's voice. "Zachary!" the voice called out, the stress on the last syllable, the word rising in mock annoyance, the way my mother said my father's name when he teased her. All other times, she called him, as everyone else did, just Zach. I looked up, and there was my father pushing a woman up against the side of a building. His building, I realized.

My father's face was buried in her neck, and she was laughing. I recognized from her reaction that he was giving her the ticklish kind of blowing kisses that I hated. I had stopped walking and was staring at them. I caught the women's eye briefly, and then she looked away and whispered something in my father's ear. His head jerked up and whipped around. I looked down quickly and started walking away, as if I had been caught doing something wrong. If my father had run after me and asked what I was doing in this neighborhood so early in the morning, I wouldn't have known what to tell him. I glanced back, and the woman was walking down the street the other way, and my father was standing at the entrance of his building. He was watching the woman. She was rather dressed up for so early in the morning, wearing a short black skirt, stockings, and high heels. She pulled her long blond hair out from the collar of her jacket and shook it down her back. Her gait looked slightly self-conscious, the way a woman's does when she knows she is being watched. Before I looked away, my father glanced in my direction. I avoided meeting his eyes and shook my head, a gesture I hoped he could appreciate from his distance. As I hurried to the subway, the only thought I had was fleeting: my man had not gotten up from bed to walk me out the door.

For the next few days, I waited for the phone to ring. Neither man called. I asked Jack, the man at work, if he had heard from his friend. "Sorry, not a peep," he said. He patted me on the knee and said that he was sure his friend enjoyed the time we spent together and that I would probably hear from him soon.

It was unusually warm that day, and I walked home rather than taking the subway. All the way home, I kept picturing myself back in the man's apartment. I saw us as someone would have if they had been floating nine stories high above the busy avenue that night and had picked out the man's lighted window to peer into: a young women, naked, moving slowly across a room to kiss the mouth of her clothed lover. It seemed that the moment was still continuing, encapsulated eternally in that bright box of space.

When I walked in the door that afternoon, my phone was ringing. I rushed to answer it before the machine picked it up. It was my mother. She had already left a message on my machine earlier in the week to call her about making plans to go home the following weekend. Whether I should tell her about my father was a question that had been gathering momentum behind me all week. My mother is a passionate, serious woman. My father met her when she was performing modern dance in a club in West Berlin. The act before her was two girls singing popular American show tunes, and after her, for the finale, there was a topless dancer. She didn't last there for very long. My father liked to describe how the audience of

German men would look up at her with bemused faces. Her seriousness didn't translate, he would say, and the Germans would be left wondering if her modern dancing was another French joke that they didn't get. After the shows, all the women who worked there had to *"faire la salle,"* which meant dancing with the male customers. At this point in the story I would ask questions, hoping that a bit of scandal in my mother's past would be revealed, or at least to find out that she had to resist some indecent propositions at one time. But my mother always jumped in to say that she had learned that if you don't invite that kind of behavior, then you won't receive it. Such things never happen by accident. My father married my mother, he would explain, because she was one of the last women left who could really believe in marriage. He said she had enough belief for the both of them. I hadn't called my mother back.

"Oh, sweetie, I'm glad I caught you," she said. "You're still going to take the 9:05 train Saturday morning, right?"

"Uh-huh."

"Okay, Daddy will have to pick you up after he drops me off at the hairdresser's. I'm trying to schedule an appointment to get a perm."

"Ahh."

"I feel like it's been forever since I've seen you. Daddy and I were just saying last night how we still can't get used to you not being around all the time."

I tried to picture myself back in my parents' house. I couldn't place myself there again. I couldn't remember where in the house we spent our time, where we talked to each other: around the dining room table, on the couch in the den, in the hallways; I couldn't remember what we talked about.

"Is everything okay, honey? You sound tired."

"Hmmm."

"All right. I can take a hint. I'll let you go."

After we hung up, I said to my empty apartment, "I caught Daddy with another woman." Once these words were out of my mouth, I couldn't get away from them. I went out for a drink.

When I woke up the next morning, I decided to cut off all of my hair. I have brown curly hair like my father's. It's quite long, and when I stood in that man's living room, I pulled it in front of my shoulders so that it covered my breasts. The man liked that, he told me afterward as he held me in his bed. He said that I had looked sweetly indecent. I lost my nerve in the hairdresser's chair and walked out with bangs instead. In the afternoon, I went to a psychic fair with a friend, and a fortune teller told me that she saw a man betraying me. "Tell me something I don't know," I said, but that would have cost another ten dollars.

I called my father Sunday morning at home. I knew when he answered the phone that he had gotten up from the breakfast table, leaving behind a stack of Sunday papers and my mother sipping coffee.

"We have to talk before I come home next weekend."

"Okay. Where would you like to meet?" He didn't say my name, and his voice was all business.

"Let's have dinner somewhere." He suggested a restaurant, and we agreed to meet the next evening after work.

"Tomorrow, then." I put a hint of warning in my voice.

"Yes. All right," he said and hung up. I wondered if my mother asked him who had called, and if she did, what he would have told her.

Next, I called up the man in whose living room I had stood naked. The phone rang many times. I was about to hang up, disappointed that there was not even a machine so I could hear his voice again, when a sleepy voice answered. I was caught by surprise and forgot my rehearsed line about meeting at a bakery I knew near his apartment for some sweetly indecent pastries.

I hung up without saying anything.

The waiter takes our empty plates away. My father refills my glass. I have drunk two glasses of wine already and am starting to feel sleepy and complaisant. My father has already told me that he is not planning on seeing the woman again, and I am beginning to wonder what it is that I actually want my father to say.

He drums his fingers on the edge of the table. I can see that he is growing tired of being solicitous. He sought my opinion on the wine, he noticed that I had my bangs cut, he remembered the name of my friend at work who I was dating the last time we got together.

"I'm not with him anymore," I explain. "We thought it was a bad idea to date since we work together." I consider telling my father about the other man, to let him know that I understand more about this world of affairs than he thinks. He would be shocked, outraged. Or would he? I'm not sure of anything anymore.

I let myself float outside the man's window again, move closer to peer inside. But this time I can't quite picture his face. What color are his eyes? They're green, I decide. But then I wonder if I am confusing them with my father's eyes.

"Someday, honey, you'll meet a guy who'll realize what a treasure you are." My father pats my knee.

"Just because he thinks I'm a treasure doesn't mean that he won't take me for granted." I take another sip of wine and watch over the rim of my glass for my father's response. I remember watching him at another table, our dining room table, where he sat across from my mother. She had just made some remark that I couldn't hear from where I perched on our front stairs, spying, as they had a romantic dinner alone with candles and wine. Earlier, my father had set up the television and VCR in my room and sent me upstairs to watch a movie. My father put down his glass and got up out of his chair. He knelt at my mother's feet, and though I couldn't hear his words, either, I was sure that he was asking her to marry him again.

"Honey. Listen. It was nothing with that woman. It doesn't change the way I feel about your mother. I love your mother very much."

"But it makes everything such a lie," I say, my voice now catching with held-back tears. "What about our family, all the dinners, Sunday mornings around the breakfast table, the walks we love to take ..." I falter and hold my hands out wide to him.

My father catches them and folds them closed in his own. "No. No. All of that is true. This doesn't change any of that." He is squeezing my hands hard. For the first time during this meal, I can see that I have upset him.

"But it didn't mean what I thought, did it?"

Right then the waiter appears with our check. My father lets go of my hands and reaches for his wallet. Neither of us says anything while we wait for the waiter to return with the credit card slip. I don't repeat my question because I am afraid that my father will say I'm right.

The next day at work, I ask my friend again about Mr. Sweetly Indecent.

"If you want to talk to him, call him up."

"Do you think I should?"

"It can't hurt."

"If we didn't work together, do you think things could have turned out differently with us?" We are in the photocopying room where, in the midst of our affair, my friend had once lifted my skirt and slid his fingers inside the elastic waist of my pantyhose.

"Oh, hell. You'll meet someone who'll appreciate you. You deserve that. You really do."

I call the man up that night. He doesn't say anything for a moment when I tell him my name. I imagine him reviewing a long line of naked women standing in his living room. "That one," he finally picks me out of the crowd. Or maybe it's just that he's surprised to hear from me.

"I had a really nice time that night," I say. "I thought maybe we could get together again sometime."

"Well, I had a good time, too," he says, sounding sincere, "but I think that we should just leave it at that."

"I'm not saying that I want to start dating. I just thought that we could do something again."

"It was the kind of night that's better not repeated. I know. I've tried it before. The second time is always a disappointment."

"But I thought we got along so well." We had talked over dinner about our families; he told me how he was always trying to live up to the kind of man he thought his father wanted him to be. He had talked in faltering sentences, as though this were something that he was saying for the first time.

"We did get along," he says. "God! And you were so beautiful." He pauses, and I know he's remembering that I really was beautiful. "I just want to preserve that memory of you standing in my living room, alone, without any other images cluttering it."

Yes, I want to tell him, I have preserved that image, too, but memories need refueling. I need to see you again to make sure that what I remembered is actually true. "Is this because I slept with you on the first night?"

"No. No. Nothing like that. Listen, it was a perfect night. Let's just both remember it that way."

As the train pulls into the station, I spot my father waiting on the platform. I take my time gathering my things so I'm one of the last to exit. He hugs me without hesitation, as though our dinner had never happened. As we separate he tries to take my suitcase from me. It's just a small weekend bag, and I resist, holding on to the shoulder strap. We have a tug of war.

"You're being ridiculous," my father says and yanks the strap from my grip. I trail behind him to the car and look out the window the whole way home.

That afternoon, I sit at the kitchen table and watch my mother and father prune the rose bushes dotting the fence that separates our yard from the street. My mother selects a branch and shows my father where to cut. They work down the row quickly, efficient with their confidence in the new growth these efforts will bring. Behind them trails a wake of bald, stunted bushes and their snipped limbs lying crisscross on the ground beneath.

After they have finished cleaning up the debris, my father brings the lawn chairs out of the garage—he brings one for me, too, but I have retreated upstairs to my bedroom by this time and watch them from that window—and my mother appears with a pitcher of lemonade and glasses. My mother reclines in her chair, with my father at her side, and admires their handiwork. Her confidence that the world will obey her expectations makes her seem so foolish to me, or perhaps it is because every time I look at her, I think of how she is being fooled.

On Sunday morning, my mother heads off to Mass, and I am left alone in the house with my father. He sits with me at the kitchen table for a while, both of us flipping through the Sunday papers. I keep turning the pages, unable to find anything that can hold my attention. He's not really reading, either. He is too busy waiting on me. He hands me the Magazine and Style sections without my even asking. He refills my coffee. When Georgie, our Labrador retriever, scratches at the door, he jumps up to let her out. When he sits back down, he gathers all the sections of the paper together, including the parts that I am looking at, and stacks them on one corner of the table. I look at him, breathe out a short note of exasperation.

"Are you ever going to forgive me?" he asks.

"Why aren't you going to see that woman again? Just because I caught you?"

He looks startled and answers slowly, as if he is just testing out this answer. "She didn't mean anything to me. It was like playing a game. It was fun, but now it's over."

"Do you think that she expected to see you again?"

"No. She knew what kind of a thing it was. And I'm sure that she prefers it this way, too. She has her own commitments to deal with."

"Maybe she does want to see you again. Maybe she felt like you had something really special together. Maybe she's hoping that you would leave Mom for her."

"Honey, when you get older, you'll understand that there are a lot of different things that you can feel for another person and how it's important not to confuse them. I love your mother, and I'm very devoted to her. Nothing is going to change that."

My father sits with me a few minutes more, and when there doesn't seem to be anything else to say, he stands up and wanders off. I realize that if I had told my father about the man during our dinner, he would have understood what kind of a thing that was before I even did.

When my mother gets back, she joins me at the kitchen table.

"Do you want to talk about something, honey? You seem so sad." I look at my mother, and the tears that have been welling in my eyes all weekend threaten to spill over.

"Daddy says you're having boy trouble."

I shake my head no, unable to speak.

My mother suggests that we take the dog out for a walk, just the two of us, so we can catch up. She gathers our coats, calls Georgie, and we head out the door. "I don't even know what's going on in your life since you've moved out. It's strange," she says. "I used to know what you did every evening, who you were going out with, what clothes you chose to wear each day. Now I have no idea how you spend your time. It was different when you were at college. I could imagine you in class, or at the library, or sitting around your dorm room with your roommate. Sometimes I used to stop whatever I was doing and think about you. She's probably just heading off to the cafeteria for breakfast right now, I would tell myself."

We are walking down our street toward the harbor.

"But you know that I go to work every day. You know what my apartment looks like. It's the same now."

"No, it's not," she says. "It's really all your own life. You support yourself, buy all your own clothes, decide if and when to have breakfast. And somehow, I don't feel right imagining what your day is like. It's not really my business anymore."

"I don't mind, Mom, if you want to know what I'm doing." We have reached the harbor, and my mother is bending over the dog to let her off the lead so I'm not sure if she hears me. She pulls a tennis ball out of her pocket, and Georgie begins to dance backward. My mother starts walking to the water. I stay where I am and look off across the harbor. On the opposite shore, some boats have been pulled up onto the beach just above the high-tide mark for the winter. They rest on the side of their hulls and look as if they've been forgotten, as if they will never be put back in the water again.

My mother turns back toward me, holding the tennis ball up high over her head. Georgie is prancing and barking in front of her. "You know what I love about dogs? It's so easy to make them happy. You just pet them or give them a biscuit or show them a ball, and they always wag their tails." She throws the ball into the water, and Georgie goes racing after it.

My mother's eagerness to oblige surprises me. I think of her dancing with men in that club in West Berlin. I had always imagined her as acting very primly, holding the men away from her with stiff, straight arms. Perhaps she wasn't that way at all. Maybe she leaned into these men, only drawing back to toss her head in laughter at the jokes they whispered in her ear.

"Mom, what made you go out with Dad when you worked in that club? You didn't go out with many of the men that you met there, did you?"

"Your father was the only one I accepted, though I certainly had many offers."

"Did he seem more respectable?"

"Oh, he came on like a playboy as much as the next one."

"Then why did you say yes?"

"Well, somehow he seemed like he didn't quite believe his whole act. Though he wouldn't say that if you asked him. I guess I felt I understood something about him that he didn't even know about himself. So he went about seducing me, all the while feeling like he had the upper hand, and I would go along, knowing that I had a trick up my sleeve, too."

She isn't looking at me as she says this. She is turned toward the water, though I know that she is not looking at that, either. She is watching herself as a young woman twirling around a room with my young father. They dance together well; I have seen them dance before, and this memory brings such a pleased private smile to her lips that I don't say anything that would contradict her.

I am quiet during dinner. My parents treat me like I am sick or have just suffered some great loss. My mother won't let me help her serve the food. My father pushes seconds on me, saying that I look too skinny. "Maybe I should take you out to dinner more often," he says.

I look up from my heaping plate of food, half expecting him to wink at me.

"That's right. You two met for dinner this week. See, honey, that's just the kind of thing I was talking about. It's nice that you and your father can meet and have dinner together. Like two friends."

My parents tell stories back and forth about me when I was young; many stories I have heard before. Usually I enjoy these conversations. I would listen to them describe this precocious girl and the things she had done that I couldn't even remember, only interrupting to ask in an incredulous and proud tone, "I really did that?" I was always willing to believe anything my parents told me, so curious was I to understand the continuum of how I came to be the woman I was. Tonight, while these memories seem to console my parents, I can only hear them as nostalgic, and they remind me of everything that has been recently forsaken.

After dinner I insist on doing the dishes. I splash around in the kitchen sink, clattering the plates dangerously in their porcelain bed. I pick up a serving platter, one from my mother's set of good china inherited from my grandmother, and consider dropping it to the floor. I have trouble picturing myself actually doing this. I can only imagine it as far as my fingers loosening from the edges of the platter and it sliding down their length, but then in my mind's eye, instead of the platter falling swiftly, it floats and hovers the way a feather would from one of the peacocks pictured on the china's face. I have no trouble picturing the aftermath once it lands: my mother rushing in at the noise with my father a few steps behind, not sure if he must concern himself, and she angry at my carelessness. I imagine yelling back at her. I would tell her that it's no use. Old china, manicured lawns, a happy dog: these things don't offer any guarantee.

I stand there holding the platter high above the kitchen floor, imagining the consequences with trepidation and relief, as if this is what the weekend had been leading up to, and with one brief burst of courage, I could put it behind me. I stand considering and strain to hear my parents' voices in the dining room, thinking their conversation might offer me some direction. I put the platter down and peak around the open kitchen door. A pantry separates me from the dining room. I can see them: they are talking, but I can't make out their words.

They are both leaning forward. My mother cradles her chin in the palm of her hand. Abruptly, she lifts her head, sits up tall, and points at my father. His arms are folded in front of him, and he looks down and shakes his head. I am reminded again of that dinner of my parents that I spied on years ago, but this time what I remember is the righteousness of my mother's posture as she sat across from my father and tossed off remarks, and the guilty urgency of my father's movements as he sank to his knees at her feet, and how there was something slightly orchestrated about their behavior, as though their exchange had a long history to it. And the next thing I remember makes me tiptoe away, as I did when I was a child, aware that I had witnessed a private moment between my parents not meant for my eyes. What I remember now is how many years ago my mother had reached down her hand and pulled my father up and kept pulling him in toward herself so that she could hold him close.

Night Train

Tony Houghton

Some winters ago Maurice Edelman, a well-known Toronto lawyer, plagued by three nights of feverish dreams, threw some clothes into a grip bag and took a taxi to the Union Station. He could not easily contemplate a fourth night alone in his city apartment above the ravine, tossing and turning so that in the morning the sheets were rumpled and the mattress pad pulled off; his temperature was already one hundred and four, and the moment he shut his eyes he seemed to hear fragments of lucid conversation. If he stayed at home he might, and cold-bloodedly, kill himself, pull open a window and throw himself into the trees. Instead, he would take the night train to Montreal. He had no business in Montreal, but he needed the metal, mechanical certainty of the night train to get him through the dark hours and deposit him in the safety of daylight. Night trains only incidentally go to places: their true destination is tomorrow.

The night train to Montreal left Toronto at eleven-thirty, though it awaited connections from the west, and sometimes lingered until well after midnight before moving stealthily out of the dimly-lit station towards the snow-blotted suburbs. Maurice did not care how late the train was. He boarded the sleeping car at eleven-fifteen, having fortunately secured the last available bedroom. It was, in that confined space, very hot, so he switched on the electric fan and splashed cold water on his face in the little washbasin. Then he headed for the bar car. This had been coupled three cars away from his sleeper, towards the front of the train. The lawyer stalked through the ghostly vestibules: two sleeping cars, then the day-niter, where tousled youths in jeans and backwards-worn baseball caps were trying to arrange themselves into sleeping positions. Other passengers were beginning tentative conversations; some were reading; there was an elderly lady half-way through a fat Danielle Steele; a young man held a library book, perhaps stolen, close to his face. Both peered at the pages under their bright reading lamps, with the single-minded intensity of people determined to read the night away.

The bar car was full. It smelled of Molson beer, warm out of cans. But it was good to be in it. Maurice Edelman was able to seat himself at a table otherwise occupied by two men in the dark olive uniform of the Canadian Armed Forces and a young woman wearing a short leather skirt and a black sweater. All three held cans of warm beer. The woman asked Maurice for a light for her cigarette but did not otherwise bother him. He ordered a brandy, and as he sipped it he noticed that the train was moving. He glanced at his watch: the night train was on time. Connections from the west had not delayed its departure.

He felt the woman's eyes on him, and drank his brandy, watching the snowbound suburbs glide past. There seemed to be few lights still on in those ghostly houses, only occasional blue flickerings from a television set; the occupants of the houses early-to-bedders, apparently. What else could one do at night in the suburbs of a Canadian city? What else could one do at night anywhere, unless one rode the night train? For the night train, its lighted windows briefly illuminating snow-banks, back-yards, garages, parking lots, was surely the only evidence of civilization left in the world. Only those who, like the lawyer Maurice Edelman, had had the foresight to purchase tickets on it had a chance of surviving this night.

The plot of the nightmares the lawyer was suffering was this: his daughter, who was thirty and whom Maurice adored, was to be executed for murder. Dreams baffle chronology, especially recurring ones, but his were vivid enough for the dreamer to piece together, in the penetrating reality that precedes full wakefulness, a sequence of events. Aboard an airplane, as it waited for clearance to take off from some hot, foreign airfield where ancient DC3s sported logos like Ingrid Air, Key Lime Airways, and World Cargo Inc, a figure in a poncho (yes, a poncho) had uttered obscure threats. He had reached out a bony wrist. Sofia, the lawyer's daughter, wearing a calf-length cotton skirt, produced from the beige folds of it a gun, and shot the man dead. The body toppled gurgling to the floor. The lawyer was shocked, though his daughter had been clearly provoked, even fingered. A steward dragged the body to the back, leaving a thin trail of blood, pushed it into the lavatory compartment, and shut the door. The aircraft took off; the shooting, it seemed, almost forgotten. Sofia was cheerful: she had not given the death a second thought. She knew these people; she lived among them. Maurice took hope from the indifference of the other passengers. Perhaps the whole incident was as trivial as everyone seemed to be treating it. Perhaps, from now on, Sofia would be able to spend more time with her father. Her mother, who lived in Florida now with a former international squash player, cush-ily installed—at Maurice's expense—in a Pompano Beach apartment overlooking the Intracoastal Waterway, had ceased to be a problem. Maurice had bought himself a house on a country hill, in Ontario, with wide views.

Sofia herself, on the flight that had begun so inauspiciously, had studied the inflight magazine, completed the crossword puzzle, and memorized the various routes flown by the airline, only to be arrested upon landing by men wearing dark glasses and gold braid epaulettes, the pilot having radioed ahead that there was a problem. Her father had been at his daughter's side throughout the public part of her trial, though not at certain private interviews, and now she was to be killed. She was, with the cool unreasonableness of nightmare, undismayed; showed little concern; and if she gave any thought at all to her coming ordeal (the manner of her death had not been prescribed, but there was a possibility of garroting) she never betrayed it in her careless conversations with her father.

The night train was slowing down for its first stop. Three motor cars were held up at a railroad crossing; their headlights blinked in Maurice's eyes. He drained the last of his brandy. His table companions did not look as if they intended sleep: the green fellows from the Canadian Armed Forces were still swallowing beer, and the woman in the tight skirt blew moody cigarette smoke through her nostrils. The successful lawyer ordered another brandy. The train was already moving; nobody, as far as Maurice could see, had climbed on and nobody was allowed off. The night train only boarded long distance passengers.

The woman said, "I'm going as far as Cobourg."

The lawyer said kindly, "I have a cousin who lives at Cobourg. Perhaps you know him. His name is Stephen Edelman."

"I don't think I do," the woman said. She was, Maurice realized, about the same age as his daughter. He saw his cousin Stephen only once a year, at a Passover seder. Most of the day trains passed Cobourg at speed; there was a factory, with a hundred lights, and at one point, where the tracks swung along the shore, you could see the two rubble-work jetties which reached out into the silent lake. At night, red and green lights winked from the stubby light-houses perched on the ends of the jetties.

"You'll arrive home at an ungodly hour," Maurice said to the woman.

Ungodly! Yes, ungodly, but all hours between dusk and dawn are ungodly. Only sailors, tossed on invisible ships somewhere out there, beyond the red and green winking lights on the jetties at Cobourg, would get through the night in godly fashion. All others, including this daughter-like girl in the tight skirt, would stumble at ungodly hours into lighted doorways, interrupting the night's slow advance, trapped by it into more or less regrettable decisions.

"About two o'clock," she said, the woman, the girl. "Mum will be waiting up for me."

"Will she?"

Maurice looked at her. He'd been aware, he supposed, of something fleshy and wanton about her, but she had a mother waiting up for her at two o'clock in the morning, in Cobourg, which gave her an innocence which the short, tight skirt, and the full lips, and the cigarette, and the beer, all seemed to belie. He wondered if she'd told the two fellows from the Canadian Armed Forces, who stared out the window in silence, holding their half-crushed Molsons, about her mother in Cobourg. Maurice suddenly felt a great desire to protect this unlikely innocent. He had a sleeping car ticket in his coat pocket; he could invite her to his traveling cocoon three cars back, rocking through the night unoccupied, but this would be misconstrued, and Cobourg, anyway, was not that many miles ahead.

Unless, of course, Cobourg, by some celestial trick, had vanished from the earth, its factory lights put out forever by the thickness of night; or unless the night train, through some human forgetfulness, or unannounced change of schedule, failed to stop there.

Sofia, throughout Maurice Edelman's nightmares, had remained blithely unrepentant, a fact which the prosecutor, an army officer, had not failed to point out to the court. Yes, there had been a threatening gesture. The figure in the poncho had certainly muttered curses, as was confirmed by witnesses; but they had been, surely, no more than the generic menaces of the poor, and aimed at Sofia only as a convenient representative of the rich. It was impossible to imagine such a lowly, oppressed creature actually rising from the tin-ribbed floor of the World War II aircraft and offering a beautiful white woman physical violence—and what kind of violence? Grapple her with angry claws, perhaps, the poncho falling off and disclosing a skull? Violate her, on a crowded plane? No. Impossible. Sofia had shot him down, simply; and Maurice, her own father, a lawyer himself, had found himself urging her, even after her sentence, to show some sign of regret. The amazing thing was that she displayed absolutely none, though she acquiesced perfectly with the decision of the court. Yes, she agreed, she had shot the man, no question, but it was as if her simple acknowledgment of the fact cleaned her conscience white, as if she was morally, while awaiting death, as innocent as the day she was born.

But how long could this state of grace, for so Maurice conceived it, last? As her execution drew near, would she not fall from it? Wouldn't dread gruesomely possess her? Wouldn't she, at some point, cling to her father (the authorities, with surprising generosity, allowed the condemned woman almost limitless time with her parent) with terror and tears?

Her father's obsession, of course, was to save her, not from execution (there was no possibility of appeal), but from this fall. Somehow he must help keep up her spirits; lead her, as once he had hoped to lead her to a waiting bridegroom, to the dread swing-doors beyond which, presumably, he would not be allowed and where, somehow, they would kill her. And Maurice was so racked by fever that he hardly realized the absurdity of this last demand on him as a father. The child he had been handed, once, by a grinning nurse, fresh from her mother's womb and bawling, to prance up and down with in a hospital corridor; the urchin he'd staggered up at four o'clock in the morning to feed, watching the little mouth slug down formula and hoping harder than he'd ever hoped anything before that she'd keep it down, not throw up, in which case he'd have to begin the process all over; the little person who'd held his hand so tightly yet so cautiously, the first time he went to see her after her mother quit on him; the angel-face he'd waited at school for every Tuesday and Thursday, his access days; the blossoming friend who laughed so much as she recounted her adolescent adventures; this beautiful, giggling, grown-up daughter of his, with the sun-bleached hair, whom every maitre d' took to be his mistress (and what pride that had given him!) And now, with the unforeseen suddenness and ridiculous finality of a highway accident, she'd killed a man, some irrelevant peasant on a jungle airplane; and the only thing left to him, the father's one remaining, unperformed duty, was to lead her cheerful to her executioners.

Maurice choked, and covered his face, sitting there bolt upright in the bar car of the night train, opposite this waif from Cobourg, and the grizzly soldiers of obscure rank noticed him, gawking over their beers.

"Is there anything wrong?" the girl said, baffled, sympathetic.

"No. No." And drying the burning tears with his fingers he said, "Where are we?" One of the soldiers glanced out the window. The night train was snaking between interminable snow-drifts. The boys must ride the train frequently, the lawyer supposed, between the city and the Armed Forces base at Trenton, where presumably they'd get off.

"Must be getting near Cobourg," the soldier decided, though he could not have based his guess on anything topographical, as the white landscape illuminated fleetingly by the night train's windows was featureless.

So there was no question of asking the girl to accompany him to his fan-cooled, speeding sleeping car for ten minutes. The thought was laughable. He took out his wallet and placed a twenty-dollar bill on the table to pay for his two brandies. He stood up and with a nod at the soldiers turned and walked in the direction of the vestibule. It only fleetingly occurred to him—another laughable thought—that the girl might follow; but he lingered on the chilly platform between the bar car and the day-niter until he was sure that she wouldn't; then made his way heavily along the corridors now illuminated by blue light-bulbs. As he opened the door of his sleeping compartment, a hand touched his elbow, but before he had time to imagine that it might be the girl the bar car attendant handed him his change.

"You forgot your change, sir."

"Oh thank you. Thank you. Ah—for you." He handed the man a crushed two-dollar bill.

"Thank you, sir. Good night."

"Good night."

It was hot, still, in the sleeping compartment, in spite of his having left the fan spinning all this time. He should take an aspirin, try to get this cursed fever down. How fast was the train going? A hundred and four miles an hour, perhaps, corresponding exactly with Maurice's temperature. He took the aspirins, swallowing them down with cool water out of one of the little cone-shaped paper drinking cups that it was impossible to put down; then he stripped off and let his clothes lie in a heap on the floor. He climbed naked between the sheets, and pushed up the blind with his toe to see if there was anything discernible outside. There was not. Only snow-drifts. But then, way out somewhere, a flashing light. He thought at first that it must be some farm building or other country light, appearing and disappearing between invisible, snow-draped trees; but then a shaft of moonlight shone on water, and the winking light proved to be a light-house far out on a reef. Maurice watched it intently until a high embankment obscured it from the train window; and at the same time he felt the brakes come on, tugging at the pounding bogies as the train lost speed. Cobourg was still some twenty miles distant, he reckoned; the soldiers in the bar car, however frequently they rode this route, had been somehow deceived; and Maurice stretched with momentary pleasure, in the moonlit privacy of his rattling room.

There was a faint tap on the door. The lawyer sat up in bed with a jerk, banging his head on the unoccupied berth above him, and covering himself with the blankets. The tap on the door must have been his imagination—but no, it came again. The sleeping car attendant? No: the attendant would press the buzzer; as he would, in a few hours' time, to announce the train's pending arrival in Montreal with the offer of scalding coffee and a sweet roll on a paper plate.

The tap again.

The lawyer swung his legs off the bed, and flicked various light switches before he found the blue ceiling light. He stepped into his pants and pulled them up, then he opened the door.

"I'm sorry. Did I wake you up?" said the girl from the bar car.

"No. I'd only just gone to bed."

"I wondered, do you want company?"

The lawyer from Toronto blinked at her. Company! Nicely put. Did he want company? He tried to weigh the question. No, of course he didn't want company.

Instead he said, "Aren't we nearly at Cobourg?"

They stood facing each other in the narrow doorway of Maurice's sleeping compartment as the night train trundled through the snow. The girl shrugged.

"I'm not sure where we are," she said. "All places look the same in the dark."

"So, you're not really headed for Cobourg."

"I could get out at Kingston and take the train back."

"We don't arrive at Kingston until three thirty-five. It's where we pass the west-bound night train. You could cross the tracks and transfer to it, but you wouldn't be home before five o'clock in the morning. And your mother's waiting up for you."

"I don't have to get out at Kingston."

"I think you should get out at Cobourg and go home."

After a moment she said, "I'm terribly sorry if I disturbed you."

She mentioned it as a prelude to departure, but she remained there long enough for him to say "Come in," under his breath. He stepped back from the door so that she could enter; and she kept her eyes fixed on him as she advanced into his narrow cabin, shutting the door behind her. He had a curious feeling she'd pull out a gun, like the daughter of his dreams, and thought, what a way for a lawyer to die, shot to death on the night train by a hooker from Cobourg.

However, she did not pull out a gun; instead she stood there, reaching out a hand to steady herself against the rolling of the train.

"I don't have to stay," she said. "I'll leave at once if I'm troubling you."

"No. No, it's all right." Maurice took a step forward, hit his head on something hard. He was suddenly awake, and drenched in sweat in spite of the aspirins he'd taken. His head throbbed. He realized he'd been dreaming again. The train had stopped, and he had no idea how long it must have been standing there.

"Where are we?" he wondered.

"I don't know," the girl would have said, if she had really followed him back to his sleeping compartment. "Why do you always have to know where you are?"

"I just wondered whether we'd got to Cobourg yet."

"I have no idea. The whole point of the night train is that you don't know where you are, until it's tomorrow."

And he was asleep again.

He walked arm in arm with his daughter, along a white, sandy trail lined with soughing casuarina pines. From far away came a long drawn-out whistle, either a distant train (if they had trains in those latitudes—perhaps some narrow-gauge antique hauling freight cars loaded with sugar cane) or a sleepless owl of some tropical species. He had begged to be allowed to see Sofia; had begged; yes, actually begged. And the officials, very troubled and sympathetic, had agreed. She had stepped out of the back of a car; two men climbed out after her but did not follow as she ran to embrace her father. The men would saunter along, of course, at a respectful distance, lugging their automatic rifles, exchanging an occasional word. But they kept at such a respectful distance that Maurice began to wonder whether a sudden run for freedom mightn't be successful. He said nothing to his daughter: there must be no false hope of escape. Sofia, chattering blithely about her childhood, and cheerfully resigned, still, to die soon, must not be allowed to glimpse the possibility of futures. As they reached a kind of cross-roads—the sandy track at this point forking right and left, with another faint trail joining at right angles—the lawyer glanced quickly about him for potential escape routes. There were none. Some way down each trail, under the casuarinas swaying to the sturdy easterly trade winds, a guard strolled, quietly enjoying the tropical peace-fulness of the spot, the sandy footfalls of his boots and the oc-casional clunk of his well-oiled automatic weapon the only sounds above the wind's murmur.

The night train had begun to move again, leaving Co-bourg—if that had indeed been Cobourg—behind in the si-lence; the train's hundred wheels ringing like cracked bells past rows of apparently abandoned freight cars. The girl in the tight skirt would have got off now; was probably slumped in the back of a taxi full of stale, small-town cigarette smoke, on the way home. Maurice Edelman was alone on the night train with a temperature of one hundred and four; and Sofia, his daughter, was spending her last night on earth in a tropi-cal prison cell. Warm night sounds would drift in through the bars of her cell window: the wind in the casuarinas, an owl, frogs, cicadas, jaunty music played on radios—tangos, rum-bas, sambas, cha chas, merengues. A gray-uniformed guard would peer through the window of Sofia's cell door, from time to time, but Sofia was sleeping peacefully; she would sleep through her last night alive as calmly and untroubled as she had slept through her first; she had never woken up her mother, had been as admirable a baby as she became a charm-ing child.

Maurice sat up in bed, banged his head again on the berth above, and got up, fumbling for the blue ceiling light. He took another of the little cone-shaped paper cups that became soggy unless drained immediately. He ran the faucet in the hope of getting cold water, but to no avail. He drank tepid dregs. The train was moving at a fine pace now, its powerful twin diesel locomotives blasting through the night. Snow-covered plains, brooding woods, shimmering, moonlit lakes coasted by. The lawyer glanced at his watch: surprisingly, it had stopped. This was unimportant, because the point of the night train was not only that you didn't know where you were, you also had no idea whether the train was on time or not. Then Maurice understood that his daughter was due to be executed just about the time the train rolled into Montreal Central Station. The next time he slept, he would dream her death. He must not sleep.

He washed himself, tugged his pants back on, pulled a sweater over his head. He stuffed his wallet into the back pocket of his pants and lurched off through the darkened vestibules in search of the bar car. He had no idea whether it would still be open; but he must stay on the move so as to remain awake; must, if at all possible, seek company of any kind, anywhere.

He reeled through the day-niter, clutching the backs of seats for support, to emerge, once again, into the brightly-lit bar car. The only occupant was the woman in the tight skirt. The Armed Forces men had gone; all the other Molson drinkers had quit, either got off the train at one of its frequent nocturnal halts, probably Trenton Junction, or curled up in the day-niter to snore the remaining miles away.

The woman was sitting exactly where he'd seen her last, facing Maurice as he came in. She nodded, but absently. After a moment's polite hesitation the Toronto lawyer sat down across from her.

"Are they still serving drinks?"

"I think so."

"You didn't get off at Cobourg, then."

"I never seem to get off at Cobourg," said the girl.

The bar car attendant appeared and Maurice ordered another brandy. He took a Kleenex and wiped the sweat off his forehead.

"I couldn't sleep," he told the girl. "I think I may have drifted off once or twice, but every time the train stopped I woke up. In the end I gave it up as a bad job. I needed to find out if there was anyone else alive on this train."

The girl parted her lips as if she was about to say something, but didn't. It occurred to Maurice that she might be on drugs, because she had the vacant, pensive look he'd sometimes seen in court-rooms.

"Do you know people in Montreal?" he said.

The girl looked at him, but still said nothing.

"I don't know anyone in Montreal either," said the lawyer. "Though I always appreciated the city. I do know some good restaurants. If you don't have any plans for lunch, I should be pleased to invite you."

The woman looked surprised, but kept silent.

"There are some good seafood restaurants. Do you like seafood?" said Maurice.

The woman reacted neither positively nor negatively to the notion of seafood restaurants.

"I have a house down south," the lawyer tried. "It's on the ocean, with three hundred feet of ocean frontage. Pure white sand beach, casuarinas. Eat a lot of seafood down there. I go out fishing with one of the locals. Big black guy, strong as a bear. We catch grouper, yellow snapper, barracuda. Shark, sometimes. Can I buy you a drink? Another beer? How many have you had?"

"Only two. No, thank you."

Seeing that she had not got off at Cobourg, and thereby lost the right to innocence, there was really no reason he should not invite the girl back to his sleeping compartment.

He sipped his brandy, contemplating the wisdom of doing that, and the night train, at speed, thundered across flat white country. It crossed frozen rivers on hollow steep bridges that echoed like waterfalls. It curled past snoring farms and townships, its enormous headlamp probing the blackness. The brakes came on.

"Now where are we?" the lawyer wondered, but the girl only shrugged. She was right. On the night train, you don't know where you are, at any time, and it doesn't matter. It is the irrelevance of things that would normally be taken for granted, like knowing where you are, that makes the night train a time capsule, hurtling towards eventual daylight.

Maurice shook himself. He was dozing, which he must not do. His daughter's life depended, now, on her father's staying alive, on the night train, somewhere in a snowy country; and his staying awake in its turn depended on this woman in a tight shirt talking to him, except that she wouldn't, or couldn't. What other desperate measures could he resort to? Suppose he got off, next time the night train halted? Stumbled into some anonymous station, blinking in the glow of one meager electric light bulb, and stayed there as the train moved off, taking light with it, and girls in tight skirts, and waiters who brought you brandy, and sleeping car attendants who would appear if you found the right button to push, and wakeful engineers in striped caps who sat up there, hour after hour, gazing into the blackness beyond the immense, unflickering headlamp. And the lawyer would be left on his own. He would have to try and telephone for a taxi, but everything and everywhere would be shut. There would be no answer, the telephone would ring repeatedly in the cold. In the end he'd have to doss down on mail-bags, in the station waiting room, unless they'd locked it, and sleep. And dream his daughter's execution. No. He must stay on the night train. He must talk to this woman.

"I have a daughter of about your age," he said.

He had hardly hoped that she'd show interest, but she said, "What's her name?"

"Her name is Sofia. It's a Spanish name. Her mother was from Cuba."

"What does she do?"

Maurice was taken aback by the unexpected questions. He put down his brandy glass, then picked it up again.

"She's a reporter."

"That's interesting."

"Yes. She works on assignments for magazines. She spends a lot of her time abroad. At the moment she's in Honduras, or perhaps Nicaragua."

"I don't have much idea where that is," the girl said frankly. "I was once in Cancún."

"Well. That's in Mexico. Same part of the world."

He felt wide awake. Glanced out the window. An incomprehensible blackness drifted past. Not much south of Cancún, where this bland, tight-skirted girl had spent a packaged vacation (made love to nightly, perhaps, by drunken fellow-countrymen or lucky locals), the lawyer's daughter slept quietly in her cell. There'd be a quiet smile on her face, and she'd look peaceful; peaceful as when, long years ago, her father had tucked her up in the pink sheets of her little nursery bunk bed. There had never been a small sister or brother to occupy the top bunk, unfortunately, because Maurice and his wife had gone their separate ways before that could happen. Sofia slept, and dreamed—perhaps—of bunk beds, while the guard squinted at her through the bars of the little window in her cell door and marveled. Not many of his wards had slept through their last night on earth so soundly; she must know, this one, beyond a shadow of a doubt, that she would very soon be in Heaven; imagined herself, perhaps, already there. Which she as good as was, hobnobbing with the Virgin Mary and all those saints. The guard found it difficult to picture this slumberer as a terrorist, which is what he'd been informed she was. His tongue slipped around his lips. It would be an easy thing to unbolt the door and slip into the cell, straddle her in her little cot. Comfort the girl, maybe, on this her last night. The guard muttered a prayer to his favorite saint, shut the little sliding window, and resumed his pacing. No. Let the gringa go to Heaven a virgin, if virgin she was; she would not go defiled by her jailer.

Maurice Edelman gripped the table. He had been almost asleep. Or was he asleep already? No. It was night still. Up ahead, the locomotive's gloomy whistle blared at a railroad crossing. Maurice looked sharply at his companion in the tight skirt. He got to his feet.

"Come with me," he said. "There are two berths. You can stretch out. It's better than sitting up all night in the bar car."

She gazed at him.

"What did you say? I'm sorry—but what did you say?"

"If you want company, why not come with me?"

The girl tried to stand up, but nearly fell. She hung onto the lawyer's elbow. The bar car attendant came by; Maurice gave him another twenty-dollar bill and told him to keep it.

"Thank you, sir."

"There are two berths," Maurice said again, as the girl held onto his arm and he piloted her through the dim blue vestibules. She needed to go to the bathroom and whimpered outside the door.

"It's all right. We have a private bathroom."

He opened the door to his compartment and pushed her inside. She saw the bathroom and disappeared. He turned down the bedclothes on the top berth for her. He slipped off his pants and sweater, climbed into the bottom berth, leaving the lights full on so that he'd stay awake.

The girl, after a long time, lurched out of the tight bathroom, still fully dressed.

"What am I doing in here?"

"Climb up into the top berth. You'll feel better if you lie down. It's difficult to sleep sitting up."

"What do you think I am? A tart?"

"I don't know what you are. At first I thought you were, then I thought you weren't. I don't care. It's not my business. I won't touch you. Just climb up there and go to sleep."

She climbed up the ladder, her legs disappearing from Maurice's view. He could hear her rummaging about, supposed she was taking her clothes off.

"I've never been in a sleeping car before. Just look at this. There's a little tin cupboard for your shoes."

"It opens into the corridor. If you want him to, the attendant will get your shoes out of the cupboard and clean them during the night."

"That's cool."

More rummaging, and then her light went off.

"How long is it until we get to Montreal?" she wanted to know.

"I don't know."

In a few minutes the girl began snoring, and the place smelled gently of used beer. Maurice felt himself falling asleep, and panicked. He sat up hastily, hitting his head, as usual, on the bottom of the berth where the girl was, but not, it seemed, waking her up. The snoring continued. Maurice was sweating again. The brakes came on: once more, the train was slowing down. How could a man be expected to sleep, with all this stopping and starting? When the train finally came to a standstill, with three huge jolts, he got out of bed and pulled on his clothes again. He went out into the corridor and strolled to the platform at the end of the car. The door was open. He peered out into the night. They were at Brockville, where the train was divided, the last three cars eventually proceeding to Ottawa. The train, as stipulated in the timetable, would stand here for half an hour. It was cold but Maurice stepped down onto the deserted station. He stood there, looking up at the height of the train. Steam from the heating pipes billowed out from under the darkened cars. He paced the platform, counting the cars. There were more than he had imagined, sixteen cars in fact, including the baggage car. A small switcher was in the process of pulling back the Ottawa-bound cars at the rear. Maurice walked the whole length of the platform. A thin yellow light glowed in the cab of the leading diesel locomotive, and he glimpsed the engineers talking to each other, sipping hot coffee from paper cups. He walked slowly back to where the sleepers were coupled and climbed back up.

She must have switched the light off. He kicked off his clothes in the dark, and rolled into his bed. The girl was there. She was still dressed, but she folded him sleepily in her arms.

"Don't go away," she murmured. "I was cold. I hoped you wouldn't mind."

"I don't mind."

"Where did you go?"

"I went for a walk."

"I was afraid you wouldn't come back," said the girl.

"I came back."

"Don't you want to make love to me?"

"I don't think so. I'm sorry."

"That's all right. I knew you were a nice man, as soon as I saw you."

She slept in his arms. The night train's triumphant whistle sounded, way up ahead.

He was allowed to be with his daughter when it was time for her execution. She was, in these last few minutes of her life, as cheerful and carefree as she had remained all the time. She said good-bye without regret, as if she was going away on vacation. Maurice hung around in silence: for her sake he would mirror her unconcern; except that now he only longed for the thing to be over so that he could walk the streets of the city and howl.

He held her hand tightly as they were led into a corridor smelling of disinfectant. She was asked to lie on a stretcher and with a last squeeze of the hand she was wheeled away from him.

Maurice Edelman awoke.

Daylight entered the sleeping compartment, under the blind. The girl in the berth above him snored peacefully.

He went out into the corridor. The sleeping car attendant was knocking on doors, offering to fetch coffee and sweet rolls. The night train was gliding quickly through the western suburbs of Montreal, in the morning sunlight.

In a Cold Climate

Ashley Shelby

My father spent his Air Force years stationed in King Salmon, Alaska. The King Salmon Air Force Base was situated near Katmai, on the Alaskan peninsula—the last mainland point before the beginning of the Aleutian chain. Dad was a skinny ex-basketball player from Indiana, with a military haircut and a girl from Phoenix to whom he wrote twice a day. He was the base's radio and television production specialist. The film morgue was about three hundred yards across the tundra from the main building, and an equal distance from the base's dump, where the grizzlies came to feed in families, four or five at a time. On midnight trips to the film morgue, it was a coin toss whether or not he'd get back in one piece. That's how he likes to tell it, anyway.

A faint madness has always replaced my father's otherwise lucid psyche during the winter months. Winter existed, for everyone in our family—except Mom, who didn't get involved in the bullshit—solely to be survived and, if things went well, to be bested.

We are a hardy family. We grew up here, after all, in this funny milk-pitcher shaped, lake-studded state. Cold weather made my sisters and me bold. Instead of contracting like metal, we expanded with winter weather, matching it step for step. We didn't hide from it, or shut it out; we joined it.

"Snow is one of the best insulating materials, if used properly," my father was fond of saying before making a winter camp in the backyard of our suburban Minneapolis home. On these occasions, he'd pull a black ski mask over his head, a fur-lined Eskimo hat on top of that and strap a hunting knife to his left calf. It was rough out there, he warned us; the arctic winds—sometimes thirty below—ran through the gaps between the subdivisions unobstructed.

"When it's this cold out, you'll feel things stiffen that you never thought could stiffen," Dad said. "The snot in your nose. The little hairs in your nostrils. Your eyelashes. It'll be the little things that'll hurt like hell, girls. Do as I say when we're out there and it'll be as cozy as cocoa."

There were few who understood my father. Cooper did. She seemed instinctively to understand the principles and the beauty of snow camping. She was sturdy, like my father, and would later climb frozen waterfalls down by the river with him, be his belay partner on weekend rock climbs and pore over books like *Harsh Winter Camping* and *Snow Caves for Fun and Survival*.

"There are whole species of birds that burrow into little snow caves," Cooper said.

"Ptarmigan," my father said. Cooper beamed.

"I was just going to say that, Dad."

But Cooper was long gone; not gone the way of all flesh, the way I feared she would go sooner rather than later. Instead she was at the South Pole, and no one wanted to be there with her worse than Dad.

Cooper was born breach and she had the biggest head of any baby ever born in the county. The doctor knew Cooper hadn't made the big pelvic somersault, but seemed untroubled. He massaged Mom's swollen belly, trying to turn Coop the right side down, but she was perfectly comfortable where she was, sitting atop Mom's hips like a little buddha.

On the eve of Coop's flight to Christchurch, New Zealand where she'd catch the plane to Antarctica, Dad had raised his glass of nonalcoholic wine for a toast.

"Coop came into life ass-first and that's the way she's continuing to go through it," he said. Everyone laughed and Coop nodded solemnly, raising her glass above her head. Agreed.

If I had taken a picture of Coop at the party that night and laid it out on the dining room table next to a picture of Coop at a year old, I'd have been amazed with the display. There has been no change in twenty-three years, not one thing different from that baby's face and the face that was half-obscured by an up-tilted wine glass. I imagined that as an old woman, Cooper would be craggy and worn from her sub-zero adventures, but would still retain that essential sweetness in the droop of her mouth. But for now I liked the way Coop hadn't changed while the rest of us grew up, grew ugly. Big hard head. Lots of freckles. Happy mouth. Good laugh. True laugh.

Both May and I had morphed over twenty plus years. I looked nothing like the happy, blonde baby with the big blue eyes that appeared in various fuzzy photographs in albums around my parents' house. That one year I had them to my-self—the year of the blue sundress, the tiny Dallas apartment, the two doting parents—was the only year of my life when I smiled in pictures. May looked like a little Mexican baby when she was born, with her coffee-colored skin, which lightened as she got older. Mom says May smiled so much that after a while, they worried about her. If they'd wake her from a nap, she'd open her eyes and smile. There are a million baby stories for May, and my mother loves to retell them at holiday dinners while May smiles smugly. The only one they ever tell about me is about the day my father snuck up on me one late afternoon as I stood in my crib on the side closest to the window, trying to grab a sunbeam that was coming through the blinds. He took two pictures—one of me with my hand outstretched towards the shaft of light and one taken an instant later when I tried to grab it. This moment has always been my saving grace, the currency of forgiveness that is passed between my parents and me.

Cooper, though, was an infant in a perpetual state of confusion. She was chubby and placid, and watched everything that happened around her with opened-mouth, drooling awe.

Before leaving for Antarctica, Cooper was living in an old apartment building in downtown Minneapolis, just across from Loring Park. She'd moved in with the boy she'd one day appeared with at Thanksgiving her sophomore year in college. He was a sculptor who wanted to be an art teacher. Mom bought one of his sculptures to be polite—it was Cooper dressed as a circus clown, balancing on a unicycle, with one leg outstretched.

"Circus Circus meets Clockwork Orange," May said when she saw it. "That's scary shit. Look at Coop on the unicycle there. She looks scared, like, what the fuck?"

"May, please," Mom said. She was only generous when someone else in the room wasn't. Randy's greatest claim to fame was the year he'd spent without shampooing his hair, but he was a gentle eccentric and loved Cooper with quiet intensity.

So Dad had just raised his glass and made his little toast and Randy's parents had hesitantly raised their glasses. I looked at their pale, expressionless faces and saw their thoughts as clearly as if their heads were transparent. They were imagining all the holidays that would be shared when Randy and Cooper made it official, as everyone knew they would, some day. They were hearing all the toasts that Dad would make that would include the word "ass" and all the weepy declarations of love my mother would make after she gulped down three glasses of wine. They were wondering if all Christmases would stack up like the one last year, when they'd given Cooper a tin of homemade Christmas cookies and Dad had bought Randy a custom-made Quetico canoe.

And then came the Antarctica business. There had been the question of financing it, through "sponsorships" and grants and fellowships. But where was money for a couple of slouches who held degrees in outdoor recreation and art education from a state school up north?

"Money like that goes to scientists who have a reason for hitting the ice," Dad said. "Folks like you have to wrangle up money the old-fashioned way. I'm talking door-to-door action with the tin can."

"And what do we promise the sponsors they'll get in exchange for their donation?" Cooper had asked.

"Framed photograph," my father said immediately. "Easy. Framed photograph of you wearing apparel with their logo on it. Let's say you're standing outside Scott's hut at Cape Evans. Slip on that Fleet Farm baseball cap, snap a photo, and you've fulfilled your obligation. They'll hang that picture above the cash register. It'll stay there for years. Maybe decades." Randy smiled vacuously at my father, who seemed to both puzzle and delight him.

"Look, Coop. I've got a name in this town," Dad had said as we lounged on the dirtied cream loveseat in Coop's little living room. "There's no doubt about that. But the question on the table is how you can use it to your advantage."

"Maybe Cooper doesn't want to use your name," May said from the dining room. "Ever mull that one over, Dad?" I am always gentle with my father, as he was always gentle with me, and I resented May's bitchy comment. Dad didn't say anything, but leaned back against the loveseat and crossed his arms behind his head.

"Dad, I just think it might be a nice test of independence to try to finance the trip on my own," Cooper said.

Coop was gone now, having financed the whole thing on her own by agreeing to wash dishes down there, and eating her heart out while the scientists drank and experimented, experimented and drank. She'd be there for a full year, eight months of which she and the rest of the base would be completely isolated. For me, I heard it like a quiet mantra: *No flights in. No flights out.*

Getting down there was an achievement. Cooper had had to undergo a battery of psychological tests. *Do you ever have pain in your chest, unrelated to indigestion? Are you often depressed? Do you have digestion problems due to stress? Do you have problems with authority?* After the psychological examinations, Cooper and Randy had been sent to Denver for three weeks of fire training.

"Antarctica is the driest place on earth," Cooper told me. "So fire is the biggest threat to life there."

"And if it's so cold, how does the water not freeze in the hoses?" I'd asked.

"We don't use hoses. Chemicals. I've gained a lot of respect for anti-inflammatories. They save human lives." She looked at me and grinned. "Maybe I'll save penguin lives. Maybe I'll save a colony of penguins and then they'll crown me as their penguin queen." She threw her head back and let loose one of her trademark belly laughs.

"But Coop, seriously, aren't you going to miss Mom and Dad?" I asked. She shrugged and nodded, but I could tell that of all the risks of this approaching isolation, homesickness was the one that Cooper would find the easiest to mitigate. She could afford it because here at home, she was the queen.

After fire training, Cooper and Randy had had to submit to a final psychological examination, in which they were told that among the precepts they had to accept before going down there was the one that stated that if they got sick and the base's nurse practitioner couldn't heal them, they'd die. The South Pole base was isolated for the entire winter, with only one plane flyover during the long dark night to drop provisions on the ice. Cooper and Randy agreed. They were told that if one of their family members were to die during the course of their yearlong stay in Antarctica, they wouldn't attend the funeral. Cooper and Randy agreed. There were provisos, if/then statements, policies. What it boiled down to was this: there was nothing more important to you than Antarctica. Coop agreed.

I'd been remembering all this before we—we, meaning the family minus Coop—ordered our drinks. On a river, in a cold state, on a cold day, my lips soldered shut and my breath escaping my nostrils in short white puffs, I looked like an angry bull facing a hero. The boat was long and elegant, a dining cruise ship called the Nordic Moon. We were all here, hungry and maybe presenting our best faces to one another. And then my father, ex-airman and Alaska outdoor survival instructor, insisted that we dine outside on the Texas deck, starboard side.

Because my father has the most recognizable voice in the state, his talk radio show being the windiest and most popular drive-time program in the state for twenty years, he was indulged. Mom refused, like I knew she would, and was sitting on the other side of the glass, sipping a glass of Merlot and smiling at me sarcastically every time she caught my eye.

"Jesus, it's cold," May said.

"Keep it secular," Dad said.

"Well, good God, Dad, this is ridiculous." Through the glass, I could see our waiter pulling on a tattered green scarf, a heavy down jacket and a wool hat. He was pulling open the door to the deck when the maitre' d stopped him and whispered in his ear. The waiter grimaced and said something out of the corner of his mouth. The maitre' d's grip on the waiter's arm tightened and the waiter's shoulders fell in angry resignation. He pulled off his hat and unwound the scarf from around his neck. The maitre' d helped him out of his coat and folded it over his arm. The waiter opened the door to the deck and walked to our table.

"Good evening sir," he said. "And ladies."

"How are you, how are you?" my father said to the waiter. "Wine, girls? Wine?"

"Do you have a house red?" I asked. May punched me in the shoulder.

"No house tonight," May said. "Dad's buying. Got anything good back there in the galleys?" It seemed the waiter's lips were turning blue.

"What do you recommend?" Dad asked the waiter.

"Well, we have an excellent *Châteauneuf-du-Pape*, if you like red," he said. There was a point in every meal I had with my family during which I felt excruciatingly guilty, and it was this point. My father hadn't had a drop of alcohol for twenty-five years. My mother had always been strangely unsympathetic to my father's ongoing battle to stay sober, despite the fact that, when he was still drinking, she had been the one who suffered the effects of his embarrassing behavior.

At home the fridge was stocked with beer and box wine and, as the years passed and the girls left home, my mother had started drinking three or four glasses of wine a night. At cocktail parties, Mom would finish off entire bottles of wine and get silly. I'd seen the way my father watched my mother's every move during dinners, keeping track of her every refill, noting the speed with which she finished a glass, and, when she got silly and loud, glaring at her stonily.

But when the wine appeared at the table, and the waiter poured that little bit into my father's glass, Dad would swirl it around and smell it so deeply that I could see his chest expand and his nostrils dilate hugely and it was almost as if he were tasting the wine just by inhaling.

"That sounds fine," I said.

"As long as it's red, expensive, and intoxicating," May said. The waiter smiled widely at her and she winked at him.

"Do you have any nonalcoholic beers or wines back there?" Dad asked. "What about that wine without alcohol that's just come onto the market?" He looked at May and me. "They say it's beat out real wine in taste tests."

May snorted. "Uh, you mean Fré?" She turned to me and stage-whispered: "He's got, like, four cases of that shit. He hides it in the laundry room."

"We have a nonalcoholic wine, sir," the waiter said.

"Well, that'll do me just fine, sir," my father said. I was trying not to look at my mother, but the maitre' d had placed her at a table for two that was flush against the glass so it would be, as he put it, "just like your mother's dining with you." She was talking to the couple seated at the table next to her, and every so often all three turned to look out the window at us.

I'd moved back home three months ago, pleasing no one. I'd been sent, with much fanfare, to New York to pursue a career in degree acquisition—first grad school, then a Ph.D. program, then an academic appointment. I'd scraped into a graduate program, but had dropped out, reenrolled, then dropped out again, and for good.

"What's the deal?" my father had asked at the time. "What's wrong?" I had no answer for him. "This isn't the right face to show the world, kiddo. You don't want people thinking you can't cut it. If you need to, pop a pill, balance your chemicals, see the world with fresh, happy eyes, get back in the game." With each concerned phone call from my father, I began to withdraw further. I was meant to *achieve*. We all were.

"Red wine gives me courage," May said.

"Know who said that?" Dad asked her.

"Um, me, just now?" May had a tendency to produce famous quotes without attribution and claim them for her own since she couldn't remember where she'd heard them. Dad looked over at me, throwing the question to me.

"Dorothy Parker?"

"Close," my father said. "Alexander Wolcott."

"No, it was Dorothy Parker."

My father appeared to think this over. "I'm fairly sure it was Wolcott."

"Why would Wolcott need courage, Dad?"

"Why would Dorothy Parker?"

"Which of us was the literature grad student?"

"Um, how seriously can we take a dropout?" May said. My hands fell in my lap and I stared at the half-empty glass of wine in front of me.

"May," my father said quietly.

"Well, I'm sorry, but how is she going to pull rank like that?" I listened to May pour herself another glass of wine and studied the zipper on my jacket.

The waiter had been allowed the green scarf, and he'd wrapped himself in it so tightly that it looked like a noose. He came to the table with the bottle of red and my father's glass of fake wine. May started laughing when the waiter poured the wine; it was steaming in the cold air. She grabbed the glass with her both of her mittened hands, and I wrapped my own numb fingers around the stem of my glass, and we clinked, and then waited for Dad to lift his glass, and clinked again. I looked over May's shoulder to see if Mom was looking, but she wasn't. The waiter took our food orders and hurried back to the kitchen, blowing on his hands.

I knew something my father didn't. I was in possession of a fact that my father didn't have access to and, worse, didn't even know existed. There was no greater humiliation for him, I knew, than discovering that he was the last to know something important. Existing in a world that contained one more fact than the one in which he lived was a new and disturbing state of being. It felt as if I were stationed atop a mountain, overlooking a landscape I had traveled my whole life and seeing him down at the foot, just a tiny speck.

And yet, one slip of the tongue and Cooper would no longer be perfect.

My mother firmly believed the secret world of women was inviolable. On their first date, my mother's menstrual cramps were so bad that she popped two aspirins at the table.

"What's wrong?" my father asked her.

"You don't want to know what's behind the curtain," my mother had said. Dad had laughed and said:

"We all have curtains."

"No," my mom said. "I'm talking about the woman's curtain."

The news my father was not privy to had come last week in an e-mail. Cooper said procedure had been successful in its objective and Randy had been there to help her recover, but the nurse, who had only performed one abortion in her life, had done some damage to Coop's uterus. May told me that Mom had been retiring to her bedroom early in the evening. When May put her ear to the door, she heard weeping.

The snow-covered banks of the Mississippi looked like the frosting on a week-old cake, cracked and brittle. The river was black and the thump of ice chunks crashing into the boat's hull sent vibrations through the deck and up my legs.

"It's fucking cold as a witch's tit. I'm going inside," May said to our father. She leaned into his face and said, as if she were talking to a man suffering from dementia: "This is insanity." Since May had returned home to live with the folks, she'd become saltier and more defiant. She'd been unemployed for many moons now and had given up the search. Mom didn't seem to mind, happy to have her best girlfriend back on her arm, ready to shop and lunch. Dad always thought something would come of her charm, if not her beautiful face. She had modeled eyeglasses to make extra cash during college, but after being rejected from every one of the talent agencies she submitted her headshots to, she decided to call it a day and come home for good. On her first day home, Mom found her in the study, feeding her headshots through the shredder.

May passed the waiter on her way inside and took her plate off his tray. He was now wearing gloves. He placed a steaming bowl of lobster bisque in front of me and a plate of king prawns and curried noodles in front of Dad. Through the window, I could see May and Mom eating fondue.

"The best way to eat hot food in a cold climate is to—"

"Eat fast?" I asked.

"That too," Dad said. "But try not to fool with it too much. Like your soup there, try to slip the spoon in so you don't break much of the skin. That way the heat is undisturbed and keeps."

"Is lobster bisque even supposed to have skin?" I asked. My father smiled faintly.

"Would mademoiselle like a warm towel for her lap?" the waiter asked me.

"Yes, please," I said.

"And sir?"

"I'm good, sir," Dad said. I watched the waiter walk back into the dining room. Inside he hugged himself and rubbed his upper arms rapidly.

"Stop calling him sir," I said. My father looked at me in surprise mid-bite, a half-chewed prawn resting somewhere on his tongue. He swallowed carefully, retaining the surprised look on his face. "It comes across as sarcasm, Dad."

My father considered this, then said: "I'm sorry." My father's apologies are so heartfelt, whether or not they are due the person demanding them, that they require a reciprocal request for forgiveness. I had forgotten about his apologies.

"Oh, Dad. Don't be sorry." He didn't say anything and I took a sip of my wine, which had grown ice cold. My bottom lip left a steam impression on the rim of the glass and I studied it for a moment. Who knew what kinds of secrets Dad kept from me? Maybe they were bad ones, like affairs. Maybe, when he was still drinking, he'd done something really terrible, and if everyone else in the world had forgotten about it, he hadn't. Maybe every action he took now—everything he offered to the world, including his daughters—was meant to be reparation. And maybe the world didn't want what he was offering.

There was only one real treasure in my father's life. It was as if Cooper were a homunculus performing marvelous, egoistic deeds at a distance, and Dad watched and admired and wanted to join her, but couldn't because he was bound by more than one tie. Coop was free, and he wasn't, and could Dad ever forgive her for that? If he found out, would he ever be able to forgive her for ruining Antarctica for him?

"This is really great," my father said. "You know, when your mother and I took that trip on the Mississippi Queen a couple of years ago, I didn't leave the deck of my cabin. Just sat there and read Twain. Just read Twain." My mother had been exasperated on this anniversary trip, having been left alone to wander the steamboat's casino and dance with the elderly bachelors to Glenn Miller on the parquet dance floor.

"This is nice, Dad. You're right." I slipped my mitten off my right hand. I reached for his hand and took it. "Thanks." He smiled and I saw his eyes move from mine to the dining room beyond my shoulder. I turned around and saw May and my mother were gathering up their things. They waved to us, and May pantomimed guzzling a beer, stroking the bottle, then licking the top. She jerked her thumb towards the boat's bar and I watched her and our mother disappear into the lounge. I turned back around. Dad was running his finger along the inside of his wine glass.

"Want some more fake wine, Dad?"

"I'm okay," he said. "Here." He poured me another glass of the *Châteauneuf-du-Pape*.

"What do you think Coop's doing right now?"

I watched him attempt to spread a pat of butter on a piece of bread. The frozen pat flew off his knife and landed on the deck near his foot.

"Apple doesn't fall far from the tree," he said. "So Coop's probably freezing her ass off."

I took off my mittens; my hands were sweating.

"Here's the thing I like about your sister. She's a doer, not a talker." My father pushed his chair back from the table to stretch his legs. I watched as the frozen pat of butter disappeared under his boot.

"Are you saying that I'm not a doer?" I said softly. My father turned his blue-gray eyes to me.

"I'd say you're more of a talker, kiddo. You need to talk things out. There's nothing wrong with that. I'm just saying that Coop uses a different kind of shrink. She's a lot like me in that; her shrink is the outdoors. That works for her."

But all I could hear was *a doer not a talker, a doer not talker* and how it was truer of Coop than he knew. I could betray her.

There were many years in between what I consider to be my life—the one I made—and the life I felt my family had made for me, the one that had petrified into hard coils of time passed under the roof of my childhood home. That was true of all of the sisters, we felt. The rigidity of our roles made us brittle. Me, the smart one. Coop the nutty adventurer. May the pretty prom queen. We were not good sisters, never looking out for the other. It was always fair game to reveal a sister's flaw, and then to point it out, in order to look better by comparison. But here's how you looked good: you liked what Dad liked.

We were all, my father used to tell us, meant to achieve important, admirable things, suitable to our roles. But then one day, my father stopped reminding May and me that we were destined to be achievers, and decided Cooper was the only one who had been listening the whole time.

A side door flew open and May came tumbling out with Mom's coat on. She was drunk. She pointed at us and smiled, then giggled, then started guffawing. Soon she was laughing so hard the tears were streaming down her eyes. I looked at Dad. He had turned away from May and me and was looking out at the river as the boat glided down its channel in the dark. I heard May's heavy boots clanking across the deck quickly, saw her body convulsing, her hand at her mouth. She leaned over the railing and vomited into the Mississippi. Dad closed his eyes tightly as May retched. Another monument defiled by one of his daughters.

There was something in the way my father was holding on to his napkin, the way his hand gripped the bottle of red wine, and the way he finally turned and looked at me with water and disappointment in his eyes that told me he knew how it had all gone down with Cooper. She'd told him, I could imagine, weeping and hiccupping, on a satellite phone. He'd listened quietly; he was there for her. But there was nothing that was uncontaminated for him anymore.

May had stopped vomiting, but was still leaning over the railing, limp as a rag doll. Mom stood in the doorway, watching, not making any move to help either of her daughters.

"I'm sorry, Dad," I said. His breath came at me in soft, frozen clouds, and I imagined they accumulated somewhere, hundreds of exhalations, every single one of them composed by sadness. These were hollow accomplishments, these tainted adventures in a cold climate, embarked upon by all of us. It was tough enough to accept our place in the family, harder still to remain a grateful tenant. And yet, I *was* grateful, because none of us were pure, and not one of us could really betray the other and even Dad knew the secrets.

For the first time in my life, I saw goosebumps on my father's skin, saw his thin lips darkening to blue. It hardly seemed real, but the chill had penetrated; my father finally felt the cold.

Lone Stars

Lan Tran

I am dressed like Texas. It is past my bedtime but I am moonstruck with the idea of being a cowgirl—after all, we live in the Lone Star State. There I am, slant eyes and a long-horn drawl, bowl-cut hair and a ten-gallon hat. I have converted my jump rope into a lasso. It hangs awkwardly around my waist. I stomp my rodeo boots and sing at my father:

"The stars at night are big and bright

Deep in the heart of Texas!"

I go for volume, not melody. He is silent, as if he does not recognize me. I have evolved from rice paddy to cow patty with this entire campfire repertoire from school that I trot out every evening. Though I push him to, my father does not sing along. Yellow is for skin, not roses.

"Di ngu di," he turns away. Go to bed.

"Aren't you going to clap?

This is our nightly ritual. We are more than an ocean apart.

One night, even though we have guests, my father does acknowledge me. My mother is still at work when he says to me, "Little One, bring out the *tra*, then you can go play." He gestures at a large teapot filled with dark herbal drink. It smells of pretty blossoms and earthy roots but I make a sour face because I am painfully shy around strangers. Our living room is packed with Vietnamese college students who have come to hear my father lecture about politics and activism.

"Go," my father says, handing me a tray. I walk into the living room first but he quickly moves around me to go to his seat. Everyone is focused on my father's words when he begins to speak. Before them he is another person than the man I know and live with. Though he is dressed plainly, as always, in brown pants and a white short-sleeved shirt, there is a charisma about him I do not often see. "We are not economic immigrants," he tells his audience, "we are political refugees." The students nod, listening raptly. I know my movements are an interruption so I nervously set the tray down and scurry back to the warmth of the kitchen. Behind me, my father's voice echoes, "We must remember our history."

History, I nod to myself, thinking of my homework. At school, we are learning about our proud Texan heritage and our assignment is to draw pictures reflecting that pride. In addition, we have been promised extra credit stars if we bring in special projects. I myself have already earned a spangling row next to my name. I am a shameless hoarder of stars.

In the previous two nights I have folded a paper fort and pony for class. My teacher has been charmed and tonight I am determined to outdo myself. I have decided to make a chuckwagon!

I take out a white sheet, making careful folds to ensure the creases are sharp and precise. Through the door, I hear my father say, "We have lost our homeland and are marooned in a foreign country."

I sit, assessing my wagon. It needs something more. In the other room, my father is saying, "Until there is no more Communism, there is no home to return to." A murmur rises from the students, the significance of which escapes me. What is the big deal exactly? Whenever I have asked, "Why do these people have to come over and listen to Dad?" I have been told he has very important ideas. But it is all vague to me; the only thing I know is that Vietnam is extremely important to my father.

Vietnam … yes! I have the perfect idea for my chuck-wagon project! Something to please both my teacher and my dad. I grab the colored markers nearby and with a few quick strokes, I color the wagon's covering so it looks like the Vietnamese flag in my classroom atlas.

Now, I know the mini nylon banner on my father's desk looks different than what is in the atlas—his flag is yellow, like our coloring, with three red horizontal stripes representing the lifeblood of Vietnam's northern, central and southern regions. But the nylon banner is old and I have learned at school that flags can change. We Texans haven't always flown our current colors: red, white and blue with a single star. During the Texas Revolution, a white cotton flag was unfurled, painted with a black cannon and the words "Come and Take It," beneath. Naturally, I want my project to have the most up-to-date emblem of my father's homeland. I want to make something unforgettable: a Vietnamese chuck-wagon!

When I finish coloring my special project, I continue drawing more pictures for school. A little later, my father comes in for more *tra*. "Are you having a good talk, Daddy?" He grunts, to indicate its acceptability. "What are you talking about?" I ask him.

"*Chinh tri ve dat nuoc. Con chua hieu duoc,*" he answers. Political matters, our national landscape. You're too young to understand.

"I know landscape," I protest, then show him my drawing of a cactus in the sun. "And look," I find another picture, "this is Texas." I hand him a purple outline of my beloved land.

My father regards the dark lines meant to convey the edges and boundaries of my home state. "*Nhung con co biet ve Viet Nam khong?*" he asks. But can you draw Vietnam? I hold an uncapped marker in my right hand, hesitant. Is he really asking me to draw it? Though I have memorized the shape of Texas, the borders of Vietnam, to me, are hazy.

"*Yeu nuoc nhu vay,*" my father chides. You're quite a patriot.

"I am a patriot," I say.

My father shakes his head sadly, a certain gesture of his disappointment.

"*Con nghi con hieu long ai quoc?*" You think you know patriotism?

I nod vigorously at first, remembering a recent field trip to San Antonio and the Alamo—our tour around the famous mission, we children wide-eyed at the stone church, the wooden barracks. And oh, the gift shop with the armadillo toys!

"Davy Crockett was a patriot," I inform him.

"*Con dau co biet.*" You have no idea what it means. "*Ong noi con yeu nuoc,*" he corrects me. Your grandfather was a patriot. He wags his finger slowly and deliberately—a wiper that sweeps my confidence away.

I clench my fists, steaming. My teacher told us Davy Crockett was a patriot and yet, my father still corrects me. Why can I never give him the right answers? Why am I always wrong because my answers are not Vietnamese enough?

When he turns his back, I see my colored wagon beneath the other drawings. Maybe this will please him. As he gets more hot water, I lift the top napkin from the tea tray and place my chuckwagon beneath. Moments later, my father carries the tray into the other room. I listen expectantly for the sounds of approval, but instead I hear the tray slamming down and my name being yelled.

When I go into the living room, I see a pool of liquid on the table where the tea has spilled, but my father is focused on something else.

"Little One, did you draw this?" He holds up the chuckwagon—two of its wheels are soggy but yes, it has the blood red covering I have colored and is emblazoned with a lone star: golden, big and bright. Everywhere I look, unfriendly eyes stare at me. I nod.

"Why?"

"Because it's the flag of Vietnam." There is a dark mumbling among the visitors and they look at each other.

My father slams his palm on the coffee table then lifts the chuckwagon higher, shaking it. *Day la co cong san, con ve co giet hai nuoc!* This is the flag of Communist Vietnam! You have drawn the flag that murdered our homeland! He points to the golden star, "This is NOT our flag!"

My chuckwagon is ripped in half. I am dismissed. The meeting ends.

In the silence of my room, I kick the wall. My sharp-toed boots leave a faint mark, which I bend at first to wipe, then decide not to. Though my father's words incite deep longing in others—a vision of Vietnam free from Communists—what I hear incites anger and shame in me. I am an activist's daughter, but from that moment on, I actively remain ignorant of his causes. For many years, I care more about Sam Houston than Saigon. I remember the Alamo. My father remembers Vietnam.

Three words. *Dien Bien Phu.* I am a college student when these words come for me, a mouthful of reprimand. In the dorms to let off steam during mid-terms, we are playing Jeopardy! in teams. There are five of us on each team and the tie-breaking answer is, "In 1954, the French lost a major battle here to the Viet Minh. This led to the north-south partition of Vietnam along the 17th parallel."

My teammates cannot believe our luck. A Vietnamese history question! They don't even bother conferring, just hand me a fat felt pen to write down our answer. Someone pats me on the back.

Across from us, the other team is deep in a huddle, whispering and glancing at me nervously. They think I am speechless because I know the answer. The only thing I know is that the northern part went to the Communists. "Hurry," a teammate whispers, "we're gonna kick some ass!" So I write down, "What is the DMZ?" because I once heard a Vietnam Vet say he traveled there.

The other team's card says, "What is Dien Bien Phu?" They jump up and down when they win. My teammates stare at me open-mouthed in disbelief.

"What the hell's wrong with you?" one of them finally asks.

I want to say, "Hey, I'm American," but I don't know anything about the U.S. in Vietnam either, except what I've seen in movies.

"You were five years old when a *what* traumatized you?"

I'm with my roommate, who's an editor for our school's African-American paper, trying to explain to her why I'm not as in touch with my roots as she is.

"A chuckwagon," I mumble.

"A what?"

I thought she would be understanding but the more I try to explain to her—

"A chuckwagon."

"How old are you?"

—the more I'm beginning to realize how foolish it all seems.

"I'm twenty."

"Exactly. That happened almost fifteen years ago. Don't you think it's time to let it go?" I just stand there fidgeting, so she says, "I mean, my parents piss me off too but you don't see me try to stop being black." She pokes me in the arm. When I don't respond she sighs and shakes her head, "A chuckwagon."

For the first time I am aware that my grievance is outweighed by my ignorance.

"Dad, what happened in Vietnam?" It is winter break months later and I have come home for the holidays.

"Happened when?" We are eating dinner together and he does not look at me as he reaches for pieces of stuffed bitter melon.

"I don't know," I shrug, "how about the twentieth century?" There, I've admitted my ignorance, now he will be really annoyed. But he looks up with a small mouthful, stops chewing, then points his chopsticks at me and says, "Come with me."

"But we're eating." I point at the food.

My father responds by holding up a finger. "It's more important," he taps his temple, "that you consume this."

So I follow him into the family room and watch as he roots inside a tall, dark cabinet to bring out an old map of Vietnam. It crinkles with history as he unfolds it. The map is so old, our country is labeled *Indochine*.

"Here," my father points at an ambiguous land mass, "this is where the Chinese invaded centuries ago. And here," he indicates another region, "is where the French came in centuries later."

As we sit on the wooly rug, I am struck by my father's patience. I thought he would be appalled at my ignorance—there were all those times as a child when he dismissed me with condescension. But tonight, it is as if he expects my questions—as if he has been expecting them for quite some time. "During the French occupation, my family and I had to dig a tunnel under our house and live there. One day, they torched our house. We sat beneath in the darkness, listening to the sounds of our home burning down. It was incredibly hot." He speaks slowly but my mind races to capture all the details.

My father then narrates a timeline and as he progresses, the names of historical figures begin bleeding into names of family. With each major battle my father also recounts a death of our kin. "In the 1954 campaign against the French, your great uncle died," he'll say, or "During a North-South battle in '67 they bombed my cousin's school, killing him." I have never met these people; they are brittle leaves on the legend of our family tree, so at the mention of each name I ask, "Did you know him well?" or "Were you close to him?"

My father nods vaguely each time and continues to describe a litany of events, each tied to another name and another and another until the distance between the past and present dissolves as it becomes clear each death has drawn closer and closer to my dad. From ancestor to great grandfather to grandfather to his generation. At times, he must grit his teeth to continue handing me this history of Vietnam, a heartbreaking tally of men he has known and loved. There are moments when I do not recognize the waver in his voice. When he finishes, I am speechless. We do not look at each other, just stare at the map—its intimate curves indicating mountains and rivers. If we could cry together, there would be tears enough to wash away all the borders between the Alamo and Dien Bien Phu.

"There is something you should know … about your grandfather's death."

"How he fell? The train? Mom said it was a horrible accident."

"Well he did fall, but it was no accident."

"Someone pushed him? Mom said—"

"Little One, your mother doesn't know this. Your grandfather originally fought with the Viet Minh for a free Vietnam but wanted to leave them when they unveiled their Communist agenda. He thought he'd be safe in Hanoi but they still went after him for 'Crimes against the people'."

"Even though he once fought with them?"

My father nods. "Your grandfather knew the Communists were determined to find him guilty—which would also condemn his children—so for our freedom, he chose to kill himself. But, he couldn't commit suicide outright since that would be admitting guilt, so he faked it. It looked accidental, but your grandfather jumped to his death for your aunts, your uncle … and for me."

My father now tears openly. I do not ask, "Were you close to him?" Instead I watch as his hand traces across the map to indicate the 17th parallel. Instinctively, I join him and we brush over borders as our fingers sweep, mine following his, across the page. In the middle of the ocean, my father stops. Why, I am uncertain. But as my hand approaches his, he reaches for me. And when I look at him, he squeezes.

They say too, at the Alamo, when they knew they were outnumbered, Colonel Travis drew a line in the sand saying, "Anyone who's willing to die, cross this line!"

The Girl in the Flammable Skirt

Aimee Bender

When I came home from school for lunch my father
was wearing a backpack made of stone.

Take that off, I told him, that's far too heavy for you.

So he gave it to me.

It was solid rock. And dense, pushed out to its limit,
gray and cold to the touch. Even the little zipper handle was
made of stone and weighed a ton. I hunched over from the
bulk and couldn't sit down because it didn't work with chairs
very well so I stood, bent, in a corner, while my father whis-
tled, wheeling about the house, relaxed and light and lovely
now.

What's in this? I said, but he didn't hear me, he was
changing channels.

I went into the TV room.

What's in this? I asked. This is so heavy. Why is it
stone? Where did you get it?

He looked up at me. It's this thing I own, he said.

Can't we just put it down somewhere, I asked, can't we just sit it in the corner?

No, he said, this backpack must be worn. That's the law.

I squatted on the floor to even out the weight. What law? I asked, I never heard of this law before.

Trust me, he said, I know what I'm talking about. He did a few shoulder rolls and turned to look at me. Aren't you supposed to be in school? he asked.

I slogged back to school with it on and smushed myself and the backpack into a desk and the teacher sat down beside me while the other kids were doing their math.

It's so heavy, I said, everything feels very heavy right now.

She brought me a Kleenex.

I'm not crying, I told her.

I know, she said, touching my wrist. I just wanted to show you something light.

Here's something I picked up:

Two rats are hanging out in a labyrinth.

One rat is holding his belly. Man, he says, I am in so much pain. I ate all those sweet little sugar piles they gave us and now I have a bump on my stomach the size of my head. He turns on his side and shows the other rat the bulge.

The other rat nods sympathetically. Ow, she says.

The first rat cocks his head and squints a little. Hey, he says, did you eat that sweet stuff too?

The second rat nods.

The first rat twitches his nose. I don't get it, he says, look at you. You look robust and aglow, you don't look sick at all, you look bump-free and gorgeous, you look swinging and sleek. You look plain great! And you say you ate it too?

The second rat nods again.

Then how did you stay so fine? asks the first rat, touching his distended belly with a tiny claw.

I didn't, says the second rat. I'm the dog.

My hands were sweating. I wiped them flat on my thighs.

Then, ahem, I cleared my throat in front of my father. He looked up from his salad. I love you more than salt, I said.

He seemed touched, but he was a heart attack man and had given up salt two years before. It didn't mean *that* much to him, this ranking of mine. In fact, 'Bland is a state of mind' was a favorite motto of his these days. Maybe you should give it up too, he said. No more french fries.

But I didn't have the heart attack, I said. Remember? That was you.

In addition to his weak heart my father also has weak legs so he uses a wheelchair to get around. He asked me to sit in a chair with him once, to try it out for a day.

But my chair doesn't have wheels, I told him. My chair just sits here.

That's true, he said, doing wheelies around the living room, that makes me feel really swift.

I sat in the chair for an entire afternoon. I started to get jittery. I started to do that thing I do with my hands, that knocking-on-wood thing. I was knocking against the chair leg for at least an hour, protecting the world that way, superhero me, saving the world from all my horrible and dangerous thoughts when my dad glared at me.

Stop that knocking! he said. That is really annoying.

I have to go to the bathroom, I said, glued to my seat.

Go right ahead, he said, what's keeping you. He rolled forward and turned on the TV.

I stood up. My knees felt shaky. The bathroom smelled very clean and the tile sparkled and I considered making it into my new bedroom. There is nothing soft in the bathroom. Everything in the bathroom is hard. It's shiny and new; it's scrubbed down and whited out; it's a palace of bleach and all you need is one fierce sponge and you can rub all the dirt away.

I washed my hands with a little duck soap and peered out the bathroom window. We live in a high rise apartment building and often I wonder what would happen if there was a fire, no elevator allowed, and we had to evacuate. Who would carry him? Would I? Once I imagined taking him to the turning stairway and just dropping him down the middle chute, my mother at the bottom with her arms spread wide to catch his whistling body. Hey, I'd yell, catch Dad! Then I'd trip down the stairs like a little pony and find them both splayed out like car accident victims at the bottom and that's where the fantasy ends and usually where my knocking-on-wood hand starts to act up.

Paul's parents are alcoholics and drunk all the time so they don't notice that he's never home. Perhaps they conjure him up, visions of Paul, through their bleary whiskey eyes. But Paul is with me. I have locked Paul in my closet. Paul is my loverboy, sweet Paul is my olive.

I open the closet door a crack and pass him food. He slips the dirty plates from the last meal back to me and I stack them on the floor next to my t-shirts. Crouched outside the closet, I listen to him crunch and swallow.

How is it? I ask. What do you think of the salt-free meatball?

Paul says he loves sitting in the dark. He says my house is so quiet and it smells sober. The reason it's so quiet is because my father feels awful and is resting in his bedroom. Tiptoe, tiptoe 'round the sick papa. The reason it smells sober is because it is *so* sober. I haven't made a joke in this house in ten years at least. Ten years ago, I tried a Helen Keller joke on my parents and they sent me to my room for my terrible insensitivity to suffering.

I imagine in Paul's house everyone is running around in their underwear, and the air is so thick with bourbon your skin tans from it. He says no; he says the truth is his house is quiet also. But it's a more pointy silence, he says. A lighter one with sharper pricks. I nod and listen. He says too that in his house there are moisture rings making Olympian patterns on every possible wooden surface.

Once instead of food I pass my hand through the crack. He holds it for at least a half hour, brushing his fingers over my fingers and tracing the lines in my palm.

You have a long life line, he says.

Shut up, I tell him, I do not.

He doesn't let go of my hand, even then. Any dessert?

I produce a cookie out of my front shirt pocket.

He pulls my hand in closer. My shoulder crashes against the closet frame.

Come inside, he says, come join me.

I can't, I say, I need to stay out here.

Why? He is kissing my hand now. His lips are very soft and a little bit crumby.

I just do, I say, in case of an emergency. I think: because now I've learned my lesson and I'm terribly sensitive to suffering. Poor poor Helen K, blind-and-deaf-and-dumb. Because now I'm so sensitive I can hardly move.

Paul puts down his plate and brings his face up close to mine. He is looking right at me and I'm rustling inside. I don't look away. I want to cut off my head.

It is hard to kiss. As soon as I turn my head to kiss deeper, the closet door gets in the way.

After a minute Paul shoves the door open and pulls me inside with him. He closes the door back and now it is pitch black. I can feel his breath near mine, I can feel the air thickening between us.

I start shaking all over.

It's okay, he says, kissing my neck and my shoulder and my chin and more. He lets me out when I start to cry.

My father is in the hospital on his deathbed.

Darling, he says, you are my only child, my only heir.

To what? I ask. Is there a secret fortune?

No, he says, but you will carry on my genes.

I imagine several bedridden, wheel-chaired children. I imagine throwing all my children in the garbage can because they don't work. I imagine a few more bad things and then I'm knocking on his nightstand and he's annoyed again.

Stop that noise, he says, I'm a dying man.

He grimaces in agony. He doesn't die though. This has happened a few times before and he never dies. The whole deathbed scene gets a little confusing when you play it out more than twice. It gets a bit hard to be sincere. At the hospital, I pray a lot, each time I pray with gusto, but my prayers are getting very strained; lately I have to grit my teeth. I picture his smiling face when I pray. I push that face into my head. Three times now when I picture this smiling face it explodes. Then I have to pray twice as hard. In the little hospital church I am the only one praying with my jaw clenched and my hands in fists knocking on the pew. Maybe they think I'm knocking on God's door, tap tap tap. Maybe I am.

When I'm done, I go out a side door into the day. The sky is very hot and the hospital looks dingy in the sunlight and there is an outdoor janitorial supply closet with a hole in the bottom, and two rats are poking out of the hole and all I can see are their moving noses and I want to kick them but they're tucked behind the door. I think of bubonic plague. I think about rabies. I have half a bagel in my pocket from the hospital cafeteria and the rats can probably smell it; their little noses keep moving up and down frantically; I can tell they're hungry. I put my hand in my pocket and bring out the bagel but I just hold it there, in the air. It's cinnamon raisin. It smells like pocket lint. The rats don't come forward. They are trying to be polite. No one is around and I'm by the side of the hospital and it's late afternoon and I'm scot-free and young in the world. I am as breezy and light as a wing made from tissue paper. I don't know what to do with myself so I keep holding on tight to that bagel and sit down by the closet door. Where is my father already? I want him to come rolling out and hand over that knapsack of his; my back is breaking without it.

I think of that girl I read about in the paper—the one with the flammable skirt. She'd bought a rayon chiffon skirt, purple with wavy lines all over it. She wore it to a party and was dancing, too close to the vanilla-smelling candles, and suddenly she lit up like a pine needle torch. When the boy dancing next to her felt the heat and smelled the plasticky smell, he screamed and rolled the burning girl up in the carpet. She got third-degree burns up and down her thighs. But what I keep wondering about is this: that first second when she felt her skirt burning, what did she think? Before she knew it was the candles, did she think she'd done it herself? With the amazing turns of her hips, and the warmth of the music inside her, did she believe, for even one glorious second, that her passion had arrived?

Sinners

Joan Corwin

To the surprise of everyone who knew of his condition in the months after the Great Wisconsin Fire of 1871, the Reverend Michael Chaston lived to a very old age. Those who became his neighbors after the event credited his recovery to the care he was given by the daughter he had saved from that terrible conflagration. Amy Chaston, they said, was fortunate to have been disfigured hardly at all by the fire: most of her hair grew back, and women of her own age observed that where it did not, the knot of pink tissue could have been disguised with some effort. But she never tried, even though she was pretty and men were always interested in her, drawn by her quiet devotion to her father. She limped clumsily, it was true, from something the cold had done to her in the water where her father had fought his pain to hold her for five and a half hours while the village of Peshtigo, on both sides of the river, burned to the ground. If she was in pain, she never complained, though Michael Chaston required her constant attendance.

The two were never seen to speak together, but appeared always to have a perfect understanding, and they must have been, people said, a great comfort to each other, for they had lost a dear wife and mother, Mariah, in the fire.

The air had been smoldering for weeks. Mostly the ash was too fine to really see, but sometimes it fell in flakes like snow, and the irony of this was not lost on the residents of Peshtigo, who had stopped scouring the cloudless sky and resolutely went about their days with set faces. Spot fires had erupted close to the town for a few days before October 8th, and the villagers were proud of the way they extinguished these fires with water from barrels and tubs placed at street corners; they even patrolled the swampy area to the west of town, where the peat smoldered as much as three feet below the surface and underbrush seemed to leap up to meet the occasional falling sparks brought on by gusts of wind from the southwest forests, which had been burning since mid-September.

So while the mood in town was tense and sometimes depressed, there was a generally held faith in the ingenuity of mankind, a vague confidence that with such efforts as those of the company men and the householders, this season of danger would pass without molesting Peshtigo's inhabitants. The explosive growth of the mill in the years since the war had encouraged an attitude of prideful optimism almost everywhere. An exception was the Reverend Michael Chaston's household, where the silent doom-saying of the Reverend's cold glare quashed all hopes, even those inspired by a recent forecast of coming rains.

Earlier that September, when the air had started to taste of char, the Reverend began reading Milton to his wife Mariah and twelve-year-old daughter Amy—the verses on Satan's humiliation. He read them over and over as though

Amy and her mother were resisting him. He read them while Amy's mother grew weary and until Amy began to worry that the poet's meaning must be more subtle than it appeared and that she was too stupid or too compromised to understand. But just when she began to be really anxious for her soul, the close hot air, the desiccating taste of it, wore out even her father. He subjected them to the poem more and more listlessly and less and less frequently. By October 8th the readings had stopped.

Only a few townspeople besides those who were members of her father's congregation saw the hand of God in the local forest fires. Amy envied those who were without sin and—though she knew this was wrong—those who were benighted in the heresy of other faiths or in faithlessness itself. They did not suffer, as she did, as her father exhorted his congregation to suffer, the guilt of one's own complicity in the drought and the fires. This was nothing new: a sense of sin had attended her for most of her twelve years. It was always associated with her father and his omniscience in such matters. Amy believed that her father knew all her sins, but it was also her belief—based on his disdainful refusal to discuss them with her—that he expected her to recognize them herself. He had not actually said so, but he implied, whether he was excoriating his flock or leading Amy and her mother in grace before their undeserved bounty, that not to detect her own sin was to ensure her captivity to it.

Amy's father had turned thirty-eight that year. He was brittle and thin and had icy blue eyes that snapped, like illtempered dogs, with disapproval. Widowed Grandmother Chaston, who had lived with them until her heart stopped in 1868, had often told how even as a boy in Boston, even as little as three and four years old, the Reverend would snap his eyes at other children and at those adults whose jolly mannerisms offended him. Grandmother Chaston told a story about a family friend, a Mr. Burling, an importer who had come drunk for dinner one evening to the Boston house, where wine was never served, and could not be dissuaded from sharing improper and gossipy stories which he found so amusing himself that he shook the water glasses with his laughter. Awakened from his bed by this guest's hilarity, seven-year-old Michael Chaston entered the dining room to witness the businessman erupting with red and humid face, a spectacle which elicited such a snap of the boy's cold blue eyes that Burling was immediately deflated and made his departure in a state of cringing apology.

For some few years before she was able to detect the self-congratulation in her grandmother's account of Mr. Burling's defeat, Amy naively imagined herself into the scene, where she would leave the Chaston table hand-in-hand with their jovial guest, accompanying him to his home, a comfortable home, she assumed, with a fire always made up, and port and cordials for gentleman and lady visitors respectively, and brandied fruits in footed glasses for the children—things her mother had described to her from a different kind of childhood. She would choose from a variety of candies which she had never tasted but had glimpsed in shops and in the hands of other children, and sit on the hearthrug warmly attentive while Mr. Burling, whom she saw in her mind as fat and plush, finished his funny stories. She did not know how to snap her eyes, which like her mother's were a golden hazel and turned down at the outer corners, giving her a constant air of sympathy. So, confident that she could not embarrass him as her father had, Amy imagined herself gazing fondly on Mr. Burling, touching his fat hand with her own baby one, kindling more and more of the warm humor that animated him.

But before she was six years old, Amy sensed that her fantasy was a voluptuous self-indulgence, and she felt she shared the shame with that ebullient guest who had been so effectively humbled by the juvenile Reverend. From that moment, Amy was continuously haunted by her sense of sin.

It was not this particular sin—her yearning for the jovial man's company, for his rich and careless life—which had ignited the forest fires, she was sure. It was not any of the small sins (as she was acute enough to rate them) in which she had indulged, or it might be more accurate to say, into which she had slipped, since her awakening to guilt. Even an accumulation of these, even the times she had shared something with her mother from which her father was by nature excluded, something sweet or gay, a touch, an idea, a joke, for a fraction of a moment—all of these together were not serious enough to warrant a plague out of Egypt as her father described the stifling smoke, the pestilential fires. Small treacheries they were, of God and Reverend, but they were not hot, not searing as real sin.

Amy might never have found out how she caused the Peshtigo fire if the big man Daniel Spence had not come to town that October afternoon.

There had been signs that something was going to happen. Infant fires blazed and died or were smothered by townspeople armed with wet blankets on the roads leading to and in the environs of the town. A haze of smoke hovered permanently along the streets. Open windows invited a layer of ash to settle like a dirty sheet over furniture and floors. Some young children became confused in the altered streets and alleys and temporarily lost their way. Then at last, where the Oconto Road entered the town from the southwest, smoke began accumulating like a thick fog, obscuring the traffic. Amy, though privately anxious, accompanied the neighbor children to the edge of town to watch the atmosphere thicken. They held hands in a line so that not one would be lost. Spanning the street like a chain of paper lanterns, they saw Daniel Spence emerging from the smoke—a *jinn* from a cloud.

Travelers were arriving in a steady stream, many from farms and cabins in the woodlands from which the persistent fires had finally driven them to the village for refuge. Most of these, men and women both, had wrapped kerchiefs and shawls around their faces, and the children lay low in the wagons with their arms around their heads, and still they could be heard choking. But Daniel Spence merely breathed in and out, making smoke eddies whirl around his nostrils. Ash clung to his auburn hair and beard. Very tall and broad and full, he was flushed and perspiring heavily as he strode forward, and when he wiped the sleeve of his coarse red shirt across his steaming face, he left streaks of black ash. He seemed like the very source of fire, like a radiant iron oven spewing smoke. All of the children dropped hands and gaped at him. Even some bowed and harassed adult inhabitants paused curiously. The big man looked hot enough to burn the hand of anyone who touched him.

Confronted with the broken chain of stupefied children, Daniel Spence exploded in laughter. They scattered, terrified, leaving only Amy, inside of whom the man's mirth had urged a small warmth, an embrous glow just reminiscent of the blaze of Mr. Burling's enjoyment. She smiled back. The big man opened bloodshot eyes very wide as he pushed toward her and lifted her off her feet in an embrace.

"You. I'd never know which was you if you had not made them golden eyes to shine."

It alarmed Amy to meet Daniel Spence for the first time in this way, and she might have struggled, she might have kicked the big man until he let her go, thereby changing the history of Peshtigo and her family, but before she could make any move at all, Daniel Spence did something that dissolved her. He buried his nose in her neck and cooed, "Let me breathe you in. Just let me breathe you in," inhaling deeply. "Yes," he murmured, "Mariah's girl."

With that, the flame in Amy changed to something, not wholly unfamiliar, but rare and intensely pleasing, so that when Daniel Spence pulled back to look at her eyes again, she clung to him tightly and he could not put her down.

His own eyes were brown, liquid brown and red-rimmed with heat.

For Daniel Spence, whom Amy loved immediately, she delivered a message to her mother without her father's knowledge. The big man had asked her that specifically—not to tell her father, the Reverend Michael Chaston, either that Daniel Spence was in town, or that he was sending a message to her mother.

She came on them arguing in the Reverend's study. Mariah Chaston was standing with a hand resting lightly on the door-handle, her eyes slightly averted. Nor did the Reverend look directly at his wife, but he stood, rather than sitting, at his desk, with a finger poised on that part of his reading where he had left off at the interruption. They appeared to be talking past one another—to other invisible and formal associates at opposite corners of the same room.

They argued quietly. The Reverend never raised his voice, but Amy's mother spoke with so little passion that an outsider would have thought she lacked conviction and that it was Amy's father who won. And it was almost always true that Mariah would pray when the Reverend said pray, and be silent when he wished it, but the same argument, quiet and steady and unaltered in its rhythm and progress would arise again as though the idea had never been discussed between them. It made him tired, said her father. Her mother would fall silent and wait until the identical quarrel could be coaxed from circumstance again.

This was an old argument, and petty. It concerned the Reverend's collar, which was always stiffly starched and raised a rash around his neck. The only time the Chastons' quarrels had ever approached violence was when Amy's mother referred to the collar as the Reverend's cross, his attempt to emulate Jesus. Then he had flushed, a phenomenon never witnessed before by Amy. In fact, until that moment she had not thought of her father as containing blood. Could it be that she had never seen him bleed? Not even once when he had shaved to the faint blue line of his jaw? No, he never bled, and no veins pulsed in him that she could discern, and he was pale as a dead man, even in summer, since he shunned the enthusiasm of the sunny day. It was only in this moment of anger that suddenly he appeared to her as something other than the Reverend. Her mother fell back a step and apologized, but even young Amy sensed that her father had lost something in the moment when his color changed.

At this time during the fires, with the extreme heat of the air, the Reverend felt compelled to change his collar several times in a day, in spite of the increasing discomfort of freshly starched linen against the skin. He could not bear to have it sag limp and sensual against his neck. "It must be cool and firm" was his stern pronouncement, and as soon as one was discarded and replaced, it was sent directly to the laundress to be restored to the cleanliness and rigidity he demanded. For the past several days the collars had been stimulating a thick angry welt like a noose burn around the Reverend's neck. The eighth being Sunday, with no one at work, Mariah had supposed that once he ran through his stock of collars, he would have to be satisfied. But she had just discovered a store of crisp new collars, which he had laid in for the Sabbath earlier that week.

So now the argument resumed, though Amy's mother was careful with her words.

The Reverend was for propriety. "I will not be thought slovenly for the sake of my own comfort," he insisted tensely, though his teeth. The welt, a sign of his unflinching standards, was also proof of his capacity for suffering. "It is an example to my congregation."

"It is a reproof to your laundress," retorted Amy's mother, but quietly, as she moved from the room, so that the flush which had alarmed her daughter and herself would not reappear. The Reverend reacted little, but watched his wife narrowly and obliquely as she left him, followed by his daughter. His lips made a thin and horizontal line.

Amy was relieved at his self-restraint: she did not wish to see her father's blood rise to his pallid face when she knew she had a message to deliver to her mother that was a secret from him.

It was a measure of Mariah's dissatisfaction with her husband that, although it was the Sabbath and a sin to perform labor, she had gone directly from his study to her sewing-room to pick stitches from a worn dress which she was dismembering for scraps. The room, situated as it was over the kitchen, was stifling, but still she had had to light the lamp and pull it close to her because so few rays of the afternoon sun were able to penetrate the ash-laden air outside her window. She sat at the treadle-table with the dress in her lap. Her hair drooped from its pins and hung limply in places, and she had unhooked her collar buttons since leaving her husband's study. Her lips were slightly parted as she worked, and tiny rivulets of perspiration made tracks down her temples. She looked up when Amy entered and absently rubbed her neck.

At that evening hour when she should have been renewing in prayer her covenant with God, Amy met Daniel Spence where she had left him, at the very spot of their embrace on the edge of town. It was harder to find than before.

There were only a few people feeling their way in the searing air, and they were becoming difficult to distinguish.

When he had read the note, Daniel Spence threw his arms out wide and his head back and howled, "Oh, yes, and oh, yes, and oh, yes, my darling!"

She wanted him to hold her again, but he took a match from his breast pocket and struck it against his shoe. When the letter caught, a passerby clucked her tongue at this display of carelessness. He dropped the burning paper and waited until it was consumed before stamping and scattering the ashes. Then he took her hand.

"I got some time to kill, Amy Chaston, and I want you with me."

They ran across the charred south firebreak toward the forest. The ground was hot. There were only a few stumps, but the smoldering roots sent smoke into the air. For a month now, it had been hard to tell when the sun was setting, an event that had been losing its visual drama as the increasing smoke softened the contrast between day and night. The haze must have lifted this night and the time must have been earlier than she thought, because there was still a glow in the west, enough to make each other out dimly as they skipped among the embers. Now and then Daniel Spence would pick Amy up and crush her to him. Once she said, "Let me breathe you in!"

"All right then." He held her tightly. She closed her eyes and breathed deeply, pushing her body against him as though she could not get close enough. She thought she heard him moan, and suddenly something happened, some hot eruption inside her, and as it did, Daniel Spence dropped her, gaping at the rosy treeline. The moaning was rising to a howl—it was the sound of the wind in the distant trees. "My God."

A huge ball of fire was jumping from treetop to treetop in the wood. Behind it, the glow which they had taken for the setting sun was growing brighter as they watched. The fireball was igniting trees with the sound of an explosion as it bounced along. Then it was joined by another.

"Christ almighty! Run, for God's sake! Run to the village!"

He had to shout above the now roaring wind. A scorching gust threw her to the ground. Daniel Spence grabbed her arm and pulled her up, and her legs dragged on burnt stubble, so that there were tears in her skirts and stockings and bloody rakings on her shins. He swung her up over one shoulder, and struggling to remain on his feet against the violent intermittent blasts, he stumbled toward the town, not stopping at the edge as he had the last time but blundering into the dark and shrouded streets.

A loud whooshing passed overhead, followed by an explosion as an unseen building burst into flames. A woman screamed. Father Pernin's bell at the still unfinished Catholic church began pealing loudly on this side of the village and then more distantly, the Congregationalists' bell could be heard in its steeple on the east side across the river, and finally, thinly, tinnily in comparison with the other two, came chiming the bell of the Reverend Michael Chaston. People began to materialize in the streets carrying children and belongings, calling for missing family. They were lit grotesquely by the proliferating fires.

"Where?" demanded Daniel, turning around wildly. He dropped her on her feet. "Where do you live from here?"

Amy tried to distinguish her father's signal from the other, fuller tollings as she peered around her. Her eyes smarted and through the dense smoke she could only make out scattered fires and a few looming shapes of untouched buildings. When a team of frightened horses pulling a wagonload of furniture and a family shuddered crazily close to them, Daniel Spence lifted her into a doorway.

She made note of the large glass globe of green liquid suspended over the street before them just as it cracked and shattered in the heat. They were standing at the door to Alpertson's Apotheca, where her mother sent her when the hired girl had the toothache.

"I know where we are, Daniel Spence."

"Good."

She started out into the street again. He drew her back.

"No—along the buildings. Don't lose the buildings unless we have to cross a street."

They held hands, running when they could see clearly enough where to put their feet, slowing when they could only feel their way. Amy had to stop often and check for signs to orient herself; she had learned to examine the entranceways: here was the Branwen Feed Store, with the freakish double ox-jawbone hanging from its lintel; here was Jorgeson's Dry Goods entrance hung with saws and files like instruments of torture; and she knew a tavern or a flop house from the drunken lumbermen and rail laborers who lay unconscious on the plank sidewalk or in the sawdust streets.

They collided with people fleeing or searching for one another; many of them Amy knew. Some of them spoke to her, but she ignored them, pulling Daniel Spence with her. Where the smoke was thickest, a face would appear and withdraw suddenly, eerily, like a ghost. She knew she was near home when she heard Mrs. Hautemann screaming for her twin sons. Then they almost stumbled over Tommy Schwarzhoff crouched with his arm around his little sister at the foot of old Miss Penny's trellised front porch; Jemma Schwarzhoff was crying with her face in her skirt, and her brother's eyes were filled with hopeless terror. After that, Amy wouldn't look at people at all.

The fires were still restricted to clusters of structures which had been ignited by the sparks that flew unpredictably, but these outriders on the frontier of the coming conflagration, fueled by the wind, were making relentless progress toward the northeast, crawling along like bright stains in the night. Now and then a fireball exploded as it struck a building.

At the end of a row of detached houses, Amy saw the outline of her father's pineboard church, gaunt and stolid, silhouetted by fires burning beyond it, and she tugged Daniel Spence desperately that direction. As they drew closer, they could make out the figure of a young girl that might have been Amy herself swaying and stumbling in front of the church. It was Agnes Meyer, one of the children in the chain who had watched Daniel Spence emerge from the cloud. Agnes was alone, but she was talking rapidly to herself as she picked goose-down from a pillow she had clasped to her chest. Overcome with dread, Amy faltered and pressed against Daniel Spence. When Agnes saw them, she dropped the pillow. Then she reached out her arm and pointed, wailing,

"Amy! Amy Chaston! Amy!"

The church exploded behind Agnes, and sparks showered down on her. She went up suddenly, like a match; she was a small human bonfire, reduced in seconds to a tarred and twisted little body. Amy screamed. Daniel Spence picked her up and carried her past the smoking thing to where he had spotted Mariah Chaston on the porch of the Reverend's house. The house was burning on every level.

Daniel Spence threw an arm around Amy's mother and cradling Amy in the other, he swept them away from the Reverend's house.

"Michael went to look for Amy!" Mariah Chaston shouted as she ran.

Daniel Spence said nothing, but made his way toward the remaining undamaged section of town. More girls and women, their skirts attracting the devouring fire like mere paper or floss, were lighting up the foggy darkness now like human candles. Amy dug her fists into her eyes so she wouldn't see them. She kept thinking how naked Agnes had been when the fire had burned down to her bones.

When it became apparent that the fire had outrun them, Daniel Spence stopped.

"The mill sits almost in the river!" shouted Amy's mother.

"It's a mill, Mariah. It's bound to go."

"It's in the river, Daniel!"

He looked around wildly, pulling his hair.

"All right. We'll go … wait!" He began to rip the skirts from the waistband of her mother's dress. Then he tore off Amy's skirts as well. He grabbed Amy and let Mariah lead them.

Amy was so hot all over she thought she would burst into flame in Daniel Spence's arms and then ignite them all so that they would burn like Agnes Meyer. The heat was even inside her, a pressure behind her stinging eyes, and her throat felt blistered when she breathed.

They found themselves caught up in a crowd as they approached the bridge. The mill was still standing, and many people had had the same idea as Mariah. Daniel Spence stopped to take in the scene. He looked doubtful.

They were standing by a well. Several of the houses even this close to the river had their own wells, not dug very deep, and it was a measure of the drought that as the river sank, the wells had gone dry one after another from the other end of town to this. Daniel Spence dropped a stone, and when it hit, it sounded a muddy bottom. He lifted Amy into the well, letting her hands slide down gripping along his arms and wrists while he lay on his stomach over the edge. The shaft was narrow, and when her feet touched down, something on the bottom felt like a wet cushion. It was a dead dog in a shallow pool of water—she knew from touching it when she sat down. Amy began to cry. She could see the outline of Daniel Spence's head above her.

"Amy! I'm taking your mother to the mill. I'll be back for you." Amy heard her mother screaming her name and Daniel Spence shouting at the same time.

"There's no room down there for more than one, Mariah! And there won't be enough air for two when the time comes. She'll be safer there 'til we're certain."

Daniel's head appeared again.

"If you have trouble breathing, keep your head down low as you can. If there's no air at all, hold your breath for as long as you can."

"Daniel Spence," said Amy, hugging her knees. "Daniel Spence." The air in the well was sour, but not smoky. The dog must have just been thrown or fallen in. It didn't smell like anything but a wet dog. When she was sure Daniel Spence was gone, she squirmed in the close well space until she was curled up and could press her face against the dog's side. She didn't know how long she had been waiting when she heard a man's violent coughing above her.

"Daniel Spence!" she called to him joyfully. A burned and blackened face appeared above in a haze of weirdly illuminated smoke. The eyeballs shone stark white against the blistered skin, and all of the hair was gone from the charred skull. Wordlessly, the man reached down and stuck the muzzle of a rifle at her. She closed her eyes, but he didn't shoot.

"Take it," he said hoarsely.

She was afraid to disobey, and with this, he pulled her out. It was her father.

She could not speak to the grotesque apparition before her. Michael Chaston must have been in terrible pain: his nose and ears were gone; the skin on his upper lip curled away toward one cheek, and the rest of his face was a weeping sore. His pale eyes took in her exposed body in an icy rage. "Where are they?" he croaked, grasping the rifle tightly. She stared. "Do you know what you've done, you bitch? Where are they?"

Amy pointed to the mill. Michael Chaston clutched his daughter's wrist and dragged her toward the building. His hand was sticky with burns. She could see that the bridge was already overloaded with masses of fleeing forms, pressing on the crowds at the building's entrance. Then a terrible sound arose behind her, and she turned to see a wind of fire, a roaring whirling column which bore down on the riverbank in fury. Her father was shouting, but she couldn't hear him. Others around her had their mouths open in screams, but she only heard the blast of the burning wind like a giant hell's engine. Her father dropped the gun and changed direction, clawing at both her arms as he pulled her down the bank and into the river.

She could not take her eyes from the fiery column as it raced across the bridge to the mill. There was a moment before the heat without engulfed the building and the windows burst inward. Then the entire structure collapsed in flames.

"Daniel Spence!" Amy screamed. There was an explosion from the burning mill, and flaming timbers flew like splinters and rained around them. Michael Chaston pushed his daughter's head under the water.

She spent the night in the Peshtigo River without her skirts, her father forcing her below the surface when the heat became too intense, or the sparks too close. They had to beware of cattle and timbers taken by the current—bodies, too, many of them partially burned, many of them small, animals and people bobbing along in a hideous burlesque. As the fire died down, the river grew icy, and Amy knew she would never be warm again.

They crawled from the water around two o'clock in the morning, and Michael Chaston's real agony began then. Amy herself could not walk on her numb legs, but lay by her father, listening to his screams, on the smoking bank where the mill workers from Menominee found them. They were taken up gently and laid in a tent until they could be carried to the Dunlap House temporary hospital in Marinette.

The Chastons, like many families, saved nothing from the fire. The church board, realizing the girl could not go out to work with her father to nurse and expecting Michael not to survive for long, made them a handsome annual pension. With it, the Chastons left their old neighborhood and settled on the opposite side of the river among new people who knew their story and watched out for them, cared for them from a distance.

For the most part they were left alone. For Michael Chaston was hard to look at, and the two of them seemed to need no one, but were sufficient unto themselves. When people did visit, they marveled afterward, at the wordless way the two communicated, at the lively snap of his lidless eyes which the weak old man could still manage when his beloved daughter entered the room, at the perfect patience of the lovely woman who grew old serving him, her heart's god. When they were both aged, newcomers mistook them for a married couple. The neighbors laughed and said there was no marriage as perfect as their affinity, for it was obvious how much the two had sacrificed for each other and how secure a place they had made for themselves in heaven.

Pepper Hunt

Kate Blackwell

"Did I ever talk to you about pepper?" he asks the girl, who is playing with the plastic pepper shaker, walking it across the table in quick jerky steps.

She is twelve, a thin girl with fine limp hair and green-painted fingernails. She has ordered an expensive breakfast, pancakes and eggs with sausage. He hasn't seen her in a few months and dislikes the new assertiveness in her high childish voice, the way she told the waitress, "I don't want my eggs runny. I won't eat 'em if they're runny."

She does not respond to his question about pepper. She merely gives the shaker a little shove and puts her hands in her lap. Her eyes roam the room incuriously, surfing, he thinks, not really looking at anyone. Their booth is in the non-smoking section of King's Family Restaurant in the suburb of Pittsburgh where she lives. It is eight-thirty on a Saturday morning, an in-between time, not that crowded.

"Pepper can be dangerous," he says and waits as the girl's vague pie eyes wander back to his face (that is how he describes her no-color eyes to himself: pie eyes). "When I was your age, my dad and me used to go out in the fields and set out white bread with a lot of pepper on it."

She is gazing at him now with what seems to be full attention, but he is distracted, seeing himself, aged twelve, an undersized boy in overalls, a cowlick of wheat-hair falling over his forehead. His mother used to sweep back his hair with her hand, to "get it out of your eyes," and there would be the ravaged battleground of his pimpled brow. His mother would freeze for a few seconds before she let the hair fall down again. Over the years, his skin has cleared, his body filled out like a tube. His face in middle age is furrowed with fatty deposits. He removes his glasses. He knows he is not a handsome man.

"What'd you do that for?" She tears a strip off her paper napkin and wraps it around a nugget of pink gum she has removed from her mouth. He thinks for a second she's asking why he took off his glasses, then realizes she means the pepper.

"To attract animals," he explains. "Rabbit and deer'd come smelling around the bread. They wouldn't catch on to the pepper at first."

His voice is low and flat, a fact-conveying voice rather than a storytelling voice. And he is conveying facts. He remembers exactly the long brown fields where he and his father used to go, the clods of bitter-smelling earth that stuck to his heels, the thorny bracken in the ditches at the edge of the fields, not far from this very restaurant where they sit.

"Where would you and your daddy be?" And he knows she means while the rabbits and deer were sniffing around the bread. He likes her question. It shows she's listening and thinking about how it was. Her question is a sign that she is not entirely lost, that she may even have something of him in her.

'We'd be ducked down behind some shrub, him over on one side of the field, me on the other." He no longer sees his father in the picture, only himself in his too-big overalls crouched behind a stand of sumac, clutching his baseball bat.

"Anyways," he continues, anxious to go on with the story, remembering the excitement he felt when the first rabbit appeared, its long ears poking up from the furrows as though it had been hiding there all along, more of them poking up like cartoon bunnies with their silly ears. And back in the scrub oak on the edge of the field, the larger, bulkier shadow that is a deer. He is laughing soundlessly, his breath coming fast.

"We'd wait there, real quiet, and after a while, the rabbit and deer'd come up and sniff at the pepper bread, and they'd start sneezing. They'd sneeze and sneeze and couldn't stop, jerking all over like they were having some kind of fit. Then we'd run up and beat their brains out."

He stops. The story about pepper is over. The girl is looking at him. Her no-color eyes have not changed. She doesn't say anything. He cannot tell what she's thinking. The waitress sets down their plates. The girl starts to eat immediately. He watches her, feeling as though he has told the story wrong. He wants her to react, to ask another question. But she's pouring syrup over her pancakes and doesn't look at him. He feels uneasy, as though he has left something out.

The waitress returns with coffee and fills his cup. The girl says in her high-pitched, newly assertive voice that she wants coffee, too. The waitress glances at him. The red of the woman's lipstick has bled into the cracks around her pinched lips. He nods. She fills the girl's cup and walks away.

He stirs his coffee, sloshing it into the saucer. He is trying to think of another story, but none occurs to him. In his mind, he is still beating the small doe to her knees. Her head is bloodied, but she continues to sneeze convulsively. He leaves off beating her and slams his bat down on a frenzied rabbit. It crumples instantly. He wants the girl to see this, too, but she is cutting her pancakes carefully into small squares.

She says, "Why'n you never take me on a pepper hunt? Your daddy took you. Why'n you never take me?"

He is stunned. She couldn't possibly expect him to take her hunting. Where would they go? The fields where he and his father went with their baseball bats are paved over with housing developments. Though there are other fields, he doesn't know the people who own them.

"Why'd you tell me that story if you weren't goin' take me?" she asks, her mouth full of pancake mush.

"I thought you might want to know something I did when I was a boy." He resents her question. He wants her to ask about the animals so he can describe the tender pink trickle of brains that oozed from the doe's smashed skull before she stopped breathing, the sneeze that came reflexively after she died. But she does not ask. Her pie eyes regard him malevolently.

"Maybe you're lying to me," she says. "Maybe you never did no pepper hunts. Maybe your daddy just told you about 'em like you're telling me."

He wonders where the girl gets such thoughts. From her mother, he guesses, though he can't remember her mother challenging anything he said. All he remembers her mother saying when he told her something was "Yeah?" until finally he couldn't stand it anymore. The girl stares in his direction and he remembers the doe looking up at him from her knees, the wet glisten of her frantic eyes as he raises his bat.

"Listen," he says, "I told you that story for a reason. You be careful what you go sniffing around. That's all I told it for."

And he leans back against the padded seat, relieved to have found this explanation for telling the story. Still, something seems awry. He can't think what it is. The girl's plate is empty. It's time to go. He wonders if she will even remember the story. She has problems remembering things in school, her mother has told him.

"Maybe I'll take you hunting," he says.

The girl's no-color eyes focus for an instant. She nods.

"I'll go," she says. "I'll go in a minute."

"Wipe your mouth," he says, easing his body out of the booth.

Everything's Going to Be So Good

Lisa Stolley

It is early spring, 1973. Olivia is fifteen and pregnant. She and her mother are walking on the sand in Myrtle Beach. They are both looking down at their feet. They are on vacation here—Olivia, her sister and mother. Her father hasn't come because he has to work, which is code for he doesn't want to be stuck in a tiny cottage with a wife he's always fighting with. It is not her mother's habit to ask Olivia to go for walks alone, but she has found out that Olivia is pregnant and insisted that they go somewhere to talk so Olivia's little sister, Kate, won't hear. Being alone with her mother makes Olivia nervous. She digs her toes into the sand at each step; it gives her something to concentrate on and makes it so they aren't getting that far from the beach house. "Who's the father?" her mother asks.

"I know him," Olivia says. This is an entirely horrible conversation. She and her mother have never talked about sex. If she hadn't thrown up every five minutes in the last four days her mother wouldn't know. It was easy to hide back in Scarsdale but the beach house is small; you can hear everything and Olivia can't stop puking, and it's obvious in the way they push at the thin material of her swimsuit, that her breasts are bigger.

"Do you need money?" her mother asks.

Olivia almost feels sorry for her. There they are, a TV picture of a mother and daughter strolling down the beach with the ocean a deep blue, the sky big and white, sea gulls crying and swooping all around. "He's paying for it," she says.

Her mother finally looks at her. Her eyes are blue and sharp. "He can afford it?"

"Yes," Olivia says. She watches the waves come in. If she weren't pregnant, she'd be out there riding them in and then swimming back out, doing the deadman's float, letting the water push her around. "You have to get me back to New York," she says. "Just get me back and I'll take care of it, I mean he will. You don't have to come or anything. I don't want you to come."

None of this is true. Erik Moss won't give her a dime. He is a cruel boy and she hates him, will always hate him, will hate him until she's old enough not to care anymore. But while she hates him, she also understands him; he is scared that his girlfriend Vicki will find out. Olivia is too, though she has less to lose. She likes Vicki, but not, obviously, as much as Erik does. She has already resigned herself to losing Vicki; you can't fuck your friend's boyfriend and stay friends. It was a fluke that she and Vicki became friends anyway. It was only because they got stuck in detention together and had no one else to talk to. Vicki, two years older than Olivia, is actually allowed by her parents to live with Erik in the apartment above the garage. The apartment is decorated with heavy wood furniture and oversized lamps that used to be in the main house before Vicki's mother redecorated. Vicki drapes scarves over the lamps and covers the walls with posters of rock bands like Alice Cooper and The Who and Led Zeppelin.

One of the best things about Vicki is that her father is a doctor and in the garage below the apartment are boxes and boxes of medicine samples. Some of the samples are good: Tuinals, Dexedrine, Seconals, Nembutal, Benzedrine, some others she's never heard of but nevertheless do the trick. Vicki steals the samples and puts the pills in a pretty earthenware bowl in the center of the coffee table unless her parents visit and then the bowl goes under the couch. Sometimes, when Vicki and Erik get stoned they start kissing in front of Olivia, which makes her uneasy and envious. They are both beautiful, dark with long hair and legs. She really liked them until Erik forgot to pull out. Even now, though she hates Erik, she still wishes she could be with someone who loves her the way Erik loves Vicki. That Erik went behind Vicki's back is something against him, but it is partly Olivia's fault. When Erik started kissing her she let him, tongued him back, put one hand on the small of his back, the other on the side of his face—all the things she is learning about sex. Sex makes guys look at you in a way that has to be love, even if it's temporary.

She told him to pull out and he did but she knew it was too late. She went and held herself up under the bathtub faucet but it was an awkward position to maintain and maybe if she just thought positive nothing would happen. Vicki is always talking about positive thinking, especially when it comes to school and tests and papers. She learned about it from *Be Here Now*, a big book with brown instead of white paper, illustrations and yoga exercises and all sorts of sayings about life. Olivia has the book, too, but doubts that she's capable of the kind of positive thinking that actually works, the way Vicki says it does for her.

Vicki, of course, wasn't there which is how she and Erik ended up on the rug in the living room and then on the bed. Olivia was stoned on a mixture of Tuinals and Quaa-ludes. She couldn't feel her vagina, but she knew Erik had been in there for too long; not enough semen was on her stomach. Erik wanted her to go when they were done. He turned off the Zeppelin record and pulled on his jeans. "Lis-ten, man," he said. "Vicki's going to be back soon. You better go." He kissed her, a long hard kiss, to make up for telling her to leave. Olivia leaned into him and then blew him a kiss as she closed the door. It is one of the rules of sex that boys want to be alone afterwards. Olivia likes to be alone, too, although she knows to pretend that there is nothing she wants more than to stay sweatily glued to them. There are so many rules she can't remember them sometimes.

Olivia and her mother go back to the bungalow. Kate is sitting on the floor playing jacks and listening to Cat Stevens on the portable phonograph, singing along, "Oh, baby, baby, it's a wild world." She stops singing and asks, "Are you in trouble?"

"Shut up," Olivia says and follows her mother into the kitchen. "Don't tell Dad," she whispers. "You have to promise me you won't tell Dad. Swear."

"How are we going to explain why you're coming home early, then, why I'm putting a fifteen year old on a plane by herself back to New York?" her mother asks.

"Tell him I'm sick, too sick to stay here. Tell him I have a really bad period. The flu. Something. Please don't tell him." This is the first time Olivia has wanted to cry since this all be-gan. Even at the clinic in the city where a woman in a white smock with a grim face said *you are positive, about six to seven weeks*, she didn't cry. She just got back on the train out to Scarsdale and went to Vicki and Erik's house. Erik didn't want her there, she could tell, but Vicki did. "Help yourself," Vicki said and Olivia dipped into the bowl on the coffee table. After awhile, she felt good and she and Vicki put make-up on each other, laughing like fools at the way they were messing it up. When Vicki went to the bathroom, Olivia told Erik and he shrugged. He asked her what she wanted him to do. He told her he didn't have any money and besides how could he be sure it was really his? Olivia stared at him. He asked her what she was looking at and she said nothing, nothing at all.

"Okay, okay. I won't tell him," her mother says, "although it looks awfully strange that you're going home because of the flu." She looks into the living room. "Shh," she says. "I don't want your sister to know about this. Now just leave me alone so I can talk to your father."

Olivia goes into the tiny bedroom she shares with her sister. The sound of the ocean fills the room. She lies down on the bottom bunk bed. Her stomach feels terrible. If this is how if feels to have a baby, she's never going to have one. She wants this one out.

She has a plan. It's the only thing she can think of to get money for the abortion. There is no asking her mother; that would be relinquishing something she'd never get back. There would be too many I-told-you-so's, countless. Olivia is surprised that her mother is letting her do this by herself. Her mother doesn't know what to do with this one. This one is over her head. But Olivia can do it by herself. She has to get back to Scarsdale so she can call George, one of her father's business partners.

When George isn't working at the publishing company he takes pictures. He's supposed to be good. Olivia's father once showed her a book of George's photographs of famous opera singers. He took them in black and white and made them look mysterious even with their fatty double chins. Last year when she was visiting her father at his office, George stopped her in the hall and asked if he could take pictures of her. "Don't tell your father, though," he said. She went over to his apartment one Sunday and he got her to take off her top, although he had her cross her arms over her chest. When Olivia saw the photographs a few weeks later, she was surprised. George had used black and white film and he made her look a way she'd never looked. "You could be a model," he said. "But don't tell your father that." She doesn't believe him but it gives her leverage; George will give her the money. He has to. There are coat hangers but she doesn't have the nerve and she's not even sure anyone has ever tried that; it seems more like a rumor invented by adults. She has tried the really hot baths and disgusting tea from a health food store. She is still pregnant. At least she doesn't have go to Puerto Rico, like one of the girls at her school did a couple of years ago. At least now you can get an abortion in New York, can even make an appointment the day before. Olivia's clinic has four scheduled sessions every morning; one of them, the receptionist told her last week, would have room.

At the airport, her mother looks at her helplessly. "Are you sure you're all right?" she asks. Kate is waiting in the car. Her mother is impatient to get back but she thinks she should hang out.

Olivia sighs. "Yes, mother," she says. "I'm fine." She makes a face so it will be easier for her mother to leave.

"I don't know what I'm going to do with you," her mother says. She kisses her cheek and leaves, her white sandals slapping the floor. Olivia can hear those sandals even after she's on the plane and it's taking off.

She takes a taxi home from LaGuardia. Her father is at work so she has the house to herself. It is raining and ugly and Olivia half longs for the itchy sunburn on her shoulders, sand in her hair, finding boys to flirt with on the beach. But she mostly hates going to Myrtle Beach and there's a certain pleasure in being alone here, in roaming through the house with the knowledge that she won't meet anyone in her family.

She goes into her parent's bedroom to use the phone. Their bed is unmade, her father's side all messy and slept in. She sits on his side and waits for George to answer and then when he answers, waits for him to stop being happy to hear from her when he understands exactly what she wants from him.

"Oh, Olivia," he says. "I'm not sure I can do that."

Olivia gets up and walks to as far as the phone cord will let her. "Please," she says. "I promise I'll pay you back." She thinks about how she's going to get two hundred dollars back to him. "I'll babysit," she says. "Or clean houses or something." She stops. Then she says, "I could model." She stops again and lets that linger between them. "You could help me do that," she says. "You said I could do it. I need the money, George. I really can't have a baby at my age."

"Olivia, how can I say yes to this? Your father is my friend. We work together for God's sake." He pauses, breathing into the phone. "Dumb," he says. "I'm so dumb, dumb, dumb."

She knows he's thinking about those pictures. He's probably so sorry he took them. Arms crossed over her chest. If she did that now it would hurt like a son of a bitch. "I don't know who else to turn to," she says.

"Okay," he says. His voice is resigned and low. "Okay, but don't tell your father, whatever you do, he'll kill me. I can't believe I'm going to do this."

"I love you," Olivia says, sinking back onto the bed. "Thank you so much, thank you, thank you, you're my savior."

"Oh, God," George says.

"I have to find out what time," she says. "I'll run in quick and then you won't ever have to see me again."

"Don't be ridiculous, Olivia. Of course I want to see you again."

The clinic can get her in at ten-thirty. "Don't eat anything after midnight," the woman says. "Have an early dinner but you can eat whatever you want." She is much nicer than the nurse, like someone that would hold your hair back while you threw up and Olivia hopes she'll be there tomorrow. "See you tomorrow, Olivia," the woman says and Olivia hangs up the phone reluctantly, wishing they could talk longer, even if there's nothing more to say.

Now all she has to do is wait. Her father won't be home until six—that's three hours. She can't stand being here by herself. She looks through her parent's medicine cabinet but there's only aspirin and Vick's and Pepto Bismol. She calls Vicki and Erik. Erik answers and when he realizes it's her, his voice gets cold.

"I'm having an abortion," she says. "I thought you should know."

There's silence. Olivia's giving him the chance to help her, to admit his part. The dead air stretches out. He's an asshole. "Is Vicki there?" she asks.

"Why," Erik says.

"Don't worry," Olivia says.

"I'm not worried."

Olivia realizes suddenly that she has nothing to lose. She doesn't have to be nice anymore.

"I want some downs," she says.

"I'm not sure we have any," Erik says.

"Let me talk to Vicki."

"All right," Erik says. "I'll bring them to you. Where are you?"

"I can come over and pick them up," Olivia says. "It'll take me about fifteen minutes to hitch."

"No," Erik says. "I'll bring them to you."

Olivia gives him directions to her house, and waits out on the front porch even though it's still raining. She sits on a lawn chair with her hands in her lap. She is wearing the same clothes she put on this morning to fly home. No one looking at her would know a thing about her. Cars go by driven by mothers with kids in the back. Most of the cars are station wagons like her mother's. When she was young, she liked to sit in the way back and give the drivers behind her the peace sign. She thought she was cool. Someday she will be. As soon as she gets this thing out of her, she'll start working on it.

Erik pulls up in his car, an old Chevy that leans a little to the left. Olivia runs out to the car and Erik rolls down the window but only a crack. He is so good looking she can feel her breath catch.

"Here," he says and squeezes a plastic bag through the slit in the window.

"You can roll down the window, I'm not going to bite you." He's looking at her the way her father looks at her mother sometimes, a look that is becoming something close to permanent. "Don't look at me like that," she tells him.

"Just do me a favor, will you?" Erik asks.

"What," she says.

"Don't tell Vicki any of this. I mean, I still don't think I got you pregnant but I don't want her to know about any of this."

Olivia shakes her head. "It was you," she says. "I wouldn't lie about that."

"How do I know?" Erik asks, and it is something men will ask her for years to come about all sorts of things and she will always be astonished that they don't believe her, even when she is lying.

She turns and walks back to the house. She will never see Erik and Vicki again, but at least she has something to get her through the next couple of days. She takes one of the red capsules. She'd take more but she doesn't want to be too high when her father gets home. She remembers that she's supposed to be sick, so she runs up to her bedroom and puts on a flannel nightgown and bathrobe and slippers. The warm material on her body is wonderful. She shivers with how good if feels. By the time she washes her face and goes back downstairs and makes some tea and cinnamon toast, she is starting to get off on the pill. This is the best she has felt in weeks and weeks.

Her father says her name when he walks in the door, and Olivia struggles awake, aware of the television blaring and darkness outside. She can't remember where she is but then she does and the tea and toast make their way up her throat. She barely makes it to the bathroom outside the kitchen. Her father says her name again outside the door.

"I'm fine," she says. "It's the flu, it's really bad."

"Your mother told me," her father says. "Can I get you anything?"

Olivia flushes the toilet, swishes her mouth with water and opens the door. Her father doesn't look like someone she knows. He is a tall stranger in a long khaki raincoat looking at her. "I'm sorry you're feeling so badly." He doesn't hug or kiss her but then he almost never does. He smiles and pats her shoulder.

She knows then that her mother didn't tell him and says thank you in her mind. She doesn't want to disappoint her father; it's too difficult. He doesn't just yell at her the way her mother does. He asks her questions in a slow, reasonable voice and looks vaguely hurt. "Why did you do that, Olivia?" he asked when she got busted for giving a girl in her 'home ec' class some hash. "Why did I give her the hash?" Olivia asked back. "I don't know, it was really stupid. She didn't deserve it." "That's not what I meant," her father said and gazed at her in a way that made her regret she wasn't better. These conversations end with him walking away and not talking to her much for awhile. She wishes she could make herself give him the right answers.

"Can I make you some soup?" he asks. He is taking off his coat, loosening his tie, pulling out the ingredients for his martini. Olivia sits at the kitchen table and watches him. He looks at her, his eyebrows raised and she shakes her head. She's still a little woozy from the down. She just wants to sit here and watch her father drink his cocktail. Afterwards, he'll go up and change into his soft corduroy slacks. Thank God her mother let her come home. Her father doesn't want to argue or pick on her or snoop. She wishes she weren't pregnant so she could really enjoy being alone with him. They could do something together, a movie maybe. Or an art gallery; he loves to look at paintings. He can spend twenty minutes in front of a single painting, his head slightly tilted to one side, then the other. Olivia has seen him do this.

She decides that she'll make him dinner while he's changing.

Neither of them say much. Olivia tries to think of things to start a conversation. What if she was to tell him? Listen, Dad, she could say, I'm preggers, knocked up, bun in the oven. He'd freak. No, he'd probably just walk away. No, he wouldn't do that either. She has no idea what he'd do. But she'd never tell him anyway. Sometimes she tries to explain to him, usually after she has fought with her mother, how she feels, how hard it is being her, how she's too old to be treated like a child, how her freedom is essential to her happiness. He says—almost every time—that all teenagers feel like that, which is anything but helpful, makes her feel common and reduced. But at least he *listens*, his eyes serious, squinting with the genuine effort of trying to understand her. Now, he taps the olive into his mouth from the bottom of the glass, chews it, and sighs. "What a day," he says. Olivia smiles at him.

"Okay, I'm going to go change and then I'll make us some dinner," he says, placing his martini glass carefully in the sink.

Olivia stands up. "No, I'll do it. I'll make something for us to eat."

"Are you sure?" her father asks. "Aren't you too sick?"

"No, I can make you something."

"Well, if you think you're okay," he says and goes upstairs.

Olivia takes out all the makings for hamburgers. She presses the ground meat into two patties and puts them in a skillet with a little butter. She is still tired but not as bad as before. Making dinner keeps her mind off tomorrow. After a few minutes, she flips the burgers and puts a slice of cheese on each. On two plates she puts a slice of tomato, onion, and hamburger buns. She starts to feel nauseated. "No," she says, but she can't help it and goes to the bathroom. Nothing comes up. It's dry retching. She hears her father come into the kitchen, hears him say, "Shit," and then the sound of the skillet being pulled off the burner. The smell of burnt meat makes its way into the bathroom.

"Why would you make yourself a hamburger if you have the flu?" her father asks when she comes out. He is scraping the burgers into the garbage. The pan is a mess.

"I don't know," she says. "I thought it would taste good."

Her father takes a Swanson dinner out of the freezer. He turns on the oven. "I think you'd be better off with toast or jello, don't you? Your mother says you know what to do." He seems annoyed.

Olivia puts toast in the toaster. She really doesn't want anything to eat anymore. When the toast pops up, she puts it on a plate and joins her father at the table where he is eating crackers and cheese and watching the mini-TV. She is acutely aware of the noise the toast makes as she chews it. All she wants to do is go to bed. Her father is talking to the television. "She's pretty," he says. He remembers that Olivia is there and says, "Isn't she pretty?" He is talking about Princess Grace of Monaco who Olivia doesn't think is that pretty, but she nods her head. Her mother is better looking than Princess Grace but her mother is a bitch and that's why her father thinks other women are prettier. She tries to eat another bite of toast. It's like swallowing glass. She stands up. "I'm going to bed," she says. "I don't feel that well."

Her father looks up. "Okay," he says. "Feel better. I'll call you from work tomorrow. Do you need anything?" He is watching the TV again. Princess Grace has been replaced by Elizabeth Taylor. "No comparison," he says.

"No, I'm all right," Olivia says.

"Thanks for trying to make me dinner," her father says as she leaves. "I appreciate the effort."

Up in her bedroom, Olivia lies facedown on the floor, her cheek pressed into the beige carpet. Her breasts are excruciating. It occurs to her that she's being punished for her sins. Not by God, that's not it. No one in the family, including her, is religious enough to believe in that. But *Be Here Now* talks about karma on almost every page. What you put out you get back, the book says. Well, she put out, all right. And look what she got back. *Be Here Now* doesn't make it sound so mean; it says that the universe, which is in charge of karma, is loving and kind. Something like that. She's near enough to her bed to dig the pills out from under the mattress, swallows dry a yellow one; they're weaker than the reds so she can wake up on time.

After awhile, she gets up to light the purple candle she keeps stashed in the drawer of her bedside table. Turning off the overhead light, she lies back down on the floor, with the candle right in front of her face. *Be Here Now* suggests you do this every day to get in touch with your inner spirit. She watches the flame flicker and weave, and plans how she'll make her father dinner tomorrow night after she has had the abortion. She won't be sick anymore. She'll feel light and wonderful, and she'll make him Coq Au Vin or Salisbury steak. Stop thinking, she orders herself. Sometimes, if she stares at the candle long enough, it makes her mindless and sleepy and calm. But tonight she's too aware of herself, her beating heart and sick stomach and swollen breasts. She blows the candle out and crawls into bed.

She is sick on the train into the city. She hangs her head over the toilet in the dirty little bathroom at the end of the car and when she's finished, she goes back to her seat and looks out the window until the train pulls into Grand Central. She wonders what they'll do to her. On her first visit, they gave her a booklet that described the process. Olivia threw it away but not before she read that they put a needle up you to numb it. She imagines it's like Novocain shots the dentist gives. She thinks about a needle going up her and her thighs involuntarily tighten. It can't be any worse than losing her virginity. Maybe it'll be like that. A sharp jolt, blood, and then some pain afterwards. It'll probably be worse than that. Not much, though, they wouldn't do it if it were that bad, they wouldn't allow it.

At Grand Central she heads straight for the Vanderbilt exit where there are always cabs. The cab driver wants to talk but Olivia pretends she can't hear. "What did you say?" she keeps asking until he shuts up. He takes too long to get to George's apartment. "Can you wait?" she asks him. "I'll pay you for this ride, but wait for me, I need to go further downtown."

The cab driver holds up five fingers. "Five minutes," he says.

George buzzes her in right away and is waiting at his door with an envelope in his hand. "Here," he says and gives it to her in the surreptitious way people give each other drugs. "Why don't you come back afterwards, honey," he says. He can't quite look at her. He lightly kisses her forehead, near her hair. "I feel terrible about this. I wish you'd told your parents."

"No," Olivia says.

"Do you want me to come with you?"

Olivia is horrified. They might think he was the father. "God, no," she says. She walks down the hall to the elevator.

It takes about ten minutes, she thinks, maybe more. The shot is the worst thing, much worse than sex the first time. The doctor, as he's giving her the shot, says, "Let's get this show on the road, you're going to feel a little prick, here we go." Then he steps back. "We'll just let that take effect." He smiles at her through his mask. "So," he says, "what is your favorite hobby?"

Olivia squeezes her eyes shut against the pain. "Hobby?" she asks.

"You know, ice skating, swimming, chess."

"I don't know," Olivia says. "I used to ride horses." She only took riding lessons for a year but she can't think of anything else to say.

"Oh, that's nice," the doctor says. "That's a challenging hobby. What do you do now?"

Olivia opens her eyes. His mouth is moving under the mask like a puppet's. "Nothing," she says. "Absolutely nothing."

Afterwards, there's blood on the paper gown. Olivia is led back to the little dressing room where she left her clothes. A nurse gives her a sheet of paper with instructions. Olivia drops the paper gown on the floor and puts her clothes on.

Her abdomen hurts. She leaves her jeans half zipped and her shirt untucked. On her way out, as she passes through the waiting room, she is hit by a wave of nausea so strong all she can do is find a corner. Everyone watches her. There's nothing to clean it up with so she leaves, keeping her eyes down. She remembers the nice woman on the phone. Maybe it's her day off.

Outside, it's still gray and drizzling and people are walking around. She joins the movement on the sidewalk. She thinks that she'll stop at George's for a minute, have a Coke or crackers or something to settle her stomach and then get the train. She puts two fingers to her mouth and whistles for a cab. She's proud that she can whistle like that, even when she's as sick as a dog. On the way to George's, she touches her hipbones again and again; she can feel the emptiness between them.

George gestures her into his apartment. "Are you all right? Let me get you something to drink. What do you want?" He is as solicitous as if she'd just had a baby. He guides her to the couch where she sat for the photographs. "I have some aspirin, do you want some?"

Olivia wishes she brought her downs. Then she remembers the Valium in his medicine cabinet from when she was here a year ago. She didn't take any; she wasn't doing as many drugs then. "Do you have anything stronger?" she asks. "I've taken Valium before for pain."

George hesitates. "Are you sure?"

Olivia puts her hands on her stomach. "Ouch," she says and closes her eyes. She can hear George get up and go in the bathroom. He comes back out and puts two Valium in her hand. They're the blues so she'll get a buzz. "Just take one for now," he says. He goes to get her water but Olivia swallows both dry before he gets back.

Later, after the pills hit, he gives her a massage. It feels good except when he gets too near her breasts, although he never actually touches them. "Stay in the middle," she says. His hands go back to the middle but then wander again. She lets him touch the sides of her breasts. That's all he does. He wouldn't try anything more.

When she wakes up, it's only an hour before her father gets home from work. "Oh my God," she says and puts her shoes and shirt back on. This morning at the clinic seems far away like something that happened when she was a child, like a nightmare. There is the smell of garlic in the apartment; George is in the kitchen, cooking something. He insists on calling her a cab to take her back to Scarsdale. "I'm not giving you a choice," he says. "If anything happened to you on that train, I'd never forgive myself." He offers her a taste of his sauce. "Try this," he says. "It's my own secret recipe. Your mother and father have been begging for it for years."

They look at each other. "You won't tell my father," Olivia says.

"No," George says. "I think he would have understood, though."

"No, he wouldn't," Olivia says. "And I won't ever tell him about the pictures."

George opens the door. He gives her two twenties. "Bye, Olivia," he says. "Take care of yourself."

They meet eyes again. Olivia wants to say something nice but all that comes out is: "There's too much garlic in the sauce."

George looks confused, then barely smiles and as he's closing the door behind her, she says, "I'm so sorry."

She gets home a half-hour before her father is due. She takes off her clothes and stuffs them in the hamper, takes two of the pills Eric gave her and then gets in the shower. She lets the hot water beat on her head until she's feeling the pills. The bathroom is steamy and damp and she'd like to just stay there all night, enveloped by humidity. But she puts on a clean nightgown and goes down to the kitchen to start cooking. Her mother's favorite cookbook is dog-eared and ripped and falls open to Coq Au Vin. Olivia gathers all the ingredients on the counter. Her head is spinning pleasantly. She will make her father an incredible meal. And she's feeling hungry herself. Her belly feels like a hole. "It's going to be infuckingcredible," she says out loud.

But the flour sifter won't sift and the onion pieces are too big and the cork in the wine bottle won't come out so she has to push it back in and now it's floating in the wine. Nothing is even close to ready when her father gets home.

There's something wrong with him. He comes into the kitchen and just looks at her and then at the chicken breasts sitting in a bowl of flour, the white wine, the onion pieces scattered all over the counter. "That bottle of wine is too expensive to use in food," he says. His voice is flat and Olivia understands that she's been betrayed. Her father knows.

"Which one should I use, Dad?" she asks. She can hear the slur in her words and her father looks at her sharply but she knows how to look straight when she has to: widen the eyes, keep the face tight, don't have too much eye contact. He takes off his coat.

Her father gets her the cooking wine from the pantry. He says, "I have to change."

Olivia puts some oil in the pan, puts in the chicken breasts and adds the wine. She shouldn't have taken two pills; she's too high. She needs to have food in her stomach, bread or something. Turning down the burner, she calls South Carolina. Kate answers. "Let me talk to mom," she says. Before her mother can even say hello, Olivia says, "You told him, didn't you. I can't believe you told him."

Her mother is silent. Then she says, "No, I didn't tell him."

"Yes, you did," Olivia says. "I can tell. He's acting different."

"What's wrong with your voice?" her mother asks. "Are you stoned again?"

"No," Olivia says. "Promise me you didn't tell him."

Again her mother pauses. "He's your father," she says. "He deserves to know."

"I hate you," Olivia says and hangs up, then takes the phone off the hook. She knew her mother would tell. Her mother thinks it'll help the marriage to not fall apart, will keep her father from having affairs with women who don't frown at him all the time—we have to stay together for the sake of screwed up Olivia.

She goes back to cooking her chicken breasts. They smell delicious even if the sauce is kind of gummy. She can hear her father moving around upstairs. Maybe if he has a few drinks, he'll forget or at least won't be so bummed-out. She rummages around the liquor cabinet for his martini stuff and pours equal measures of vermouth and gin into his favorite glass, then drops in three olives, just like he likes it. The chicken is sizzling away on the stove, the salad is pretty with its green romaine lettuce and baby tomatoes and the bread is covered in tinfoil, warming up in the oven. All she has to do is set the table. Her mother would kill her but Olivia uses the good china and cloth napkins, lining up the salad and meat fork the way she learned in girl scouts a million years ago. Her head is clearer now, and she's suddenly nervous; if her father weren't coming down the stairs, she'd run up to her bedroom and take another yellow pill.

She's putting the chicken onto the plates as he comes into the kitchen, pauses to hand him the martini and turn on the television so he can watch the news. He gives her a little smile that looks fake and she rushes to dish the salad onto his plate, trying to keep it separate from the chicken sauce, which is, she realizes abruptly, all wrong, thick as pudding, nothing like her mother's. And the salad has too much dressing, which is bleeding into the sauce to create an oddly yellowish color. The French bread, though, is okay, thank God, warm and crusty with pats of butter melting between the slices.

"This is nice, Olivia," her father says and puts his napkin on his lap. His movements are stiff and formal, as if he's someplace he'd rather not be. He takes a bite of chicken and chews for a long time.

Olivia tries to eat, too, puts a piece of bread in her mouth but she's too acutely aware of her father who is staring at the television even though it's just a commercial. Pretending to cough, she spits the bread into her hand and drops it under the table. She wants to make her father understand that the abortion doesn't mean anything, that it was just something she had to do, that he wouldn't want to be a grandfather and it was the right thing to do. She wants him to like her and not just because she's his daughter. She starts to talk. She tells him how she's going to re-join the swim team, take up riding lessons again. "Remember that time I fell off?" she asks. "And the instructor told me I didn't have to get back on but I did?" That's the sign of a real rider, she says. That's what the instructor told her. "And I saw the swimming coach last week in the grocery store and he asked me when I was coming back." She tells him how much her English teacher likes her. "He says I'm a really good writer." Her voice isn't as wobbly anymore, she feels profound and ambitious. When her father looks at her, his face doubtful and a little suspicious, she keeps her eyes trained on his, willing herself not to blink. "I'm going to change everything," she says.

"Well," her father says, "your mother will be glad to hear that."

"Yeah, I guess." But she wants to say, I'm telling this to *you*, not mom.

Her father takes a big sip of his martini and makes a face. "Good God, what's in here, Olivia?"

There's the tiniest hint of amusement around his mouth and she widens her eyes in mock innocence, wanting to laugh out loud, to hear him laugh. But it's not the right moment. Not yet.

"I really mean it, about changing my life," she says. "I'm going to make a list of goals and I'll give it to you and you can check each goal off." She doesn't tell him about the other list he won't see because it's in only in her mind. That list that has things on it like: don't ever let anyone pull out again and go on the Pill and after the downs Erik gave her are done, no more. "Do you want more chicken?" she asks. "I can make some more."

Her father smiles at her, an almost normal smile and Olivia sashays to the stove, singing out, "More Coq Au Vin coming up." Her slippers slide on the linoleum and it's like ice skating, it's fun so she bypasses the stove and skates around the kitchen. "Maybe I should take up ice skating," she says. "That can be my hobby." But the pills are still in her even if she can't feel them much and one foot shoots out, dropping her to her knees. She laughs at herself until she catches her father's expression. "Don't worry," she assures him, struggling to her feet. "I'm fine."

"Are you sure?" he asks and she wonders what he'd say if she said, no, I'm not.

"I'm so sure," she says. "Everything's going to be so good, Dad. Just wait."

"Is it?"

Olivia feels almost trapped by his gaze, the way his eyes flicker back and forth intently to keep contact with hers, waiting for an answer. Holding onto the counter, keeping herself up, she doesn't say anything, just smiles wide and toothy, hoping that'll be enough.

Smash & Grab

Michael Knight

At the last house on the left, the one with no security system signs staked on the lawn, no dog in the backyard, Cashdollar elbowed out a pane of glass in the kitchen door and reached through to unlock it from the inside. Though he was ninety-nine percent certain that the house was empty— he'd watched the owners leave himself—he paused a moment just across the threshold, listened carefully, heard nothing. Satisfied, he padded through an archway into the dining room where he found a chest of silverware and emptied its contents into the pillowcase he'd brought. He was headed down the hall, looking for the master bedroom, hoping that, in the rush to make some New Year's Eve soiree, the lady of the house had left her jewelry in plain sight, when he saw a flash of white and his head was snapped back on his neck, the bones in his face suddenly aflame. He wobbled, dropped to his knees. Then a girlish grunt and another burst of pain and all he knew was darkness.

He came-to with his wrists and ankles bound with duct tape to the arms and legs of a ladderback chair. His cheeks throbbed. His nose felt huge with ache. Opposite him, in an identical chair, a teenage girl was blowing lightly on the fingers of her left hand. There was a porcelain toilet tank lid, flecked with blood, across her lap. On it was arrayed a pair of cuticle scissors, a bottle of clear polish, cotton balls and a nail file. The girl glanced up at him now and he would have sworn she was pleased to find him awake.

"How's your face?" she said.

She was long-limbed, lean but not skinny, wearing a sweatshirt with the words *Saint Bridget's Volleyball* across the front in pastel plaids. Her hair was pulled into pigtails. She had on flannel boxers and pink wool socks.

"It hurts like hell." His nostrils were plugged with blood, his voice buzzing like bad wiring in his head.

The girl did a sympathetic wince.

"I didn't think anyone was home," he said.

"I guess you cased the house?" she said. "Is that the word—cased?"

Cashdollar nodded and she gave him a look, like she was sorry for spoiling his plans.

"I'm at boarding school. I just flew in this afternoon."

"I didn't see a light," he said.

"I was in the bathroom," she said, waggling her fingers at him. "I was on my left pinky when I heard the window break."

"Have you called the police?"

"Right after I knocked you out. You scared me so bad I practically just shouted my address into the phone and hung up." She giggled a little at herself. "I was afraid you'd wake up and kill me. That's why the tape. I'll call again if they aren't here soon." This last she delivered as if she regretted having to make him wait.

Cashdollar estimated at least ten minutes for the girl to drag him down the hall and truss him up, which meant that the police would be arriving momentarily. He had robbed houses in eleven states, had surprised his share of homeowners, but he'd never once had a run-in with the law. He was too fast on his feet for that, strictly smash and grab, never got greedy, never resorted to violence. Neither, however, had he ever been bashed unconscious with a toilet lid and duct-taped to a chair by a teenage girl.

"This boarding school," he said, "they don't send you home for Christmas?"

"I do Christmas with my mom," she said.

Cashdollar waited a moment for her to elaborate but she was quiet and he wondered if he hadn't hit on the beginnings of an angle here, wondered if he had time enough to work it. When it was clear that she wasn't going to continue, he prompted her. "Divorce is hard," he said.

The girl shrugged. "Everybody's divorced."

"So the woman I saw before—" He let the words trail off into a question.

"My father's girlfriend," she said. "One of." She rolled her eyes. Her eyes were a curious, almost fluorescent shade of green. "My father is the last of the big time swingers."

"Do you like her?" he said. "Is she nice?"

"I hardly know her. She's a nurse. Regina something. She works for him. I think it's tacky if you want to know the truth."

They were in the dining room, though Cashdollar hadn't bothered to take it in when he was loading up the silverware. He saw crown molding. He saw paintings on the walls, dogs and dead birds done in oils, expensive but without resale value. This was a doctor's house, he thought. It made him angry that he'd misread the presence of the woman, angrier even than the fact that he'd let himself get caught. He was thirty-six years old. That seemed to him just then like a long time to be alive.

"I'm surprised you don't have a date tonight," he said. "Pretty girl like you home alone on New Year's Eve."

He had his doubts about flattery—the girl seemed too sharp for that—but she took his remark in stride.

"Like I said, I just got in today and I'm away at school most of the year. Plus, I spend more time with my mother in California than my father so I don't really know anybody in Mobile."

"What's your name?" he said.

The girl hesitated. "I'm not sure I should tell you that."

"I just figured if you told me your name and I told you mine then you'd know somebody here."

"I don't think so," she said.

Cashdollar closed his eyes. He was glad that he wasn't wearing some kind of burglar costume, the black sweatsuit, the ski mask. He felt less obvious in street clothes. Tonight, he'd chosen a hunter green car coat, a navy turtleneck, khaki pants and boat shoes. He didn't bother wearing gloves. He wasn't so scary-looking this way, he thought, and when he asked the question that was on his mind, it might seem like one regular person asking a favor of another.

"Listen, I'm just going to come right out and say this, okay. I'm wondering what are the chances you'd consider letting me go?" The girl opened her mouth but Cashdollar pressed ahead before she could refuse and she settled back into her chair to let him finish. "Because the police will be here soon and I don't want to go to prison and I promise, if you let me, I'll leave the way I came in and vanish from your life forever."

The girl was quiet for a moment, her face patient and composed, as if waiting to be sure he'd said his piece. He could hear the refrigerator humming in the kitchen. A moth plinked against the chandelier over their heads. He wondered if it hadn't slipped in through the broken pane. The girl capped the bottle of nail polish, lifted the toilet lid from her lap without disturbing the contents and set it on the floor beside her chair.

"I'm sorry," she said. "I really am but you did break into the house and you put my father's silverware in your pillowcase and I'm sure you would have taken other things if I hadn't hit you on the head. If you want, I'll tell the police that you've been very nice, but I don't think it's right for me to let you go."

In spite—or because of—her genial demeanor, Cashdollar was beginning to feel like his heart was on the blink; it felt as thick and rubbery as a hot water bottle in his chest. He held his breath and strained against his bonds, hard enough to hop his chair, once, twice, but the tape held fast. He sat there, panting.

The girl said, "Let me ask you something. Let's say I was asleep or watching TV or whatever and I didn't hear the window break. Let's say you saw me first—what would you have done?"

He didn't have to think about his reply. "I would have turned around and left the house. I've never hurt anyone in my whole life."

The girl stared at him for a long moment then dropped her eyes and fanned her fingers, studied her handiwork. She didn't look altogether pleased. To the backs of her hands, she said, "I believe you."

As if to punctuate to her sentence, the doorbell chimed, followed by four sharp knocks, announcing the arrival of the police.

While he waited, Cashdollar thought about prison. The possibility of incarceration loomed forever on the periphery of his life but he'd never allowed himself to waste a lot of time considering the specifics. He told himself that at least he wasn't leaving anyone behind, wasn't ruining anyone else's life, though even as he filled his head with reassurances, he understood that they were false and his pulse was roaring in his ears, his lungs constricting. He remembered this one break-in over in Pensacola when some sound he made—a rusty hinge, a creaking floorboard—startled the owner of the house from sleep. The bedroom was dark and the man couldn't see Cashdollar standing at the door. "Joyce?" he said. "Is that you, Joyce?" There was such sadness, such longing in his voice that Cashdollar knew Joyce was never coming back. He pitied the man, of course, but at the same time, he felt as if he was watching him through a window, felt outside the world looking in rather than in the middle of things with the world pressing down around him. The man rolled over, mumbled his way back to sleep, and Cashdollar crept out of the house feeling sorry for himself. He hadn't thought about that man in years. Now, he could hear voices in the next room but he couldn't make out what they were saying. It struck him that they were taking too long and he wondered if this wasn't what people meant when they described time bogging down at desperate moments.

The girl rounded the corner into the dining room trailing a pair of uniformed police officers, the first a white guy, straight out of central casting, big and pudgy, his tunic crumpled into his slacks, his belt slung low under his belly, the second, a black woman, small with broad shoulders, her hair twisted into braids under her cap. "My friend—" The girl paused, shot a significant look at Cashdollar. "—Patrick, surprised him in the dining room and the burglar hit him with the toilet thingy and taped him up. Patrick, these are Officers Hildebran and Pruitt." She tipped her head right, then left to indicate the man and the woman respectively.

Officer Pruitt circled around behind Cashdollar's chair. "What was the burglar doing with a toilet lid?"

"That's a mystery," the girl said.

"Why haven't you cut him loose?"

"We didn't know what to do for sure," the girl said. "He didn't seem to be hurt too bad and we didn't want to disturb the crime scene. On TV, they always make a big deal out of leaving everything just so."

"I see," said Officer Pruitt, exactly as if she didn't see at all. "And you did your nails to pass the time?" She pointed at the manicure paraphernalia.

The girl made a goofy, self-deprecating face, all eyebrows and lips, twirled her finger in the air beside her ear. Officer Hildebran wandered over to the window. Without facing the room, he said, "I'll be completely honest with you, Miss Schnell—"

"Daphne," the girl said and Cashdollar had the sense that her interjection was meant for him.

Officer Hildebran turned, smiled. "I'll be honest, Daphne, we sometimes recover some of the stolen property but—"

"He didn't take anything," the girl said.

Officer Hildebran raised his eyebrows. "No?"

"He must have panicked," Daphne said.

Cashdollar wondered what had become of his pillowcase, figured it was still in the hall where the girl had ambushed him, hoped the police didn't decide to poke around back there. Officer Pruitt crouched at his knees to take a closer look at the duct tape.

"You all right?" she said.

He nodded, cleared his throat.

"Where'd the tape come from?"

"I don't know," he said. "I was out cold."

"Regardless," Officer Hildebran was saying to Daphne, "unless there's a reliable eyewitness—"

Officer Pruitt sighed. "There is an eyewitness." She raised her eyes, regarded Cashdollar's battered face.

"Oh," Officer Hildebran said. "Right. You think you could pick him out of a line-up?"

"It all happened pretty fast," Cashdollar said.

And so it went, as strange and vivid as a fever dream, their questions, his answers, their questions, Daphne's answers—he supposed that she was not the kind of girl likely to arouse suspicion, not the kind of girl people were inclined to disbelieve—until Officers Hildebran and Pruitt were satisfied, more or less. They seemed placated by the fact that his injuries weren't severe and that nothing had actually been stolen. Officer Pruitt cut the tape with a utility knife and Cashdollar walked them to the door like he was welcome in this house. He invented contact information, assured them that he'd be down in the morning to look at mugshots. He didn't know what had changed Daphne's mind and, watching the police make their way down the sidewalk and out of his life, he didn't care. He shut the door and said, "Is Daphne your real name?" He was just turning to face her when she clubbed him with the toilet lid again.

Once more, he woke in the ladderback chair, wrists and ankles bound, but this time Daphne was seated cross-legged on the floor, leaned back, her weight on her hands. He saw her as if through a haze, as if looking through a smudgy lens, noticed her long neck, the smooth skin on the insides of her thighs.

"Yes," Daphne said.

"What?"

"Yes, my name is Daphne."

"Oh," he said.

His skull felt full of sand.

"I'm sorry for conking you again," she said. "I don't know what happened. I mean, it was such a snap decision to lie to the police and then that woman cut the tape and I realized I don't know the first thing about you and I freaked." She paused. "What's your name?" she said.

Cashdollar felt as if he was being lowered back into himself from a great height, gradually remembering how it was to live in his body. Before he was fully aware of what he was saying, he'd given her an honest answer.

"Leonard," he said.

Daphne laughed. "I wasn't expecting that," she said. "I didn't think anybody named anybody Leonard anymore."

"I'm much older than you."

"You're not so old. What are you, forty?"

"Thirty-six."

Daphne said, "Oops."

"I think I have a concussion," Cashdollar said.

Daphne wrinkled her nose apologetically and pushed to her feet and brushed her hands together. "Be right back," she said. She ducked into the kitchen, returned with a highball glass which she held under his chin. He smelled scotch, let her bring it to his mouth. It tasted expensive.

"Better?" Daphne said.

Cashdollar didn't answer. He'd been inclined to feel grateful but hadn't the vaguest idea where this was going now. She sat on the floor and he watched her sip from the glass. She made a retching face, shuddered, regrouped.

"At school one time, I drank two entire bottles of Robitussin cough syrup. I hallucinated that my Klimt poster was coming to life. It was very sexual. My roommate called the paramedics."

"Is that right?" Cashdollar said.

"My father was in Aruba when it happened," she said. "He was with an AMA rep named Farina Hoyle. I mean, what

185

kind of a name is Farina Hoyle? He left her there and flew all the way back to make sure I was all right."

"That's nice, I guess," Cashdollar said.

Daphne nodded and smiled, half-sly, half-something else. Cashdollar couldn't put his finger on what he was seeing in her face. "It isn't true," she said. "The Robitussin's true. Farina Hoyle's true. Aruba's true."

"What are you going to do with me?" Cashdollar said.

Daphne peered into the glass.

"I don't know," she said.

They were quiet for a minute. Daphne swirled the whisky. Cashdollar's back itched and he rubbed it on the chair. When Daphne saw what he was doing, she moved behind the chair to scratch it for him and he tipped forward to give her better access. Her touch raised goosebumps, made his skin jump like horseflesh.

"Are you married?" she said.

He told her, "No."

"Divorced?"

He shook his head. Her hand went still between his shoulder blades. He heard her teeth click on the glass.

"You poor thing," she said. "Haven't you ever been in love?"

"I think you should cut me loose," Cashdollar said.

Daphne came around the chair and sat on his knee, draped her arm over his shoulder.

"How often do you do this? Rob houses, I mean."

"I do it when I need the money," he said.

"When was the last time?" Her face was close enough that he could smell the liquor on her breath.

"A while ago," he said. "Could I have another sip of that?" She helped him with the glass. He felt the scotch behind his eyes. The truth was he'd done an apartment house just last week, waited at the door for somebody to buzz him up, then broke the locks on the places where no one was home. He was in and out in less than an hour. Just now, however, he didn't see the percentage in the truth. He said, "I only ever do rich people and I give half my take to Jerry's Kids."

Daphne socked him in the chest.

"Ha, ha," she said.

"Isn't that what you want to hear?" he said. "Right? You're looking for a reason to let me go?"

"I don't know," she said.

He shrugged. "Who's to say it isn't true?"

"Jerry's Kids," she said.

She was smiling and he smiled back. He couldn't help liking this girl. He liked that she was smart and that she wasn't too afraid of him. He liked that she had the guts to bullshit the police.

"Ha, ha," he said.

Daphne knocked back the last of the scotch, then skated her socks over the hardwood floor, headed for the bay window.

"Do you have a car?" she said, parting the curtains. "I don't see a car."

"I'm around the block," he said.

"What do you drive?"

"Honda Civic."

Daphne raised her eyebrows.

"It's inconspicuous," he said.

She skated back over to his chair and slipped her hand into his pocket and rooted for his keys. Cashdollar flinched. There were only two keys on the ring, his car and his apartment. For some reason, this embarrassed him.

"It really is a Honda," Daphne said.

There was a grandfather clock in the corner but it had died at half past eight who knew how long ago and his watch was out of sight beneath the duct tape and Cashdollar was beginning to worry about the time. He guessed Daphne had been gone for twenty minutes, figured he was safe until after midnight, figured her father and his lady friend would at least ring in the new year before calling it a night. He put the hour around 11:00 but he couldn't be sure and for all he knew, Daphne was out there joyriding in his car and you couldn't tell what might happen at a party on New Year's Eve. Somebody might get angry. Somebody might have too much to drink. Somebody might be so crushed with love they can't wait another minute to get home. He went on thinking like this until he heard what sounded like a garage door rumbling open and his mind went blank and every ounce of his perception funneled down into his ears. For a minute, he heard nothing—he wasn't going to mistake silence for safety a second time—then a door opened in the kitchen and Daphne breezed into the room.

"Took me a while to find your car," she said. She had changed clothes for her foray into the world. Now, she was wearing an electric blue parka with fur inside the hood and white leggings and knee-high alpine boots.

"What time is it?" he said.

But she passed through without stopping, disappeared into the next room.

"You need to let me go," he said.

When she reappeared, she was carrying a stereo speaker. He watched her into the kitchen. She returned a minute later without the speaker, took the parka off and draped it on a chair.

"It's a good thing you've got a hatchback," Daphne said.

For the next half hour, she shuttled between the house and the garage, bearing valuables each trip, first the rest of the stereo, then the TV and the VCR, then his pillowcase of silverware, then an armload of expensive-looking suits and on and on until Cashdollar was certain that his car would hold no more. Still she kept it up. Barbells, golf clubs, a calfskin luggage set. A pair of antique pistols. A dusty classical guitar. A baseball signed by someone dead and famous. With each passing minute, Cashdollar could feel his stomach tightening and it was all he could do to keep his mouth shut but he had the sense that he should leave her be, that this didn't have anything to do with him. He pictured his little Honda bulging with the accumulated property of another man's life, flashed to his apartment in his mind, unmade bed, lawn chairs in the living room, coffee mug in the sink. He made a point of never holding on to anything anybody else might want to steal. There was not a single thing in his apartment that it would hurt to lose, nothing he couldn't live without. Daphne swung back into the room, looking frazzled. She huffed at a wisp of stray hair that had fallen across her eyes.

"There," she said.

Cashdollar said, "You're crazy."

Daphne dismissed him with a wave.

"You're out of touch," she said. "I'm your average sophomore."

"What'll you tell the cops?"

"I like Stockholm Syndrome but I think they're more likely to believe you made me lie under threat of death." She lifted the hem of her sweatshirt to wipe her face, exposing her belly, the curve of her ribs, pressed it first against her right eye, then her left as if dabbing tears.

"Ha, ha," he said.

Daphne said, "I'll get the scissors."

She went out again, came back again. The tape fell away like something dead. Cashdollar rubbed his wrists a second, pushed to his feet and they stood there looking at each other. Her eyes, he decided, were the color of a jade pendant he had stolen years ago. That pendant pawned for $700.00. It flicked through his mind that he should kiss her and that she would let him but he restrained himself. He had no business kissing teenage girls. Then, as if she could read his thoughts, Daphne slapped him across the face. Cashdollar palmed his cheek, blinked the sting away, watched her doing a girlish bob and weave, her thumbs tucked inside her fists.

"Let me have it," she said.

"Quit," he said.

"Wimp," she said. "I dropped you twice."

"I'm gone," he said.

Right then, she poked him in the nose. It wouldn't have hurt so much if she hadn't already hit him with the toilet lid but as it was, his eyes watered up, his vision filled with tiny sparkles. Without thinking, he balled his hand and punched her in the mouth, not too hard, a reflex, just enough to sit her down, but right away he felt sick at what he'd done. He held his palms out, like he was trying to stop traffic.

"I didn't mean that," he said. "That was an accident. I've never hit a girl. I've never hurt anyone in my whole life."

Daphne touched her bottom lip, smudging her fingertip with blood.

"This will break his heart," she said.

She smiled at Cashdollar and he could see blood in the spaces between her teeth. The sight of her dizzied him with sadness. He thought how closely linked were love and pain. Daphne extended a hand, limp-wristed, ladylike. Her nails were perfect.

"Now tape me to the chair," she said.

Brave Girl

Peter Ho Davies

Fillings were good for groans. There was something about that contrast between the low, jumbled moans and the high-pitched whine of the drill, not quite drowning them out. Sometimes the mewling would sound almost like words, like Chewbacca in *Star Wars*, full of feeling, but without meaning. It was impossible to form real words with the steel tang of my father's instruments on your tongue, his rubber-gloved knuckles pressing into the corners of your mouth.

Fillings were good. Sometimes there were even tears. But extractions were better. Extractions made kids scream.

My father would stand back a little after the first examination and say, "Rinse now," and then when the patient was lying back in the chair, try to break the news gently. "I'm not going to hurt you," he'd tell them, and they'd pale. "You don't believe me, but you will. Promise. You want to know why?" He'd put his hand on his heart. "Because it's the *tooth*." That might even make them smile, but soon there'd be tears and they'd just be the start. My father would say something about an injection, but even that wouldn't do it. Kids who'd never had an extraction thought that an injection meant a shot in the arm. The real moment was when he held up the silver syringe, with its glistening tip of novocain shining wetly in the bright halogen lights. "Just a little pinch," my father would say. "Open wide." That was when the yelling would start, the needle bearing down on you, vanishing from sight into your mouth.

I was ten that summer, almost eleven, old enough to look after myself at home, but my father insisted on taking me with him to work. In the spring my mother had moved to London with her captain from the Territorial Army (he was a gynecologist in real life) and my father didn't like me being alone in the house. He'd demanded I finish the term at my old school and spend half the summer with him, but now it was the second Friday in July and on Sunday I would go away to live with my mother and Captain Cunt.

My mother had left me her white overnight case. It was round and silk lined, and just the right size for me. It had a vanity mirror in the lid where I loved to stare at myself. Soon I'd be packing it.

"I could fight her for custody, sweetheart," my father had told me. "And I'd probably lose. But I want you to know I love you and if you want to stay, I'll do everything in my power. No ifs and buts about it. It's your choice; you just say the word."

I told him I knew he loved me. And I did. But I also knew I was the only one left for him to love and when he said things like that it made me worry that I didn't love him enough. I didn't want to choose. I already felt sorry for him that my mother had left. I tried to make up for it by being good.

It wasn't so bad at the surgery. I even had my own room, a tiny cubical intended for gas extractions but rarely used by my father who referred most of that work to the hospital. There was still a high bed, upholstered in blistered red vinyl, and a tall stainless steel instrument tray which I could use as a desk. Every morning, before he opened, my father would let me into the waiting room to take my pick of the new comics and magazines. I would come back with yellowed dog-eared armfuls of *Mandy* and *Jackie*, and the occasional copy of boys' comics like *Battle* or *Warlord*, the ink smelling like pee. Buried deep in the pile would be one or two slippery editions of *Cosmopolitan* or *Elle* that my father's Australian nurse, Sylvia, subscribed to and left in the waiting room for mothers. At the start of the summer I had read my way through most of the girls' comics and grown bored. The boys' comics with their tales of torture and heroism had entertained me briefly (I was especially struck by a strip called "Sergeant Steele" about a self-sacrificing NCO with a bullet next to his heart—"like a timebomb in his chest!"—who stayed on at the front to perform weekly feats of suicidal bravery.) But lately I was onto a steady diet of slick grown-up magazines. I would close the blinds on the window and skim through the pages to see how many stories there were about sex. I tried to memorize all the tips: seven secrets of office romance; nine lives of modern women; ten tell-tale signs he's interested. I couldn't imagine my parents doing any of the things the stories described, so I pictured blond Sylvia, in her short dental nurse's uniform and white tights, winning and keeping men, enjoying a career and multiple orgasms. Sylvia would be good at all that, I thought, and I admired her. If there were no new *Cosmo's* or *Elle's* I'd settle for the duller articles in *Woman's Own* about family life.

The only thing that would tear me away from a good article about sex were moans or cries from the other room.

The girl in the chair on my last day at the surgery had been ice-skating with friends. It was her birthday party. Most of them hadn't known how to skate and they'd been circling the rink hanging on to the sides and making short staggering runs back and forth across the ice. On one of these, the birthday girl had dropped behind the others. They'd reached the barrier and slumped across it and in her hurry to catch up she'd stumbled and slid on her stomach towards them. Someone had lost their balance and the back of a skate had slipped out and caught the fallen girl in the face. Her two front teeth went *snap* like a pencil lead.

My father was pushing cotton wadding into her mouth, his fingers working quickly like a magician's, shoving in more and more of the short, white swabs until her cheeks bulged like a hamster. Then just as fast, he was pulling them out one after another, limp with blood. He dropped them with his tweezers into the metal pan that Sylvia, his beautiful assistant, held out for him.

The girl was lying almost horizontal and raised up for my father to work on without straining his back. My head, when I took my usual position in front of the chair, was at her shoe level. It took a moment for her to see me standing there, staring, and her eyes grew huge around her tiny pupils.

I never said anything when I watched my father work. I never really showed any expression. I just wanted to let the kids know I was there. I liked to think I was helping him. Sometimes he told them how traveling dentists in olden days often drew a crowd. I was sure my presence could shame some of the kids into not going mental. It was a playground thing. What I held over them, like a knife at their throats, was my contempt.

"Hello, darling," my father said, but his glance at me was so fleeting his expression didn't change. He picked up his drill and thumbed it for a second to get the girl used to the sound. "Now, this will only tickle, sweetheart," he told her over the whirr of the motor. He showed her the air-blower and the water jet and called them his toys. A little later, he held up an injection and told her it would only sting a bit. He said these things so often that I thought he believed them. You couldn't see his lips move behind his mask, but if you looked closely you could see the paper crimp at his mouth.

My father talked to all his patients. He asked them their names and then he used them as though he'd known them all their lives. This girl's name was Marie. He told Marie how good she was. What a big girl Marie was being. He told her how proud her parents would be. He called her mother *mummy* and her father *daddy*. It was odd hearing him talk like that to a stranger. It reminded me of how he had sat down one evening and answered my questions about the divorce.

"The tooth?" he lisped, but I didn't smile. "Mummy and Daddy fell out of love." The way he said it made me think of falling out of treehouses, or swings, off bicycles or ponies—all the ways kids ended up in his surgery. "People change," he said. I told him I'd never change, but he said I was being silly. "Don't you want to grow up?" he asked me gently, and I shook my head till my temples ached and he caught me and held me.

I glared up at the girl. She was older than me, twelve perhaps thirteen, and she had lipstick on—a dark cherry that seemed almost black against her pale skin. She wore tight designer jeans and a white blouse freckled with blood. I could see her bra through the polyester and I watched her small chest heaving.

She was in too much pain and shock to scream, but she was shuddering with sobs and whinnying nasally. I wanted to tell her to stop having an eppy. But my father spoke to her softly as he worked, while Sylvia stroked her forehead, her shiny nails in the girl's fringe. The three of them reminded me of a funny sort of family. After a little while the girl's moans became weaker and fuzzier and I knew the injection was taking effect. My father reached into her mouth with his shiny pliers and pulled the broken stubs of teeth out of her mouth one at a time. He had long, strong fingers, only slightly hairy, and I saw them go white, straining. He held each tooth up, streaky with blood, and studied it for a second. He looked like a doctor in the westerns he loved who'd just extracted a bullet from deep in the hero's leg. Then he dropped the teeth into a kidney-shaped bowl where they made a dull ping on the stainless steel.

"All done," he said, cheerfully. "There's a brave girl."

She smiled at him, numbly, her cherry lips opening over the dark gap in her teeth.

For as long as I could remember I had been the bravest kid I knew. Everyone else was afraid of the dentist—even boys. My father's surgery was close to school and most of my friends were his patients and I was sure they were scared of him. It made me secretly proud.

That summer, though, I had started to be afraid. I knew that my father would never let me go ice-skating now. The year before he'd had a girl come in who'd lost several teeth playing hockey and he'd made me take netball at school. Last spring the police had used his records to identify the body of a boy who'd drowned and I'd had to give up piano and take swimming lessons instead. It had bothered me then, but now I knew that when he banned skating I would be glad. Even if my mother let me, I decided I didn't want to.

I was afraid of other things too. My friends had begun to get their ears pierced and I wanted to, but I was frightened. They all had their mothers to take them and give permission for the man to place the gun to their ears. I couldn't imagine my father there with me. Sharon Clark in my class had gone with her mother and she said proudly it *hurt like hell*. That made me feel faint. I thought of buying bras. I thought of getting my period. I didn't want to leave my father, but I knew I'd go to my mother. I loved her, too, of course, but next to fear, love just didn't seem like a useful way of choosing between your parents.

My mother called me almost every night and because we couldn't talk about her and my father, we talked about the Captain. I asked her what he did in the TA, and she said she wasn't sure. "Only he can't be a gynecologist," I said. I'd only learned the word recently. Guy-neck-ologist. I liked to say it. "There's not much call for gynecologists in the army. I mean what would a gynecologist do at the front." She laughed a little and told me she didn't know, but I had my suspicions. He was handsome, the Captain, tall and fair. He looked like the Nazi interrogators in my comics. The kind of man who made people betray their comrades. Everyone cracked under torture, sooner or later, I knew.

Sometimes the Captain would come on the line. I liked to call him "Sir." He thought I was very polite. He used to tell me how much fun we'd all have together. "What do you like to do?" he asked and I told him I liked going to work with my Dad. "Could *we* do that, sir?" But the Captain just coughed. "I mean when you're being a soldier," I said. "Not looking up people's *fannies*."

During the days I read *Cosmo* and tried to make friends with Sylvia. I told her I liked her nail polish and she showed me how to put it on in long tapering strokes. She was younger and prettier than my mother, just like the Captain was cleverer and richer than my father. I wanted to get her alone, to make her a confidant. I would tell her how nice my father was. I thought if he had her I wouldn't feel so bad about leaving. Perhaps I could even stay. But I could never find the right moment. Sylvia insisted on treating me like a kid even though I knew all her sex tips.

"My Dad likes nail polish," I said.

"Really?" She took my hand in hers. "Let's just see what we can do with these nails of yours, eh?"

"Don't you think he's good looking," I asked her coyly and she whispered back, "Fair Dinkum. If he was my Dad, I'd be really proud of him." I wasn't sure who was trying to convince who.

In between patients, my father would slip the mask down around his neck and try to entertain me. Sometimes he would pull out a matchbox, empty the matches into a pocket and drop a shiny globe of mercury into the tiny drawer. He would tip it back and forth under my nose. "See," he'd say. "A little mouse." And I'd go, "Oh yeah." I preferred it when Sylvia gave me the used drill bits to collect. They were diamond tipped, and came in tiny plastic cubes, the size of jewel boxes. "Your first sparklers," Sylvia whispered to me and I told her that diamonds were a girl's best friend.

Once I heard my father tell her she was good with me and that he appreciated it. "She has a bit of a crush on you," he said, which made me furious. After that I stopped trying to time my trips to the loo to coincide with hers.

The last patient that day was a boy called Barry, so scared he refused to sit still. His mother had to come in with him. As soon as she placed him in the chair and my father began raising it, he squirmed off. "I'll be good," he blubbed. "Honest." *What a spaz*, I thought. I would have liked to help, but when parents were in the surgery my father liked me to keep out of the way. I satisfied myself with sitting in Sylvia's swivel chair, studying the chart on her clipboard, sucking her Bic.

"I promise this won't hurt," my father said soothingly, but the boy's mother was losing her patience.

"You'll just have to learn to put up with a little pain," she said and I saw my father give her a sideways look. In the end he asked her to get into the chair with Barry in her lap. He tilted the chair back until mother and child were almost horizontal and then he raised the chair to work on the boy.

My father only worked on children. He preferred it that way. So when Barry pleaded, "Mummy first," and she said, "Oh, why not?" he paused for a moment. She had already closed her eyes and laid her head back in a pantomime of calm resignation. "Open wide?" Sylvia suggested, and my father began the examination. He was silent, though, as he probed the mother's teeth. He hadn't worked on adults for years and he didn't know how to talk to them. When he bent over I could see his bald spot, not much bigger than a ten pence coin, was flushed. I hoped Sylvia wouldn't notice.

At five o'clock my father hung his white coat on the back of the door and looked suddenly smaller and older in his shirt and creased tie. "What a day," he said, dropping into the chair opposite Sylvia's desk. I was spinning around on an adjustable stool, holding my arms out and then bringing them into my body and speeding up like a figure skater.

"You were a trooper with that Marie," Sylvia said, looking up from the chart she was completing.

"Thanks for your help with Barry and his mother," he told her, and she looked down as she passed the chart across to him. "Really," he said.

She got up and began collecting instruments from the trays.

"I'm lucky to have you, Sylvia," he said. I let my feet scuff the floor until my spinning came slowly to a rest. "You're the best nurse I've ever worked with."

"Well." She dropped the instruments into the sterilizer with a clank. "Cheers."

Her mask was lying on her desk where she had taken it off to answer the phone. It was still bowed from her face and leaning over I could see, in the center, a smudge of lip-stick. I slipped it over my mouth and smelled her perfume. I wondered if the lipstick would rub off on me. There was no make-up at home since my mother left.

"We make a good team, I think," my father went on. "The two of us."

He's paying her a compliment, I thought. It was a sign.

But Sylvia just shrugged her coat on. "Oh yeah," she laughed. "Torville and Deane. That's us all right." She didn't look back at him, but at the door, she stopped to blow me a kiss. "Be good, you. Ciao."

"See ya," I called through the mask, but my father just went back to his paperwork, pressing his signature firmly through the carbon paper.

Before he closed up, I made my father examine me. I could tell he was unhappy. After all the cowardly kids, the cry-babies, I thought I could cheer him up by being the perfect patient.

"That Marie," I said scornfully, climbing into the chair. "They were her baby teeth, right?"

He shook his head. It seemed like a crime to lose your permanent teeth and I was suddenly angry at the girl, although I also understood a little better why she had cried so much. My father had stickers that he gave out to his best patients: a bright shining cartoon smile with the words, "Teeth are for life."

I lay back while he pumped the pedal and felt myself floating up towards him. It was like being held in his arms, even better than the magic carpet feeling of wafting down to earth later. He smiled at me over his mask—I could tell from the way his eyes went—and asked me to open wide, "wide as you can," and told me what a good girl I was, how brave I was. Just like he talked to any of the other kids. For once, I liked that. It was good to know he would love me even if I was a stranger.

He'd even cried when they'd identified the body of the boy, his missing patient. I remembered it because it was the last time I'd seen my parents touch. We'd watched the announcement on the local news and when I looked at my father the tears were dripping from his chin. He told us that the boy's father had called him that morning, wanting to know if there could be a mistake. My mother reached across and stroked the tears from his cheeks. "He asked me how I could be so sure when he couldn't even recognize his own son."

On that last evening at the surgery, I'd already made up my mind that if he found no work to do I'd suggest he take an impression of my teeth. He'd fill two horseshoe shaped troughs with pink goo, slip them into my mouth one at a time, and make me bite down hard. I liked leaving a perfect ring of tooth marks. The worst thing about it was that you felt as though your mouth was being stretched, as if you'd smiled too long like Miss World. Afterwards, he'd ask me if it was yummy—it was supposed to be strawberry flavor—but I'd tell him it tasted like a plastic spoon left in a bowl of fruit-salad and make him laugh.

But that afternoon, he found a slightly loose baby tooth and asked me if I wanted him to take it out or if I wanted to just let it work free.

"It's up to you. But it'll mean an injection." I swallowed my spit and told him to take it out anyway. I didn't know when he'd get another chance and I didn't like the idea of another dentist doing it.

"Okay," he said. "If you're sure you're sure?"

I'd never had an injection before, but I watched coolly as he showed the needle to me and told me it would just pinch. "I know." I watched it get closer until I couldn't keep it in focus any longer. Just for a second I thought about changing my mind, and then the needle was gone, out of sight, into my mouth.

Later, on the way home in the car, I couldn't stop touching my slack face. It felt different, I told my father, smoother, softer.

"Because you're feeling your face through your fingers. What's missing is the feel of your fingers *on* your face." I turned that over for a long moment.

"So this is how I feel to other people when they touch me?"

He nodded. I had been rubbing my face, trying to overcome the numbness, but now I stopped and touched myself, my lips, my chin more gently.

It made me shiver. I blew my cheeks out and slapped them as hard as I could in time to the song on the radio then I folded down the vanity mirror and admired how rosy they were. I couldn't feel a thing. After the needle went in I lost all sensation in my jaw, except that at the last second I felt a sharp stabbing pain. For a second, when it hurt, I thought something was wrong with me. I thought it was my fault. I was less brave than I should be. And then it came to me: you couldn't be brave without being scared. Sergeant Steele knew it. "I'm no 'ero," he'd growl gruffly, turning down medals. "I've just got nuffin' to lose ..."

But it also occurred to me in that moment of wincing pain that my father was a liar, that he lied every day of his life. And I was suddenly, enormously relieved.

At dinner, he tried to say how much he'd miss me. I was drinking my milk through a straw and was distracted by the idea that the straw had a hole in it. When I realized it was lying in the new gap in my teeth, resting against the gum, I set the drink down quickly. "We'll still see each other on weekends and holidays," he was saying, and I nodded vigorously.

Afterwards, I washed the tooth—an incisor, my father told me—under the kitchen tap and looked at it in my hand. It was funny to think it had been part of me. He asked me if I'd like to leave it under my pillow for the tooth-fairy, but I told him I was too old for that and he tried to smile. I didn't say, but I thought I'd show the tooth to my mother. I put it in a jam jar and shook it to hear the tiny sound of it beating on the glass. I decided to keep all my teeth.

But when my father came up to tuck me in I told him I'd changed my mind. I gave him the tooth and told him I'd like to put it under my pillow. For a second it lay like a tiny bone in his hand and then he folded it in his hanky and slid it under my head. He bent down to kiss me goodnight and then he was gone, pulling the door to within an inch of closing the way I liked it. He smelled of tears.

I lay awake a long time after he left. In the bathroom, before bed, I had run my tongue, tangy with toothpaste, over the hole where the tooth had been, flicking the tip back and forth, not wanting to keep it there too long. There was something thrilling about the tingling feeling I got from that raw, tender spot. I looked at it in the mirror and it looked very pink and shiny with saliva. I touched my finger to the gap and it felt moist, slick. Now I lay there and thought of my new incisor pushing up into place and I couldn't wait. I started checking the rest of my teeth, grabbing them one by one between two fingers, tugging, testing to see how firm they were.

Green Cubes

Amy Day Wilkinson

Donna, my boss, slept with my dad. I'm sure of it. They used to work together, it's how I got the job, and Donna's married, has been, but it doesn't matter. They slept together.

Mom, when she came to visit me in New York, didn't act like she suspected a thing. "Donna sure is pretty," she said. "Is she married?"

This woman's nails scratched Dad's naked back. They *did it* under fluorescent office lighting.

Dad has been in prison two years now. He's there on fraud charges. He had a company; there was a contract for services he provided. Then the people he had the contract with said, "Don't worry about the contract. Do this thing not on the contract." So he did. But the people he had the contract with got in trouble, and this thing they told him to do was no longer good, and they came around, then, pointing fingers. The federal government got involved and this is fraud. A real recipe for fraud. Don't do this.

Donna likes mentioning my dad's trouble in business meetings. It was in all the papers. It's not like she's spilling the beans. Here's what she does though: she says, "Emily's Dad's a real genius. He revolutionized patient access," then she pauses. "*Before*," she says and looks meaningfully around the conference table, "he got in trouble."

I hate her for the fucking pause. I hate her more, though, for sleeping with my dad.

Woody, my boyfriend, asked why I thought they'd slept together. "It doesn't take long in business," I said, "to figure these things out. Sales meetings and conferences are like college spring break," I said. "Except the company picks up the tab for the alcohol and it's not a problem, finding a room to go back to."

"Un-fucking-believable," Woody said. Woody's a conceptual artist. It's easy to convince him corporate America is pure evil.

When I was a kid, Mom used to call Dad and me "two peas in a pod." She's full of dumb expressions, but it's true our interests are the same. We used to take special trips together, me and Dad, to the Civil War museum and Monticello. I'm the one Dad gave a nickname. He calls me Bug.

Once we went to Jamestown, Virginia. I was nine. We took our bikes and rode along cement paths and wood plank bridges. As we circled a field full of building foundations Dad said, "Look Bug. A deer." I had a plastic kid's version of a camera. The deer ran away; I took a picture. I said, "Wow Dad. That's going to be pretty." I said, "You can hang it in your office, Dad," and he laughed. When I got the photo back, it was nothing but a white dot on a swirl of green.

Maybe I'll be an artist. Woody has me thinking these sorts of things. He's amazing, really. I'm really in love with him.

Woody's not like people I've dated before. The last boyfriend considered himself a deviant, wearing a bowtie to his job as an investment banker. Woody works with broken car glass he finds on New York City streets. He keeps a garbage bag full of it in his kitchen. When I'm there I like to sink my hand in. Car glass, when it's smashed in accidents and break-ins, is not sharp. It collapses into tiny green cubes. "Careful," Woody says, "there are all sorts of things mixed in there." Dirt and hair, dried blood. I like the texture of the glass, though. The way it swallows my hand up and the chill.

Here, I'll describe Donna. She is forty-two years old and wears suits like she's twenty: short skirts, tiny jackets, filmy blouses with scarves billowing around her neck. Her perfume cloud is nauseating and she must spend half her day reapplying lipstick.

I tried this look for a while. I admit it: I was enamored. The first time I went to visit Dad I was wearing my favorite gray suit. It has a jacket that cuts in at the waist and shows off curves.

"I hope the guard doesn't give us any trouble for your skirt," Mom said. "They can just be so picky, and skirts are supposed to be past your knees, and it would just be such a shame if they sent you out because they found a problem with your skirt."

Mom was wearing a blue jean jumper like the kindergarten teacher she is. I got a charge out of this: maybe being too sexy for prison.

At Petersburg, which is what we call where Dad is, he lives in a minimum-security camp. It's a three-story tan building with thin windows running from the ground to the roof and no fence. It looks like an office you might see outside a city, on a newly paved road by the mall.

"He has a bottom bunk in a room like a cubicle," Mom said. "His window faces the parking lot."

I imagined Dad behind a strip of glass, watching cars come and go, and not being able to leave a place. I'd want razor wire fences.

The visiting room is a trailer with rows of coffee tables, each with four plastic chairs tucked close. Along one wall are vending machines. Stretched across another is an oil painting of a mountain and waterfall scene. Mom and I were at a table in the middle when Dad came in, winked. I stood and watched as he talked to the guard.

"He looks okay, right?" Mom said. She was beside me. The clothes the inmates wear are solid green, like steamed artichokes. The color made Dad seem older. "Yes," I said. "The same."

When he got over to us Dad said, "Look at my little Bug," and hugged me. He held on for a while and I could feel his fingers clasp onto the back of my suit jacket as he squeezed. This was fine with me. As a girl, I'd been the one to not want to let go, like those monkeys with Velcro hands and feet: me, on Daddy's side, against him, warm.

That visit Dad and I talked business. "I'll sit over here," Mom said from the far side of the table, "so you two can hear each other." I used phrases like Post Merger Integration and Revenue Cycle. Dad chuckled and nodded. I told him a story about a company with two Directors of Accounting. "Their titles were different," I said, "but they were doing the same thing." Dad said, "It's crazy, isn't it? The things you see." I loved all this. The shared vocabulary, getting what Dad did, his listening, now, to me.

I blame Donna. I've seen her at work on other men. She used to take me to meetings with her to push buttons and forward her PowerPoint presentations, the PowerPoint presentations I made, my thoughts, my ideas. It's nauseating: watching her touch male arms, guffaw and talk sports. It's not so hard, Donna, to like the Yankees. News flash, Donna: they win, the Yankees. Harder is liking the Atlanta Braves because Dad does and not really giving a fuck about sports.

Woody and I met at Barnes and Noble. Isn't that funny? Woody, who's so against corporate America, at the corporate American bookseller. He explained, "Frank McCourt is here." He held out a copy of 'Tis. "My mom, she's Irish." I was sipping a café crème in the Starbuck's café.

"We do what we must," I said in a judgmental way. What did that even mean? I, too, was at Barnes and Noble.

I liked the way Woody looked: tall and weirdly skinny. His hair, lop-sided like he cut it himself, seemed perfectly messy. He was in form fitting, dark blue jeans, a tight, long-sleeved T-shirt, and his toes, I noticed and liked, curled up at the end of flip-flops and were very dirty. I asked him to sit with me.

Woody has been, over these past six months, a wel-come addition to my life. On our first date, he asked what art-ists I liked. I said, "Van Gogh and Picasso"; he said, "But any-one living?" He introduced me to art galleries in Chelsea, flea markets on Sixth Avenue, and sidewalk book venders around the city.

One day we were talking about Robert Smithson and I commented on what he accomplished in a day. The photo-graph we were looking at was of white rocks arranged in rust red earth. "It seems much more important than what I do," I said. "Placing rocks."

Woody hugged me. He said, "I love how you just put that." With Woody I feel like someone learning.

My job is this: boring. I am a Senior Consultant. I make PowerPoint presentations. I also build customer service data-bases, write press releases, balance checkbooks, make messes in the ladies' room, steal salad dressing. And for this I get $1,800 every two weeks, which is a lot of money. I'd say more than I know what to do with, but come now.

I expected, when I started, a lot out of business. Dad always spoke so highly of it. I'd done many things the same as Dad. I went to the same college, majored in math. It was the only place I applied. For four years I walked around campus thinking: Dad was here and here and here.

I called him once my senior year. It was after midnight and I was drunk as a skunk. I got my ability to drink from Dad, too. I said, "Dad, which Beatles record do you like best? *Sergeant Pepper* or *Revolver*?" I said, "It's important, Dad. I need to know."

He said, "Are you all right, Bug? Do you want me to come up there?"

"Fine," I said. "Of course not, Dad. No."

Now Dad calls me. Twice a week. Wednesday and Saturday mornings. The calls open with a beep and then a mechanical voice: *This call is from a federal prison.* We have fifteen recorded minutes.

We used to talk business. I'd tell him about meetings; he'd ask me to research companies. I've tried to get away from this, though. I say, "Work is fine. Dad, I did this interesting thing last weekend." I ask, "What are you reading? Do you have friends there that play bridge?" Our conversations sputter and stall more than they used to but they're getting there; I make Dad laugh. Though he'll ask each time, "How's Donna?"

I've thought about how Mom and Dad get along. With my mom it's incessant chatter. I think she's afraid of silence. Dad, he's a stoic. He can manage to look interested in all the kindergarten—Charlie did this to Paul today—crap. Most of the time her monologue, though, hinges on worries: "What are we going to do about the lawyers? Are we in danger of being foreclosed upon?" Here Dad is like a fireman squelching fires.

I take after Dad in relationships. More nights than I can count I've gotten to Woody's apartment to find him curled up under his sheet, rocking himself and in a panic about art. I know that he needs me to lie behind him, wrap my arms around him, and say, "It's going to be all right. You are fine. It is important and scary, what you're doing." In this way I give back.

I do, you should know, recognize that Woody can be an asshole. Like with this whole work thing: I do, he doesn't. Sometimes he makes fun of my suits, which I stopped wanting to wear ages ago. He says, "Good God Emily, look at you."

"This," I say, "is not nice." It's not like I like myself in blue pinstripes and milky white hose. It's not like I have a fucking trust fund, Woody.

But I'm glad Woody does. Woody makes beautiful things. His latest project, for example, is truly brilliant. He sculpted tiny cars—they'd fit in your hand—out of broken car glass; in the centers, he installed pulsing red lights. The cars are battery-operated and Woody places them on New York City sidewalks on top of mounds of broken glass. So the effect, then, is this: cars, beating red that look like they pulled themselves up and out of rubble, living. Woody hides with a video camera in sunken doorways to record reactions.

I have a cardboard box of things I made when I was a kid. I've been going through it lately. There was this:

Run and play outside today.
Blow all your troubles away.
And when you come in, again,
Do your best in every way.

I sang it over the elementary school announcements but can't, now, remember the tune.

There was a poem I wrote about Dad and me alone in the woods with silly squirrels. And though I wish it were more than it was, I said, "You see. I can do more than math."

I figured out Donna and Dad slept together when I was in Vegas with Donna, at the e-Healthcare Conference a year ago. Plexiglas arches topped with company logos divided the conference space, a ballroom. Magicians worked to lure doctors and healthcare administrators into areas marked off by company-colored carpet.

I was the steady at our consulting company's table.

Donna would leave and come back with men, bubble-blowing pens dangling from their necks, her hand tucked in the crook of their arms.

I'd give private PowerPoint presentations. Tapping through slides, I'd say, "We make using online information easy." Men in golf shirts and khakis would leave business cards in my fishbowl.

Nights at conferences the plan is this: find another exhibitor to take you to dinner. Donna taught me well. In Vegas, the two of us went for sushi at the Bellagio with Andy and his friend from Merck, the shorter version. We ordered three rolls and three pieces each and Andy said, "No way that's enough." His friend laughed and patted his pocket, "Company card."

Over dinner, Donna told stories about hospital work she'd done with my dad without mentioning my dad. She fanned her face and said, "I always overdo it with the wasabi." Andy's friend made a show of passing her his water; Donna reached across the table, grabbed his hand, smiled. I thought, She's yours, short guy.

Andy said, "Emily, right? What do you do for fun in New York?" We were sitting across from each other. He was older, bald but well-groomed with one silver tooth in the back that, when he smiled, caught light.

I talked about restaurants and bars. "The Hudson," I said, "makes a great martini."

Andy said, "I'm a vodka connoisseur! I'll have to check it out sometime. I'm in New York a lot, on business."

Donna and Andy's friend were laughing. He pulled out his wallet. I thought, Slipping back to the room early where she'll climb on top of you, go down on you, like I'd often suspected, what with all her touching. Andy put his hand on my knee under the table and I thought of my dad. I pushed Andy's hand away. Don't mistake me for Donna.

The waiter walked by then and Andy ordered another round of sake bombs. Outside the restaurant a slot machine's sirens sounded. Lights flashed and quarters shot out. A big man in a cowboy hat stood smugly as his little wife jumped, shrieking, around.

"Not for me," Donna said as she thumbed through school pictures of kids—if Andy has one, she's likely eight or nine—Donna smiled at that short guy: "Very cute." She handed him his wallet. "I've got to run gang. I'm expecting a call from my husband." She said, "Emily, can you get home all right?"

Donna's married to a Colonel. He's been stationed this past year in Afghanistan, a regular American hero. I told Andy all about him. About the picture Donna keeps on her desk in a camouflage frame, how she makes a show of kissing it. Andy said, "Aren't you something?" Andy snores with his mouth slung open, I could see that tooth, refracted street light. It isn't relevant.

I know Donna slept with my dad. It's what happens.

Mom came up to visit once. She shared my bed and went into the office with me. "Oh Emily," she said, "your cube is very nice. Your view is very nice. Your file cabinets are very nice. It's nice that you sit next to the copy machine and there's a plant there. Plants are nice."

I'm working with Woody, now, on an art project. Me! In art! Again, it is with the glass. This time, the idea is transformation.

It is night. We are on 10th Street by Tompkins Square Park. A square of asphalt, lit up by streetlamp, is marked off with orange cones. East Village hipsters linger at the crosswalks or stop, in the middle of walking their dogs, on sidewalks. Woody had me wear a suit. He hands me goggles and says, "Okay Emily, go lie in the middle of the street."

We don't have long to do this as taxicabs are honking and Woody is convinced cops will be here any second. He begins pouring shattered auto glass around me. It's heavier hitting my skin than I expected. Pieces get lodged between my lips and ping as they bounce off the goggles. I feel the outline of my body grow—it's this chilly glass thing—and I smile, resisting the temptation to make the car glass equivalent of snow angels.

The shower stops and Woody says, "Here, I'll help you up." I open my eyes to a green, distorted version of him at my feet.

From the sidewalk I see this shape that's me. In the streetlight it's a sparkling version of the lines drawn at murder scenes, around corpses. Woody collects the orange cones and races back to his camera, which is recording on a tripod beside me.

Cabs full of drunken men and women—pouring out, now, of Alphabet City bars—tear over me. It's about one car after another turning this green glass shape into dust and as I watch I want this: To be standing in the parking lot at Petersburg where Dad can see me, but I'm just out of reach.

Dry Falls

Heather Brittain Bergstrom

1.

It had been almost five years since Gil Hanson had seen Nattie, his middle daughter. Still, he felt little enthusiasm on the ninety-minute drive to the airport in Spokane to pick her up. He stopped three times along the way for a cigarette, the first time before making it out of Grant County, before even making it past the potato factory at the edge of town where he'd worked steadily his first decade out of high school. Lingering on the tailgate of his Dodge truck, the second and third times, he watched traffic crisscross in front of him on I-90. As usual, more cars were heading west towards Seattle than east to Spokane. Only a few times in his life had Gil wished to follow the traffic west over the Cascades, leaving behind the desert country of his childhood: the deep-cut coulees and scablands, the irrigated flats and dusty slopes of the Columbia Basin.

This was one of those times.

His wife Linda didn't understand his hesitation. Excited by Nattie's visit, she'd taken the rest of the week off work, but thought the ninety-minute drive home from the airport alone in the cab of his truck with Nattie would do both father and daughter good, force them to get reacquainted. She'd even suggested they stop at Washtucna Cafe in Ritzville—halfway between Spokane and Moses Lake—for a late breakfast. Eggs Benedict. Pancakes. Blueberry waffles. But Linda wasn't Nattie's mother, or she would've known all Nattie would order in a restaurant like that, with wheat fields surrounding them on all sides and big rigs blowing their horns and an American flag the size of an island flying overhead, was maybe some dry triangles of toast.

At least his oldest daughter, Rose, who also hadn't been home in five years, called and sent pictures and had invited him to visit her in San Antonio last spring before it got too hot to walk through the missions. Nattie hadn't even called to say hello in three years. She sent Birthday and Father's Day cards, but never picked up the phone when he called to thank her.

Nattie was coming to tour Dry Falls and the dams—Chief Joseph, Wanapum, Grand Coulee. Or so she'd claimed on the phone ten days ago. "Of course, Nattie," he'd said, clearing his throat. Hearing her voice, he'd wanted to cry. "Of course," he'd said again when she'd reminded him that she goes by Natalie now, never Nattie.

"Of course."

When he'd called his youngest daughter, Sarah, to ask if there was any chance she could drive to Spokane with him to pick up Nattie, she'd said she would have to find a sitter for the kids first. Which meant no. It was the same excuse she gave every time Gil or anyone invited her to go places. Even when Gil would suggest bringing the kids along, like he had this time, she would decline. She hardly left the trailer. She had never left town like her sisters—a fact that used to console him.

"She writes poems about the Columbia, Dad," Sarah had said when he'd asked why in the world she thought Nattie wanted to visit the dams. "She's working on a book. I thought you knew." Gil could hear her kids—his four grandkids—screaming in the background.

"How would I know?" he had wanted to ask angrily. But he'd taught himself over the years to be careful with Sarah. "I hadn't heard," Gil said. He thought she just read other people's poems.

"She's not for the dam busters, Dad, if that's what you're afraid of."

"I'm not afraid of anything." He sounded like a toddler.

The truth of the matter was he'd been afraid of all three of his girls—at one time or another—since their mother abandoned them all so many years ago, running away with a truck driver who was twenty years older than Gil, though in better shape.

At first it was his oldest daughter, Rose, who had scared him with the way she stepped into her mother's shoes so quickly, taking over the cooking and cleaning duties, staying home from her best friend's house to fold his underwear into neat little squares and stack them in his dresser drawer. By the time both Rose and Nattie left town—Rose to Bible college in Texas, Nattie to California to search for her mother—he'd married Linda from Lewiston, Idaho, and it was his youngest daughter, Sarah, who started to frighten him. It was the way she went after the boys, swimming in the canals in her cut-off shorts and bikini tops, her black eye makeup smeared down her cheeks when she got home, shoulders

sunburned and breath stinking like beer and God knew what
else.

Now, for the last three years, it had been Nattie who
kept him awake at night: twenty-eight and still unmarried,
living all alone in an apartment in California, without a steady
job, but plenty of student loan debt.

Ten years ago Nattie had found her mother living with
a different truck driver in an RV park in Sacramento. Somehow she'd talked her mom into leaving the trucker and getting an apartment with her—right beside an almond orchard,
Nattie had bragged on the phone. Then eventually, a few
years later, after Nattie had started taking classes at the state
university, claiming tuition in California was the cheapest of
any state, she'd persuaded her mom into giving up her wait-
ressing jobs and enrolling in some sort of technical school
where she'd majored in medical billing. But then her mom
had gotten breast cancer and died. Since then, Nattie had been
on her own and rarely called home. Gil wondered if maybe
her mom had told her something in the last months of her life
when she was hallucinating on morphine, something about
him or the town that repulsed or angered Nattie, and that's
why Nattie never called him anymore. Maybe that's what she
was coming home to talk to him about, and the dams were
just an excuse, the poems about the Columbia just a romantic
idea to please her little sister—whose life in that run-down
trailer was depressing even to him, though he'd learned to
live with it.

2.

"Mom *did* mention you often her last weeks," Nattie
said, before taking another large bite of her Eggs Benedict.

Gil hadn't asked.

They were sitting in a booth at Washtucna Cafe. He'd suggested they stop for a bite to eat after Nattie had hugged him for a long time at the airport—like she used to as a girl— and he'd noticed she'd put on some extra weight. He'd already asked her about school, if she was still taking graduate classes at the university, and she'd asked him about his job at Basin Irrigation, so he should've been thankful for a new topic. Why she hadn't called in three years would've been preferable.

As for the topic of his first wife, there had always been an unspoken rule between him and the girls that they didn't bring up their mother around him. She'd torn his heart out plain and simple—torn all their hearts out—and the memory of that first week after she'd left town when he'd searched every inch of the house for clues, opening and closing her empty dresser drawers for hours each evening, still made his knees weak and his stomach knot.

"And the Columbia," Nattie continued. "The river and you." She smiled. "It's all she talked about."

He put down his fork and watched Nattie take another bite of her eggs.

Swallowing, she said, "That's why I'm here. To research." There was a piece of pepper between her front teeth. "And to visit."

He needed a cigarette. He didn't want to feel excited or vengeful at the thought of his first wife thinking so much about him at the very end of her life. But he was curious. His heart quickened. Maybe she'd thought about him every day like he had her. Maybe she'd also imagined him in that Sacramento apartment by the almond orchard. Probably not. It was the morphine.

"I'm glad you came, Nattie," he said.

"Natalie."

"Sure. " It was impossible for Gil to call his middle child by her real name. Natalie sounded so much more feminine than Nattie, and growing up she'd been more like a son to him—or what he'd imagined a son to be like—than his other girls. Even Nattie's mother used to say they should've nicknamed their daughter Nate instead of Nattie.

"Where do you want to go first?" he asked. "I make sales calls to Wanapum and Priest Rapids Dams every Tuesday or—"

"Sarah's. I'm staying with her."

"She didn't tell me that." He tried not to sound surprised. Or hurt. Linda had already reorganized her sewing room, Nattie's old bedroom, clearing away bobbins and bolts of fabric. She'd even hung up one of Nattie's old Bon Jovi posters as a joke.

"Sarah doesn't know I'm staying with her," Nattie said. "I wanted to surprise her. Besides, you know Jason. He would've made her say they didn't have room or that one of the kids had a fever."

Gil felt his knees go a bit weak again and even his hands as Nattie explained to him the third and most important reason she'd returned to Washington. It had been her mom's last wish that either Nattie or Rose return to Moses Lake to take care of Sarah, get her on birth control, help her leave her husband Jason, and maybe even the state. Nattie had never mentioned this request to Rose, with her being so into religion and all. It had taken Nattie two years to raise the money—she'd completed only one graduate class in two years—and to get up the courage. Her mom had also left her some money for the cause. In the meantime, she'd started researching the Columbia and writing poems, even getting a few published in small literary journals.

Gil should've known Nattie's visit had absolutely nothing to do with him. Just like her move to California to search for her mother ten years ago had nothing to do with him—or so Nattie claimed at the time, barely eighteen, standing beside the small car he'd bought her and she'd helped him sand and paint, the trunk packed like a giant suitcase with all her clothes, books, and stuffed animals. She had always been his favorite daughter, the most spirited, easily comforted, interested in his job at the potato factory and then at Basin Irrigation. It had been Nattie who seemed the least affected by her mother's abandonment, assuring her sisters, and even him at times, that they would be all right.

As for her mother's last request, he wished Nattie luck. She'd need lots of it. Hadn't his first wife known him better than to assume he hadn't tried to get Sarah to leave her husband? Or at least to better her living conditions? For years he'd tried to talk Sarah into making Jason pull the weeds and sagebrush around their trailer and plant grass seed for the kids, or to allow him to come over and do it, or even to hire someone. Her place looked as desolate as homesteads had fifty years ago, before Grand Coulee Dam, when people used to clean the dust out of their rickety houses after wind storms, not with brooms, but with shovels and buckets.

When Gil pulled into the driveway of Sarah's place to drop Nattie off from the airport, he noticed the shocked look on her face as she surveyed the empty beer cans and broken flower pots all over the front steps, the tangled mini blinds in the windows, the weeds as tall as corn. Before even getting out of the truck, Nattie told Gil she wasn't going anywhere until she helped Sarah clean up the place. Jason could go to hell if he didn't like it.

For the rest of the week Nattie stayed holed up with Sarah in her trailer, much to Linda's disappointment. She was hoping to tour the dams with Gil and Nattie and had taken— she reminded Gil half a dozen times—the rest of the week off work to do so. They did get to see Nattie every day, but only for a couple hours when they went to Sarah's for dinner, at Nattie's invitation.

The first evening they found Nattie sitting outside alone on the front steps of Sarah's trailer smoking a cigarette. The steps had been hosed off and the dead flowers in cracked plastic pots replaced with small trees. "I bought them at K-mart," Nattie said when Linda commented on how nice they were. "Martha Stewart Lawn and Garden." They ordered pizza and drank a few beers. Gil tried not to count how many Sarah drank in the two hours they were there—seven. Thankfully Jason was working late, so Gil didn't have to hear the ugly words passed back and forth between Jason and Nattie. He'd just as soon leave before things started to heat up, though he'd promised himself—and Linda—he'd help in any way he could once push came to shove, especially if Sarah decided to leave Jason.

His favorite grandkid—the calmest, and also the youngest—sat on his knee for half an hour while the other three ran through the trailer screaming and dripping chocolate milk all over the carpet before Nattie suggested they sit at the table and color for a while. She'd bought them new packs of crayons and coloring books, promising if they finished the books before she left, she'd buy them each a new puzzle or game.

When they walked inside the second night, Gil was shocked at the transformation. The million small toys that usually lay scattered all around the house were organized into bins, the larger ones lined up neatly against one of the bare walls of the living room. There was even a small bookcase with half a row of books. Nattie and Sarah made dinner, Fettuccini with grilled chicken and salad. They weren't the cooks their older sister Rose was. They took after their mother—and stepmother—but Gil cleaned his plate and even had seconds.

Sarah's cheeks looked pink for once instead of pale, and she drank one less beer than the night before. Gil left feeling happier than he had in years. Maybe his first wife *hadn't* been that befuddled on morphine before she passed away. Her final request was making more sense to him. But then Jason had worked late again.

The fourth evening Nattie met them in the driveway. Jason's truck was there with the boat still hooked up. It was Saturday. Gil had hoped he'd still be fishing.

"I'm eight weeks too late," Nattie said. "Sarah's pregnant."

3.

Early Monday morning—after consoling Linda, who had to return to work at the school district where she did payroll—Gil picked up Nattie. She climbed into his truck, wearing a backpack and carrying a notebook and a small stack of books. The title of the top book put Gil a bit on edge: *A River Lost: The Columbia*. He didn't understand why Nattie would be carrying around a book like that—written, no doubt, by yuppie environmentalists in Seattle or Portland who couldn't begin to comprehend how important the Columbia really was to farmers east of the Cascades, people who went outside not just to play, but to earn a living.

As they drove along Highway 17, he suggested they stop at Dry Falls on the way up to Grand Coulee Dam, but Nattie wanted to save it for the trip home. "The ancient path of the Columbia," she said excitedly. "Let's see the man-made stuff first."

He'd hardly call the most massive man-made structure on earth "stuff," nor refer that way to Lake Roosevelt behind the dam, which happened to be the second largest man-made lake in the world. But he'd been on enough tours of Grand

Coulee to notice the men were more impressed than the women. While the men listened in awe to the tour guide telling them how the dam holds the record for the most concrete poured in twenty-four hours or how it's still the largest producer of hydroelectric power in the nation, the third largest in the world, the women usually started talking to each other about their kids or hair color, or worse—like he hoped to God Nattie *wouldn't*—the salmon.

He wondered if his daughter realized he'd be out of a job if those radical environmentalists and Indian sympathizers ever got the government to start busting down the dams like they threatened, so would Jason, so would everyone in the area, all Nattie's cousins and uncles and aunts who worked at the various food processing plants in the Basin. Then how would Sarah ever better herself? He supposed she could hightail it out of Washington like her mom and sisters, follow Nattie to "The Golden State" with all its druggies and tie-dye-clad tree huggers. Weren't there any dams in California Nattie could write poems about?

Gil looked over at his daughter. She was flipping through the pages of one of her books. Each time they drove past a new body of water, she asked him what the name of it was—Soap Lake? Banks Lake? Lake Lenore?—and if it was natural or a reservoir.

He wished, now, that he'd stuck on at least one of the bumper stickers his boss had given him a few months ago. *SAVE THE DAMS* one said. *FOOD GROWS WHERE WATER FLOWS* was Linda's favorite. And then there was one about hydroelectricity being good for the environment—*HYDRO FOR ENVIRO*. Ever since the local newspaper had announced how important it was to show support for the dams so their licenses with the federal government would be renewed, Gil had been seeing the bumper stickers everywhere, especially on pickup trucks. He hadn't put one on the bumper of his own Dodge truck, but *only* because he was hoping to trade it in on a new one real soon.

He tried to calm down. Nattie was writing poems after all, not letters to newspapers or congressmen. And Sarah had assured him Nattie wasn't a dam buster. Sarah would know. She was the only one Nattie called somewhat faithfully. Once in a while she told Sarah to say "hello" to him—as if they were merely old acquaintances, not father and daughter.

At Grand Coulee's Visitor Arrival Center, built in the shape of one of the dam's giant generators, Nattie stood a long while in front of FDR's wheelchair displayed behind glass. "It gives me chills," she said. "How symbolic it is."

"Yes, we have him to thank for all this," Gil said.

"Maybe," Nattie replied.

Gil didn't want to go where he thought Nattie was headed, at least not here, so he kept quiet.

"Roosevelt wanted to give small potato farms to poor veterans," she said, "*not* McDonald's french-fries to the world."

"Come on," Gil said, looking around to see if anyone had heard his daughter. "I want to show you something."

"One minute, Dad," she said, pulling a pen out of her backpack and opening her notebook. "I'll catch up."

Gil wandered around a few of the other displays without her—mostly black-and-white photos of the workers building the dam, lean-looking men suspended high in the air from ropes that seemed no stronger than yarn. There were also dozens of photos of eastern Washington, before and after the dam. Gil had seen plenty of photos of the Columbia Basin Project. They were displayed in every restaurant, factory, and small business throughout the area. But they never ceased to thrill him, especially since his own father had worked all his life at various pumping plants, helping to bring river water to the desert, to the poor farmers. He wondered if Nattie remembered this about her grandfather.

He'd explained it all to her one of those first times she'd accompanied him to work at Basin Irrigation, but she may have been too young then to remember. Which might actually be a good thing since he'd more than likely been overly emotional considering he'd gotten the job the same summer his father died. He remembered walking with Nattie through the supply yard, showing her the different irrigation pipes, valves, and sprinklers, explaining how he was carrying on his father's work. He should probably remind Nattie again in case she wanted to mention her grandfather in some of her poems about the Columbia.

One of the largest displays—and also Gil's favorite, the one he wanted to show to Nattie—was a floor to ceiling photo of an old abandoned farmhouse, fields of dust and weeds surrounding it. The size of the photo always gave Gil the sensation that he'd been physically transported back in time. He could feel the harsh wind that had tilted the two-story house to one side, hear it blowing through the dark rectangles that used to be windows, taste the dust and even the disappointment of the family who'd tried to make a go of dryland farming. It seemed to him so symbolic, as symbolic, perhaps, as the wheelchair had been to Nattie. She'd said it gave her chills, but hadn't really explained. She hadn't explained what symbolic meant either, but luckily Gil knew from those few years he'd attended church faithfully right after the girls' mother left town and again with Linda the first six months of their marriage.

He walked slowly past the giant quilt of the western half of the United States where he noticed some women had gathered, where Linda would surely be hanging out if she'd been able to come. But Nattie wasn't among them. She wasn't standing in front of Roosevelt's wheelchair anymore either.

Maybe she was already buying souvenirs for Sarah's kids like she had mentioned on the ride up here.

Gil winced when he found Nattie across from the gift counter, which sold hats and T-shirts and bibs and thimbles with Grand Coulee depicted on them. She was hunched over a card table speaking to an old Indian. A paper banner was taped to the wall above their heads: COLVILLE CONFEDER-ATED TRIBES.

"Can I help you sir?" the woman at the souvenir counter asked Gil.

Not taking his eyes off Nattie or the Indian, he said, "No thanks." Nattie seemed to be writing every word the Indian said into her notebook. Would she do the same if her grandfather were still alive, if she could interview him? Instead of moccasins, the Indian wore white tennis shoes, similar to the ones Gil had on, but his hair was long and braided.

"Not many people stop to talk to him," the woman said. "He sits there every day, staring. A good guy. He brings me coffee sometimes, but never says a word." Gil turned and smiled briefly at the woman. She was middle-aged, like Gil, and about as pudgy. She laid the paperback book she was reading on the counter. "He made me so nervous when I first started, I used to refold the T-shirts all morning. Now I read."

"Give me four of your kid T-shirts," Gil said, pulling his wallet out of his back pocket. "And a bib."

Walking the T-shirts out to his truck—so he could have a quick smoke—Gil realized maybe he should've also bought a T-shirt for Linda. But then she'd wear it to bed every night with her sweatpants instead of the silky nightgowns she used to wear when they were first married, when he still went to church with her every Sunday instead of only every third Sunday when it was her turn to play the organ. He'd buy her a thimble when he went back in.

Nattie and the Indian were both standing now. He was pointing to one of the colored flyers taped on the wall below the banner. Gil had to admit he never would have stopped to talk to the old guy. Even at Wanapum Dam, where the Indians had their own heritage center, not just a card table, he'd never stopped to look at their artifacts or to admire the long canoe displayed there. His interests lay with the irrigators. He could better understand Nattie's curiosity if she had any Indian blood in her, which she didn't. Maybe her mom had told her she did. When he cleared his throat, Nattie turned around.

"Dad," she said. "Sorry."

"The movie's about to start upstairs."

Nattie gathered a bunch of flyers from the Indian's table and put them into her notebook. "Thank you," she said. The Indian nodded.

They sat through two films about the dam, during which Nattie took no notes. She opened her notebook once, but only to glance quickly through one of the flyers the Indian had given her. It was right after the film showed a couple of Indians in full head dress blessing the dam. Gil had been worried maybe there'd been additions made to the films—government enforced additions—since he'd last seen them, additions that explored the history of the Indians, their take on the dam, or the loss of salmon in the rivers. He was relieved there hadn't been. In fact, the Indians were only mentioned that one time. The only photo of an Indian he'd seen downstairs was the one of some chief holding a stake while Governor Martin drove it into the ground to signify the beginning of construction. Maybe that's why he'd been startled when he'd turned the corner and seen his daughter talking to a real life Indian.

The tour of The Third Powerhouse didn't begin for an hour, so Gil and Nattie decided to have lunch first. Gil halfheartedly suggested they try and find the Indian museum the old guy had told Nattie about instead, or maybe even drive to Chief Joseph's grave, if Nattie *really* wanted to. But she claimed it would make her too sad. "I would like to go out to Grandpa's grave, however," Nattie said, "before I go back to California. Last time I didn't get a chance."

Last time Nattie was in Washington, five summers ago, she was one semester from her BA in English and her head was filled with quotes from poets Gil had never heard of, though Nattie bragged they were famous Americans, as famous as George Washington or Abe Lincoln. Always wearing her SACRAMENTO STATE UNIVERSITY backpack—which she made a point of telling everyone was stuffed with poetry books—Nattie had snickered, last time, at how small the county library's poetry section was when he'd driven her there, at her request, to get books for Sarah. She'd snickered at the thin newspaper delivered each day to his doorstep. She'd even snickered at the one-page menus at most local restaurants. It had been hard at the time not to remind Nattie how she used to order the same item, biscuits and gravy, at every restaurant when she was a girl, proudly telling the waitresses she didn't need a menu.

Nattie had tried like the dickens the last time she was in town to get Sarah to enroll in the junior college. She'd even asked Gil and Linda if they'd mind watching the kids—there were only two at the time—on Monday and Wednesday evenings so Sarah could take a class. But Sarah wouldn't hear of it. She'd told Nattie if she took any classes at all they'd be at Belinda's School of Cosmetology, so she could finish the program she'd started in high school, before meeting Jason.

That last time Nattie had been in town her mother was still alive, though already diagnosed with cancer. Whenever Gil had tried to bring up the subject, Nattie had quickly changed it—to poetry, or her future teaching jobs, or the beauty of the orchards all around Sacramento, or, much to Gil's irritation, the shabbiness of her hometown, the lack of growth, the dust that was impossible to keep off her shoes or the wind that never seemed to let up. "Isn't that why they built Grand Coulee, to change all this?" she had asked, wetting another paper towel to wipe off the tips of her shoes. She'd said, at least a dozen times, that she wished she'd grown up in Seattle.

She may as well have, he'd thought then. His little girl had turned into a snob.

But now here she was, five years later, ordering biscuits and gravy again in a hole-in-the-wall cafe, which also happened to look over the Grand Coulee Dam. What had happened? Why the sudden interest in eastern Washington and the Columbia? It must have something to do with her mother's death. But Gil didn't remember his first wife being that interested in the river. When they'd gone camping with the girls, they'd always headed down to the Oregon coast, where Rose and Sarah hung out on the beach with their mom, gathering seashells, while he and Nattie climbed the smaller cliffs, waving down to them below.

They talked a moment now about the view outside the cafe window, how the color of the granite was so much lighter than the dark basalt cliffs they'd traveled past to get here. He was getting ready to explain to her how basalt was softer than granite, when she changed the subject to Sarah and Jason. "Plan B," she said. "I use the money I've saved, and the money mom left me for Sarah, and have sod put in and some poplar trees planted and maybe buy a swingset for the kids and some patio furniture for Sarah. I saw a decent set at K-mart with a big umbrella."

"Martha Stewart is a far cry from divorce," Gil said. "And I've already tried to get Sarah to let me help her with the yard."

"She won't leave him," Nattie said. "Mom had been away too many years. She didn't know Sarah anymore. Besides, she never realized the effect her absence had on Sarah. I don't think any of us did. Sarah was only eleven."

"I know how old she was," Gil said. Why couldn't Nattie just pray for Sarah like Rose did in that Catholic church she attended with her husband, like Linda did for all three of his girls each evening before dinner?

"And do you know how old she was when she started sleeping with Jason?" Nattie asked.

"I don't want to know." He said that too loudly. He felt heated. He drank the cup of water in front of him.

"If only Sarah had half Mom's courage."

That hurt. Gil had to admit. He looked back out the window at the dam. Nattie looked with him. Not much water was spilling over it today or maybe more people would be looking out the window instead of staring at them.

"See how the river bank is lined with concrete chunks?" Nattie asked, pointing. "Makes it look more like a giant irrigation canal, doesn't it, than the 'River of the West'?" He wished the waitress would bring their food. The Columbia might have eleven dams on it, but it was far from an irrigation canal. The concrete chunks helped erosion. They weren't piled there for looks.

He'd tried his best with his girls. Linda always told him that. She even told him once—right after the one and only time she'd asked him to reconsider their agreement to have no children together—that she knew he loved his three girls better than her. Which was true, in a way. He loved them more because they were part of their mother. He'd loved their mother, Margaret, more than he'd ever loved anyone. Still did. He'd loved her since the first afternoon he'd seen her, swimming in a canal, like Sarah in her cut-off shorts. She was beautiful, no doubt about it, but it also *was* her courage. He'd never seen a girl dare the Sinkiuse Canal and Spillway before. They usually stood far back on the concrete shores of the canal, holding hands or biting their nails or smoking nervously while they waited to see if their boyfriends or brothers would be able to grab the one rope tied between two rusty poles at the end of the canal before being thrown over the edge of the rushing spillway, crushed by cement slabs that jutted out to further divide the irrigation water.

He should've known that afternoon, when Margaret missed grabbing the rope with her right hand, but caught it with her left, and his heart almost leapt out of his body, that she'd one day tear it out. If only she'd done it before they'd gotten married and had three daughters who adored her as much as he did, especially their once curly-haired youngest, who looked more like her mother every day.

Feeling a bit perturbed now at his middle daughter, and wondering if she'd ever been in love herself, Gil tried to explain how it hadn't always been bad between Sarah and Jason. "He used to take Sarah out on the lakes and rivers," Gil said. "You were gone. They'd fish together all weekend. Even on the Columbia. He used to make her bring along her homework. He'd quiz her for her tests."

"He was a man, Dad. She was a sixteen-year-old girl. She should've stuck to swimming the canals."

"Nattie, I don't believe—"

The waitress was standing beside the table with their steaming plates.

"Thanks," said Nattie, "and I'll take the check when you have it ready."

They ate half their lunch in silence.

"Why Natalie instead of Nattie?" Gil asked. He'd been curious since the last time Nattie—Natalie—was in town and had informed him of the name change.

"I thought it might be easier to get my poems published with a more sophisticated-sounding name."

"And your love life?" Gil blushed as he asked this.

"Little improvement."

"Let me get the check," he said.

During the incline elevator ride down the front of the Third Powerhouse, Nattie took Gil's hand for a second and squeezed it. Was she afraid? Or worried that he was? She used to walk past him in his chair in the living room after her mother left and do the same thing: squeeze his hand for a second, then let go.

4.

When they climbed out of his truck at Dry Falls, it was windier than it had been at Grand Coulee. Nattie didn't seem to mind the wind this time, maybe because she'd put on weight, and it helped keep her cool. With the wind pushing her hair out of her face, she looked a great deal like she had as a toddler, only without the goofy smile that had been captured over and over in the countless family photos Margaret insisted they pose for. Margaret hadn't taken any photos with her when she left, not even those from her own childhood. Linda had reorganized them for Gil a few years ago, the Christmas after Margaret died. She'd even sewn matching photo album covers with lots of lace and ribbons. Gil kept them in the hall closet with his old high school yearbooks and the girls' babybooks containing locks from each of their first hair cuts.

"Can we go through the Interpretive Center first," Nattie asked, "before looking down at the falls?"

"Whatever you want, honey. It's your day," Gil said. Did his daughter's voice sound shaky? Maybe it was the wind. Or maybe the pills he'd seen her pop at the cafe—for her allergies, she'd said, claiming everyone in California had allergies, and not because of smog, as non-Californians probably think, but the numerous plants and fruit and nut tree pollens. Gil hoped that's all the pills were for.

A girl about Nattie's age stepped from behind the information counter when Gil and Nattie entered the building. She was wearing khaki shorts and a T-shirt and had the tanned muscular legs of a hiker. "I'll start a video in the back room," she said with little enthusiasm. "It lasts twenty minutes."

When it was over, Nattie asked the girl to replay it. She'd been so enthralled, she said to the girl, that she'd forgotten to take notes. Maybe that's what had happened at the dam. But Nattie hadn't asked Gil if they could stay and watch the Grand Coulee films again. He would've. They replayed every few hours.

The short film they'd just watched was about J Harlen Bretz, the geologist who first took an interest in the strange scablands and coulees that mar Eastern Washington. He was the one who first proposed that a gigantic flood had carved the landscape, including the four-mile wide, 400-foot high Dry Falls. He'd estimated at the time of the flood that the drop of the falls was ten times the combined flow of all rivers on earth.

"And just think, Dad," Nattie said after they'd watched the film a second time, "it was the Columbia that carried that flood to the sea."

Her voice was definitely shaky. Maybe they'd been diet pills that Nattie had taken. He'd heard they give women the shakes—the caffeine in them or something. Probably everyone in California took diet pills.

The woman at the counter suggested Nattie buy the video they'd just seen and the book also. She did, charging them on her visa, and five other books, and two topographical maps. Did she even know how to read topographical maps? And how was Nattie going to pay the visa bill if she didn't have a steady job? How was she ever going to pay her student loans? He should've offered to buy the books and maps.

Nattie told Gil she'd bought the book *Desert of Dreams* for him. One of the books she bought for herself was about Chief Moses. She held it up. "I bet you'd recognize this Indian's face anywhere," she said, "with the way it's painted and engraved all over town."

"Sure," he said. Of course he would. The town and the lake were both named after Chief Moses. His face was engraved on the front of all Gil's old high school yearbooks and Nattie's. What was his daughter's point? A wooden Indian in his likeness had even been the high school's mascot, up until a few years ago when the school district had to change it to a wooden buffalo instead. They were even considering changing their name from the Moses Lake Chiefs to the Moses Lake Bison. Which didn't make a lot of sense. Had there ever been bison around here? The Indians might try to claim so—that way they could get more compensation money from the government—but Gil doubted it. The Moses Lake Jackrabbits would be more realistic.

"Remember how his picture was painted on the side of the high school gymnasium?" Nattie asked, but didn't give him time to answer. "I used to eat my lunch alone by that painting. It reminded me of the picture of Mom you kept next to your bed after she first left."

Gil didn't know what to say. He was embarrassed about the picture. Embarrassed that his daughter had known then how much he'd missed Margaret. He was also embarrassed, thinking back, by how a few times he'd stayed awake all night, seriously contemplating leaving the desert, even planning how he'd pack up the girls, rent a U-haul, and head west over the Cascades, never coming back or sending word.

As far as Nattie eating lunch alone, he'd always thought his middle daughter had lots of friends in high school. She hadn't been shy like Rose or a boy chaser like Sarah. She'd even been in the FFA for a while and then the Drama Club or Key Club or something.

"Have you ever noticed how there's no pictures of Mom hanging up at Sarah's?" Nattie asked.

"I hadn't noticed," he said. Though, of course, he *had*. He'd noticed there were no pictures of anyone on Sarah's walls, except an unframed snapshot of Jason holding up a fish he'd caught years ago.

Gil remained quiet for the next half hour or so as they walked together through assorted rock displays and past various relief maps. There was also a small chart of native grass and plant species—which Nattie was most likely comparing to the billboard-sized charts they'd need in California. Actually, Nattie was so busy writing in her notebook and asking the yawning information girl questions, that Gil felt certain she wouldn't have even noticed had he gone to wait for her on the bench by the door so he could rest his feet. But he didn't want his daughter to think he was bored or old.

"I forgot to get Sarah's kids something," Nattie said as they were finally heading out the door.

Following Nattie back to the gift section, Gil noticed how her backpack didn't have SACRAMENTO STATE UNIVERSITY embroidered in red on the front like the backpack she'd worn the last time she was in Washington. This one was plain brown and didn't look as stuffed with books. "I don't want ordinary souvenirs," Nattie said. "No T-shirts for them to stain or toys to throw down."

Gil would keep the Grand Coulee Dam T-shirts and bib behind his truck seat until Nattie left town. Sarah's kids were-

weren't picky. They liked any present Gil gave them, and he gave them a lot. Probably because he didn't get to see them that often. Sometimes Gil wasn't even sure they knew he was their grandpa. How could they know? Sarah had quit coming to holiday dinners a couple of years ago, and when Gil would call and invite himself and Linda over to her trailer, one of the kids always had a fever and so Sarah would suggest waiting until the next weekend.

Maybe instead of Nattie buying Sarah's kids a swing set with her mom's money, he'd build them one, a sturdy wooden one with a lookout fort on top. That would give him a chance to see his grandkids more often, at least while he was building it. He'd take his time—do a real nice job. Nattie would be surprised the next time she visited. If she ever visited again.

Nattie bought each of Sarah's kids a chunk of petrified wood over 15 million years old and a series of bookmarks based on sketches from Lewis and Clark's journals. She told Gil she'd make Sarah keep them up on a shelf until the kids were older. But *not* in the built-in curio cabinets in the dining room with the three hundred or so Beanie Babies Jason's mom had sent Sarah over the years—maybe because she felt bad for the way her son treated his young wife.

Gil bought two bottles of the apple hand lotion he hadn't noticed before, one for Sarah and one for Nattie. His oldest daughter, Rose, made her own herbal lotions. She'd explained to Gil about curative herbs when he'd visited her in San Antonio last spring, when they'd sat more often on her front porch talking—thank God—than indoors holding beads and praying with her husband and his family and their priest. Her porch was covered in ferns that she'd dug from the banks of the Guadalupe River, and also statues of Mary. Gil had tried not to look at the statues, having raised the girls as Protestants. Sometimes, though, like now, he wished he was still sitting there with Rose.

Gil stood with Nattie a few minutes looking down at the dark scalloped cliffs of basalt—"the skeleton of the greatest waterfall in geological history," the film had said. Several of the plunge pools, where the falls had landed at the end of the last ice age, still contained water. A few of the pools looked as large as lakes, though nowhere near the size of Grand Coulee's reservoirs. The film had said the rumble of the falls might have been heard for miles away. On days less windy, Gil supposed the silence of this place, now, might be heard for miles also. It was almost eerie.

"That geologist, Bretz," Nattie said, turning away from the cliffs to look at Gil. "I read a book about him."

He looked over at his daughter. She was twisting a strap of her backpack between her fingers. "You did?" he asked, a bit surprised. Gil had never heard of Bretz before today, but he was relieved Nattie wanted to talk about him instead of Chief Moses or Sarah.

"Yes," she answered, explaining to Gil how Bretz was ousted from his profession for over thirty years for claiming a catastrophe had shaped the landscape of eastern Washington instead of slow processes and weaker forces operating over long periods of time.

His daughter sounded nervous, but knowledgeable. "Really," Gil said. "That's interesting stuff."

Nattie quit twisting the strap of her backpack and continued talking. She told Gil how on his deathbed, Bretz got a telegram from a crew of prominent geologists who'd just finished exploring eastern Washington for the first time. "Do you know what it said?" she asked.

He shook his head. Neither the film nor the information girl had mentioned it.

"It said, *We are all catastrophists.*"

"Wow," Gil said. He wondered if Nattie was still planning on teaching English after she finished graduate school, if she *ever* finished graduate school. She hadn't mentioned teaching once this visit. Maybe she could move back to Washington and work at Dry Falls, instead, like the girl inside. She might have to lose a little weight first, take up hiking, but she was definitely more engaged with the subject than the girl had been. He could imagine Nattie walking groups of tourists around, explaining about Bretz, offering to replay the movie or interpret topographical maps.

"I guess Bretz was the opposite of Noah predicting a great flood," Gil joked.

Nattie laughed, saying she'd have to write that one down.

Her smile quickly faded. "Grand Coulee Dam was the Indians' catastrophe," she said with as much determination in her voice as there'd been the day she told him she was moving to California.

Despite what his middle daughter had just said, Gil waited for her to keep talking. It was the sound of her voice. He'd missed it so much over the last three years. But she didn't. Instead, she started twisting the strap of her backpack once more. Why was she so nervous? Maybe she was waiting for him to respond—to argue or agree. He'd rather not. He would ask her a question about Bretz instead. But what? In San Antonio he'd asked questions to keep Rose talking, questions about herbs, even questions about Catholicism, anything to keep Rose and him out on her porch alone for a few minutes longer. But what to ask Nattie about Bretz? He looked back at the falls where afternoon shadows were beginning to deepen and define the already dark layers of basalt.

Nattie cleared her throat. "Mom always loved you," she said, her voice still as determined as a moment ago. "I'm sure she would've wanted me to tell you that somewhere along the Columbia."

The plunge pools on the coulee floor suddenly seemed a lot nearer. Gil felt dizzy. "Don't," he said.

"But that canal where the two of you first met," she persisted, "that was Columbia water."

He gripped the lookout rail with both hands. Maybe he should tell Nattie how Sinkiuse Canal and Spillway had been dried up for years now, fenced off by the county so that farm animals and stray dogs wouldn't fall in, a new canal and spillway built. He wondered if it was as quiet beside the old spillway as here at Dry Falls. He hadn't driven past Sinkiuse Canal in years, not since it had been drained, not since teaching Sarah how to drive on the same country roads where he'd taught Rose and Nattie. Only when he'd taught his two older girls to drive, he hadn't pointed out Sinkiuse Canal as the very one where he and Margaret had met. He hadn't parked the car beside the canal and asked them, like he had Sarah, to walk with him down its concrete shores towards the spillway, walking until Sarah asked if they could please turn back. Gil hoped to God that day didn't have anything to do with Sarah never leaving town. He hadn't asked Sarah that day *not* to leave town—had he?

"I should've told you sooner about Mom still loving you," Nattie said, her voice softening. "I wanted to. I just didn't know how. That's why I never called."

Was Nattie telling the truth about wanting to call him? Had she wanted to pick up the phone when he'd called her? Maybe his daughter had missed his voice also. Had Margaret ever? When Gil used to call California after Nattie and her mom first moved in together, he'd always hoped Margaret would one day pick up the phone. She never did, as if she knew, somehow, it was him.

"Mom *did* still love—"

"Stop," he said a bit firmer. "Please." What was his daughter trying to do? Margaret would've come back if she'd loved him. Plain and simple. Margaret knew—she must have known—he would've taken her back.

"What Mom did to you, Dad, really haunted her at the end. She'd mumble your name, sometimes, all night."

Gil was still gripping the lookout rail with both hands. He closed his eyes. He should've been there when Margaret died. Even Linda had suggested at the time that they drive down to California. But if he'd gone, he wouldn't have wanted Linda along. Maybe Nattie was trying to get back at him now for not being there. It must have been frightening for Nattie, all alone with her mom at the end.

Interrupting his thoughts, Nattie said, "That's why I decided to tell you *here.*"

"What?" Gil asked, opening his eyes. Had he missed something? Nattie was staring straight at him. Did she have more to say? He waited for her to go on. She'd probably been planning this moment for years, finally ready now to tell him the truth as *she* saw it. Nattie deserved this moment. Probably all his girls did. He hadn't really done his best with them, not *always.*

He closed his eyes again, this time in preparation.

But Nattie didn't yell at him for not coming to California and helping her nurse her mom, for sending flowers instead, and then a check to help pay for Margaret's burial in a graveyard Gil hoped was close by an almond orchard, like Margaret's and Nattie's apartment had been, but would never dare to ask. Nattie didn't rebuke him for not supporting Sarah more, for not encouraging Sarah to better her living conditions. Instead Nattie squeezed his hand with one of hers, then let go. Her palm was sweaty, as sweaty as his own palms still holding the lookout rail.

"Don't you see, Dad?" Nattie asked. "I decided to tell you *here* at Dry Falls because like the Columbia, Mom changed paths." Gil wanted to respond, if only he could open his eyes. "She changed paths, Dad. That doesn't mean she didn't still love you."

If only he could open his eyes, Gil would reach over and put his arm around his daughter—to comfort her, to tell her it was okay if Margaret hadn't continued loving him, like he had her. It was what he should have done that day with Sarah, put his arm around her and told her it was okay if she left town like her mom and sisters. But it was too late now. His feet ached and he was falling, no, sliding, sliding down Sinkiuse Canal, heading for the roaring spillway, Margaret beside him in her cut-off shorts.

Myself as a Delicious Peach

Heather Sellers

I was balancing on the curb, having sex. Pretending. In my mind, I was doing it.

Oh, baby, I said.

Even to me *oh baby* sounded stupid.

My dad was always late. My brother said they weren't visitation rights, they were visitation wrongs. My brother was having nothing to do with "el traitor." My mother sent me down to the corner for Dad to pick me up.

"I don't need the man in my driveway," she said. She was very against sex. She said things like *why buy the cow when the milk is free?* To that I said Ma, I'm not a cow and I'm not wanting to be bought anyway. "Oh, yes, I know all about it. Free love. Give me a *break!* Don't even think about pulling anything, Georgia."

She and Sid both harangued me about seeing my dad. "He's a loser," Sid said, which hurt my feelings. "Honey, your father—" my mother trailed off. She was only fierce when she was telling me to not have sex. The rest of the world was vague, she only had the first of the rest of the sentences.

I didn't care that they'd thrown in the towel on my father. I loved him. I loved everyone in my family. Equally. If I started getting down on one, like my mother, I tried to like the others a little less, so it balanced out.

And so I stood there, on my toes, leaning against the kumquat bush, bending into it, and pretending it was my husband. I had my eyes closed. Cars whipped by on the busy street. The day was hot and sticky. I was at a somewhat major Orlando intersection, Summerlin and Topaz; I felt invisible.

I wondered what would become of me.

I wanted a hundred men to see me naked so that I would get used to it, and stop hating my pointed pink body.

My father was on time, shocking.

I'd been deep into it when he roared up. Squeezing my butt cheeks together, I pretended my husband was right there, *right there*. My body bent over, into the bushy tree. Waiting for my Pops, thinking of him pressing on me, pressing on me. Not him, as in my dad, but him, my husband.

But my father was on time, which was so weird. The other two times he'd come for Visitation, he was hours late. Once I'd fallen asleep on the curb, and the other time I had gone home and taken a bath that lasted to the next morning. I went to school a pickle, and he picked me up there, and took me to Steak and Shake for lunch at 9:30 in the morning.

Dad was a busy guy. He had a lot of business interests. This was the year he was in pencils. Last year it was wine bottle holders. The year before, gold.

"Hi, Buck," I said. "Welcome to my world!" I was serious. I climbed in the car, yanking my underwear back discreetly into its place. I fastened my seat belt.

My father gunned the Olds. He hadn't looked at me, hadn't said hi.

"Are you ready?" he said. We passed a car around the curve and sped past the lakes.

"Born ready," I said. I hated the sound of my voice. My butt was still stinging. I felt caught, caught in the act. Settle down, I said to the lower half of me. I felt wet and juicy.

Whoa, girl.

I thought about sex all the time and I didn't even know what it was, precisely. But I was fourteen, and thought I should sure know by now, every one else did, so I kept on thinking, *oh, push, push it to me, yes, I love you.*

"Why are you sticking your butt out like that? What's wrong?"

"I'm not," I said. I had it perched off to the side of me, trying to let the air conditioning whoosh up my legs, to my crotch, which I worried was abnormally damp.

We zoomed up onto the highway, past Lake Ivanhoe, all choppy and foamy and steamy in the hot June sun. Little boats, like letters from lovers. I thought that, *little boats like letters from lovers,* and felt I would be famous someday.

I smiled.

"How are you, baby, I missed you," he said. He gave me a slobbery kiss as he veered into the opposite lane; a truck's horned screamed. "Are you okay?" he was squeezing my kneecap, hard; I hated that.

"I know you miss me."

"You're a snot," he said. "What do you mean you know? You don't know. I might not really miss you at all."

"I know," I said. "I know that too."

No way would I ask him where we were going.

In the back seat, I saw he had a suitcase. My mother would go out of her mind at that. Perhaps he was kidnapping me, one of those custody battles.

"Cop," I said, as we passed by a black and white car on the freeway. "Is this the passing lane?"

"Confine your comments to the matters at hand," he said.

Confine your comments. Gotta love that shit, as Oscar, the boy I loved, would say. Confine your comments! Lock your words in little cages.

"Remember," I said to my dad, who was drinking a highball, "when we were walking through houses going up, and I stepped on that snake?" I contorted so I could look up at the sky through the windshield, big blue pajamas with white splotches, so sweet. I opened my mouth and let the sun in.

"What?" he said.

"It's a beautiful day," I shouted, over the radio and the blasting high air conditioning. "Where we going?"

"Classified. You're on a need-to-know basis, First Daughter. I have told you that."

"Oh, Daddy, I waited all week to see you!" I reached up and kissed him, just as he was bringing his cigarette to his mouth. It burned my cheek.

"Ouch!" I shrieked. I rubbed my cheek.

I rolled down my window to let the smoke out, and he turned the radio louder. I rubbed spit on my cheek, and watched it reddening in the side view mirror as I tried to guess. The beach? His father's? J.G.'s ranch down on Matlacha, the tawny island in the gulf where you couldn't swim because it was all *spiney*? Every goddamn thing on my grandfather's entire island was spiney. The boys, the sea, the food, the trees, the boats. But we were flying down the highway the wrong way for Matlacha.

"Where are we going, tell me, Daddy, I get to know these things. I am *along*!" It was just that we had left Orlando, we were into Ocala.

"Where's your brother, what's going on this time, do you want to enlighten me? Why the hell doesn't he come? Do you have any insight into that situation?" My dad finished his drink at the end of that, and put it on the floor between his feet. "I can't believe he killed three cats. Does he try to get out of weekends with his poor old daddy on purpose, do you think?"

"Well, you don't really like cats that much, Dad." I pulled my hair back into a ponytail, coiled it, and leaned into the rearview mirror to see what that did for my facial bone structure. Good things, as it turned out. It made me look eighteen. Cheekbones, I thought. Blowjob, I thought. What the hell was a blowjob? My father would know, but I wasn't asking him. I had said at recess I knew. I nodded when asked. I nodded to blowjob and suck-off. I didn't have a clue. And I was fourteen years old. It was pathetic.

"Gonna be a beautiful sunset," I said, laying my head back down on his lap, and sticking my feet out my open window. We flew along. I honked the horn, wondering who was I signaling, who was I scaring as the traffic whipped past us.

"Cut it out," he said, and he popped me on the nose.

It always hurt when he pinched and hit me.

I watched my shoelaces snap in the wind. "Sid's Sid," I said. "My brother is my brother. I know not what makes him tick." I was looking at my father's bottom portion of chin, stubbly, red.

A weak chin, my mother always said.

I suddenly knew what she meant.

Once, years ago, we'd taken a road trip as a family, zipping up I-75 north, up the spine of Florida, just like this. We'd gone to Kentucky, before their divorce, our one and only official family vacation.

My mother slept in the car because she found my father's relatives, and their shacky houses, too dirty, too shack-like. The Clampetts, she said. Which I didn't understand. We didn't have a television. But later I saw a cartoon book of *The*

Beverly Hillbillies, and there were some apt comparisons. Those being: Zena Mae my cousin did fix us possum, which was fun to eat, because it was possum, and my Uncle Clarence did keep his money under his mattress.

I slept on my Aunt Stella Mae's floor on a pallet of old flowered wool blankets with Sid. In the middle of the night, when my cousin Dale kissed me, for a long time I just stayed very quiet. It felt good and I thought about his lips and the little cool fur above them every day for a long time. I thought I'd marry Dale. I thought about him the whole way back to Florida that trip.

It was funny how road trips made you think even more about sex, more than you already were.

North of Gainesville, me and my dad drove through a patch of rain, hard thunderous drops, a sheet of gray, for about seven seconds, then it was blazing sun again.

"Oh, Daddy," I said, "I am simply dying of thirst." Suddenly I had a Kentucky accent. "Parched!"

"What?" he said.

"Rest stop," I commanded.

"Oh, God," he said. "You have to wait. Come on. Really?" He said we were going to a great party, a convention, and we had to make time.

"I'm not packed," I said.

We were speeding into the late afternoon. He was steering with his knee. His gin sparkled like crystals in his glass. He clicked the tuning buttons, looking for the game.

I slouched against the door, which wasn't locked. If you sat against an unlocked door in a car like this, my mother would fairly lose her mind. It was too nerve-wracking, so I quit.

My father passed every single person—we were flying up the highway. "You're doing eighty," I said. I was trying to say it neutral.

"You got the angle," he said. "It's not eighty."

Another time, Buck'd taken me to Daytona to watch the 500, only we didn't get tickets, and ended up in a pink cement block one-story motel on the beach, the Neptune Star, with a woman who had a son my age. He and I sat on the sand while my father and Ginger or Gretchen or Gretel took naps. She had a tiny German accent. The boy, whose name I forget, had a small dirt bike. I think it was Derry. Derry or Dusty.

After it got dark, we waded into the ocean. The little motel was dark behind us.

"Why you hikin' your dress up, because you think you're sexy?" he'd said, this boy my age.

I had thought he was about to kiss me. I felt sick to my stomach when he said that. I was burning, my face and palms red. "I was just saving it," I said.

The ocean crashed around our ankles. I don't remember who slept where that night, or if we even had dinner, or if I threw that dress—it was white gauze with beige embroidered trim around the skirt—in the dumpster behind the Neptune Star.

"Please tell me," I begged. "Maybe I have brought the wrong stuff?"

"You're happier worrying than you are having a good time, that's the problem with you, Georgia. You are exactly like your mother."

"No," I said. "I'm nothing like her. I just don't have good stuff," I said. "I didn't really bring anything except one pair of underwear and my bathing suit."

I looked at my brown grocery bag, on the back seat, by his brown flagging suitcase. "She would never wear a bikini and I wear a string bikini," I said.

"I would like silence." My father lurched us onto the shoulder and at the same time, he curled himself off to the side, and let out an enormous episode of gas, and then started cussing, and tears came to his eyes and the car smelled damp and doggy.

I kept my eyes on the road. I didn't know what was happening.

He grabbed the wheel, we swerved into the oncoming lane again, the Olds kind of like a giant sled; there were horns blaring, and he pulled over to the side of the road, the crazy shoulder sounding like thunder, and the terrible smell of gas, skunk, and beer.

All I could think was *I thought you wanted silence.*

He wouldn't sit back down. He remained kind of hunched up over the seat, over the wheel, and we idled in the emergency lane. Then we started rolling along, towards Exit 74B, Lake City.

"Godman it. Bum-fuck Egypt. This bullshit again. Goddamn it. Where's the nearest goddamn port-o-potty."

I stared straight ahead. I wished I hadn't been thinking of sex. I wished I was on the route to becoming a nun, a good person. Not this kind of person. The terrible smell filled the car, and I rolled down my window all the way.

"What can I do?" I said, staring straight out the window, as though my gaze kept the windshield from imploding. I was holding the wheel, so was he.

I hoped the car would blow up—me standing, no, sitting, no, draped, in tatters, on the evening news, oh the tragedy on I-75 continues to leave the beautiful young Georgia Jackson in shock—shot of me standing there by the burning car, my hair gold like Cinderella's, the car a pumpkin on fire, and my mother and Sid watching this, realizing how stupid they had been, how unkind, how selfish, how fearful, oh their beautiful Georgia. She was perfect.

Til she blew up.

We were close to the Stop 'N Go. But not that close. We were more askew on the exit ramp. The cars that passed us slowed down and I waved them on. It really did smell awful. Buck threw himself out of the car. There was a stain the shape of Africa on the seat. I wanted to touch it with my hand so I sat on my hands.

He walked around the front of the car, and slid down into the ditch.

His beer had spilled. The empty tinkled out onto the pavement after him.

On the highway above, cars blazed by.

Quickly scooting around, I herded other bottles, the empties scattering round the pedals and stuck them firmly, wedging them so they wouldn't roll, under my seat, case a cop came up to help us out.

Then my father, who'd been into the ditch of weeds and rushes and back already, yelled at me to pop the trunk. He was back there, and I couldn't see him, for a long time. The sky was starting to get dark and bright purple, with peach stripes, the way it did at seven o'clock every evening in summer in Florida. Dark, like beautiful curtains being drawn. A flock of birds flew over in their sharp perfect V. What the hell were they? Geese? Gulls? Pelicans? I strained to see something I would recognize, but they disappeared behind the brown pines at the edge of the highway.

A trucker yanked on his horn, long and low, and then when Dad flung himself back into the car, he had a drink. I noticed that first, because it was in a highball glass from my mother's good barware.

But the main thing was he was naked from the waist down, his sport coat flapping at his thighs, and that whole dark weird business down there—when I realized my father had been standing in an emergency lane naked from the waist down, except for socks and shoes.

Naked.

"Whoa," I said. I looked away, it's what you do. I looked out my window. "Wow," I said. He was naked. He'd been standing out back of the car, taking his pants off?

He slammed his door, and we jerked back into the traffic. He didn't agonize over merging like my mother did, he just went for it. One thing you can say about my dad.

I wondered where the pants were. Where the next ones were coming from?

"Hotlanta! Hotlanta, here we come." He belted it out.

2.

"Are you doing okay, Daddy?" We were near Macon before I spoke. I was unsure exactly what had happened—sitting there with him. The bad smell, the accident itself. Things smelled like a hospital, not a good hospital, and I wondered if was true that baby's diapers aren't stinky to the mother.

"I said Hotlanta, Georgie, did you hear me, Hotlanta, do you know what that is?"

"Of course," I said. I tried to smile. I patted him on the leg, but it was so bare, pale, and hairy. His suit jacket sort of covered the whole serious business frontal area, sort of not. I didn't care where we were going anymore.

He drained his drink, set it on the seat between us, in a nest of Kleenex, flashlights, a hammer, a Hustler, and a pouch of fish gravel. He grabbed my knee, squeezed it in the way I most hated.

"Okay?"

"Great," I said.

After a bit I said "Should I call Mom?"

"Fuck her off," he said.

"I know, I know." I banged my head into the dashboard.

"We gotta stop anyway because I need a bathroom," I said.

"Why didn't you go at the pit stop?"

"I needed a bathroom," I said. "Not a ditch."

"You kids are spoiled, you know that?"

"Yeah," I said, and folded myself over, laying my head on my knees.

Right before Milledgeville he said for me to run in and get him a six-pack. I'd been sleeping. His hand was on my bare thigh. My skirt was pushed up.

"Get me some beer, honey."

I woke up with his words in my ears like little hairs.

"Yeah," I said. "Sure I can." The tears were coming and I tried to think of sex, so I would stop crying.

"Get yourself something, get me a sixer, and go ahead and get me a pig knuckle too." The little shack station was strung with all-colored Christmas lights. Two men were talking and wearing overalls. They had a deer strapped to the back of a giant red Ford. The deer didn't look awake and it didn't look sleeping.

"Daddy," I said, taking the twenty. "I don't want to get a pig knuckle. They are so disgusting. I'll feel like a dip. I'll puke. I *will* get carsick and puke all over creation if there is the joint from a poor innocent porcine being in this vehicle. Pig knuckles are too weird."

"Oh, for God's sake. Just pluck out a good one, with the tongs. You don't have to touch it. Get a big one. Get one with a lot of gristle on it." He smiled. I don't think he really liked them. I think he liked making me buy them.

"It's too gross," I whined. I went from looking at his white socks, to his sunglasses, which had thousands of me's, all looking worried and tiny and birdish. "Are you going to wait in the car?"

"Do you always ask so many questions?"

"Excuse me," I said, flouncing into the store.

"You're a Southerner, aren't you?" he shouted. The deer men were staring at us.

"Oh hey," I said, but my throat was pretty closed up and no words came out.

I tried to remember to wiggle my butt the whole way around the store which is not all that easy to do when you are about to buy a pig knuckle, believe you me.

"Oh boy," I sighed as I flung open the heavy glass door and grabbed his beer, the first one I saw. I hooked the plastic ring thing on my index finger, and slung it over my shoulder and wiggled.

There was the knuckle jar, by the cash register, all pink and gleaming. They're freaking hooves, I said under my breath. Two women in tube tops with two babies each on their hips were laughing. They weren't buying anything. They were just standing there by the cokes, laughing.

"Party time," the red-haired one said to me.

I looked out into the parking lot. I had no idea if they could see his pale hairy thighs, the dark nest between his legs, the sports coat ending so soon. My father with no pants on.

"One of those," I said, pointing with my pinkie to the slimy floating knuckles, "And could you please direct me to the nearest rest room?" I paid and took my items into the bathroom, vowing to do it in the other order next time. There was a phone between the men's and ladies. Out back behind the shack, I stood there with my purchases, feeling damp,

sticky and dirty. If I called my mother, she would call the police, start driving to Atlanta.

The man who flung himself out of the men's room was
one of those good-looking guys, tan, curly hair down his neck,
broad lazy grin.

"Hey, sugar," he said. "What's up?" He stood in front
of me, looking at the phone and my eyes.

"Hey," I said.

He stood there, and I just wanted him to keep looking
at me. He ruffled his hair, like he was just getting out of the
shower.

"Oh. Man. Look at you." He looked me up and down
again. "Do what it takes to make it a good one, honey."

I felt like he was divorcing me when he hopped on his
motorcycle without me. Back in the car I opened the Cheetos.
The bag let out a huge popping gasp and my father snatched
it, resting his juicy knuckle on his bare naked leg.

"Here," I said. "You need a beer. God, that thing is
dripping all over!"

I popped the top—they had been on sale—and handed
it to him, sliding it across the seat so any police wouldn't see
all this we had going.

"You could have gotten a quieter snack," he said. He
flung the Cheetos into the back seat. You could smell the orange powder of them everywhere.

"Daddy. Cheetos?"

"They're driving me over the edge."

"Daddy, shouldn't you put some clothes on?" I flicked
off the radio.

He took a big suck off his knuckle.

"I messed myself, honey," he said. His eyes were
damp, big. He was pushing the buttons on the radio, looking
for a ball game, even though the sound was off. "You can get
me a fresh set of duds at the next stop. I don't want to be

stopping every goddamn minute. We want to make the banquet. There's a cocktail hour."

He explained about the convention, his old IRS buddies, how it worked, the dance, the sessions, the bag of goodies waiting for us in the hotel suite. It was a three-day party and I would be his princess.

I saw herons, and gators in the drainage ditch by the side of the road. Lolling in the deep purple light. I wondered how long I could wade there before I got nipped. I wondered if people could tell I was still a virgin just by looking at me. I put my feet on the dash, and opened my legs, to let the hot Georgia night on my thighs.

A trucker laid on his horn as he waddled past us. We'd been driving so long, it seemed really slow now.

"You could flash 'em," he said. And he leaned forward over the wheel, and we sped up.

I thought about that. Wondered if that kind of thing might encourage my tits to grow. They weren't coming in. If they stayed as small as my mother's, I could see suicide, I could see dying in eleventh grade. I would give them that long. Then I was taking steps. I was not going through life flat as a board. Flat as a board, Sid always said.

Then about five minutes into Macon, he hauled off and whacked me across the face. Just out of the blue.

"Daddy!" I gulped, and then started coughing and tears blurted out of my face.

"Goddamn Near Beer," he yelled. He threw the beer I'd bought him way back there into the back seat. He swerved, cars honked, the pig knuckle rolled onto the magazine on the front seat, and he leaned over me, steering with his bare knees, rolled down my window, reached in to the back seat with the hand that had just socked me, I was cringing back into my door, sure it would fly open. He flung the entire six-pack, out my window.

"Goddamn Near Beer. No wonder I feel like shit," he said. "Goddamn it, honey, do you pay attention? What were you thinking? Near Beer?"

We parked underneath the hotel. The smells of fumes and rubber made my stomach swirl.

"You got any money on ya, honey?"

"I want to go back home, Dad. I'm just not wanting to do this. I don't feel well."

"I'm going to pretend you didn't say that, honey. I really am." He stood in the dim purple light of the parking garage and pulled his bathing suit on.

"You can have a good time without me."

"Honey, godammit, you're pushing the limit here." He was patting himself down, searching for the missing wallet. "This is your debut! Get up for it!"

"Daddy—"

"I want to show you a good time, honey. I don't do it enough. You're going to love Hotlanta, we're going to have a great night, a great weekend." In his suit coat and tight little green bathing suit, he yanked his luggage out of the trunk, and then he yanked me out.

"I'm going to go call mom," I said.

"Oh for God's sake, don't even think about that."

"But I just don't really—" I wanted to be in my crazy mother's house, sitting on my bed, reading a long book. I wasn't trying to be mean. I just wanted to be there, that's where I wanted to be. My own bed.

"Don't start pulling Belle on me."

"Dad, do you even have your wallet? What about your wallet?"

"You are ready for a sugar daddy, aren't you? Listen to ya, jeez. Future Homewreckers of America." He lurched off, his white legs sticking out under the suitcases and suit coat, his dress shoes damp, his hair like a wild patch of fire.

Peachtree Plaza was the most beautiful hotel I had ever been in. It had an atrium. I knew this because there were peach plastic signs everywhere on little stands, like little butlers, saying in gold script, *Atrium.* The middle of the hotel was hollow, and shot straight up to the sky, way up! Balconies wrapped around each floor, and I could see all the peach doors to all the rooms, story after story. It was like one of those Escher drawings Oscar liked so much. I could never see the appeal. Until now.

I followed my father, in his bathing suit and suit coat across the lobby. Fake peach trees, with gold peaches and pretend money dripping from them. Fancy parrots swarming around in cages suspended from ten stories above. Everyone seemed dressed up, even the plants, which had little white lights in their branches. I felt like I was on stage. Like I was making my debut. No one knew who I was. I could be anyone.

"Oh, paradise, here we be." Buck threw his hands back into the air, dropped his suitcase, and I picked it up. It was like I was in a movie, by myself, in a city, checking in.

Women were barelegged, sandaled, made up, dripping gold beads and hair-sprayed feathered hair—big blonde woman, every single one of them with great boobs. I stood by the fountain, where my father had planted me with his luggage. I had no luggage. I had been picked up for a pizza date with my dad, and ended up in the middle of downtown Atlanta with water and conversations crashing around me, glass elevators making me dizzy, giant birds whistling and fluttering around the atrium, and the Bee Gees cooing and hollering in their soft peach way.

"We're in Room 1212," he said when he returned. "My lucky room."

"You've been here?"

"Honey, I've been a lot of places." He brushed his damp hair back off his shiny forehead.

"Is this that auctioneers' convention?" I said, pulling on my dad's sleeve, but carefully. I had this feeling around him that if I pulled too hard, his whole clothes would unravel, like a blanket, or a sweater, one tug, and he'd be buck-naked. "You went to last year?" That was a stretch when Mom had had us calling hotels after him.

We got on Elevator Six, even though it was packed with people. I pressed myself to the back, which was glass, like a capsule. And as the whole city whizzed past, a man asked my dad what time he was planning on gettin' to the ball.

"I reckon we'll be there right on time. S'long as the little woman here doesn't take too much time paintin' her face."

I felt frozen, cut-off, we were going so fast. He was making like I was his wife? We were going to a ball? What the hell was I going to wear? I wouldn't go, I guess. But what was I going to do? This was my movie! I wanted to slap him. And I wanted to stand right next to him, see if people really were fooled into thinking we were husband and wife.

"Excuse, our floor." A clot of people exited, and I had a clear view of my father, who was lighting a cigarette. He looked like some kind of emu, those skinny hairless legs poking out of that big feathery body.

"We're really on the thirteenth floor you know," he said when we got off. I could smell us.

"Then why does it say twelve?"

"Think about it," he said, and I followed him down the corridors, looking down into the atrium, where people glided about, as if they were being filmed.

"I should call Mom," I said.

He couldn't get our room open, but I could. "You just have to turn it, really hard."

"I'll be in the bathroom," he said, and he took the phone book in there with him. And there were the terrible sounds of his gas. I opened a window, and turned on the television.

I pulled the phone into the giant bed with me, and read its little face carefully. I decided just to use the *collect* option.

I could imagine the kitchen at my mother's. Bare light bulb, Sid's Auto Traders covering the kitchen table, processed veal patties thawing in the sink.

The phone rang and rang.

A loud explosion of noise came from the bathroom, and my father groaned.

"Are you feeling okay?" I said to the wall.

On the television, it was still one long, long commercial for Peach Orchard, the hotel's gift shop. They had everything, mints, shoes, champagne, cigars.

"It's awful quiet out there!" he yelled. "You didn't fall out the window, did you?"

I walked over to the window, and leaned out. I remembered Sid hanging from the balcony when we were little. "Oh, boy." I took a deep breath, and let my body buzz with the thought of me falling through the air. Would I be conscious as I went down? Who would find me? Would I linger for a few days? Would I fall like a dinner napkin, a kite, or a bird? Would I look beautiful?

I jumped on the bed. It was huge. It was the biggest bed I had ever seen. I flung myself at the phone, and dialed the collect call to my mom's again. This time I said it was urgent, it was her daughter.

Sorry, there's no answer.

My father flushed the toilet, and I was just about to hang up when my mother said to the operator, "Calling collect? She's calling collect?" My mother sounded furious and rushed.

"Do you accept the charges?"

"This better be a terrible emergency."

My father still hadn't come out. More gas. I was going to have to take him to the doctor as soon as we got back to Florida. This was not normal. Accidents, and all this gas. He never ate food. He just drank.

"Well, you won't believe what he is doing now," I said. This was *not* what I had planned to say. I was going to ask if I could buy a dress, a dancing dress. "I'm in Atlanta and I don't think I should be here, Mom. It's a business convention."

"What are you saying, Georgia? Honey, I am in the middle of sweeping out the garage. I can hardly hear you. Can I call you back? This is the most expensive way to call."

"Mom, he's got me in Atlanta. I just don't know. I don't know what to do."

"Atlanta? What Atlanta. What exactly do you mean, Atlanta?"

"Atlanta, Georgia." I spelled out the words, and was suddenly not crying. I tried to think about sex. If I had a husband, how would I be acting? I would not be spelling.

"Oh, for crying out loud. What do you mean?"

"I don't know. Forget it."

"Well, you called. If you called, then I guess you should tell me what is going on. What is going on?"

"I guess I just feel like something bad could happen? I don't know. I'm not sure. Mom, I am not sure. I don't feel like I am old enough."

"What kind of tone of voice are you using with me, Georgia?"

"I said just please forget I called." I was yelling now. My father yelled something from the bathroom. I heard the shower come on.

"If I come up there, you are going to have to be waiting out front of that hotel, Georgia. You can't pull a stunt like this, you can't just keep doing this kind of thing. This back and forth, back and forth, playing one of us against each other. It will take me five hours. At least. Oh my gosh in heaven."

"Mom, we're in this hotel room. People think I am his wife, and he lets them. He encourages them." I started to swell up with tears.

"You made your bed, Georgia." When she said this, my father came out of the bedroom.

There was this big long silence. I could feel the clicking of the phone—the money I was costing my mother. I tried to smile up at him.

"Who's that?" he barked. He was naked, with just a small towel wrapped around his body, and it was about to fall off.

The shower water was still running.

How was I going to sleep in the same bed as my dad? Maybe we could order a bunch of extra pillows, and make a beam down the middle. Like me and Sid used to do.

"I gotta go," I whispered.

"I'll come up. I'm coming up. I'm getting upset just thinking about it." She let out a big stream of air, like a teakettle. "I'm going to have to turn around and come back down here with you, because I can't be late for work. It's going to be quick, Georgia. No monkeyshines. I'm going to drive up, then turn around and come straight back. I'm going to be a wreck tomorrow."

I hung up the phone.

"It that your mother?" He was reaching down now, trying to grab the phone. He had my hair in one hand, and was grabbing on it.

"No," I said. "Of course not. Why would it be her?"

He plopped down on his side of the bed. His towel fell open.

I skittered across the room like a spider or a baby, keeping low.

"I couldn't really reach her," I said.

And I was able, perhaps, to convince myself, somehow, that this was true.

At the reception, in the Golden Fruits ballroom, a huge cavernous plaza of a room, dripping with peach chandeliers, lined with mirrors, and dotted with waiters in black coats, walking around with platters of champagne flutes, I pickpocketed my father.

Buck had made out my nametag, slapped it on my breast, which still stung, like a bruise. I was feeling like the stupidest girl in the world, I was hating myself, my shorts, my T-shirt, my nametag that said, in my father's shaky downslant hand, "Mrs. Jackson."

"Dad, it doesn't seem like we should be here," I said. That's when I slipped my hand into his back pocket; it was a joke. But when he didn't notice, I put the wallet in my pocket. "Dad," I said. "Did you hear me?"

My father ran into a woman in a slinky blue dress with butterflies made out of sequins. "Shit," she said.

A man in a green suit coat and red pants boomed, slapping my dad on his back, "Ya hear the news? Shit like that?"

"Man. She was born to be fucked," he said.

The waiter guy went by and my dad told me grab two, like he did. I reached for one of his, but he pulled his hands away. He hoisted the flutes into the air. We were standing in a little group of men.

"God, there's your butt-ugly girlfriend, Bucky," the backslapper green coat man said to my dad. Two of the other guys, both in navy ties with big gold peaches on them, laughed.

"Oh, the uglier half of the what-her-name sisters, oh yeah, hell yeah."

"Nothing like a dumb dutch broad."

I looked around, like I was trying to find someone I knew. Someone who read books, I was thinking.

A cluster of women next to us, a cluster of men, burst into the tinkly laughter that I associated with fancy movies. All the women had boobs, and dresses, and there I was, like a boy or an animal or a ghost, my dad's wallet bulging out of my back shorts' pocket.

"You sure do like them young, Buck! Every year they're younger!"

"Marry me, honey, I'll treat you right, not like old Hoss here," a ruddy man with pinkish eyebrows said, leaning to me.

"I'll be back," I whispered up into my dad's ear. He smelled faintly of walnuts and grass.

"What are you talking about?" he said gruffly.

"I'll be right back," I said. I was stern.

"Ten minutes," he said, looking at his watch, but I could tell he couldn't focus on the face.

I smiled and curtsied and dashed through the throngs of dressy folks. I ran down the hallway.

"Hey," one of the waiters said to me, and I didn't hear the rest. A warning, or an invitation?

I scooted down the spiral staircase, into the lobby. I pretended I was famous and alarmed, for a very important reason. Ten minutes, I thought. I headed for the elevators. I peeled off my nametag, and threw it into the fountain, which had a monkey in a cage dancing around, right above the plumes of water. I saw the letters melt away, and it was just a sticky piece of blank paper, with a little blue border, like a window, like a window floating in the water.

Overhead, the parrots, who looked very dressed up, seemed to think it was a good idea for me to go to the gift shop. To get some gum.

What I bought was a purple dress, out of silky stuff that wasn't real silk, "but acts just like," Marvelle the clerk said. It had a large parrot embroidered onto the hip, and it was a wrap dress, very low cut and sexy and it tied at the shoulders and the waist. I liked all the strings. I liked feeling like a package, a present. In the gauze dress, I felt safer and gorgeous, both of those. I felt quite flaming bright.

"Shall I bill to your room?" she said, and I decided that was the best way to go.

"Twelve twelve," I said.

"Lucky numbers," she said.

I wore the dress out of there. I left my shorts, and my shirt in the dressing room. I felt like a new woman. Marvelle had put a little rouge on my cheeks. It was really just her lipstick, which she had also used on my eyelids.

I minced along through the lobby like a colt in the new silver plastic high heels, feeling vampy and stupid and brilliant all at once. I trolled through the lobby looking for plate glass mirrors. In them all I could see was that I had no boobs, and this was a boob dress.

I took the elevator to the Ballroom floor, and two men in tennis shirts and tennis shorts got on. They smelled like leather, expensive. "Hello," they said. "Going up?"

I wondered how much a prostitute got paid, as I looked at each of them, looking at their faces, the skin there.

I pushed out my tits with all my might. Grow, dammit. Hurry up and grow before I give up and throw myself out a window.

"Have a good one, hon," they said when I got off.

I smiled back and tried to shake my hips, swivel them, the way I saw women walking, as I went into the party.

It was like I was in a music box, turning, only no sound was coming out.

3.

"What you got that shit all over your face for?" Buck said as we over to the bar at the back of the ballroom. "Wipe off that glop."

"What can I have to drink," I said, wiping my eyelids. I handed him his wallet. I didn't even know how much the bill was. I wondered what kind of time my mother was making.

"A daiquiri for the Mrs. and a double Jack for me," he said. "Make that two of everything, would you? These lines are bullshit."

Well maybe she would turn around. She had done that before. Miami, Matlacha, the Key West trip—she hadn't ever made it to any of those, she had turned around and gone back home. What I would do was, at eleven, I'd run down and just see if she was out there, and if I didn't see in three minutes, no five minutes, if I didn't see her in exactly five minutes, I'd run back up to the party.

We stood in another line and got oysters. I listened to one of his friends tell some long story-like-thing about guys in New Orleans coming out of their graves and wanting dirt thrown on them. I had no idea. I just watched his little nose hairs touching each other every time he said a vowel, his ruddy face widening and shrinking with the story. The party was lots louder than it had been half an hour ago. A man cupped his hand around my butt but I couldn't tell who it was.

My father made a big show of dropping the oysters down my throat. Everyone watched and laughed. I played trained seal, and ducked and bobbed in my purple wrap dress.

The oysters were so good, so slippery and salty and expensive tasting, I just loved the weirdness. And the attention. Until my father said, "Your goddamn tit is hanging out."

A woman tinkled up to me, with a beautiful cold porcelain face, a high forehead, and dyed hair. Her Indian bracelets tinkled, she had coins on her sandals. I straightened up, and wiped off some of the juice on my face.

"The kids are all out by the pool," she said.

I stared at her, dumb.

My dad slapped her on the back. "Open wide, BJ," he said.

"Okay," I said, and I looked at my dad for a clue. Wondered what time it was. What I was going to do with the rest of my life.

The kids. The kids. That sounded so funny.

I said sure, but she had already wafted off, and I got up, my father was yelling, really really yelling at a guy way across the room who wasn't paying any attention to us at all, and so once again I walked down the stairs, and out to the pool.

The sky was the color of peaches set on a purple flannel bed sheet. This Georgia sky was rolling over the downtown buildings, which were silvery in the light, and I couldn't believe how beautiful it was. I sat down on a chaise. The others were standing in a group by the diving board. Three kids, a girl in a white dress, "age appropriate," my mother would have said. Sailor collar, short, with blue piping. She had dark hair, and a queenly look, all tan and perfect and groomed. I felt my lipstick on my eyelids, my plastic shoes seemed to be melting, my hair was kind of like hay gone bad. The two guys looked at me, and then looked back at linen girl.

I kicked back. I missed my brother. And my mom. And my dad. He was not who he used to be. Then the tall dark-haired cutie pie came over to me, smiling, his big teeth askew.

"So do you like to have fun?"

He smelled like steak and stupidity.

"What?" I said. I spoke from the dress—I thought it seemed kind of snotty. I could feel the plastic slats of the lawn chair imprinting on my thighs and butt. But still, I let the dress talk. "Of course I like fun," I said. "What do you think I am?"

Down at the beach he said, just like that boy from before, "Why you trying to hike your dress up like that? Do you think it's sexy or something?"

I wished he wasn't such a mean tall dumb boy. He was rich. I could see it would be very difficult for him to get into heaven. We went out into the waves. I threw my shoes, soaked, into the dry sand.

"What's your name," he announced, as though he had said this hundreds of times before.

"Oh, I never tell in these situations," I said, and I flung myself on him.

I put my tongue in his mouth, but it hurt to stick it out that far. I put my hands on his back, his slippery white polyester. You taste just like Heinz gherkins, I wanted to say but that was not very put-outy.

"What is your name? How old are you?"

"Those are the questions I asked boys in kindergarten," I said.

"Oh, grow up."

I laughed, and pushed him, and he lost his balance and went down.

"Bitch," he said, not getting up.

"Howdy, howdy," the queenie girl called, from the deck, far up the beach. You could just hear her voice, like a shell in the wind.

"Fucking bitch." He splashed water on me. "You're a fucked up chick."

"I'm here with my husband," I said.

I imagined my mother dead, in a car wreck, and ran, fast, back to the hotel, past the queenie girl and her toady boy—my boy's little brother, perhaps, and into the lobby, again, this time barefoot, wet, running down the staircase, like I was late, but not for something I had really been invited to.

I had no idea what time it was. People stared at me as I ran past the lanai. Two women reached out to me. Maybe they thought I'd been raped.

I ran through the lobby. The parrots squawked. I started crying, kind of. Since I had been running it was more like a leakage.

The doorman asked if he could help me and then out of the darkness at the exact same moment I saw her truck, the pea green Datsun parked between two long white limos, like a little lima bean.

She got out and jumped up and yelled across the truck, "What happened to your face?"

"Mom!"

"What on earth!"

I looked back. I worried "the kids" would see her.

She stood there, like a military person, in a blocking stance. She had a yellow umbrella with her. She was in her uniform, her khaki jumpsuit, and she had a kerchief over curlers.

"What!" I said. I kept running. I ran right past her, down the circular driveway that was under the hotel's front. Past the potted palms.

I was so shocked to see her. I got to the busy street, truly outside, and I turned to go back into the hotel, which was a kind of awkward move, since it was only one-third of my body participating.

"Your face!" She was coming after me. The doorman said can we valet your truck?

"Oh," I said, and I did a kind of vaudeville face check. "It's on!"

"What's your father doing, where?" She was vibrating. The bellman, a fat black man with a gorgeous and perfect head was standing a foot away, listening to all of this. What if he was my father, and Marvelle was my mother? Would I be happier or sadder and would boobs come in? Oh, I'd be happy.

"Ma, I can't believe you made it. Wow. Fast." She stopped short and stared at me really mean.

She stood hands on her hips. "When my children call me, I am here. I do not like to see my children, either one of them, endangered, and I am here to take you home, Georgia. Where's your things? Where's your father? What's wrong?"

"Just wait here. Okay? I'll be back."

"Georgia! You can't possibly go out into public in that outfit, that thing is falling off of you and it hikes up. This is insanity."

"You're telling me."

"What's going on up here?"

"You're telling me," I said again because it had sounded so good the first time.

I dashed past her, and dove into the revolving doors. I dashed up the beautiful curving lobby stairs again. Each time I ran up or down those stairs, I forgot the misery of the world. On those stairs, I felt destined to wear a crown or something. Even barefoot. I felt like I owned the hotel. *Oh, look, she's late!*

That woman, she must own the hotel and be wanted up in the penthouse.

"Georgia!" my mother's voice hollered across the lobby, got all the parrots going, saying "Come back y'all.

I ran faster. I couldn't believe she had come into the hotel in those curlers!

I knew my mother, in curlers, and carrying a fraying yellow umbrella, would not follow me into a swanky cocktail party.

I pushed my way to the back. I wanted to order a drink. Blend into the crowd. The hand grabbed my bottom as people swirled around us.

"Agh," I said. I jumped back.

"Your daddy said to tell you he's up in the room, and you are late and get your hiney up there." He winked.

I turned, trundled to the edges of the ballroom and there was my mother and her cold stiff tiny arms.

I took a long last look at the party. I wished so much to be the girl dancing in the middle of the parquet floor to Frank Sinatra, but that was the other girl.

That was the not me girl. In the right dress with the right father and the perfect dance steps to the right music.

My mother's voice was steely. "Georgia, gather your things."

4.

In Room 1212, my father and three other men, old men, white haired, slack, shirtless, all are stretched out on the bed, our bed, me and my dad's bed.

"Hey," I say. My mom and I are walking in the room. I am holding her hand.

"Buck," one of them says. "Company." His voice is soft.

I hear a woman's voice. I can't tell if it is coming from the bathroom, or the television. I don't want my mother to hear women in this room or see the things that go on in here.

"Did you ever think Jesus committed suicide?" my father says. He speaks to the stale smoky air. The men are watching the television, their eyes jelly. I feel like I'm in a morgue. "Because that's what happened." He is lecturing the room. No one is listening.

"Mom," I say, turning to her, "Just wait in the hall." I push against her chest, like in a car, when the people are flying towards the windshield.

She stands firm in the doorway, bracing the door open with her foot.

I go stand by the television. They are watching it intently. My father is in his bathing suit, no suit coat.

Two men are lying on my grocery bag, my little jacket, as if my things aren't on the bed. As if nothing is under them. I screw my body around and look at what they are watching. It's an animal program: anemones, starfish, something pink and squishy inside something else gross. Then I see hair. Then I see it.

"Dad," I say. "What are y'all doing?" I pretend I am not seeing. He is fiddling with the remote.

"Where've you been?" he says, suddenly sitting up, coming to, taking a breath. "I said ten minutes. You're a hell of a lot later than ten minutes." To me his face looks to be in pieces.

"Georgia," she hisses. "Please." My mother leans against the hotel room door like a hurricane is trying to press it shut.

"Honey," he says. He is still fumbling with the remote. One of the men stands up. I think I remember him from when I was a little girl.

"Guess who is here," I say.

"Don't you knock?" he says. He is pointing the controls at the television, but it only gets louder.

"What are you watching?" I say, but I don't mean to ask. It's the only thing I do not want to say. Pops right out. I cover my face.

"Where the hell have you been?"

"I'm just getting my bag, sir. You're lying on it. It's probably pretty uncomfortable." Two men not on the grocery bag go out to the balcony and light up cigarettes.

"Daddy, we're leaving now. I think you can understand that." My mother says this, and the men look at her. She puts her hands on her head, to cover her curlers, or keep from screaming. "I'll be in the hall. Georgia, make it snappy."

Has she seen what I have seen?

"Who needs refills?" the standing-up man says. The bag-squisher one lights a cigarette and the mustache one turns on a light by the bed. I snag my jacket and tug on the little tote bag.

"Your butt hangs out of that," my dad says. "What is that?"

On the television I can't help but see two women are crawling all over a hairy naked brown-haired man who is butted up against a pink shell-shaped man. They open the parts between her legs and the camera moves in for a close-up. Sea creatures! It's so strange to see this. It's not pretty at all. Why would we be watching?

"Daddy," I say. "I'm going to go with Mom, okay?"

The light-turning-on man comes over, stands between me and television, and shuts it off.

"I'm gonna go take a crap," he says and he shuffles past me and leaves by the other door. I hear my mother's voice out in the hallway. "I can't wait very much longer. I'm about at the end of my rope." She is talking way too loud. The bellhops are going to be flocking the place and Dad is going to be pissed at me.

"Oh, for God's sakes," Daddy says. He walks over to the door in the bathing suit. You can see everything about him. "I try to do something nice. Look what happens. What the hell did you go and call her for?" He has his ashtray in one palm.

"I didn't!" I say. I run to the door. He grabs my arm.

"Mom," I say.

"I'm leaving," she says. "I don't know what you're doing."

My face is burning. I feel gherkin boy's sweat in the rubbed parts, and it hurts, but it hurts good, just like I imagine these things. I think of him in the bushes, waiting for me, this perfect innocent woman who loves him.

"I shouldn't have to pick between two parents," I say.

"What? Why don't you both come in here and sit down and let's talk. Can we talk like adults? Then we can go down to the party, as a family, be a family for a change. Or what the fuckever you want. As long as you are here, you may as well try and have a good time, woman. Both of you. That's one thing you two were never very good at. Having a good time."

"Not me, Daddy," I say.

"Do you know your daughter has been drinking? Do know what she is doing? The kind of activities she is engaging in?"

"Mom," I shake her by the shoulders, and my father tries to put his arm around me, like we are friends. "Stop, Mom. Stop saying that stuff."

"I don't need the aggravation, I don't goddamn need it." My dad, it turns out, is holding an ashtray, which is fortunate, because his cigarette is all ash, a wand that is about to scatter into thousands of particles.

"Are you going to hit me? Go ahead. These are your friends?" Her face is grim and stoic.

Then he hurls the glass square into the hotel room, over the heads of the men. I watch it hit the window above the television, and I see the glass slowly move into a web of frozen lines.

"That's enough, knock it off," the mustache guy says. He comes to the door.

"Come on back in now, Buckster," the guy says. He doesn't look at us. "Let's go."

A woman in high heels is teetering up the hallway.

"Bye, Daddy," I say.

Another woman comes out of the bathroom.

I don't want my mom to see.

I take my mother by the shoulders, and steer her gently down the hall.

I just stay quiet, and we walk on past her, the silvery teetering hallway woman. Of course she walks into Room 1212. We both look back. I think, oh no, this is the turning to salt thing. She knocks and walks in, one motion. I see the hem of her little slinky dress slink in after her, just a glimpse of purple fabric.

I don't know why my father wanted me around. I don't know what he wanted me on this trip for.

In the elevator, my mother is hard as a wire. She grips my hand, hard. The elevator is crowded and I pretend I don't know her. I'm at that age, I guess, where I can still pull that kind of thing off in my own mind. Everyone else knows I know her. I know they know. But I am still able to stare out the glass, into the black and gold night of Atlanta and the city, stretched out like a sea with all those people going to all their normal and all their fucked up lives. And think: I don't know this woman. I am not related to her. I am not going to be turning out anything like her. I'm going to turn out great.

I follow her, at a distance, out of the elevator, out in the lobby and we leave the Peachtree. I think to myself, *oh that beautiful child, she must be visiting from another country. Perhaps she is the queen's daughter, look at that beautiful hair, she could sell it. It's virgin hair, I bet. Look at it shine! Is she all by herself?* That's what I'm thinking.

The bellman yells at my mother that she said she'd only be there a minute and it's been half an hour.

"Please, please, please, please, I beg of you," she says wearily, and she gets in, and sits there, slumped over the wheel.

"Y'all need to move that vehicle. I have already called the tow service," the man says to me.

At the edge of Atlanta, we get stopped by the longest train in the world. She has trouble getting the car to stay running at the railroad tracks. Car after car of cows and coal and lumber and barrels goes by. I should thank her for coming to get me, but I can't. I can't.

When the train finally ends, and the gates lift up, she makes a big deal of checking for more trains, and then we finally cross the tracks, into this darker and even more desolate warehouse district at the edge of town.

"Can you see a street sign at least?" she barks.

"Nope," I say. "They don't have them in Georgia."

Driving to Atlanta with my father. Driving back home from Atlanta with my mother. What if I had stayed? Would the men have been nicer if I'd been around? Was my father driven to wildness because I just didn't pay enough attention to him? What's the worst thing?

She has trouble seeing the road, trouble with her clutch.

"You have to cover up. I can't stand it." She hands me a white sweater she keeps under the seat. I will not put it on. She hands me newspaper. "I can see everything," she says.

"I have no breasts," I whisper. Sort of thinking she won't hear.

"That's not the point."

"Well how could it not be?" But I don't really want to fight with her. I don't really want to make her sad. I love her. I love her for showing up, ready to rescue me.

I stare out the window. We drive slowly, 45 miles an hour, back across Georgia and back down to Florida.

"It's a pretty night," I say.

"It really is," she says.

We get fried chicken at the Popeye's in Cairo. Then it gets light, all at once. The sky is peach. I keep thinking about that woman, the shell between her legs. Why was she doing anything in the world like that? It doesn't seem pretty enough a business to show all creation. On television! What makes men pretend to act as though it was beautiful? This monstrous shell.

I think of my mother's. I think of the woman's, the woman who took our places in 1212, the silvery fancy dancer woman who walked in when we left. I think of the perfect linen girl's, the girl who will be a bride. What's between her legs? I can't imagine any of us have *that* nasty thing in common. I can't imagine it being the same at all.

We eat the chicken in the car, trolling slowly home. After we are all cleaned up, with HandiWipes, and the chicken bones hidden underneath the seat with the awful acrylic white old lady sweater, I start to breathe, and I don't feel so wet between my legs anymore. A little calmer. A little less of everything. But it's not until we are pulling into our driveway, slowly, slowly steering, stopping, that I have the courage to ask her.

What do you like about me best, I ask my mother. For real, I'm asking. What is your very favorite thing?

Falling Backwards

Dan Chaon

Age 49:

This is a braid of human hair. The braid is about two feet long, and almost two inches wide at the base. It seems heavy, like old rope, but is not brittle or rough. Someone has secured each end with a rubber band, so the braid itself is still tight—the simplest braid, which any child can do, three individual strands twined together, A over B, C over B and A, etc. It smells of powder. There is a certain violety scent which over the years has begun to reek more and more of dust. The color of the hair is like dry corn husks. At first, Colleen thought it was gray.

But it must have been blonde, she now thinks. There was a newspaper clipping among the effects in her father's strongbox, concerning the death of a girl who would have been Colleen's aunt: her father's older sister, though he'd never mentioned her, that she could remember. The clipping, which is dated October 9, 1918, is a little less than an eighth of a column. "Death came to the home of Julius Carroll and wife

Sunday evening and claimed their daughter, Sadie, aged eleven years, who had been ill with typhoid fever for two weeks. All that loving and willing hands could do did not save the child." The article goes on to describe the funeral, and to offer condolences. Perhaps erroneously, Colleen has come to believe that the braid belonged to that long-ago girl. There is no one to ask, no one alive who can confirm anything. She found it recently, curled in the bottom of a trunk along with some of Colleen's grandfather's papers. The braid wasn't labeled. It seems to have been removed rather abruptly, or at least uncarefully. The edges at the thickest end of the braid are ragged and uneven, as if it has been sawed off by a dull blade.

It reminds her of a conversation she'd had with her father years ago. She'd been very interested in genealogy at the time, and had sent him a number of charts, which he'd dutifully filled out to the best of his ability, but he'd really wanted no part of it. When she'd asked to interview him about his memories of their family, he'd balked. "I don't remember anything," he'd said. "Why do you want to know about this garbage, anyway? Let the dead rot in peace," he said. "They can't help you." She'd made some comment then, quoting something she'd read: Genetics is destiny, she told him. Don't you ever wonder where the cells of your body came from? she asked.

"Genetics!" her father said. "What's the point of it? All that DNA stuff is just chemicals! It doesn't have anything to do with what's real about a person." Anyway, he said, a cell is nothing. Cells trickle off our body all the time, and every seven years we've grown a new skin altogether. The whole thing, he said, was over-rated.

Nevertheless, for years now she has carried the braid with her. She keeps it in an airtight plastic bag, in a zippered compartment of her suitcase. No one else knows that she carries it with her, and most of the time she herself forgets that it is there. She cannot recall when, exactly, the braid began to travel with her, but it has become a kind of talisman, not necessarily good luck, but comforting. Occasionally, she will take it out of its bag and run it through her hands, like a rosary. The braid has traveled all over the world, from Washington, D.C. to the great capitals of Europe, from Mali to Peru. She supposes that this is ironic.

For the last ten years, she has worked for an international charitable organization which gives grants to individuals who, in the words of the foundation's mission statement, "have devoted themselves selflessly to the betterment of the human race." For years, she has anonymously observed candidates for the grants, and written reports on them. Her reports are passed on to a committee which divides its endowed monies among the deserving. It is a great job but it leaves her lonely. She is divorced and she rarely speaks to her grown son. Most of the relatives that she remembers from her youth died a long time ago. There are a number of regrets.

Age 42:

She is in a motel room in Mexico City when her son, Luke, calls. "Mommy?" he says, in a voice that is drunk or drugged. He is twenty years old, telephoning from San Diego, where he had been a student before he dropped out. The last that Colleen had heard, he was working as a gardener for a lady gynecologist from Israel and living in a converted greenhouse out behind the woman's house.

"She's really weird," her son says now, trying to carry on a normal conversation through his haze. "Like, when I'm clipping the hedges or something, sometimes she lies out on a lawnchair, totally naked. I mean, I'm no prude, but you'd think she could wait until I was done. It's not a pretty sight, either. I mean, my God, Mom, she's older than you. I'm starting to wonder if she's trying to come on to me."

He *is* drunk, Colleen thinks. What sober person would talk about this kind of thing with his mother? But the comment about her age sinks in, and she hears her voice grow stiff: "It must be really grotesque, if she's older than me," Colleen says.

"Oh, mom!" Luke says. Yes: there is the petulant slur in his voice, a wetness, as if his mouth is pressed too close to the phone. "You know what I mean." And then, as is Luke's habit when he is intoxicated, his voice strains with sentiment. "Momma, when I was little, I thought you were the most beautiful woman in the world. I just idolized you. You remember that blue dress you had? With the gold threads woven in? And those blue high heels? I thought that you looked like a movie star." Any minute now, Colleen thinks, he will start bawling, and it disturbs her that she can't muster much compassion. He has used it up, expended it on the histrionics of his teenage years, on the many, many ways he has found to need "help" since going off to college. He has already been treated once for chemical dependency.

"Oh Mommy," Luke says. "I'm so screwed up. I'm so lost." He takes in a thick breath. "I really am."

"No you're not, Honey," Colleen says. She clears her throat. He is still a kid, she thinks, a child yearning for his mother, who has been cold. But what else can she say? They have had these conversations before, and Colleen has learned that it is best to simply pacify him. "You'll find your way," Colleen says, soothingly. "You've got to just keep plugging away at it. Don't give in." Of course, Colleen thinks, the truth is that Luke is clearly wasting his life. But he'd never listened to any advice when he was sober, and to say anything when he was drunk would only lead to an argument. She considers asking Luke if he is on anything. But she knows that he will deny it—deny it until he is desperate. What could Colleen do for him at such a distance, anyway? "Are you all right, baby?" Colleen whispers. "Is everything okay?"

Luke is silent for a long time, trying to regain his composure. "Oh," he says. And his voice quavers. "Yes—I'm fine, I'm fine. I'm not doing drugs, if that's what you're thinking."

"I'm not thinking anything. You just sound—"

"What?"

"Sad."

"Oh." He thinks about this. Then, as if to contradict Colleen, his voice brightens. "Well," he says, "How are things going for you? Anything exciting happening?"

"No," Colleen says. "The usual." He is her son, and she has failed him.

"How's grandpa?" Luke says. "Is he still holding up?"

"He's okay," Colleen says. She pulls the shade, shutting out the lights of Mexico City. There is nothing special about this place, nothing particularly outstanding about the candidate she is observing, a man who runs a free AIDS clinic for street people but who is not nearly selfless enough to be awarded money by her firm. Does Luke realize how endless the world's supply of sorrow and hard luck stories is? Does he ever think that even if he were a saint, he might not be worthy of notice among a planet of billions? She is so tired. She can't believe how far away she is, how distant from the people that she should love.

Age 35:

"Why does everyone have to be so smart-alecky," her father says, and throws his tennis shoe at her TV screen. "That was a steaming pile of crap."

He has been drinking a lot since he came to her house, sitting alone in her guest room—the only place he is allowed to smoke—sipping at a never-empty tumbler of Jack Daniels. She has seen him drunk before, but he has never been this belligerent, this temper-prone.

"That didn't even make any sense," he says. He is referring to the video they just watched together, which she'd loved, and which she'd thought he would like too. "Why can't they just tell a good story anymore," he says sullenly. She can't believe that he actually threw his shoe at her television.

"Dad," she says. "You can't just throw things! This is my home!"

"Jesus H. Christ," he says, and stalks out of the room.

He has been staying with her for almost a month. She hadn't known he was coming: he just pulled into the driveway one morning. He'd been trying to get ahold of her for over a week, he said, and Colleen had frowned. "How did you try to get ahold of me," she wondered. "Smoke signals? Telepathy?"

"Well," her father said. "Your damn phone's always busy. How many boyfriends do you have, babygirl?" He tried to smile, tried to ease things a bit by evoking this old pet name from her childhood. But he knew that things were not as simple as that. The last time he'd stayed with her, they'd fought constantly; he'd left one night after an argument and hadn't called her for almost two months.

The argument had been about her son, Luke. Her father thought she was spoiling him; she said that she didn't dare to leave Luke alone with him because he drank so much. Each had hurt the other's feelings, which was how it often was. Neither one could bear the other's disapproval.

After a time, she goes to his room. He is sitting on the bed, smoking, and he looks at her balefully as he lifts his tumbler to his mouth. He has taken off his toupee and it lays beside him on the bed, like a fur cap. She could have never

imagined him wearing a hairpiece; he has always been embarrassed and scornful of male vanity, but she sees that he is
right to wear it. He is completely bald, except for a few fine
tufts wisping here and there over his pinkish scalp, like the
head of a four-month-old baby. Without the toupee, he looks
awful—frightening, even.

He is going to live a while longer. The cancer, much to
the doctors' surprise, is gone. It is not merely in remission; as
far as they can tell, it has completely left his body. Sometimes,
he seems aware that something miraculous, or at least
vaguely supernatural, has happened to him. But not often—
more frequently, he seems frazzled, even haunted by his good
fortune, and he turns even more fiercely toward his old habits.

"I brought your shoe," she says. He looks at her, then
down.

"I'm sorry I didn't like your program," he says. "I
guess I didn't understand it."

"Well," she says. "You've never been one for ambiguity."

He frowns. He knows these "two-dollar words," as he
calls them—he has done crossword puzzles all his life—but he
disapproves of people actually using them. He thinks it's
showing off.

"*Ambiguity*," he says. "Is that what you call it?"

"Dad," she says, quietly. "What's wrong with you?
You never used to … go off on little things like that. It's not
good."

He shrugs. "I guess I'm just getting old. Old and
cranky." His hands shake as puts the nub of a Raleigh cigarette to his lips, and she thinks of how badly she needs him to
be normal and happy, to be an ordinary father. *Don't be this,*
she thinks urgently. She is a divorced woman with an eleven-
year-old son and she works forty hours a week as an adminis-

trator at a charity organization, where all she thinks about is helping people, helping, helping, helping. She does not want him to need her, not right now. But she can see that he does. His eyes rest on her, gauging, hopeful.

"I don't have anywhere to go, Colleen." he says. "I don't know what to do with myself.

I'm sixty-two years old, and I'm damn tired of working construction."

"Well," she said. "You know that you can stay here …" But she hesitates, because she knows it's not true. He can't stay here if he's going to drink and smoke like this. He knows this, and his eyes deepen as he looks at her. She doesn't love him as much as he'd hoped—she sees this in his eyes, sees him think it, struggling for a moment. Then he lifts his tumbler and tastes his drink again.

"That's all right," he says.

Age 28:

From time to time, she loses her temper. Like this one time, he pushed her, for no reason, teeth gritted: "Leave me alone!" he said, and that got to her. Oh, I'll leave you alone, she thought. See what it's like, see how you like to be alone.

She knows it is wrong, even as she presses her back to the bark of the tree that conceals her. It is a bad thing, but her anger buoys her, makes her breathing tight and slow. She isn't hurting him, she thinks. She is teaching him a lesson.

It takes him a while to realize that she is gone. It is a warm day in early summer, a little breezy. From her hiding place, she can see the wobbly reflection of the sun and clouds floating in Luke's inflatable swimming pool. Luke plays without noticing for some time. Then, as if he's heard a sound, he stands straight and alert. "Mom," he says. He scopes the yard and the roads and the pasture beyond. They live a few miles outside of the small college town where she is studying for her Master's degree; the nearest neighbor is a mile away. "Mom?" He says again, but she doesn't move. An army man drops from his hand into the grass, near where the hose made a sinewy, snake-like curve through the lawn. "Mommy?" He says, more anxiously. Her heart beats, quick and light, as she presses herself into the shadows. She has the distinct, constricting pleasure of having disappeared—a pleasure that, since her divorce, has occupied her fantasies with odd frequency: to leave this life! To vanish and be free!

And, more than that, as he begins to panic—there is a kind of tingly relief. For what if he hadn't noticed that she was gone? What then?

She lets it go on too long, she knows. He is almost hysterical, and it takes a long time to get him calmed down— rocking him, his face hot against her shoulder, whispering: "What's wrong? It's okay. Don't cry!" A kind of warm glow spreads through her. "I thought you wanted Mommy to go away," she whispers—Horrible! Horrible!—she can sense that it is wrong but she keeps on, running her hand through his hair, long-nailed, thin fingers: vampire fingers. "I thought you wanted Mommy to go away," she murmurs. "Isn't that what you said?" And then she begins to weep herself, with shame and fear.

Age 21:

She is just out of college, staying at her father's house for a week or so, when the tornado hits. It is the most extraordinary thing that has ever happened to her. Parts of the roof are whisked away. The windows implode, scattering shards of glass across the carpets, the beds, into the bathtub. Apparently, there had been a beehive in the upper rafters, because dark lines of honey have run down the kitchen walls.

Colleen and her father have been hidden in the cellar, among rows and rows of dusty jars: beets and green beans and apple sauce that Colleen's mother had canned, or that her grandmother had canned, when her father was a boy. Some of the jars go as far back as 1940, their labels written in a faded, arthritic cursive. Her father has been planning to get rid of this stuff for as long as Colleen has been alive. She had been warned, as a child, never to open anything from the cellar. Her mother had heard of poisonous gas coming out of ancient, sealed containers.

She recalls this, sitting on the cool earthen floor that reminds her of childhood. As the storm roars overhead, she and her father huddle close together.

When they come up to see the world, after the howling has stopped, it is raining. There are no trees standing as far as they can see, only the flat prairie and branches and stumps everywhere, as if each tree had burst apart—as if, Colleen thinks poetically, there were some terrible force inside them that they finally could not contain.

"Jesus H. Christ," her father keeps saying. He goes to the door of the house, and Colleen follows after him. The rain is falling into the kitchen, dripping off scraps of insulation that hang down like kudzu. Her father touches the kitchen wall and puts his finger to his mouth. "Honey!" he says, and laughs. The room is full of the smell of honey and the sound of water. She doesn't know what to say. It is the house that both she and her father grew up in, and it is destroyed.

Her father finds his bottle of Jack Daniels under the kitchen sink; he finds ice, still hard, in the refrigerator's freezer; and he pours them each a drink.

"At least the liquor's okay," Colleen's father says. "There's one blessing we can count."

Colleen smiles nervously, but accepts the drink that's offered to her. She had thought that this would be a rest period in her life—that it would be the last time she really lived at home, and that there would be a number of conversations with her father that would bring closure to this stage of her life. She had been a psychology major and was very fond of closure. She likes to think of her life in segments, each one organized, analyzed, labeled, stowed away for later reflection: Another stage along her personal journey. Nevertheless, a tornado seems a melodramatic way to end things. She would have preferred some small, epiphanic moment.

Her father settles into the kitchen chair beside her, leaning back. The sky is beginning to clear; cicadas buzz from the dark boughs strewn about the lawn. Through the hole in the roof, they can see a piece of the evening sky. The constellations are beginning to fade into view.

"Well," her father says. He puts his palm on top of her hand, then removes it. He sighs. "Now what?"

Age 14:

"Here's babygirl, with her nose in a book!" Colleen's father crows. "As usual!"

She is stretched out on her bed and looks up sternly, closing the book quickly over her index finger, hoping maybe that he will let her alone. But it is not likely. He is standing in the doorway, in a clownish, eager mood. He does a weird little dance, hoping to amuse her, and she is terribly embarrassed of him. Still, kindly, she smiles.

"What good is sitting alone in your room," he sings, and capers around. She leans her cheek against her hand, watching him.

"Dad," she says. "Settle down."

She takes a tone with him as if he is a little boy, which has become their mode, the roles they act out for one another. Her mother has been dead for a little over a year, and this is how things go. They have accepted that she is smarter than he, more capable. They have accepted that things must somehow continue on, and that she will leave him soon. He says that she is destined for great things. She will go on to college, and become educated; she will travel all over the world, as he himself wanted to; she will follow her dreams.

They don't talk about it, but she can see it—in the morning, as he sits hunched over his crossword puzzle, sipping coffee; after dinner, as he sits, watching the news, rubbing salve onto his feet, which are pale and delicate, the toes beginning to curve into the shape of his workboot. She can feel the weight of it as he stands in her doorway, looking in, trying to get her attention. He dances for a moment, and then he stands there, arms loose at his sides, waiting.

"Do you want to go out to Dairy Queen and get a sundae," he says, and she looks regretfully down at her book, where the hobbit Frodo is perhaps dead, in the tower of Cirith Ungol.

"Okay," she says.

She is a pretty girl. Older boys have asked her out on dates, Juniors and Seniors , though she is just a Freshman, and she is flattered, she takes note, though she always turns them down. Her hair is long, the color of wheat, and her father likes to touch it, to run the tips of his fingers over it, very lightly. These days, he only touches her hair very rarely, such as when she's sitting beside him in the pick-up and he stretches his arm across the length of the seat. His hand brushes the back of her head, as if casually. He believes that she is too old to have her father touch her hair. He will kiss her only on her cheek.

Their little house is just beyond the outskirts of town, and as they drive through the dark toward Dairy Queen, she wonders if she will ever not be lonely. Perhaps, she thinks, being lonely is a part of her, like the color of her eyes and skin, something in her genes.

Her father begins humming as he drives. The dashboard light makes his face eerie and craggy with shadows, and his humming seems to come from nowhere: some old, terribly sad song—Hank Williams, Jim Reeves, something that almost scares her.

Age 7:

On Saturday after supper, Colleen's father asks her if she'd like to go on over and see his place of employment. He tilts his head back, draining his beer. He smiles as he does this, and it makes him look sly and proud. "It's a nice night," he says. "What do you say, babygirl?" He seems not to notice as Colleen's mother reaches between his forearms to take his plate. He is not inviting *her.*

Colleen is not sure what is going on between them. It is an old story, though, extending back in time to things that happened before Colleen was born—things Colleen's mother should have gotten, things she is still owed. Every once in a while, it begins to build up. Colleen can feel the heat in her mother's silences.

But her father doesn't appear to notice. He gives Colleen's hair a playful tug, and makes a face at her. "I'm only taking you, babygirl, because you're my favorite daughter."

Colleen, who is sensitive about being teased, says: "I'm your only daughter."

"You're right," her father says. "But you know what? Even if I had a hundred daughters, you'd still be my favorite."

Colleen's mother looks at him grimly. "Don't keep her up too late," she says.

Colleen's father works for the Department of Roads, and he drives her out to a place where a new highway is being built. The road is lined with stacks of materials, some of them almost as tall as houses, and with heavy machinery, which looks sinister and hulking in the dusk.

Her father stops his pickup near one of these machines, a steamroller, which she has seen before only in cartoons. He wants to show her something, he says.

Just at the edge of the place where the road stops, they are building a bridge. The bridge will span a creek, a tiny trickle of water where she and her father occasionally come to fish. Every few years or so, the creek has been known to flood, and so it has been decided that the bridge will be built high above it. The bridge, her father says, will be sixty feet off the ground.

The skeleton of the bridge is already in place. She can see it as they walk toward the slope that leads down to the creek. Girders and support beams of steel and cement stretch over the valley that her father tells her was made by the creek—over hundreds of years, the flowing water had worn this big groove into the earth. They have cleared earth where buffalo and Indians used to roam, he says, and then he sings: "Home, Home on the Range."

She is only vaguely interested in this until they come to the edge of the bridge. It *is* high in the air, and she balks when her father begins to walk across one of the girders. He stretches his arms out for balance, putting his one foot carefully in front of the other, heel to toe, like a tightrope walker. He turns to look over his shoulder at her, grinning. He points down. "There's a net!" he calls. "Just like at the circus!"

And then, without warning, he spreads his arms wide and falls. She does not scream, but something like air, only harder, rises in her throat for a moment. Her father's body tilts through the air, pitching heavily, though his arms are spread out like wings. When he hits the net, he bounces, like someone on a trampoline. "Boing!" he cries, and then he sits up.

"Damn!" he calls up to her. "I've always wanted to do that! That was fun!" She watches as he crawls, spider-like, across the thick ropes of net, up toward where she is standing, waiting for him. The moon is bright enough that she can see.

"Do you want to try it?" her father says, and she hangs back until he puts his hand to her cheek. He strokes her hair, and their eyes meet. "Don't be afraid, babygirl," he says. "I won't let anything bad happen to you. You know that. Nothing bad will ever happen to babygirl."

"I know," she says. And after a moment, she follows him out onto the beam above the net, cautiously at first, then more firmly. For she does want to try it. She wants to fly like that, her long hair floating in the air like a mermaid's. She wants to hit the net and bounce up, her stomach full of butterflies.

"You're not afraid, are you?" her father says. "Because if you're afraid, you don't have to do it."

"No," she says. "I want to."

Her father smiles at her. She does not understand the look in his eyes, when he clasps her hand. She doesn't think she will ever understand it, though for years and years she will dream of it, though it might be the last thing she sees before she dies.

"This is something you're never going to forget, babygirl," he says. And then they plunge backward into the air.

Contributors' Notes

STEVE ALMOND's collection, *My Life in Heavy Metal*, is out in paperback. His stories have been published in *Zoetrope, Tin House, Playboy*, and widely anthologized. He is also the author of a nonfiction book, *Candyfreak: A Journey Through the Chocolate Underbelly of America*. A second story collection is due out from Algonquin in Spring, 2005. See *www.stevenalmond.com*.

AIMEE BENDER is the author of two books: a short story collection, *The Girl in the Flammable Skirt*, which was a *New York Times* notable book of 1998 and a *Los Angeles Times* pick of the year; and a novel, *An Invisible Sign of My Own*, also a *Los Angeles Times* pick, for 2000. She has published short stories in *Granta, Harper's, The Paris Review, GQ, Fence, McSweeney's, Other Voices* and many other journals, as well as NPR's "This American Life." She is the recipient of a Pushcart Prize for 2002, and is at work on a new novel and new stories.

HEATHER BRITTAIN BERGSTROM's prose has been published in *Fourth Genre* and *The Greensboro Review* and is forthcoming in *Manoa*. She won the Willard R. Espy Award in Fiction from the University of Washington and one of her stories recently received Honorable Mention in *The Atlantic Monthly*'s Student Writing Contest.

KATE BLACKWELL lives and writes in Washington, D.C. Her stories have been published in literary magazines, most recently in *New Letters*, *The Literary Review*, and *The Nebraska Review*, as winner of its 2001 fiction prize. "Pepper Hunt" won *So To Speak*'s short-short contest in 2001.

BLISS BROYARD's stories and essays have been anthologized in *Best American Short Stories*, *The Pushcart Prize Anthology* and *The Art of the Essay*, and appeared in *The New York Times*, *The Washington Post*, *Ploughshares*, *Grand Street*, and elsewhere. Her first book, the short story collection *My Father, Dancing*, published in 1999, was a *New York Times* notable book. She is currently a contributing writer for *Elle* magazine.

DAN CHAON is the author of two collections of short stories: *Among the Missing*, which was a finalist for the 2001 National Book Award; and *Fitting Ends*, recently reissued as a Ballantine paperback. His novel, *You Remind Me of Me*, will be published in June, 2004. Chaon's stories have appeared in many journals and anthologies, and have been included in *Best American Short Stories* of 1996 and 2003, *The Pushcart Prize 2000, 2002*, and *2003*, and the *O. Henry Prize Stories, 2001*. Chaon lives in Cleveland Heights, Ohio, with his wife and two sons, and teaches in the Creative Writing Program at Oberlin College, where he is the Houck Associate Professor in the Humanities.

SANDRA CISNEROS was born in Chicago, Illinois, in 1954. She and her six brothers grew up in Mexico and Chicago. Cisneros earned a B.A. in English from Loyola University of Chicago and an M.F.A. from the University of Iowa. She is the author of three books of fiction: *Woman Hollering Creek and Other Stories*, which won the Quality Paperback Book Club New Voices Award, the Anisfield-Wolf Book Award and the Lannan Foundation Literary Award; *The House on Mango Street*, which won the American Book Award in 1985, has sold over two million copies and is required reading in classrooms across the country; and *Caramelo*, which was selected as a notable book of the year by the *New York Times*, the *Los Angeles Times*, the *San Francisco Chronicle*, the *Chicago Tribune* and the *Seattle Times*. It was also nominated for the Orange Prize in England. Her books of poetry include *Loose Woman, My Wicked, Wicked Ways, The Rodrigo Poems*, and *Bad Boys*. Cisneros is also the author of a bilingual children's book, *Hairs: Pelitos*. Her articles and reviews have appeared in publications including *Glamour*, the *New York Times*, and *Revista Chicano-Riquena*. Among her honors are fellowships from the National Endowment for the Arts and the MacArthur Foundation. She has taught at many colleges and universities, including the University of California, University of Michigan, and the University of New Mexico.

JOAN CORWIN has a Ph.D. in English from Indiana University and has published a number of essays in her area of special interest, nineteenth-century travel writing. Her short story "Hindsight" was a winner in Chicago Public Radio's "Stories on Stage" competition and subsequently appeared in the *River Oak Review*. Currently, she is at work on a collection of interrelated stories that take place in a Pacific Northwest college town. She lives in Evanston, Illinois.

PETER HO DAVIES is the author of the story collections *The Ugliest House in the* World and *Equal Love*. His work has appeared in *The Atlantic Monthly, Harper's, Granta, The Paris Re-*

view and *Ploughshares*, and been selected for *Best American Short Stories* and *Prize Stories: The O. Henry Awards*. Born in Britain, Davies currently directs the M.F.A. Program at the University of Michigan.

GINA FRANGELLO is the Executive Editor of *Other Voices* magazine, and Editor-in-Chief of the new *Other Voices* imprint, OV Books, which will come out with its first short story collection in 2005 (for information see *www.othervoicesmagazine.org*). She is also a writer and has published numerous short stories in venues such as *Swink, Prairie Schooner, Hawai'i Review, Fish Stories, two girls review*, and *American Literary Review*. She has taught literature and fiction writing at several universities in Chicago, contributed book reviews to the *Chicago Tribune*, written widely for the *Chicago Reader*, and recently completed a novel. She is also the mother of identical twin girls.

KAUI HART HEMMINGS is a Wallace Stegner Fellow at Stanford University. She has finished a collection of stories set in Hawaii and is working on a novel about a resort town in Colorado. She graduated from Colorado College in 1998 and received an M.F.A. from Sarah Lawrence in 2002.

TONY HOUGHTON is Canadian and currently divides his time between Kingston, Ontario, and the south of France. After a stint as Peter Sellers' ghostwriter and another as science fiction correspondent for the *London Sunday Times*, Houghton took a temporary job with an advertising agency in an attempt to ward off starvation. The attempt was successful. He left the agency thirty years later, retiring to the Bahamas and set out to teach himself to write seriously. *Memoirs of a Croiss-Eyed Cat* was published in Britain in 1998, and "for reasons unclear enjoyed a modest success in New Zealand." His short fiction has been published in *Other Voices* and *StoryQuarterly*.

With four daughters, Houghton believes himself as well qualified as any as a contributor to *Falling Backwards*, though "the girls themselves may disagree. They usually do."

PAM HOUSTON is the author of two collections of linked short stories: *Cowboys Are My Weakness*, which was the winner of the 1993 Western States Book Award and has been translated into nine languages; and *Waltzing the Cat*, which won the Willa Award for Contemporary Fiction. Her stories have been selected for the *Best American Short Stories*, the *O. Henry Awards*, the *Pushcart Prize*, and the *Best American Short Stories of the Century*. A collection of essays, *A Little More About Me*, was published by W.W. Norton in the fall of 1999. In 2001, she completed a stage play called *Tracking the Pleiades*, which was produced by the Creede Repertory Theater. Houston has edited a collection of fiction, nonfiction and poetry for Ecco Press called *Women on Hunting*, and written the text for a book of photographs called *Men Before Ten A.M.*. Her first novel, *Sighthound*, will be published in 2004. Houston is the Director of Creative Writing at U.C. Davis and she teaches at many summer writers' conferences and festivals in the U.S. and abroad. She has appeared on *CBS Sunday Morning* from time to time doing literary essays on the wilderness, and has been a guest on the *Oprah Winfrey Show*. She lives in Colorado, 9,000 feet above sea level near the headwaters of the Rio Grande.

MICHAEL KNIGHT is the author of a novel, *Divining Rod*, and two collections of short stories, *Dogfight & Other Stories* and *Goodnight, Nobody*. His fiction has been published, among other places, in *Esquire*, *Five Points*, *The New Yorker*, *The Paris Review*, and *StoryQuarterly*. He teaches writing at the University of Tennessee.

ANTONYA NELSON is the author of seven books of fiction, including *Talking in Bed*, *Nobody's Girl*, and her most recent, *Female Trouble*. She is the 2003 winner of the Rea Award for the Short Story. She holds the Cullen Chair in Creative Writing at the University of Houston.

ELISSA SCHAPPELL is the author of *Use Me*, a novel-in-stories, which was a runner-up for the PEN/Hemingway award, a *New York Times* notable book, a *Los Angeles Times* Best Book of the Year, and a Borders Original Voices selection. She is also co-founder and editor-at-large of *Tin House* magazine and a contributing editor and book columnist for *Vanity Fair*. Her fiction and non-fiction have appeared in places such as *The Paris Review*, *SPIN*, the *New York Times Book Review*, and *Vogue*. Currently she is co-editing an anthology, *The Friend Who Got Away*. She teaches in the low-residency M.F.A. program at Queens in North Carolina and lives in Brooklyn.

HEATHER SELLERS was born in Florida and now makes her home in Michigan with her husband and two sons. She is the recipient of an NEA fellowship for fiction, the author of a collection of stories, *Georgia Under Water* (which won a place in the Barnes & Noble New Discovery Award Program in 2001), and of a collection of poems, *Drinking Girls and Their Dresses*, as well as the memoir *Page After Page*. Her textbook on creative writing is forthcoming, as well as a children's book, *Cubby and Spike: Ice Cream Island Adventure*. Nearly fifty of her poems have appeared in journals, anthologies and literary magazines including *Louisiana Literature*, *Ascent*, *The New Virginia Review*, *Gulf Coast*, *Hawai'i Review*, *Barrow Street*, *The MidWest Quarterly* and *So To Speak*. Recent prose has appeared in *The Sun*, *The Madison Review*, *The Southeast Review*, *The Writer*, *Writer's Digest*, *Beloit Fiction Journal* and *Five Points*.

ASHLEY SHELBY's work has appeared in *The Sonora Review, Post Road, Gastronomica, collectedstories.com, Identity Theory* and *Carve*, among other publications. She is the recipient of the William Faulkner Short Fiction Award, and author of the non-fiction book *Red River Rising: The Anatomy of a Flood and the Survival of an American City*. Shelby grew up in Minneapolis and lives in New York, where she works in publishing and is the co-director of the KGB Bar Nonfiction Reading Series.

LISA STOLLEY is currently working on her Ph.D. in English at the University of Illinois at Chicago in the Program for Writers. Her short fiction has appeared in literary journals and anthologies including *Hawai'i Review, Florida Review, Washington Review, Fish Stories: Collective III, Gulf Stream, Passages North*, and Simon and Schuster's *Scribner's Best of the Fiction Workshops, 1999*. She received an award from the Illinois Arts Council in 1999 and was recently nominated for a Pushcart Prize. Her nonfiction has appeared in such publications as the *Chicago Reader, Playboy Inc. Publications*, and *Today's Chicago Woman*. She teaches at Roosevelt University and DePaul University in Chicago, is an avid horsewoman, and is currently at work on her second novel, set in the world of horse barns and shows.

LAN TRAN was born in Austin, Texas and raised in Southern California. She uncovered her familial roots when researching her Master's Thesis on the socio-political evolution of Vietnamese cuisine. "My grandfather did indeed commit suicide by jumping in front of a train to protect his family. At first my father, who also writes, was reluctant for me to use this in a story. But when he eventually gave me his blessing because he trusted my words, I felt as if a torch were passing from father to daughter." Lan's creative writing has been featured on NPR, published in literary journals, and produced off-

Broadway and in numerous festivals. Her one woman show, "How to Unravel Your Family," played to a sold-out audience at HERE Arts Center's American Living Room Festival 2002, sponsored by Lincoln Center Theater. Lan also likes food that no one else likes to eat.

AMY DAY WILKINSON's work has appeared in *3rd bed, Pindeldyboz, Comet, Hobart, 96 Inc.*, and other places. She just finished the Master's program in fiction at the University of Southern Mississippi and is a Ph.D. candidate in English and fiction at the University of Missouri-Columbia.

Hourglass Books
... time to read

How much richer are our lives because of short fiction? Imagine a world without the classic short stories written by the past masters of this form

To enter into other lives, other worlds, and to visit them for a brief time, is a wonderful gift, one that perhaps too often falls to movies or television.

Today's busy readers need an alternative, quality short stories that can be read in one sitting, to avoid slipping into the trap of easy entertainment.

Such short stories are still being written by all kinds of authors, both established novelists and new writers who are honing their literary art. They appear regularly in hundreds of literary magazines.

Our mission is to pluck these stories from the specialized world of literary journals and bring them to a wider audience of everyday readers. We do this by focusing on the anthology—short stories from different authors, with each book assembled around a common theme.

Mark Twain is often quoted as saying about one of his works: "If I had more time, I would write a shorter story."

Short fiction indeed takes a long time to write. But the good news is it takes less time to read, and therefore it is more accessible. By focusing on quality fiction of shorter length, the publishers hope to make a small contribution to contemporary literature.

CENTRAL

Printed in the United States
21367LVS00004B/13-15